The Shylmahn Migration

David R. Beshears

Greybeard Publishing
Washington State

Greybeard Publishing
P.O. Box 480
McCleary, WA 98557-0480

ISBN 0-9773646-0-7

The Shylmahn Migration

Chapter One

Two hundred transparent canisters lined the shadowed rows of Compartment One. A golden glow emanated from the containers, the only light in the chamber. There was no need for more. ShahnTahr cared for them and saw to the needs of the occupants. Each held a single Shylmahn colonist suspended in a buoyant, golden fluid. Vital signs were monitored and adjustments were made to the fluid nutrient levels to maintain optimum conditions. At current state, the Shylmahn bodies were aging at the rate of one half million of normal, a definite improvement over the deterioration rate of the colonists during those first years following departure. ShahnTahr had made, and continued to make, significant refinements. At the completion of the journey, the colonists will have aged somewhat less than two new-world hours.

During the long journey, the education of the Shylmahn colonists continued, for while their bodies will have aged but two hours, the minds were often active. ShahnTahr brought them up as new data was acquired, providing to each colonist the data deemed pertinent to the specialty of that colonist. Each Shylmahn knew Earth. Each individual's knowledge of the new world was greater than the knowledge many of the new world's inhabitants had of their own planet.

Data continued to arrive, traveling back along the migration path from the new world to the line of colony ships, to that part of ShahnTahr that resided within each, and on to Shylmah. By now, the sole inhabitant of Shylmah was that part of ShahnTahr that could be called the First, that part which had initiated it all, that part of ShahnTahr that had been responsible for the survival of the Shylmahn people and saw this as the only way.

Information was processed, sorted, provided to the colonization specialists as necessary.

Canister Twelve.
ID 1-1-12.
Name: EsJen.
Field: 065:102.

ShahnTahr isolated information recently arriving from the new world that would aid 1-1-12 in successfully performing her duties upon arrival and thereby aiding in the successful migration and assuring the survival of the Shylmahn people.

EsJen dreamed. She walked the narrow streets of home, amid the bustling crowds rushing about their early morning business, hurrying in all directions at once. Each had much to do, and what was not done now must be added to the afternoon chores, and the afternoon would be no less busy than the morning.

She stopped, uncertain, in the middle of the thoroughfare, blinking; her large, round eyes moistening. The whites held the hint of gold, the iris the darkest brown and filled with bright, gold flecks and large, deep pupils. She looked about her at the masses jostling past and realized that she had nothing to do, no place to go.

The *dahlseht* was home, but it had pushed her away and would have nothing more to do with her. The faces of those around her did not turn to her, and would not acknowledge her presence. Their eyes, Shylmahn eyes, with whites that held the hint of gold and irises of the darkest brown, did not see her standing there, alone and frightened, in the midst of the crowded streets of the *dahlseht*.

She was thin, with thin, delicate bones. Her skin was a pale gold, soft and smooth to the touch. Her hair, as with all the Shylmahn, was a shimmering golden brown. Her face was attractive; her nose, mouth and chin were fine featured; her neck was narrow and slight.

The crowds continued to hurry past her; past this frail, insubstantial figure, strangely numb now with this odd sensation of being a small child lost in a foreign land.

And no one could see her.

Looking up, EsJen saw the slate-gray sky beyond the tops of the precariously tall, narrow buildings that made up her *dahlseht*. Each yellowish wall was dotted with small, dark windows behind which thousands of her fellows lived and worked.

As she stood there, turning slowly, gazing at the black windows, the faded walls, the gray sky, sensing the crowds swarming around her, feeling their shadows all around, a sudden numbing sensation washed over her, through her.

The sounds. The noise. The noise was wrong.

The wind that normally whistled through the deep, narrow streets was still and silent. And the buildings—there should have been sounds from the buildings. There was always sound from the buildings.

She brought her gaze back to the Shylmahn in the streets. There were sounds, but they were fading away. The street noises were dying, were growing dull and distant. The people, still moving about her, were quiet now. They did not talk, but more than that, their movements, their footfalls, the noises that must be there, were not. It was quiet. It was dead quiet.

One by one, the people left the streets. She did not notice at first, but as the slow, enveloping seconds passed, the streets cleared. EsJen stretched out an arm, tried to touch one of her fellows, one of her *dahlseht*, but he was not there. He was there, then he had never been there. She reached out again, to another, and her hand was held out in the open air. With each desperate reaching out of her hand, EsJen grew more and more alone.

She stood then on the empty street. She took a step; the sound echoed against the walls of the canyon-like thoroughfares of the *dahlseht*. She turned her head and felt the slight breeze brush against her face, comb through her long, wavy hair. She could smell the walls and walks, the odor of life behind the windows.

From around one of the buildings came a shadow. A thick, green vine crawled along the foot of the building and moved in her direction, in all directions. It branched and spread, branched and spread again. Wide leaves vibrated in the ever-increasing breeze. The vines crawled up along the walls, branched into windows, curled up over the rooftops and reached across from building to building. Quickly, yet unhurried, everything was blanketed in vine and leaf.

Then...stillness. The gray sky reached down to her from the gaps in the vines overhead, creating strange, alien shadows. She was alone but for the faintest touch of the breeze on her cheeks, the slightest rustle of the leaves.

EsJen turned in alarm at a tearing, ripping sound.

Black void. Black void, black void...

Soothing warmth. She lived in warm, soothing comfort. She was held in great, unseen hands. New knowledge surrounded her, enveloped her, was absorbed by her. She closed her eyes to the tranquilizing wash that pulsed against her, seeped into her pores.

Ship was talking to her...

§

The colony ship was one of five in the advance fleet. It had been traveling for almost 200 years, following after one of the sleeper probes sent out a hundred years before, chasing after the thin messages of hope the probe sent back toward home.

The original probe, an eight-sleeper, had itself followed an earlier automated probe. The probes fed data back to Shylmah, all they had discovered of this new planet, their new home. They told of abundance. Flora, fauna, air and water, mountains, valleys, glaciers, rivers and streams, seas and great oceans. They told of varieties of climate, of the moon in the night sky, of the warm, yellow sun that gave life to it all. They told of Earth and of Earth's inhabitants.

Through the many decades, the two probes sent back whatever could be learned. From the beginning, though, there had been no doubt that, finally, one of their shots in the dark had paid off. All those auto-probes and sleeper probes that had been sent out into the cold, cold dark. Auto-probe 7A and its sleeper probe companion had done it. They had found the new home world for the people of Shylmah.

They named their new world Chehno. The migration had begun almost immediately after the first messages began coming in from across the great expanse between Shylmah and Chehno. First had come those brief cryptic streams from the auto-probe, followed several years later by the ecstatic first messages from the awakened sleepers. The first of the advance fleet was being readied as the sleepers were just settling in. They remained hidden from the local inhabitants. In those early years, it was easy for them to move relatively freely about the planet, gathering important initial data and establishing automated information-gathering stations. Once this was complete, a central post was established and the more routine business of information retrieval and transmission was begun.

So, also, was to begin the ever-greater restrictions on their freedom of movement. As the years passed, it became increasingly difficult to keep their presence hidden from the locals. The human population grew at a frantic pace, as did their technological advances. Still, there were no regrets. Far from regret, their joy was beyond measure. Their sacrifices were badges of honor, worn with pride. That they would not live to see the planet colonized did not matter. Their children, who would be born for the sole purpose of carrying on the work, would welcome the first arrivals. This they knew. What greater purpose could there be to life than this?

§

March 04

Joseph sat down on the bench. The small park behind him was empty. It straddled the hilltop, and from here he could see the community spread out below him. The sun was just setting and the fading rays streaked through the winding streets of the middle-class neighborhood, one of the many small towns surrounding Seattle.

This time of year, the sun disappeared early and the air quickly grew cool. Joseph stuffed his hands into his jacket pockets and pulled it tightly around him. He watched as windows in the homes below turned yellow and bright, his neighbors settling in for the evening, preparing dinner, watching television, getting ready for the next day.

Far to his left, the horizon was turning bright, the glow of the big city, beyond his view but ever-present in the northwest. Much nearer, within walking distance when he was willing to put up with the uncertain weather, was the plant where he worked.

Closer still, he could just make out his house. The windows were dark.

A short distance from his house was his sister's place. It was just on the other side of a small rise, and he couldn't quite see it from the park. Nonetheless, he knew light would be shining through curtained windows. There would be a flickering of shadows coming from the television. Elizabeth would be starting dinner soon.

Joseph leaned back and glanced up at the darkening sky. From recent news stories, he knew that a handful of meteors were up there somewhere, coming this way. While the approach would be close by astronomical standards, they weren't supposed to come anywhere near Earth.

Still, it sure generated a lot of talk.

Joseph let out a tired sigh and looked back at the spreading vista below him. More lights shone from more houses as more of his neighbors arrived home.

He yawned, he let out another long sigh; he closed his eyes to rest them... just for a moment...

Joseph opened his eyes... and found himself staring at a devastated landscape.

An illusion, hallucination... a dream... a vision of a post-apocalyptic world; His world, his town, his neighborhood.

It was daylight. In the small community below, lawns had overgrown and some were beginning to turn brown. Shrubs and hedges shown signs of neglect.

The homes looked lonely. Windows were dark and lifeless. Doors stood ajar. All was eerily still...

Abandoned...

Over the nearby hill, somewhere near Elizabeth's house, smoke rose from one of the homes lining the empty streets. Just as the rising smoke came into Joseph's view, a slight breeze caught it and wisped it slowly over the neighborhood.

Further in the distance, though Joseph knew that in reality he couldn't see it from the hilltop park, Seattle was clearly visible. Skyscrapers were now broken spires rising up into a sky of smoke and fog. Streets were silent, strewn with rubble.

And then Joseph found himself rushed back, hurled back, into the real world.

He stood, stepped forward, stared down at the familiar world below him. Everything looked normal.

Night had fallen. Below him, lights shone warmly through the windows of homes lining the neighborhood. Streetlights and traffic lights glowed in the misty evening air.

He could smell dinner even before his sister opened the front door. Elizabeth pulled him in, gave him a motherly hug, and called out to the family that Joey had finally made it.

Elizabeth was a few years younger than Joseph, five foot six and a fraction overweight, had pretty green eyes and thick, reddish-brown hair that encircled her face. She loved her life and it showed. It emanated from her. She loved her brothers and her sister. She loved her husband and her two sons with that extra zeal that caused her to smother them. Still, all were happy and a little smothering couldn't hurt.

William and Sean, seven and four, ran into the entry hall and took hold of Uncle Joe. They led him into the living room, where Robert waved lightly from his chair. Joseph's presence was a regular enough occurrence that he needn't make a big deal about it.

"How are things at the plant, Joseph?" This was the most common phrase those who didn't work at the plant used to greet those who did. He picked up the television remote and pushed the mute button. The screen was showing a diagram of the solar system. "I hear things are picking up."

"So they tell me. I'm not seeing any difference. How's the store?"

Robert shrugged. He was the manager of a quick-stop. His lean frame sagged from the weight of the pressure that he was under. His pale eyes looked heavy and tired.

Joseph glanced at the television. The diagram of the solar system now included the image of a yellow arc cutting across the lines of the planetary orbits.

"Interesting stuff, those meteors."

Robert gave a slight, confident smile. "They're really overplaying it, though, don't you think? They're going to miss us by a long way."

"Still, the whole thing gives me the willies." Joseph looked from Robert back to the television. "You look tired. When are you going to take a vacation?"

They could hear the children playing in the other room. Robert nodded in the direction of the noise. "I'd need a vacation when I got back."

Elizabeth came in from the kitchen and handed Joseph a cup of coffee. "A vacation is just what he needs," she said, resting a hand on her husband's shoulder. He really did look tired.

"Maybe come summer. I just can't right now."

"The store can spare you, Robert," said Elizabeth. "The bank can certainly spare me. We should go, at least for a few days. Maybe across to the peninsula."

Robert always had a tough time when Elizabeth began to put the pressure on. He ran his fingers absently through his hair, stared at the muted television. The solar system was being shown against the backdrop of a much larger area. An astronomer was pointing out the belt of comets that orbited far beyond the orbit of Pluto.

"We'll see how things are in few weeks, Liz," Robert said, finally. "Maybe then. Maybe we can take a long weekend."

Elizabeth squeezed her husband's shoulders. "What am I going to do with him, Joey? What am I going to do with my Robert?" Anxiety and pride mixed in her voice. "He's going to work himself right into the grave."

At some point in the conversation, the kids had disappeared down the hall. Joseph could hear the sound of the crashing and scraping of plastic toys being bounced off walls and dragged across the floor.

Joseph loved it here. The warmth and the closeness. Stability. Security. This was his tie to normal existence. When all the rest of his life would spin and blur, he could come here. This was what the world was supposed to be. This little piece of the world brought Joseph back to earth.

"You kids stop that roughhousing!" Elizabeth cried out, then she too disappeared, heading into the kitchen. Robert clicked the mute off the television, and the sound of the news helped drown out some of the noise coming from down the hall. Joseph followed Elizabeth into the kitchen.

Elizabeth was closing the oven as Joseph came in. She stood at the counter and began cutting up the ingredients for the salad. When Joseph grabbed at a slice of tomato, she brought the knife down as if to stop him, but was noticeably slow and to one side. He tossed the tomato slice into his mouth.

"Have you heard from the rest of the family?"

"Carolyn called," she said.

"Yeah? How's life in Australia?"

"She's bored. Stuck out in the middle of nowhere."

"She was so excited about that job. Programming for a big company in 'exotic locales', snorkeling the Great Barrier Reef, jaunts to South Sea Islands—"

"Well, she's not too happy with the work, and from what she says, the only activity she's getting is fighting off other bored programmers."

"At least there's wildlife."

"Oh, I got a letter from Kenneth day before yesterday. He's been stationed in Kansas."

"Back stateside. That's a bit closer to home."

"That's what he said. Should be his last duty station. He'll be out in a year and a half."

"He's not going to re-enlist?" Joseph grabbed at another slice of tomato, got away clean as Elizabeth turned her back.

"Bril offered him a job in the boat charter."

"Better off in the army," Joseph mumbled.

"Joseph..."

"Working for Bril?" Joseph gave a dramatic shudder. "I thought he went into the army to get away from dear brother Bril."

"Yeah, well," Elizabeth looked side-glance at Joseph. "Jim's wife saw Barbara yesterday."

"Let that go," said Joseph. Jim was one of Joseph's friends from work. He and his wife could also be a nuisance.

"I'm just saying... It has been more than a year, you know."

"Exactly. It's long over."

"Okay, okay..." Elizabeth handed Joseph the bowl of salad and turned to the oven, "Try not to eat all of it on your way to the table. Tell them dinner is ready."

After a lively and spirited dinner, the family sat around in the living room, sometimes watching television, sometimes talking over the sound of it. By evening's end, the lights were turned low, and the room was filled with moving shadows made by the television screen. A local news reporter was conducting an interview outside a domed building with a large telescope jutting out its side. The reporter wore a broad, cheery grin. The astronomer looked uncomfortable.

William and Sean were asleep on the floor, and Robert was sleeping in the chair. Elizabeth walked Joseph to the front door and saw him out.

He stuffed his hands into his jacket pockets as the door closed behind him. Despite the cool night air, Joseph felt a warmth inside him. It had been a pleasant evening, and now, looking up at the night sky, it looked as though even the weather was going to be kind to him. The pavement was wet, but the rain had stopped. The walk home should be dry.

He slept well and was in a good mood when Jim picked him up for work the next morning.

Such mornings were not to last much longer.

Carolyn Britton stared absently at her computer monitor, her mind only partially on what was passing in front of her. A job as a maintenance programmer wasn't the most exciting assignment in the world, even if the project did get her a free trip to Australia.

Australia. They had neglected to tell her that the communications center they were sending her to was out in some primitive wasteland. Quite beautiful in its own way, but one could only admire these wide open spaces for so many hours a day. Sooner or later you had to do something more with your free time than smile woodenly and mumble niceties about Mother Nature and Her wonders. The main problem was, there was nothing for an attractive young American woman to do but fight off young, old, single, married, attractive, not-so-attractive, American and non-American men, and the occasional daring woman.

Oh, please... give me something more...

She continued to stare dully at the monitor.

There were bugs in the system, and it was her job to find them and get rid of them. The table beside her was piled high with the console printouts of the past three weeks, all of which she had gone over, again and again and again. They hadn't been any help in identifying the problem, but they were something to stare at when she could no longer stare at the code or the log files.

No explanation. Communication devices were shifting targets without warning, leaving data transmissions hanging until the devices were reset. The resets were automatic, and were almost instantaneous in human terms, but in computer time communications were down an eternity. Even so, the problem had only surfaced when a maintenance technician compared send-receive time logs from two locations.

Something was definitely wrong. Carolyn's company suspected corporate sabotage. Yet nothing had been stolen or destroyed. Any data lost in transit was retransmitted automatically. The problem had caused zero impact on operations and customer service.

The code looked clean. Cleaner than clean. These were tried-and-true programs, stable and on-line for some time. Hardware people had gone over everything a dozen times. No evidence of any problems on that side.

Sure. Kick it back to software.

Well, whether the bugs were hardware or software, she had the bastards now. Carolyn wrote a program of her own to track down the little buggers the next time they reared their ugly little heads. This program would identify exactly what was going on during that brief moment when the computer glitched and did something it wasn't programmed to do... which, by definition, could not happen.

John leaned into Carolyn's cubicle, admired what he saw, which was rather attractive. Her long, straight hair was pulled back into a ponytail.

"How's the family, John?" asked Carolyn, not turning from the screen.

"They're fine, Carolyn. Thanks for asking." John slid the rest of the way into the cubicle and stared at Carolyn's monitor. "So?"

"Nothing," she said, nodded at the empty chair.

John sat down and sighed heavily. "It's gotta be hardware."

"Well, hardware says no."

"Of course they say no. They always say no. That's the way it works. They say no. We say no."

"And?"

"These are stable programs. Stable. They don't just start not working. Communications hardware, on the other hand, can just start not working."

"We can't kick it back to hardware again. They'll freak."

John rubbed tiredly at his face. "We've been dragging code for three weeks. Do you really think we've missed something?"

"Of course," she said precisely. "I've found a dozen bugs in this code. None related to our problem, but for every bug I've found, how many have I missed?"

John stared at her a moment, finally sat up with a groan.

"Oh, hell," he said dejectedly. "No. It's not hardware, it's not software."

"Don't say it. Not again."

"Unauthorized access."

"You said it."

"Yeah, well..."

"We've been there. We have firewalls, security utilities, and a hundred safeguards." She rubbed absently at her forehead. "And who? And why?"

"You kidding? A communications network? Could be a thousand reasons." John frowned, then grew studious. "Can't be sabotage. Any data dropped in transit is resent in microseconds once auto resets kick in. We haven't lost anything. Zero impact to operations."

Carolyn sat silent, watching John, waiting for him to sort through his thoughts.

John stared down at his hands. "It's not hardware, and it's not software."

Chapter Two

April 09

Joseph had had his car back for a couple of weeks and was back on his regular schedule. It was fifteen minutes before the shift and he liked to relax in the break room with a hot cup of coffee before starting the workday. He was surprised to come in and find most of the tables, chairs and benches filled. Looking curiously around the room, he put his lunch box into one of the refrigerators and sat down at one of the few remaining chairs.

He seldom saw so many others here so early. Most of these guys showed up with just enough time to toss their sack lunches in the fridge and get out onto the floor... unless, of course, there was an unpleasant new rumor grinding its way through the plant. The excitement level told him this was probably the case, but he was having a hard time sorting out what was being said.

"What's goin' on?" he called out, to anyone who might hear and give him an answer.

Those nearest to him turned and looked at him as though he was an idiot. At that moment, Jim came hurriedly in, tossing his brown lunch bag into the refrigerator. "Man, so waddya think about that?"

A dozen enthusiastic responses, none of which Joseph could understand.

"Think about what?"

"Don't you watch the news?" Jim was near bursting.

"Yeah," defensively. "Usually." The radio in his car wasn't working.

"Those things in space, Britton!"

"The meteors," Joseph said flatly. The story of approaching meteors had been on the news like forever. Of course he had heard about them. He and Jim had talked about 'em thirty times.

"Aliens, man!" someone cried out.

"What!?" *What the hell were these guys talking?*

"Okay, okay... we don't know what they are." Jim was trying to speak calmly now, but was having a tough time of it. "But they are not meteors."

"Meteors," said Joseph, flatly.

"They're moving faster than any goddamned meteors," grumbled Old Doc.

"Says who?"

"And course corrections," someone put in.

"And they're slowing down," said Old Doc.

"Come on, Doc. Where'd you hear that?"

"The news, man," said Jim. "The news."

Joseph was waiting for the end of the gag. "Come on. We've known about these things for weeks. They're meteors. And they're not coming anywhere near us."

Jim leaned forward, "Meteors do not make course corrections."

"With all the planets and moons and the sun and stuff pulling at them? Are you watching the news or gossip shows?"

Jim allowed a long, dramatic pause, then leaned in and spoke conspiratorially, "They're comin' for ya, man. They want ya. Their planet has no men, and your reputation spans the galaxy."

There were loud guffaws around the room, and then speculations started being tossed around as to what the aliens might be like and what they were doing here. Much of it was light and filled with bravado, but under it all Joseph could sense unease in the room. They all believed it. The aliens were coming.

The aliens were coming????

Joseph fell silent. He just wasn't ready to accept that those things out there might really be space ships. There were too many rational possibilities to consider first. And since he hadn't heard the news that morning, he couldn't know for sure what had gotten everybody all stirred up. He certainly wasn't going to take on faith what <u>they</u> were saying. That'd be crazy.

The horn sounded and everyone started out of the break room. Several dozen others were already on the floor and heading for their machines. It was the same talk everywhere.

The aliens were coming.

Kenneth Britton had actually had some measure of success in the army, despite his rather vulnerable, some might say childlike appearance. He was just twenty years old and looked even younger. He had joined the service as a private rather than a buck private, and had quickly made rank to PFC. In the accelerated program, he had recently made corporal.

The sphere of responsibility of this young corporal was at present limited to a foxhole out on the Midwestern plains of the United States. This duty he shared with another young corporal several years older than Kenneth and rather more worldly.

"This shit sucks," said Bobby. He squatted down in the foxhole, rifle held between his legs. He glanced up at Kenneth, who continued to survey the terrain their foxhole was responsible for. "Let me know if you see any bad guys, hey, Britton?"

"You got it," said Kenneth. "A-ffirmative. Bad guys come, I tell you. No problem."

"Yeah," Bobby grumbled. *Goddamned alerts.*

"You have many alerts like this?" asked Kenneth.

"Nothing better for us to do, stateside. They're always jerking on us."

"We were always on maneuvers in Europe, but this? This is just weird."

"Overseas, you're already where you need to be. It's different here."

"I suppose."

"What the hell am I saying?" Bobby cried out, "Look around! Does this look like they've brought us to where we need to be? What the hell are we doing out here?"

"Gettin' paid big bucks to protect the citizenry," said Sarge. His shadow appeared in the foxhole and Bobby slowly rose to his feet.

"Thanks a lot, Britton," said Bobby.

Kenny shrugged, fought down a grin.

Sarge grunted. "They can hear you three foxholes away, Bobby Boy. Do you know what that means?"

"Not really, Sarge."

"Well," Sarge squatted down, "then it's a good thing I'm here to tell ya', isn't it?"

"Yeah, Sarge." Bobby could feel it coming. *Sarge is going to give another of his-*

"That's right, kids," said Sarge. "Who better to advise you as to the scientific concepts that govern the world around us, to aid you in your education, to assist you in acquiring those skills that will help you in keeping your scrawny little asses out of the grinder?"

"And I do thank you, Sarge. It is deeply appreciated. Really."

"Not at all. Not at all. Now, son, if you'll just turn about there and look out yonder, I'd like to show you something..."

"Saaaarge," Bobby groaned. *Crap. I hate when he does this...*

"Please. Do bear with me."

Bobby turned towards the perimeter, grimacing.

"That's right," Sarge continued. "Now, I think even you can see that we are out on what is sometimes referred to as 'the prairie'."

"So I understand."

"Stick with me, son. This is important. Now, do you know what happens out on the prairie?"

"Nothing. Not a damned thing." He was definitely in it up to his *scrawny little ass* this time.

"That's right. Exactly. And that nothing of which you speak is a very dangerous and tricky force. You see, Bob, in the midst of all that nothing, in which not a damned thing happens, sound carries. It carries a long damned way. A helluva long, damned way." Sarge adjusted his footing, tilted his head slightly and raised a brow.

"Now, while it is quite impossible for an entire company to maintain total silence for an indefinite period of time, I truly believe it to be in the realm of possibility for *you* to keep your yapping trap closed for that afore-mentioned period of time. Am I clear? Corporal?"

"Oh, absolutely, Sergeant. You want me to shut the hell up. Sarge." *Spends three minutes telling someone to be quiet because sound travels...*

Sarge smiled menacingly. "I would be oh-so-grateful."

Kenneth waited until he was sure Sarge had finished. "Um, Sarge?" he asked.

"No news, Britton," Sarge said, anticipating Kenneth's question.

"What goes on?" Kenneth persisted.

"You know what I know."

"We don't know jack," said Bobby.

"That pretty much sums it up."

"We've been out here for four days," said Kenneth. "We haven't had mail in two weeks. This isn't just an exercise, Sarge. This is different. Something's up."

"That may be. But if there is a crisis, it's not immediate. Brass may be nervous, but no one down here is panicking. We shouldn't, either." Sarge stood up. He was in his late twenties, and those few extra years were filled with experiences that Kenneth and Bobby hadn't had. He was young, slim and strong, and his experiences showed in his manner. He was confident and ran his squad well. He was not a big brother to those in his squad, nor a father. He was a squad leader, and nobody could lead his squad better than he. He knew it, his platoon sergeant knew it, and his troops knew it.

"Be alert, kiddies," he said. "And don't sweat it. I hear anything, you'll hear it next. Meantime, keep it down. And, nothing gets by you."

"Nothing by us. Got it," said Kenneth. "Bad guys come, I tell Bobby."

"Right..." Sarge moaned, moved off to the next foxhole.

Bobby looked sharply at Kenneth. "You are such a suck-up."

Kenneth turned and leaned against the wall of their foxhole. He watched the sergeant kneel down near the next foxhole.

"I don't think he'd have given you the LWP if he really thought there was a serious threat," he said. LWP was their short-speak for 'Long Winded Professor'. "Do you?"

"Of course not," grumbled Bobby. "That great insight doesn't make you any less a suck-up."

EsJen...

EsJen looked from side to side. This was a new place. The warmth and comfort were here, but it held a different feeling. There was a *newness* about it.

EsJen. It is time.

Ship? She asked, but there were no words.

It is time...

We are here? she asked. She peered more sharply into the darkness. There was the hint of a breeze, though she knew this was not possible. There was a slight fragrance. It reminded her vaguely of home.

You must prepare.

I understand, she stated firmly. She knew that some would panic during the awakening, and she didn't want to be one of them.

Over the next few hours, the fluid nutrient in her canister was modified, which in turn caused her metabolism to change, and EsJen's body began its journey back. Ship, ShahnTahr, spoke softly to EsJen, helping her mind along on its return.

EsJen.

I am ready.

When I direct, you will open your eyes. You are at rest in your sleeping canister. There is no need for alarm. I am with you.

I understand.

Open your eyes, EsJen.

Her eyes opened. For the first time in two hundred years, she saw with her eyes. There was a golden swimming wave before her.

My eyes! she cried, before realizing that of course she was seeing exactly what she should see.

All is well... It is time for you to roll over.

Of course. Yes. I am ready.

It was a difficult task, as she knew it would be. The size of the canister, and the fluid itself, made it very awkward. EsJen struggled, slowly rotating her body around until she was face down. Her golden hair swam as a mist about her head.

Your movements should be slow and smooth. Into position now.

EsJen slowly pulled her knees up to her chest. She wrapped her arms about her legs.

Very good, EsJen. I am going to remove the nutrient fluid.

I am ready.

I will be with you. Remember.

Yes, Ship.

The fluid level is falling now.

EsJen could feel the change. It came slowly, as she knew it would. She felt her knees touch the bottom of the canister. Unwrapping her arms, she spread her knees and held her hands out before her. She felt the weight of her body shift to her hands and knees. She grew anxious.

I am with you.

Determination.

All is well.

All would be well. She would get through this and step out onto Chehno. The new world. Her new home.

Her hair dropped before her face as the fluid level continued to fall. Her lungs fought. They were filled with the fluid. Her mind fought at this, struggled with this. She convulsed, but nothing happened.

Ship! Ship!

All will be well.

I am going to drown!

There was no response. The fluid had drained. The connection was lost. She was alone in the canister. She was wet, and naked, and all alone.

I'm going to die!

A spasm, retching, and she heaved fluid up from her lungs. She fought for breath, forced up more of the fluid, and took in great gulps of air. Yes! Yes! Reaching out in both directions, her hands worked their way up the sides of the canister. The top had opened and she raised her head. With one hand, she brushed her hair back from her face, leaned out and looked down the row of canisters. It was calm and quiet, but there was some movement. In the golden glow, she could see several of her companions peering out of their own canisters. These few, and their counterparts in the other compartments, were the Stage One personnel aboard this ship. If all went as planned, the others would be awakened in the hours and days to come.

She coughed, wiped fluid from her nose and mouth. It took several minutes for her breathing to normalize, then she found the button to lower the side wall of the canister, and climbed out onto the floor. It took her several more moments before she had the confidence to let go of the canister.

"EsJen tyh muhtla," she heard someone say. *Very good, EsJen.*

EsJen raised her head, proudly nodding to the shaky figure standing beside a canister four meters away. Along with the glow of the canisters, ShahnTahr had now activated soft lighting along the rows.

"TohPeht fa buhn," she said. *And you, TohPeht.*

TohPeht turned to the several Shylmahn behind him, giving each a few words of encouragement. When they all felt able, EsJen led the way to the shower stall, where each washed and dressed. They joined those from the other compartments in the mess, where they collected food and drink from the dispensers. Almost silent at first, their excitement eventually got the best of them and they were soon talking frenziedly.

They had done it. They had traveled far, these Shylmahn pioneers. A journey begun centuries earlier. They were as excited now as they had been back then, boarding the great ships and preparing to enter the sleeping canisters. Now they were preparing to embark on the next stage of their great adventure.

Showered, clothed and fed, as per instructions, TohPeht led the way to the main control center, from where he was to communicate with ShahnTahr and receive the assignments for the Stage One personnel. They had not been in connection with ShahnTahr since leaving the canisters and many were beginning to feel uncomfortable.

TohPeht stood before the communications station, rested his fingertips on the glass panel inlaid into its surface. A faint, glowing shimmer enveloped his hand.

"All is well," he said finally, turning to the others, now crowding in where there was really not enough room. He turned quickly back to continue communication with ShahnTahr. EsJen had to remind herself to breathe. She clutched her hands before her until her fingers began to throb. GahJen, a distant cousin to EsJen, stood beside her and mumbled nervously until someone standing behind him smacked him on the back.

"Tek!" *Stop!*

TohPeht stepped away from the panel at last. His broad smile told them that the news was good.

"Ship is proceeding splendidly. The braking sequence is good. Reports continue to arrive from Chehno and are being processed and assimilated. We arrive soon. For now, after we perform our standard visual checks of all systems, we are asked to begin assisting ShahnTahr with the awakening of the Stage Two personnel. So come, let us hurry about our business so that we may welcome more of our companions to our great adventure."

Chapter Three

April 15

Elizabeth came into the living room with a cappuccino in each hand. She held one absently to Robert as she sat beside him on the couch. They each clutched uneasily to their mugs as they listened anxiously to the television. The reporter looked thoroughly excited to be a part of it all, if not a bit lost and bewildered by the events that he was detailing. Elizabeth tapped Robert on the knee when the sound of the children down the hall threatened to drown out the TV. Robert reached out to the remote and clicked the volume up a couple of notches.

"Although it is becoming increasingly difficult to locate and talk with experts in the field, we do have confirmation that there are at least five large ships approaching Earth." The reporter was speaking through his headset to the anchor back in the studio. *"We are receiving secondary confirmation, though from less reliable sources, to the earlier rumors that astronomers have identified yet another group of ships just entering the solar system, and this group of ships is following along the same trajectory as the first. This second fleet reportedly several months away."*

"Jesus Christ," said Robert. "It's an invasion, all right."

"We can't know that," Elizabeth said quickly. "Not for sure. Not yet."

"News of a second fleet does force us to look at this first group of ships with greater concern."

"Paul," said the anchor back in the studio, *"Do you have anything more about the ships themselves? Something that might give us a clue as to the intentions of the occupants?"*

"Well, as I mentioned a moment ago, experts are increasingly difficult to find. Private interests and government agencies have spirited them away to secured locations... research facilities and the like." The reporter held a clipboard out to where he could glance at his notes. "What we believe we know at this point is that the volume of each ship may be twelve to fifteen times that of our largest aircraft carriers."

He lowered his clipboard again and looked into the camera, as if looking directly at the anchor back at the studio. "We have no information as to their design, or of the material used in the manufacture of these craft, or we may have been able to infer something from that. What we can say for certain is that they are very large, and they have traveled a very, very long way to get here."

"But from where, Paul?" His tone implied that he was not expecting an answer.

"No one is willing to put a finger on a star chart and say here is where they come from. Not even as a guess. There are just too many variables."

"Not even a shot in the dark, then..."

"Again, the people most in the know just aren't accessible. Those we are able to talk with, amateurs like myself, are quite able to focus their lenses up there, but we are just not able to gather the information necessary to provide an answer."

"And the U.S. government is saying—what?"

"As Brad stated in his earlier report, there are only the standard releases that tell us very little. We can assume that the experts they have gathered together are continuing their analyses, but there is really not much that anyone can do right now but watch the skies... as they say."

"And what about the military?"

"All military forces throughout the world are in a heightened state of readiness, as you have already heard. This is to be expected, but it has many U.S. officials quite nervous. The United States has cautioned other nations to use all possible restraint. The last thing anyone wants is for an action on the part of an anxious foreign military to endanger mankind's first contact with beings from the stars."

"How do government officials interpret the continued silence from the visitors?"

"They try to put the best face on it, of course, as was evident in this morning's press conference. We've heard everything from incompatible communication equipment to speculations that they may be life forms so different from our own that there may not be a way for us to communicate with them at all."

"Could they still be deciphering our messages of welcome?"

"That continues to be put forward as a possibility. The most optimistic of options."

"It's the one I'm holding out for," said the anchor. "And what of the ordinary citizen on the street? I know you've been talking to them as well. How are they taking all of this?"

"Many are hopeful," said Paul, "but the continued silence is of considerable concern to most. Any acknowledgment at all from the visitors would be comforting. The comment that I'm hearing most often is that the space travelers must know that their arrival would cause apprehension to the inhabitants of this little planet and they should have at least attempted to make contact by now. Whether or not they understand our messages, they must have received them and should have at the very least acknowledged that fact—if their intentions were in fact friendly."

Elizabeth reached out and grasped Robert's hand. She could hear the children playing down the hall. She felt an ache inside, pulling at her, gripping at her.

Jim eased his car around the curve, took the exit and came to a stop at the light. He was driving by habit, paying little or no attention to his driving. He and Joseph were listening to the chipper, cheerful radio announcer as they drove home from work. The tone was lightweight. He seemed to be taking none of what he was talking about at all seriously.

"And now, folks, we have some unconfirmed rumors for your afternoon contemplation. We have small scout ships hovering over people's homes. We have people being abducted, and we have people returning from trips to the space ships bearing messages from the aliens. We have people in communication with the aliens via HAM radios, CBs, cell phones, and yes... tooth fillings. My, my, oh my...

"Oh, crap..." Joseph groaned.

"Really though, ladies and gentlemen, can any rumor be too wild these days? Two months ago, these little slices of life wouldn't have received a moment's airtime, at least not on my show. These people would have been laughed at even by their nearest and dearest friends. Now, however, any of these stories might actually be true, or none of them."

"None of them," said Jim.

"Everyone's gone crazy," said Joseph.

"Yeah, but really, can you blame them?"

Joseph just shrugged.

"Don't you feel weird going to work?" asked Jim. "I mean, here we are, driving home from a mundane eight hours at the plant, and all the while we have this stuff going on. Doesn't this—stuff— make everything else seem just a bit unimportant?"

"Everyone should stop their lives, then? Quit their jobs?"

"I'm for that." Jim absently swerved around an empty pop can that was bouncing around on the pavement. "No, of course not. But I wouldn't mind putting it on hold for a while. When someone drops by your house, don't you stop what you're doing and say hello?"

"Depends on what I'm doing."

"Well, naturally..."

"Banks are gonna love you."

"Let 'em sweat. Do 'em good." Jim turned the car onto Joseph's street. He pulled down the visor to shade his eyes, leaving his face covered in shadow. "I may go see Jack for a while."

"Jack? Your brother, Jack? Jack's crazy."

"He's looking a wee bit less certifiable than he did a couple of weeks ago."

"He lives in a shack in the woods, surrounded by barbed wire."

"Exactly." Jim pulled up in front of Joseph's house.

"One noted astronomer has informed us that an alien attack base has been under construction on the dark side of the moon for several months."

Joseph growled, "Now how the hell would he know that? Noted astronomer, my ass."

"Joey, don't you think that if these aliens had good intentions, they would have said something by now?"

Anna Broderick says that she was taken aboard a—a"

"Perhaps they have. Who knows what we're not being told?"

"If they had sent a message, a million amateurs would have picked it up."

"Depends on how the message was sent," said Joseph. He glared at the radio, then turned his gaze out the side window, "One thing I can tell you for sure—what we're picking up now is a lot of crap."

"Thank you, Miss Broderick. And we have dozens of reports that aliens already on the Earth have been sending coded messages out to the alien fleet for years. From our affiliate in—"

Joseph knew as soon as he opened his front door that he was not alone. He sensed a presence there... something that wasn't quite right, something that wasn't normal. Something was different than when he had left that morning. A tingling, prickly wave swept over him. He stood unmoving, not breathing. An unreasoning paranoia born of all that had been going on these days threatened to consume him.

He saw a shadow in the chair in the corner by the window.

"Joey?"

Joseph jumped at the voice, slapped at the light switch on the wall. Carolyn was sitting with her hands in her lap; quiet, withdrawn.

Joseph struggled to calm himself enough to speak.

"Carolyn?" Joseph managed, took a step, "Carolyn, what are you doing here?"

Carolyn stood. They met in the middle of the room. Holding her, Joseph felt her twitching nerves and the tightness of her muscles, despite his own adrenaline rush and still-racing heart. He had thought that if anyone would be able to hold up through all of this, it would have been his sister.

"Hey, no reason to panic, Sis. Not yet, anyway."

"Oh, I wouldn't say that. You don't know what's going on."

"We do have television here in the States."

"You don't know," she said firmly.

"All right... I don't know. So, tell me." They sat side by side on the couch.

"Oh, crap," was all she could get out. Joseph took her hands in his, held tightly to them.

"No rush." He loosened his grip on her hands, sat back and gave a comforting smile. "It's good to see you."

Carolyn smiled then, brushed a loose hair from her face, leaned back and rested her head against the back of the couch. It had taken everything she had just to get here, and she hadn't thought much about what she would do when she actually made it. Now that she had, there was a peculiar emptiness inside her. Joseph waited.

When she was finally able, after Joseph rambled about all the craziness going on at the plant and with Jim making plans to go see psycho Jack, she told him of the problem they had been having, and of the program she had written to track it down. He knew just a little of her assignment in Australia, that she was maintaining some sort of communication software that her company owned, or operated, or something. What she actually did, though, he hadn't a clue.

"Okay, okay..." he said, waving a dismissive hand. "You lost me. Again. I'll take your word for it. You did something, wrote something, and you found out that the aliens are using some system to talk to the fleet."

"Yes," she said. "Incoming bursts, milliseconds long, redirects the comm apparatus, sends out a coded message burst, resets the apparatus..."

"Uh, huh."

"And wipes its trail as it backs out."

"I got that. But aliens?"

"The outgoing message was on a narrow beam, not directed at any of our satellites. It was directed along the path of the alien fleet."

They were never able to trace the incoming trigger back to its source, but its method had been clear enough. It went around access procedures and used maintenance routines to reset the apparatus.

Joseph again waved a hand in surrender.

"Okay okay, wait a sec." He thought about what this implied. "They've been using your company's equipment to send messages to their fleet."

"Right."

"But... that would mean... you're saying—"

"They're already here."

Joseph and Carolyn sat at the kitchen table, each with a glass of iced tea in front of them. They hadn't said much since Joseph took Carolyn by the hand and led her into his small kitchen.

She stared down at her glass. "Who knows for how long?" she asked.

"How long, what?"

"Who knows how long they've been at this? Before the station, even before we had communications. Once we developed the technology, it was probably less conspicuous for them to use ours instead."

"That's a lot of assuming, Carolyn."

"They might have been here a long time. A really long time."

"Carolyn—"

"I think those ships up there right now are following others that came before them. They may have been here a year, a hundred years, or a thousand years."

They again both fell silent. Joseph stood finally and went to the refrigerator. He opened the door, then looked back to Carolyn in a desperate plea.

"Pizza," she said.

"Good choice." He closed the refrigerator and reached for the wall phone. Instead of picking up the receiver, however, he picked up the cell phone he kept sitting on the wall phone. He pushed a button. Speed dial. He turned back to Carolyn and gave her a guilty grin.

He gave his order, then closed the phone and set it back on top of the wall phone.

"You didn't tell them where—" Carolyn started, then stopped. "Never mind."

Joseph gave another guilty shrug and started to make a pot of coffee.

"I'm glad you're back," he said.

"You and me, both." She sat back heavily in the kitchen chair. "You should've seen all the suits floating around down there once it started looking like... you know."

"I can guess."

"I was lucky to get out when I did."

"Whatever your motivation, glad you're here, and safe."

The five ships drew farther and farther apart as they moved nearer the new world, sliding into high orbit one by one; two hundred thousand kilometers out, slowing, spiraling ever nearer. The Shylmahn were all awake, excitement so great that each thought he might burst from it. All were eager to begin the colonization of Chehno.

TohPeht was now in constant communication with ShahnTahr. He would occasionally lift his head, turn a cloudy gaze to GahJen and provide instructions for one or another of the colonists, generally regarding procedures once they were on the surface. On each of the other ships, there was a counterpart to TohPeht—a Shylmahn leader answering only to ShahnTahr.

There was but one ShahnTahr. At any given moment the information and knowledge in Ship One might be different than that in Ship Two, or any other ship within the advance fleet, and the data currently being processed by the advance fleet would not be processed by the second fleet for some time and not by any of the other fleets trailing back towards Shylmah for some time beyond that, but it was no less true that *they* were but *one*. The ShahnTahr residing in each ship, within each fleet, all the way back to the First, on Shylmah, was one, and the *one* was ShahnTahr.

May 01

Carolyn practically hurled herself at the television set, dragging the chair beneath her as she went. "Joseph! Joseph!"

The room was dark but for the glow of the television screen and Carolyn shimmering before it, with shadows stretching out behind her. Joseph came in and stood beside her.

The television screen was displaying a still graphic with the phrase 'Breaking News'. Finally, the graphic was replaced with the set of the local news desk. A female news anchor was sitting stiffly behind the desk.

"We have breaking news regarding the arrival of the alien fleet."

"She looks scared," said Carolyn.

Joseph, nodding slowly, sat on the arm of the chair.

"This may be our last opportunity to provide you with important information. Communication satellites and ground communication facilities are being destroyed, as are power installations. We will not be on the air much longer.

"We have lost our network feed... We know that our own military forces are attempting to strike back, but we have no word on the effectiveness of those strikes.

"Alien craft are leaving the large ships. Prior to our loss of network feed, it was reported that these smaller craft were attacking locations throughout the world.

"Military installations throughout the world are being attacked at this time. Eyewitnesses to the attacks report a bright flash prior to the explosion. Destruction is said to be complete and alien weaponry is described as extremely efficient."

The reporter's eyes searched frantically from side to side as a scrambling of feet went on behind the cameras. She turned then, calmly, toward the camera. She straightened her posture and spoke precisely.

"That's it, then. Good luck to all of –"

The image swam, then static. Joseph and Carolyn stared dully at the screen, now filled with a loud, hissing snow.

The television went dark. The room was black.

Joseph reached for the light switch.

Click. No response.

Click, click, click.

"It's started," he said.

"She said military bases. God, Joseph—"

Puget Sound was one military base after another...

The room went suddenly, explosively, white. Instant, total light washed everything of all color. In the next heartbeat every window in the house imploded into thousands of tiny, glittering, glassy raindrops. Walls cracked and buckled, doors vaporized into splinters. Joseph was struck with a violent, crushing pressure that hit him from all sides at once, then lifted him into the air and brought him down hard onto the floor. His house collapsed down around him.

Chapter Four

May 02

The morning held dull, gray skies and threatened rain. Joseph stumbled out of the splintered rubble and fell clumsily onto the lawn. Carolyn crawled up next to him, pulled her legs around in front of her and wiped loose strands of hair from her face. She saw the blood under Joseph's nose, wiped her own and looked at her own bloodied sleeve.

"Oh, yeah," she nodded clumsily, sniffed. "This is good... yeah."

"Sorry," Joseph droned. "Afraid I don't see it."

"You and I of the way, Joey. Taken care of. The way is now clear for them to take the planet."

"Ah. Cynicism."

Joseph looked up and down the block. Most of the homes were destroyed, though a few had one or two walls still standing. There were half a dozen chimneys still up. He could see a few of his neighbors searching among the rubble. He looked at Carolyn and himself, then rolled over to get to his feet.

"We have to get to Liz's." Standing now, he reached down to help Carolyn up. "You okay?"

"Do I look okay to you?" She managed to get to her feet. She appeared to have no broken bones, but her chest felt as though she had been crushed. Looking back at Joseph's house, she realized that she had. They cleaned themselves up at a broken water line and put on some clothes that had survived the disaster. They put extra clothes into cloth laundry bags, along with a few supplies and what few canned goods Joseph kept on hand. Carolyn found her cell phone, but as expected, there was no signal. Joseph searched in vain for his, holding out some hidden belief that his memory dial would somehow be able to reach Liz where Carolyn's phone could not.

They walked down the center of the street where there was less debris. Some of the homes they passed were smoldering, showing an occasional flickering flame, but most were simply piles of broken wood and wallboard, with curtains and clothes and furniture and appliances twisted in amongst splintered timber. Cars had no windows. Some had the paint blown off, leaving primer or bare metal. Some of the cars lay on their side or top, and a few were sitting on the rims, the rubber tires themselves gone.

They passed a car parked askance in the street with a man slumped over behind the wheel. As they drew nearer, Joseph could see that the skin and flesh on the left side of the man's face was gone, and the eye socket was empty. The exposed bone was dark.

It was the first body. The first death. The destruction was everywhere, and Joseph knew that he had only seen a few quiet streets and that the devastation was likely worldwide; but he hadn't seen any bodies. Not out in the open. Not until now.

He and Carolyn hurried around the car. Joseph absently ran his fingers across his own face, as if to make sure his was still flesh and blood. They continued on, more anxious than ever to get to Elizabeth's.

The utility poles were gone. A few dead wires lay across the road. As they approached the main thoroughfare, Joseph and Carolyn found the service station at the intersection had gone up. In place of the building and pump station was a deep crater. The fuel tanks must have exploded. The empty field behind the station was now barren and black. They passed by quietly and turned up the next street.

The homes on this street were intact but for a few shattered windows and doors. A large bush in the middle of one yard was charred. The house itself, however, and the car in the driveway, looked almost untouched. Taking this as a sign of hope, they picked up their pace. Liz and Robert's house was one more block up, one block over.

"We get Liz, we'll head to a private marina a couple of miles south. There are usually twenty or thirty boats tied up there."

"I'm not too comfortable about going out onto the Sound in the middle of an invasion."

"Until we figure out what's going on, Bril's looks like the safest place to be."

"Setting aside the whole issue of being trapped on a small island with our dear brother, first we have to actually get there."

"We'll get there."

"Over big water. With aliens flying over our heads."

"We'll get there."

Damn fine mess we're in now, and it'll take more than pointing the front of the boat at Bril's island to get us out of it...

Yet, if there was one thing the Brittons were good at, it was pulling together in a crisis. That was what had brought Carolyn all the way back from Australia. With the Britton family, it had always been unite and conquer.

Bril must be eating this up.

Joseph glanced over at his sister. She looked to be struggling against collapse. She had to be emotionally and physically drained, yet she refused to surrender. Here he was, hands shaking, fighting for control, fighting against an almost overwhelming urge to go screaming into oblivion with arms flailing.

Halfway to the top of the hill he waved for Carolyn to slow down. He had made the walk to Liz's house dozens of times and never had a problem with this hill; but today... today...

I'm about ready to go out of my mind. If the aliens will just sit back and wait, we should all be blithering idiots in a week...

Carolyn saw it first. Making the top of the ridge, she stopped, took a stumbling step forward, and stopped again. Joseph felt a numbing sense of foreboding as he moved slowly up beside her, knowing what she was seeing, not wanting to see it, and unable to stop himself.

He had always loved the view from here. To the north lay the Seattle skyline, with Bellevue to the northeast. To the south lay Tacoma. Directly below and spreading to the east, three small bedroom communities lay snug in the valley.

Tacoma was smoldering, dark and misshapen under a huge, gray-brown cloud. The cloud glowed and pulsated as if feeding off the ashy corpse below it. The army and air bases to the south were certainly gone, and Bremerton with its shipyards and the nearby naval bases.

To the north, the Seattle skyline was now half a dozen broken spires, though Joseph thought he could see the stadiums still standing. Perhaps it was wishful thinking.

The streets and homes directly below looked torn and scattered amidst the smoke, fires burning unchecked everywhere, and the valley was being smothered in the heavy smog.

Millions, thought Joseph. The face of the man in the car came back to him, unbidden. *Millions. Millions and millions...*

And then... *I've seen this... I've seen this...*

That weird dream or vision or whatever it was... that night at hilltop park.

Where the heck had that come from?

Joseph's thoughts crossed and re-crossed, and he couldn't quite organize them, couldn't quite put things in order. Moving through a numbing, mental fog, he and Carolyn started down the other side of the hill, turned finally onto Elizabeth's street. It wasn't until he saw that her house still stood that he began to think coherently.

Her house had a few broken windows, and inside they found the walls bare, with all the pictures thrown to the floor, but it was standing. Some of the walls were cracked. Cabinets were emptied with their contents strewn about. There was no sign that anyone had been seriously hurt.

"No one here," said Joseph, moving hurriedly from room to room.

"Here!" Carolyn called from down the hall. Joseph hurried after the voice, followed it into the bathroom. There he saw a message neatly written on the cracked mirror with lipstick:

Gone to Bril's.
Find Barbara!
Love, Liz.

Joseph leaned back against the door jamb and let out a heavy sigh of relief, as if he hadn't breathed since coming into the house.

Elizabeth must have taken her family away during the night. It wouldn't have taken her long to decide on the best way to take care of her family, and once the decision was made there would have been no reason to wait. Not even for Joseph. Besides, she apparently had other plans for her brother.

Well, he wasn't about to go looking for Barbara now. She lived forty miles away, and had probably gone to her father's, which was even farther. Joseph would follow Elizabeth to Bril's. Once he knew that Liz and the kids were safe, then he would think about finding Barb.

They rummaged around the house for anything that might come in handy, to add to their collection of supplies from his place. They found an empty plastic bottle they hoped to use for water, and picked up a few cans of food and a box of cookies the kids must have missed. Ready then, they went out the front door. It started to rain. Light at first, it grew heavier with each step they took.

Elizabeth pulled her children back under the dog-eared eave of the metal building just as the dark sky opened up and the rain began falling in earnest. Robert stepped in beside them, large suitcase in hand.

"We'll make it," Elizabeth said to him. "I promise."

Robert nodded curtly. He wiped the heavy drops from his face with his free hand and looked out at the rain. He set the suitcase down and pulled the long coat more tightly about him. Elizabeth had bought it for him last Christmas. This was the first time he had worn it.

"You boys all right?" he asked the children. He struggled to keep his voice from betraying his own fears, which threatened to overwhelm him. His sense of duty to his family was all that kept him from curling up in a dark corner somewhere.

"We'll make it," said William, echoing his mother.

"Yup," said little Sean. Confidence shown strongly on his face. He was soaked to the skin.

Elizabeth looked calmly at her husband. He was quiet, cold and anxious. He glanced back at her, finally showed her an empty smile. She smiled, reached across and pulled him closer, squeezing the children between them.

Several minutes passed and there was no sign the rain was going to let up. Elizabeth looked impatiently in the direction of the dock.

"What do you think, Robert? Let's make a dash for it."

Robert reached down for the suitcase. "Why not..."

Elizabeth looked down at the children. William had gotten a bump and a nasty little cut on the forehead when the family picture had fallen from the wall. His head was wrapped in a wet, dirty bandage. "You kids ready?"

They looked up at her, nodding, and she pushed them out into the rain. The four of them rushed down through the heavy downpour, their footsteps hollow splashes in the growing puddles. In the distance they could see the short, narrow pier and just make out several boats bobbing up and down in the water.

Chapter Five

May 12

Kenneth dropped to the ground beside Bobby and elbowed his way above the sticky weeds until he could just see over the small hillock. An alien transport craft rested some five hundred yards farther on, and there were loud noises spreading out into the darkness beyond the range of the blazing lights. They were unloading personnel and supplies, and didn't seem concerned about possible attack.

This location had become a regular disembarkation zone for the aliens. Once it had been identified, Kenneth's company had been assigned to attack the next ship to land there. It was about time, as far as Kenneth and the others were concerned. It had been a week and a half, and they had yet to get into it with the bastards.

Still too far away to get a really good look, Kenneth was near enough to feel the *alienness* of it. Small, golden figures were unloading gray crates from large open bays. All the figures wore the same light brown, loose fitting shirt and pant outfits. The ship was big, but he knew it was small compared to the mother ships in orbit. The attack craft they had caught a few glimpses of were smaller yet, more sleekly designed, and mean as hell. By contrast, this was just a big box with huge wings strapped to the top of it.

Bobby tapped Kenneth on the leg and waved him down. He pointed to his watch and gave the sign for one minute.

Looking from side to side, they could see the others of the platoon readying for the assault. Together, the four platoons formed an arc along one side of the alien ship. They would move in behind the mortar blasts.

According to those who had already faced the aliens, air assaults brought against the invaders had either been beaten back by the energy blasts or were destroyed by alien attack ships long before they got near their targets. Artillery barrages had been found to be useless. As the shells approached, the energy blasts emitted from the alien craft detonated the charges too far out to do any damage. These blasts were smaller and more concentrated than the more extensive detonations like those of the first days of the invasion, and were more surgical in purpose. The aliens had eliminated most of the military installations in the first hours of the original attack, and since then had reserved the larger energy discharges for any large forces they found remaining. Because of this, troops and supplies had been divided into smaller, less conspicuous units.

As the final seconds ticked away, Kenneth pressed himself into the ground, anticipating the mortar blasts to come. It was hoped that using mortars at this close range would give them a greater chance of reaching target. In any event, Kenneth and the others would be following right behind.

He heard the mortars go, followed immediately by a second barrage. He and those around him jumped to their feet and began the charge toward the alien ship. They could see the blasts near the ship, and for a moment were heartened and pressed on.

At three hundred yards, several of the soldiers around Kenneth began firing. Kenneth continued charging. Tiny flashes of light erupted around him, almost blinding. Another hundred yards closer and the intensity and concentration of the alien energy blasts drove Kenneth to the ground. He pushed his rifle out in front of him and began firing at the figures near the ship. The aliens looked calm, almost detached from the attack.

The small, explosive flashes continued. Kenneth could hear human cries behind and beside him. He pulled the empty clip from his rifle, slapped in a new one and began firing at random locations around the ship. There was no way to tell where the energy blasts were coming from, nor where they were going to strike. There were no visible emissions or trails. A burst of light would suddenly blossom, as quickly vanish, and anything within the small target area was destroyed.

He pulled out the emptied clip and put in another full one.

"Fall back! Fall back!" Bobby was crying out.

Kenneth rose to his knees, then stood. Backing away, he made controlled, carefully aimed shots: at the ship, at the crates, at the aliens themselves. It was a long three hundred yards back to the hillock from which they had begun their charge, and he spent the time observing the result of each of his shots. He was the last to return.

The energy blossoms did not stop. The hillock was not safe.

"Retreat! To the trees! Retreat!" The panicked order came down the line. The platoons made an orderly run, occasioned by what appeared to be random blasts that hollowed out the troops two, three, five at a time.

Sarge laid a hand on Kenneth's shoulder. "You okay, corporal?"

Kenneth was sitting on the ground with his elbows on his knees. His helmet sat beside him, his rifle lay on a cloth in front of him, disassembled and partially cleaned. A young private walked by with a box under one arm. He tossed a ration packet to Kenneth, another to Bobby, and continued on his rounds.

Kenneth nodded.

Bobby said, "Britton here tried to walk up and shake hands with 'em. Think we could get a little closer next time?"

"I'll pass your request along to Command," said Sarge, continuing on.

Bobby tore open his ration packet and began digging into his dinner. Kenneth continued cleaning his weapon.

"Suck-up," he mumbled.

"John Wayne," said Bobby.

In their first attack on the alien force, Bravo Company had lost a third of its troops outright, and a number of others had been wounded. The walking wounded stayed with the company, while those with major injuries were taken to a centrally located field hospital that served all the forces in the area.

As exchange for the casualties, some information was acquired through debriefing of the troops. The information was passed on to other companies, just as information had been given to them. Such was the way it was going to be. A battle's success wasn't calculated by comparing casualty counts or whether or not a hill was taken. A battle's value was to be measured in the information obtained. Information was more valuable than... than just about anything.

May 16

The small motorboat moved noisily northward, always staying close to the shoreline. Joseph was ready to make a hurried dash to land at the first sign of the aliens.

For him and Carolyn, the way here had been difficult, and it did not appear that it would get any easier. After leaving

Elizabeth's house, they had nearly stumbled right into an alien ship as it came in to land. They had cut through a yard and as they stepped into the next street were caught in the blast of air cushion beneath a small shuttle landing in the middle of the roadway. Hurrying back between the houses, they crouched down and waited. The ship landed, and after several moments four creatures stepped out.

They were all five foot three to five foot four, very thin, and wore brown shirts and pants. The shoes looked soft and cotton-like. Their skin was a golden yellow, and they had long, golden brown hair. They each had large, golden eyes, and delicate nose and mouth that looked like those of a human child. The ears, if they had ears, could not be seen for the hair.

The four aliens had moved single-mindedly to a house directly across the street from where Joseph and Carolyn were hiding. Approaching the front door, the door, its frame, and the area immediately surrounding it vanished in a cloud of splinters and dust. The four never slowed pace. They stepped into the house and disappeared for half a minute. Coming back out, one alien indicated for two of its comrades to go around to the back as it and the fourth moved to the front door of the next house. The front door of this house also exploded as they neared, as before, and they went inside.

Joseph heard the family of the house attempting to resist. They had tried to escape out the back, and were being herded from the back yard by the group of aliens. The humans looked bewildered, confused. Everything that was happening to them, to everyone, was so foreign and so beyond any sense of reason or reality, that all their actions and responses were uncertain and half-hearted. Two of the aliens were using what looked like small sticks, a foot and a half long, to prod the family along. The sticks obviously caused some discomfort, as the young couple and their two small children moved more quickly when prodded.

As the group stepped into the street, a fifth alien came out of the shuttle and approached the human family, now being formed into a line. The children were crying, and the mother bent down to comfort them. As she did, one of the aliens pushed the stick to her back and she jumped in pain. The father lunged for the alien and was set upon by the others who prodded him into submission.

A gunshot rang out. Joseph couldn't tell from where, but he was glad to hear it.

The aliens, rather than showing any fear, looked about curiously. One of them pointed to a house several doors down from where Joseph and Carolyn were, on the same side of the street. Another of them nodded and spoke into a box.

Again came the bright, blinding light, and there was an explosion from within the suspect house. Another shot rang out and one of the aliens went down, wounded.

There were several more energy bursts within the house.

There were no more shots. After a few moments, the house slowly collapsed in on itself.

Several of the aliens knelt down to examine their wounded comrade. They helped it up and one of them assisted it into the shuttle.

The fifth alien, meanwhile, had begun a cursory examination of the human family. It nodded finally to the alien that had been leading the search team and indicated that the family should be taken aboard the shuttle. Within moments of the family being loaded inside, the shuttle lifted off and headed south. Joseph and Carolyn stepped out into the street, out to where the shuttle had been just seconds before.

"The ground's not hot," Carolyn noticed.

"They bleed," said Joseph. There were drops of blood, red blood, where the wounded alien had fallen. Carolyn knelt beside Joseph, reached as if to touch the red drops with her fingertips, thought better of it. She stood then, looking at the blasted doorway of the one house, then at the collapsed house down the street.

"Energy blasts," she said thoughtfully. "Smaller than before, but definitely energy blasts."

"They can level a city or knock out a door with the same weapon. Same type, anyway."

"Those sticks we saw them use are probably based on the same thing."

A few people had stepped cautiously out of their homes, some standing on their lawns, others in the street. One ran to the collapsed house, tossing wallboard aside in an attempt to find the gunman who had tried to fight back.

"They had no fear at all," said Joseph. "Did you notice? They didn't even try to take cover."

"Maybe this invasion stuff is as new to them as it is to us."

"But they didn't even know to be scared," Joseph continued, not quite believing. "They can be hurt. Their lack of fear doesn't come from invincibility."

"Like... religious fanaticism."

"They're so damned calm. It's scary." Joseph wiped his hands on his pants. "Let's get our stuff. Let's get out of here."

Later, nearing the dock, they heard a whistling sound coming from somewhere above. Before they could step into the shadows, a sleek alien craft, much different than the shuttle they had seen earlier, sped overhead, leaving a cracking thunder behind it.

The sun was trying to burn through the high clouds. Joseph and Carolyn approached the small pier and found just one boat tied up. It had been well cared for and looked like just what they needed. They tossed their bags in and climbed aboard.

Before they could do any more than that, three quick shots rang out, and plastic and wood shattered around them. They dove into the water and swam beneath the pier. Moments later, heavy footsteps pounded down the walk.

"Who the hell you goddamned sonsofbitches think you are!" a man called out angrily. He sounded large and very upset. "Think you can steal a man's boat? Is that it?" Another shot rang out, but they couldn't tell where it had been aimed. "Fuckin' chickenshit sonsofbitches!"

They heard him jump into his boat and start the engine. He continued to grumble angrily. They waited until the man and his boat were well away before coming out from under the dock.

"Wow," said Carolyn, climbing back up onto the dock.

"I gotta get me one of those things."

"What things?"

"A gun."

"What would you have done? Would you have shot the guy? Joey, we were going to steal his boat."

"There seems to be a helluva lot of shooting going on. I think I'd rather be on the trigger-pulling side of it. That's all."

They were walking up and away from the pier. The clouds were darkening up again.

"Are you ready to start killing people?"

"He got all of our stuff."

Carolyn decided to change the subject. "Isn't there another dock down that way?"

"Yeah." Joseph pulled wet clothes away from his wet body.

In getting to the next dock, they would be passing not far from Jim's house. They decided to swing up his way and, if they hadn't gone to psycho Jack's survivalist cabin, see if he and his wife wanted to join them.

The homes on Jim's street had been hit hard. Standing on his friend's front lawn, Joseph could see the front door and all the windows had imploded, most likely from the initial attack. Wet drapes hung limp and dirty on either side of the opening where a six-by-ten front window had once been.

Carolyn continued toward the porch while Joseph remained standing in the yard. Reaching the front door, she took a single step inside, and stopped.

Joseph could see that something was seriously wrong, but couldn't move. He watched silently as Carolyn moved calmly away from the house. Reaching her brother, she took a final step and stood behind him.

"He must have been standing right in front of that big front window."

Joseph managed a curt nod, nothing more.

"Come on," said Carolyn. She reached back and rested a hand on his shoulder. "Let's go." She walked off the lawn and started up the sidewalk. Joseph straightened and slowly followed after her.

There was a small neighborhood strip mall at the next intersection, where Jim's street met a four-lane boulevard. It held a small grocery, a pharmacy, a western clothing store, and a used paperback store. They hit the clothing store first, finding dry clothes to replace the wet clothes they still had on, and western dusters to put on over their fresh clothes. They stuffed extra clothes into two garment bags. Joseph looked for a weapon behind the counter, but came up empty.

They loaded up on groceries and medicine in the grocery store and pharmacy, again no weapons, before continuing to the dock. It was near dark by the time they got there. They found a boat, small but worthy, and decided to make the trip across the Sound despite the late hour. They reasoned that it would probably be safer making the crossing at night anyway.

Alien aircraft flew overhead several times during the trip over, but either the invaders didn't see them or didn't care. A small boat in the Sound with two humans aboard wasn't really much of a threat and would probably be more trouble than it was worth.

They arrived safely on the far shore just before midnight. They made camp twenty yards inland, built a small campfire, and spent the night. The next morning, and on subsequent mornings, they moved northward, staying close to shore. They occasionally stopped at beachfront homes, most of which had been abandoned and a few of which had been destroyed. They were chased away from one upon threat of death by the owner. At least, he said he was the owner. Joseph didn't really think the gentleman had the look or manner of the owner of a three million dollar beachfront property, but you never knew, and who was he to argue with a man holding a big gun? Again with the guns...

On the sixth day, they pulled the boat ashore a few hundred yards south of a little community that before recent events had earned its livelihood from tourists and a small dock and boat launch. The town was little more than a half dozen stores, with homes scattered across the hillside above.

It was midmorning, the sun was out, and Joseph and Carolyn hoped to get a few supplies and maybe some news. They crossed the back parking lot of the general store. The sign above the back door read *rear entrance, welcome.* Joseph led the way in. There was the tiny tinkling of the metal bell as the door opened. The shelves were shoulder high. They each chose an aisle and started searching the shelves.

Joseph began to grow uncomfortable, and not because the store was empty of people. It would have been odd to find a clerk behind the counter these days. It was something else. There was something... he felt that increasingly familiar tingling along the back of his neck. He froze.

He was looking over the tops of the shelves. A shadow moved across the far wall. Without moving, Joseph looked side-glance at the front window.

A small alien figure was right outside, in front of the big plate-glass storefront window, taking oh-so-slow steps, as if on a Sunday stroll. Joseph dared not move. The alien was not looking inside the store, but it would certainly catch any movement. If it did look in, movement or not, it would see Joseph standing there in the middle of aisle 3 beside the tomato paste.

Where's Carolyn?

Joseph's eyes darted hurriedly about, searching frantically. If she hadn't seen it... Hell, what if she says something?

Don't move! Don't talk!

The alien stopped.

Shit, shit, shit, shit.

The alien turned its back to the window, faced the street.

Joseph went down to his knees, hands palm down on the cold linoleum. The alien's head turned to the left, then the right. It turned about again, stepped away from the window. Joseph heard shuffling in the next aisle, caught a short breath when he saw Carolyn appear near the front window, on hands and knees and looking out into the street. She waved for him to come to her.

He would much rather be going out the back door. Still, he crawled over.

Four trucks, U.S. Army trucks, were lined up at the end of the street. There was an alien shuttlecraft parked beside them. Aliens were everywhere, all up and down the street; many more than could have arrived on the one shuttle. A group of humans was being prodded into the back of one of the trucks with those sticks. A sharp piercing sound made Joseph turn his head and look toward the boat ramp at the other end of the street.

What looked to be an alien-made hovercraft was hurtling across the surface of the water and up the launch ramp. It settled onto flat ground and two aliens with prod sticks approached the slowly opening side door. Three human men and a small boy were brought out and herded up the street. Joseph and Carolyn ducked down and out of sight as they passed by the store window.

There was more movement in the hovercraft, and Joseph saw three aliens being carried off on small stretchers. Their clothing was splattered in blood. Two looked to be alive, the third was obviously dead. All three were taken into the building across the street, to what had once been the restaurant. The hovercraft started up again, slid back out above the water and away.

Back up the street, the shuttlecraft lifted up and left. The trucks themselves stayed.

Joseph and Carolyn backed away from the window and went to the back door of the store. Joseph opened it a few inches, gently closed it again. He shook his head. Carolyn opened it a fraction to see for herself.

A number of aliens were leading several dozen humans across the field beyond the parking lot towards town.

They would have to wait.

They returned to the front window when they heard the sound of a shuttle coming in. Over the next several hours, Joseph and Carolyn watched as hovercraft, shuttlecraft, and quite a few foot-bound aliens came into this little town and loaded up truck after truck with humans. Trucks came and went, but there were always at least four or five parked and ready. The shuttlecraft weren't limited to landing on the roadway, either. They were forced to land behind the general store every now and then, whenever the street was occupied.

Wounded aliens continued to arrive as well, and were taken away by larger shuttlecraft on two occasions. They were handled carefully by their comrades; there was genuine concern for their well-being. So while these bastards were willing to die, they didn't necessarily want to, and had no desire to see their fellows killed. It was difficult to relate this to what they had witnessed in the street days earlier.

Darkness came, and Joseph and Carolyn found themselves trapped. The back parking lot was being used regularly now; the aliens even set up lights. Joseph took a stack of towels and made up a bed of sorts behind the counter, and the two of them managed to fall asleep some time after midnight.

In the morning they were alone.

The aliens had left sometime before dawn. Carolyn suggested that maybe they were moving from area to area gathering up humans. With this area cleaned up, they had simply moved on. This seemed as likely a possibility as any. Joseph was glad just to be able to get out of there.

They continued north. Travel was slow, and Joseph was all the more cautious now that it appeared the aliens were picking up humans. There was more human activity about, and more alien activity as well. They often heard gunshots, and occasionally the sound of the small energy blasts. More rarely, they heard the larger blasts that shook the ground beneath their feet. The shuttlecraft were common overhead, and even the assault ships were seen several times a day. Once they heard what they knew to be a group of jet fighters, manmade, flying low and fast. Joseph doubted that aliens would be flying jet fighters.

There was no mistaking Bril's island once they finally saw it. They had been fooled three times before, thinking that they had simply missed the mainland dock, and so started out towards the island, turning back once they could see they were wrong.

There was no way this was not their brother's island. One of the more normal-looking small dots of land on the Sound, yet very obviously Bril's. Verification was the small dock jutting out from the nameless collection of buildings on the mainland peninsula. They started out from the dock, moving slowly away from the protection of the shoreline.

The island was a quarter of a mile wide and a quarter of a mile long. About fifty acres or so, and it belonged to Bril Britton. It was little more than a hilltop rising up out of the water, covered in fir and alder. A narrow spit of land ran along the north side, creating a small, interior cove. From the east bank of the cove, there was a slow rise for several hundred yards before rising sharply to form the east ridge of the island.

Joseph brought the boat up along the spit, then around and down into the narrow inlet. He was several hundred feet inside before he spotted the camouflaged boathouse, within which Bril's charter boat and sailboat must be hidden. If he hadn't known it had to be there, he probably wouldn't have seen it.

He came around the bend and could see the house halfway up the slope. It was set low to the ground and the back of the house was actually set into the hillside. It was attractive yet inconspicuous, blending in well with the surroundings. As he ran the boat up onto the shore, Joseph noticed mounds of freshly turned earth, freshly finished bare wood and low concrete walls some thirty yards east of the house.

It wasn't till he and Carolyn were out of the boat that Joseph spotted the figure in the trees a few yards to his left. He saw movement then off to his right.

"Who be ye!" came a deep, resonant voice from the trees, spoken in a cheesy, pirate twang. The voice could belong to no one other than Bril.

"I be Joseph the Exhausted," Joseph called out. He reached into the boat for the bags of supplies, tossing them one by one onto the shore.

"And who be the appetizing wench beside ye', Joseph the Exhausted?"

"She be Carolyn the Irritating. I offer her in trade for safe passage through your lands."

"A tempting offer, traveler. Perhaps my men might find use for her. Come forward then, and bring the young morsel with ye'."

"It's not too late," Carolyn mumbled. "Let's get back in the boat and get the hell outta here."

Joseph was already starting up the slope. "It be the price we pay, Sis."

"Grrr," she grumbled tiredly in her own monotone pirate, following after Joseph. They each had several of their bags in hand, leaving still others sitting beside the boat. Bril stepped into view.

He was a big, strong man. He actually *looked* loud. He had a blustering, independent air about him. His hair was light brown, cut short and severe, and he wore a thick, trim, reddish beard. His face was weathered from long days spent outside. Nearing forty, he was the oldest of the Britton clan.

Bril wrapped his heavy arms around Joseph, squeezed hard and pounded his back sharply.

"You made it, brother!" he said, then reached out for his sister. "Carolyn!"

Elizabeth had come out of hiding, weapon in hand, then Robert. Elizabeth rushed up and hugged them both.

"I see you guys made it all right," said Joseph.

"Not an easy trip," said Elizabeth. She stepped back to get a better look, nodded in Bril's direction. "Sorry about that. When we saw that it was you, I wanted to warn you, but, you know."

Joseph smiled. "Kids all right?"

In answer, Elizabeth indicated the action just up slope. Bril's seven-year-old son Peter was running down from the house, followed by Elizabeth's two children, and they all huddled around the new arrivals. Bril's wife Kathryn stood on the front porch of the house and watched the spectacle below, smiling broadly. She looked and acted the part of family matriarch—a stout, hard-willed pioneer of a woman.

"I began to wonder if you were going to make it, Joseph," said Bril. "But then, Liz said that you were going after Barbara."

Everyone gathered up the supplies Joseph and Carolyn had brought and they continued working their way up towards the house. Joseph ignored the Barbara comment.

"We had some trouble, but we're all right."

"I am glad to see you." Bril looked back at Carolyn, "And damned surprised to see you, little one! I figured you for still Down Under and feared we'd never see you again."

"You don't think a little thing like an invasion can keep the Britton family apart, do ya' Bril?" She spoke with just a hint of sarcasm.

Bril didn't pick up the sarcasm. "Abso-damned right!" he called out proudly.

Kathryn stepped off the porch as they reached the house, held out her arms for a hug; first Carolyn, then Joseph.

"Joey," she said, pulling back then wrapping an arm about his waist.

"Kathryn. Sure glad to see you." He gave a look around. "Have any of the others shown up?"

"Not yet," she said.

"Kenny was in Kansas at last word," said Bril. "I imagine he's knee-deep fightin' the bastards right now. Jason, well, who knows where the hell Jason is? Could be on any of six continents."

"Daryl? Susan?"

"I hoped they'd be here by now. With Suzy and the kids, expect he's being particularly cautious."

"He may have decided to stay put," said Carolyn. "It might be the safest thing, with a family."

"Safer than here?"

"It's rough out there, Bril," said Joseph. "Traveling's getting tougher every day."

"Enough of this," said Kathryn. "You just got here. Come on inside."

Once inside the house, they told the story of their journey to the island, of their encounters with the alien invaders. Joseph was glad to hear that Elizabeth and her family had had a much easier time of it, and had found the island right off. When Joseph asked Bril what he had heard on his radios, he was told that the aliens were managing to jam the airwaves most of the time, but Bril continued to monitor them regularly and occasionally picked up information. He refused to be cut off from the rest of the world. Keeping his HAM antenna up may have been a little risky, but it was well camouflaged. He seldom sent out messages, again because of his concerns about being discovered. He managed to get local info through his CB, despite the interference, and occasionally news came up from California and Oregon and, more rarely, from the east. Information was given and received generously and at great risk. In addition to information being transmitted across the airwaves, there was still a lot of traveling going on. As radio operators gathered data in, from whatever source, they immediately passed it on.

The aliens called themselves *Shylmahn*, or something like it. It was estimated that they numbered only in the thousands in this first fleet, but they had managed, in those first hours, to shut down most of the governments in the world. They had destroyed many of the larger cities and virtually wiped out the military structures of the greatest nations on the planet, had shut down power, communications, transportation, emergency services, everything, all over the world. Assaults on the Shylmahn ships had been unsuccessful, and Bril detailed several attacks that he had heard about, and the methods the Shylmahn used to defend themselves.

"So," Carolyn frowned, "basically, we have no communications, we're defenseless against their weapons, and our only offense is a bullet at close range."

"That's the picture," said Bril.

"This is crazy," said Carolyn. "Joey and I have seen them standing out in the street, just standing there... literally watching the bullets coming at 'em."

"And we outnumber the little buggers a million one." Bril leaned forward melodramatically. "Yes, they can be killed. They are being killed. But they learn. And what one learns, they all know. It's like they have a shared brain. And they did know a helluva lot about us to start with."

Joseph decided to slip away and go out onto the porch, as it sounded as though the conversation was going to go on for some time, as Britton conversations frequently did, but without much new being discussed.

The sun was above the hill behind the house, shining down onto the cove below. Everything looked peaceful. Elizabeth came out, stepped up beside him and took his arm.

"I was worried about you," she said. "I was afraid they might have killed you."

"Never," he said in a poor imitation of Bril. He pointed to the construction off to the right, "What's going on?"

"A bunker. There's a tunnel leading to it from the back of the house. And he's dug a few more rooms in the back of the house, right into the side of the mountain."

"God help us, was Bril right? Who builds a house into the side of a mountain?"

"Will we never learn?"

"Will he ever let us forget?"

Elizabeth chuckled lightly. She looked out at the cove, squeezed his arm tightly. "Joseph... We have to find Barbara. And Daryl. We have to get them and bring them back."

"I know. I'll be heading out soon," Joseph said quietly. He took in the view, the sight of the sun shining on the water. "But you, you need to stay here with the kids."

"They're safe enough with Bril and Kathryn. As safe as anyone can be these days. Around here." A faint trembling ran through her. "I get the feeling we're in a nest of those things... gives me the creeps."

"I'm not about to help get their mother killed. Besides, if these, these *Shylmahn*, show up here, don't you think you should be with William and Sean? You and Robert both? You stay. I'll go."

Chapter Six

May 20

It was a miserable, gray evening. It had drizzled all day. The ground beneath Kenneth's boots was soft and there were patches of muddy ooze that sucked at his feet and sapped what energy he had left.

Today was better than yesterday. Yesterday had been colder and wetter, and they had come off an overnight battle with the Shylmahn. 'Battle' wasn't really the right word, though it had started out promisingly enough.

Alpha, Bravo and Charlie companies had moved in on a cargo ship. With Alpha on one flank, Kenneth's Bravo Company on the other, Charlie went up the middle. This time they made it all the way into the ship. The roaring cheer of the troops at the moment the first men of Charlie Company stepped onto the alien platform could be heard all across the battlefield. The other soldiers pushed forward with newfound strength and determination.

They were beaten back. The concentrated energy blasts, the CEBs, as they had come to be called, became more intense and more tightly packed as the main attacking body neared the ship, forming a virtual shield around it. The troops of Charlie Company were littered about so thickly that it was obvious not many had survived to make it inside the ship.

None ever came out.

That was the night before last. There were twelve left now in Kenneth's platoon, forty-eight in all of Bravo. Alpha Company, now a few miles south and west, was down to forty. Together, Alpha and Bravo *were* the battalion. More than eighty percent casualties in eight days.

The last orders given to the battalion were to search out and destroy all alien concentrations. Any information gathered was to be passed on to any remaining forces. Bravo's radio operator said that over the last two weeks the airwaves had been clear enough for transmission and reception just three times. The captain took to sending out runners on foot. As these runners encountered humans, whether military or civilian, they told everything the company knew about the aliens and about the situation in the area. And they listened. They listened to everything these people had to say and then brought back what they heard.

Alpha and Bravo moved slowly west and north, coming across fewer and fewer people with each passing day. And with each day, the soldiers of Bravo Company grew more somber. Their numbers continued to dwindle, and there seemed little hope that there would be victory before the last of their number perished.

It probably hit Bobby harder than Kenneth, for though he was the more worldly, Bobby had never really had to deal with the world's darker side. His few years had been easy and he had seldom turned his head to bear witness to any of life's unpleasantness. He was self-taught and had been quite successful at avoiding the dirty little scenes. When finally confronted with the dirtiest and the darkest of all situations, and forced to come face to face with it, he had trouble dealing with it.

Kenneth had somehow found the strength, though he had grown harder as a result. There really had been no choice. He grew hard, fought down the emotions, the feelings, and existed day to day. Their lives were so beyond any normal experiences that Kenneth lived now in an otherworldly dream. His was a nightmare from which he long ago had decided he was never going to wake. He knew, too, that this was just beginning. All that had been before, would never be again. They had left all known and familiar life behind. There would never be a return to normalcy, to a life of movies and restaurants and blind dates and barbecues and noisy neighbors and dances and yard sales and television commercials.

Kenneth thought of home, of Bril and the island. There was Joseph and his calm, quiet way. There was Elizabeth and her family. Since his breakup with Barbara, Joey spent a lot of time with them.

Kenneth didn't see much of Daryl. He and Susan kept mostly to themselves. Bril said that Susan was turning Daryl into a snob, but Kenneth didn't think so.

He wondered a lot about Carolyn. She was down in Australia, and he was afraid that he would never see her again. But maybe things were better down there. Maybe she should stay right where she was.

He had to smile when he thought of Jason. Jason was exciting. Jason was cloak and dagger. Most important, Jason listened to him. There was no telling where Jason was.

If they continued traveling in this general direction, and if they survived long enough, Kenneth figured he might someday see his family again. If they were alive, those that could make it were probably on Bril's island by now. He hoped so.

May 21

Daryl Britton stood beside the curtained window, his back to the wall. On the street below, he could see the Shylmahn loading humans into several manmade trucks, herding them along with stun sticks. The humans looked dejected and compliant, with no fight left in them. Their captors took it all matter-of-factly.

Daryl and his family had been trapped here in this second floor hotel room for three days. He glanced over at Susan, who sat unmoving on the couch. She was a young, dark, striking woman, though the last three weeks had taken their toll. The exhaustion, fear and burden showed painfully around her eyes. His own anguish was all the worse for seeing her and the kids like this.

Sharon and Little Daryl sat on either side of their mother. The little girl, five years old, looked exactly as her mother had when she was five, yet Sharon had a haunting, watchful, silent air about her that her mother never had, and it tended to make others uncomfortable when they were around her. Little Daryl, a year older, was a tiny fireball and very protective of his little sister. Daryl could imagine his little boy climbing off the couch now to defend her to the end, terrified though he obviously was.

The Shylmahn on the street below made way for a shuttle that eased out of the sky and landed at the end of the row of trucks. Humans coming out of the shuttle were herded toward the trucks, along with others being led up the street from somewhere beyond Daryl's view. One of the Shylmahn pulled a middle-aged woman out of the line and pushed her toward another waiting truck that was parked off to one side. Daryl had noticed that over the past three days some prisoners were separated from the main body. He hadn't been able to spot any difference between these and all the others, couldn't tell if they were randomly selected or if there was in fact something different between these and all those taken to the other trucks.

Daryl looked up at the sky. The sun would be setting soon. Another long night of bright lights on the street below, late night shuttle landings, convoys of trucks disappearing into the dark, going who knew where.

One of the Shylmahn turned suddenly, looking sharply in the direction of the hotel.

My God, did he hear something?

Daryl held his breath. He and his family had come into the hotel after the Shylmahn had emptied it of its occupants, and had been fortunate that the aliens had made only brief, cursory searches of the surrounding buildings since.

The Shylmahn moved its head slowly, eyes searching one window, then the next, and the next. At Daryl's window, it paused only briefly before moving on to the next. A companion moved up beside it and spoke. The alien nodded, and the two of them started toward the entrance of the hotel, several others joining them.

No, no, no. God, no. Daryl slid quickly away from the window, his back still against the wall. He looked to Susan.

She could see it in his eyes. A breath caught in her throat, she stiffened, her body quivered, she grasped the children tightly and pulled them even closer to her. She shook her head just the slightest from side to side.

Daryl looked at the children. There was desperation in his eyes. The children...

He looked again to his wife. Their eyes locked.

The children.

Daryl spoke the words silently to her. *I love you...*

Her blood went cold. Her chest felt tight.

I love you, she said silently. There was no other way. It was for the children.

Daryl moved quickly then, to the door and out of the room. Susan pulled her children from the couch and hurried to the closet. Crawling in, she buried herself and the kids under clothes, hotel blankets and towels.

Daryl appeared suddenly in the lobby, stood before the aliens and feigned surprise. He turned then and raced to the back of the hotel. He didn't make it far. The stun sticks, painful when pressed against the body as a prod, could actually strike someone down at a distance of fifteen feet or more. Daryl had seen it before, watching as a Shylmahn held the stick in the direction of a fleeing man, the man collapsing to the street, his muscles twitching.

He felt it now, himself. All the muscles in his body were shot through with fire, twisted and contracting. He didn't notice until he was lifted to his feet that his nose was bleeding. It must have struck the floor when he went down. Within a matter of seconds he sensed his muscles coming back to him, enough to wipe the blood with the back of his hand.

Two Shylmahn half-carried Daryl out the front door and into the street. He dared not look back, dared not take away what little chance there might be that the Shylmahn would think that he was alone. It was quite likely though, that even if they didn't go back inside now, they would probably be more thorough with any future searches of the buildings on this street. Susan would have to get the kids out quickly.

A burning pain shot through his side and seemed to strike out to all the nerves in his body, forcing him to jump forward. The Shylmahn at his left pulled the stun stick back and pointed ahead. Daryl obligingly picked up the pace and marched on his own toward the line of trucks. As he drew closer, another of the aliens stepped up and pointed to Daryl. He was pulled out of the line and led to the lone truck parked off to one side.

So, he was to be one of the select few. If nothing else, he was going to find out what this was all about. Climbing into the back, he saw four fellow humans sitting glumly on the wooden benches. Nothing special about them. Just people.

What makes us different?

As he sat down, he braved a glance at the hotel. The Shylmahn who had brought him out were going back into the building. Tearing his eyes away from hotel, he stared down at his feet.

God, no. Please, please, please...

Several minutes later, the aliens came out of the building alone. For the moment, anyway, Susan and the kids were safe.

A few minutes after dark, with ten more prisoners crowded in with Daryl, the truck started up and headed away from the collection point. Having had very little sleep the past days, Daryl pulled himself into a ball and let the sound and feel of the truck engine, and the warmth of the bodies pressed tightly around him, lull him into a fitful sleep.

Jason Britton had a dark look about him, smooth and neat. The same could be said for his personality; dark and smooth and neat. He was confident, quiet. He never talked about his work, the silence itself being part of the game that he played. It was this game that irritated some in his family, in particular his oldest brother Bril; but he had been born for it, he lived for it, and he had found it, becoming a part of the U.S. Special Investigations Unit, an organization as dark and mysterious as he liked to imagine himself to be.

His home was ostensibly in Seattle, though he was away from it more than not. The Northwest was a great place to come back to, and when home, he usually made an effort to see the family.

There was Bril, of course. The man who would be king. Overbearing, argumentative, and an all-around pain in the butt. All in all, a hell of a guy to have as a big brother.

And Joseph. Next in line to the throne. Dear brother Joseph. Quiet lad, as caring as they came. Joseph was born to be a target.

Younger brother Daryl, a teacher at one of the community colleges. He and fellow teacher and wife Suzan seemed rather distant from the rest of the family, but they did make most of the obligatory appearances at the family gatherings.

Elizabeth. Yes. The temperamental one. When those fiery green eyes locked onto you, you were done for. It didn't matter; she was still a great sister to have around. As far as her being a good mother, Jason was reminded of the nature documentaries that he liked to watch on PBS.

Sister Carolyn... Cliché come to life, for sure. The free and independent one. Rebellious, self-sacrificing, oh so outspoken. A woman in search of a cause. The wild little sister. Bril went nuts trying to keep a rein on her. He had failed utterly.

Finally there was baby brother Kenneth. Wide-eyed, naive, little Kenny. Shy, trusting, vulnerable almost beyond belief. He ran blindly into the army in a desperate attempt to get out from under Bril's dominating, suffocating weight. Everyone else had the strength to stand against Bril's great wind, but Kenny hadn't had a chance in hell. So, with a little encouragement from Jason and Joseph, and bit of prodding and pushing, the kid ran. Kenneth Britton became a soldier. Having him join the army was almost as terrifying for his brothers and sisters as it was for Kenny himself. A lamb being tossed into a wolves' den.

Unbeknownst to everyone else, though, Jason had kept an eye on young Kenneth, and pulled an occasional string when it needed pulling. Nothing unethical, nothing illegal, but when opportunities showed themselves, Jason made sure they were taken. Nothing more.

Jason wondered where baby brother was right about now. He'd lost track of him after those first days of the invasion.

He looked up at the dark night sky overhead, inwardly pulled himself closed against the weather. Not a star shone, not a single star. The night clouds threatened to drop more rain on him. Wherever Kenny was, he had to have it better than this.

From his hillside perch, Jason looked through night-vision goggles down at the squat, square building below. A truck, formerly the property of the U.S. Army, pulled up in front of the building and three Shylmahn climbed out of the cab. About a dozen men and women were hurried out of the back of the truck, followed by another Shylmahn that had been back there with them.

Third truck in two hours, thought Jason.

It started to rain. Lightly at first, it became heavier by the second. He wiped his face, continued his observations.

The front door opened as the group approached. Bright light escaped from inside, streamed out across the scene. The prisoners were led in and the door closed. Two minutes later, the Shylmahn who had accompanied the humans came back out, climbed into the truck, and left.

Jason wiped the rain from his face again, stuffed the goggles into his jacket, and slid back from the hilltop.

Chapter Seven

Jason moved slowly across the room and sat in the only available chair. The room was cold and filled with shadows. There were no windows. The walls were faded and bare. Mr. Johnson was sitting behind a small, time-worn desk in the middle of the room. He nodded without looking up, and Jason began to speak. He calmly detailed the results of his mission, stating the facts and including his thoughts and opinions where he felt they were appropriate. His voice was flat and dispassionate. For the moment, emotions had no place.

Mr. Johnson stopped him twice with questions, but beyond these he let his agent make his report uninterrupted. He occasionally scribbled notes in his small notebook.

As they finished the debriefing, Mr. Johnson poured two drinks from a large bottle sitting on the floor beside the desk. He handed one of the glasses to Jason. As Jason took a drink and swallowed, Mr. Johnson emptied his own glass, poured himself another and rubbed at his aching neck. This second drink he planned to nurse along slowly.

"Why don't you ever bring me good news, Jason?" he asked tiredly.

"You just don't know how to put a positive spin on the material being provided."

Mr. Johnson's expression remained unchanged. Sometimes, he had no sense of humor.

"We're not causing them much of a problem, are we?"

"No sir."

He looked into his drink, brought it hurriedly to his lips and tossed back the warm liquor. He reached to the floor and picked up the bottle. Staring at it, he grimaced and set it on the desk, unopened.

"How can we change that, Mr. Britton?" Mr. Johnson leaned back in his chair and rubbed his eyes with the heels of his hands, again worked his way back to his neck. "There has to be something."

Mr. Johnson drove himself as hard as he drove his agents. He would not stop. He could not stop. Not Mr. Johnson. He may bitch and complain, but he was constantly digging, constantly probing, constantly trying to come up with that something that *had to be there*, that *one* thing that would turn things around. Jason knew also that Mr. Johnson was in communication with the army patrols that roamed the area, and was sending them into situations he knew full well they wouldn't be coming out of, hoping against hope that with their sacrifice he might discover the key that could later be used against the Shylmahn.

And there were probably a dozen others out there just like him.

"What do you hear from the others?" asked Jason.

"You mean those who are still active?" Mr. Johnson eyed Jason. When Jason said nothing, he cleared his throat and continued. "The same as what you're telling me."

Mr. Johnson pushed himself forward. "Hit and run resistance tactics, Jason. Futile? As futile as they are... shit, large scale assaults are worse than useless." He raised and lowered a brow, "If these creatures are considering us at all, they gotta be laughing their scrawny little butts off."

"We are at the very least an irritant to them. They notice us, all right."

"Reflexive scratching will not long their victory delay..." Mr. Johnson grew thoughtful. He stared at Jason, at first not seeing him, then noticing him as if for the first time. "We have to find a way in, Mr. Britton, and we have to find it soon. Major confrontations have proven rather disadvantageous, and these smaller skirmishes aren't slowing them down at all."

"And giving us less and less intel."

"And giving us less intel. While they may be incurring some minor casualties, I don't believe we're doing them any serious harm."

"Perhaps not."

"Chemical, biological, *something*. I know we've looked at them before, but..."

These creatures had rather bizarre personality quirks; perhaps one of these could be exploited, could be put to use...

There has to be something...

He grabbed at the liquor bottle, then pushed it aside. That shit only made it worse.

The Shylmahn are tightening their grip, taking hold of us so damned fast. There just isn't time...

The more hurriedly he juggled the possibilities, the more likely the possibilities were going to slip away from him unseen. If only he could establish a reliable communications network. Different cells could work on different possibilities and he wouldn't have to explore the dead ends that others had already traveled. They could share information more readily, and with a thousand sets of eyes from a thousand viewpoints, the solution might be seen.

"The Shylmahn did their homework. If they can keep us off our feet, we won't have a chance."

"We'll need to make a few miracles, sir, but we have a chance. If nothing else, we humans have... I don't know... spirit? Gall? We won't be giving up."

Mr. Johnson couldn't hold back a guffaw. "Jesus, Mr. Britton! Sentimentality? I wouldn't have expected it of you."

"I do try to keep it to myself, sir." Sentimentality notwithstanding, over the past few weeks he had seen self-sacrifice beyond anything he could have imagined before the arrival of the Shylmahn. He had seen strangers rushing into certain death to aid their fellows. He had witnessed men, women and children bravely fighting battles they knew they couldn't win, yet never giving up.

Mr. Johnson smiled weakly, and when he spoke, it was with a calm, controlled voice.

"Very stirring, Mr. Britton. But a glorious death is nothing more than death. An honorable defeat is still defeat. While it may be comforting to you that we are dying in our Sunday best, right now I'd rather our spirited, self-sacrificing fellow humans scurry away into the night. Cockroaches hiding in the dark are difficult to exterminate."

May 23

Bril was the last one back to the house. He washed up at the basin on the porch, then sat with the rest of the family in the front room. Kathryn had a stew simmering in the kitchen and the smell gave the whole house an atmosphere of family. The sound of the children playing, and fighting, was pleasant and soothing to the ears. The kids had to be as tired as the adults, working right alongside them day after day, but they sure weren't showing it.

The bunker was coming along more quickly now that Joseph and Carolyn were here, and the tunnel from the back of the house to the bunker was being shored up.

Joseph was continuing the work on the concrete pillbox that had been begun out on the spit. Anything coming into the inlet would have to pass directly beneath it. Another gun emplacement was being constructed on the hill up behind the bunker. This one looked out over the slope from the house to the cove.

In the meantime, Bril had been placing booby traps all over the island. The alien slimeballs may get 'em, but it wasn't going to be without cost.

The house was crowded, just the way he liked it. Sitting in his big, heavy chair, Bril sipped the hot coffee that his wife had brought him and let the warmth work its way through him. Through the lull in the children's noisy activities, he heard the sounds of dusk coming from outside. At this moment, all was right and proper.

Carolyn and Kathryn went to the windows and door just then and pulled closed the dark, heavy curtains that held in the light and shielded the family's presence here from the aliens. With that, reality lay heavy across Bril's chest.

"We're going to California," said Elizabeth, blurting it out as she sat in the high-back chair beside the cold fireplace. The statement struck Bril hard.

"What the hell would make you think of such a thing?" Bril turned from Elizabeth and looked at Robert. He must be the cause of this. Robert stiffened and said nothing.

Truth be told, Bril knew better. Elizabeth was the power in that pair.

"If we don't get out now," she said, "I don't think we ever will."

"Think it through, girl! You can't make it to California. Even if you did, you're no better off. A sight worse, I'd say. There's family here. Have you forgotten that? And this island is defendable."

"They'll come soon enough, and there's nothing any of us can do about it. Not for all the work we're doing."

"We're doing what we can." Bril nodded sharply. "We'll hold our own."

"No. You won't."

"Elizabeth—"

"This place... the whole damn state..." she swallowed heavily. "Everywhere... they're like rats..."

"Elizabeth..." Robert started, quickly faded.

"They scurry around like rats. You can't fight rats."

"We damn sure can."

"Robert has family in Eureka. It's quieter there," she said, in full voice once again.

"You don't know that," said Bril. "You're not going, and that's that."

"When the weather improves. A few weeks. No more."

"Liz," Joseph spoke up, thinking to be the voice of reason. "Remember what it was like out there? Remember what you went through to get here? A week ago Carolyn and I saw them gathering people up and hauling them off to who-knows-where."

"Turning them into crackers, most likely," grumbled Bril.

"Liz, you can't seriously be planning on taking the kids back into that?" asked Carolyn.

"I'll take them through Hell if there's a safe place on the other side."

"You're tough," said Joseph, "but that won't be enough to get you and the children all the way to Eureka."

"I can't stay here, Joey... I won't."

Joseph leaned back and took in a long, deep breath. He watched as she scratched absently at her arms, brushed at her nose as if to push away the stench.

"I need some air," he said. He grabbed his jacket from the hook beside the door, pushed his way through the curtain and went outside. The sound of Bril's raised voice, laying down the way of things to Elizabeth, followed him.

Night was coming fast. Some of the brighter stars were already out and their reflections shone in the tiny lagoon below. The spit of land across the cove was a black shadow lying across the water. To the side of the house, the bunker was a splay of dark amidst other shades of dark.

Joseph sat on the step and zipped up his jacket. He watched the night sky. As it grew darker, more stars appeared, slowly at first, then quickly, in a rush to fill the heavens. It was beautiful; peaceful, relaxing. When had the night sky ever been so bright?

He would have to let Liz go. He wasn't sure what had brought this on, but they each had to pick their own place to stand, and she might be right about not making hers here.

With that, Joseph felt the tight muscles in his back ease.

He considered going with her, but quickly decided against it. To be honest with himself, she probably had as much of a chance without him as with him, and he had his own journey to undertake. Elizabeth had certainly reminded him of that often enough these past days.

He could think of three or four likely places he might find Barbara, if she wasn't at her father's. As bad as things had gotten between them, the thought of her all alone out there, surrounded by the Shylmahn, when the end came...

He would give it a couple of more days, until after he finished the east ridge bunker. Then he was going to have to leave the island. He was going to have to try and find her, and if she wanted, he would bring her back here.

Bril wasn't going to like everyone leaving like this, and he dreaded having to tell him. He was going to feel abandoned. But there was no choice. He had to go. Bril already knew that.

Still, it didn't make telling him any easier.

Joseph noticed then that one of the bright stars overhead was moving. He leaned forward. There was another. And another. He rose to his feet, walked out into the middle of the yard and stared up at the suddenly alien sky.

It was filled with moving stars.

Chapter Eight

June 03

EsJen pressed her cheek against the window to better see the large Chehnon city below. The shuttle hit a down draft and there was a jolt as it dropped sharply, then rose again, compensating. EsJen did not appear to notice. Her thoughts were scattered in a hundred different directions, all demanding her attention. The past few weeks had been absolutely fascinating, and these short jaunts into the Chehnon environment were particularly so. This was her third time out and her large, dark eyes gleamed with excitement and anticipation.

The shuttle passed over a large structure that had been identified as a gathering place for the Chehnon, the Earth People, where they would conduct various sporting or other entertainment activities. This aspect of Chehnon culture was something EsJen and several of her colleagues had been researching together. She spent most of her time, however, in independent study, and was currently exploring several distinctive elements of the Chehnon psyche that manifested themselves through Chehnon activity. During the long journey from Shylmah to the new world, she had examined countless examples of Chehnon endeavors in her attempt to define and chart the mind of these curious creatures. She had been able to identify very few parallels between the Chehnon and Shylmahn individual, even fewer between Chehnon and Shylmahn society and culture. On the whole, the two races were as different as could be imagined.

This made it all the more interesting, and EsJen leapt at each opportunity for hands-on contact, hands-on study. Several of the creatures had been brought on board for her to examine, and she had managed some communication, made some inroads into the Chehnon disposition, before they had been turned over to others for ongoing study. She felt, though, that any real success lay in examining Chehnon habitation and the Chehnon individuals as they went about their lives within their own environment. ShahnTahr had agreed completely and had actually encouraged her to take her studies into the field.

Her companions on this trip, other than the pilot and standard support and escort complement, were MehnTec and NehLoc. EsJen didn't know MehnTec very well. He was an overly large, rather quiet sort who had tried very hard to serve as EsJen's protector on their last trip out together. As a consequence of his own studies, which had something to do with the changing Chehnon social structure resulting from the Shylmahn migration, MehnTec had made quite a number of excursions into the field and had now taken it upon himself to serve as guide and mentor to young EsJen.

NehLoc was young and arrogant and thought himself quite attractive. He fancied himself a leader on the way up. He was aggressive in his dealings with others and in his work, which was to effect the Chehnon transition to the new order. Such a position suited him. It was very visible and could possibly lead to positions of influence.

NehLoc was watching her. Several times he had started to speak, each time restraining himself. Finally, he could take it no longer.

"EsJen. You behave as though this was your first trip out into the wild."

"It is my third," she stated flatly. EsJen did not like him very much. If there was a downside to this trip out for EsJen, it was that NehLoc was along. If she allowed herself, just the thought of him being in the same shuttle made her uncomfortable.

"We each have duties necessary to the success of the migration, EsJen. Be careful not to use your responsibilities to your own benefit. These excursions can be dangerous and are not intended for enjoyment."

"I am watching after her, NehLoc," said MehnTec. "I have been out many times in the past few weeks."

"I do not need watching after," said EsJen. "I do nothing less than my duty."

"As do we all, EsJen," said MehnTec. He turned his head in an apologetic gesture.

"And if I enjoy my *excursions*, NehLoc, that is my business. The fact still remains, they have been approved. My success is dependent upon hands-on study."

"We have returned several of these creatures for you to examine."

"I do not answer to you, NehLoc. My activities have been approved."

"Which is why you are here." said NehLoc. He looked over at MehnTec, then back to EsJen, spoke coolly. "I do not care at all about Chehnon social structure, or how or what the creatures think. If you can help me with the transition, so much the better. Anything beyond that is a waste of time."

"ShahnTahr does not believe so."

"That is exactly what ShahnTahr believes."

EsJen felt her blood turn icy. The chill ran through her. She turned back to the small, oval window and surveyed the cityscape below, but the magic was gone.

She did not like NehLoc at all.

Joseph stood on the dying lawn and watched the small, alien shuttle as it approached from the north, from Seattle or perhaps beyond. In the week since leaving the island, he had grown accustomed to such sights, and had seen a number of the Shylmahn creatures up close, most recently in his brother Daryl's neighborhood. According to the note left behind, Daryl and Susan had left some time ago. They were going to try to make it to Susan's sister. Well, good luck to them. They would have had a better chance getting to Suzy's sister than to the island. She lived in a cozy little out of the way neighborhood enough off the beaten path that it was probably as safe a place as any other here in the Northwest. Joseph hoped that one day he could contact them to ensure that all was well.

The neighborhood in which he now found himself was little damaged, but dead quiet. Lawns were becoming overgrown from weeks with no attention, the grass beginning to brown and shrubs starting to pale and hang limp from the recent warm dry spell.

A car sat in a driveway several houses down, looking as though the owner had arrived home only moments before, had just gone inside, turned on the TV and switched to the news, which would then be offering up the events of the day. Perhaps there were children in the background, now fighting for attention, wanting to let the owner of the car know all that had happened to them during the day.

None of this was so. The car had sat there untouched for weeks. The last time the television had been on, it had warned of invasion. If anyone remained in the house, they huddled now quietly in unlit gloom, fearing the Shylmahn would come, would take them away as they had so many of their neighbors. At this very moment they held their breath, staring anxiously at the ceiling as the alien craft passed overhead.

Joseph stepped slowly back under the eaves of the house behind him, stood motionless in the shadows. He calmly watched the shuttle fly over, no more than forty feet above him. It landed seconds later; two streets beyond, he guessed. On impulse, he decided to check it out. Hurrying through the yards, he came out onto the next street. As he crossed, a family rushed passed in the opposite direction, desperate to get as far away from the aliens as possible.

I should follow them, he thought, but did not. Instead, he cut through the next set of yards and crept cautiously along a collapsed house facing the next street, keeping low to the ground. The shuttle had landed in the middle of the street and sat now directly in front of him. Two aliens, armed with the stun sticks they often carried, looked to be playing bodyguard to another as they walked up the street. A fourth stood unmoving beside the shuttle. Four more, two under escort by two military types, strolled along the sidewalk directly in front of him.

They passed by Joseph, the two out in front jabbering away like tourists, pointing and nodding and gesturing. All they lacked were cameras, Mariner baseball caps and Seahawk T-shirts. They disappeared into the house one property up. Once out of view, Joseph turned his attention to the one remaining Shylmahn, left alone beside the shuttle. A male, Joseph assumed, feeling confident that he could now discern the differences, minor though these differences sometimes were. This one was about five and a half feet tall; about as big as any Shylmahn he had seen. A golden complexion, delicate features. Thinner than human, but this one looked to be heavier than most other Shylmahn. Relatively speaking, this one was a brute.

After several minutes, the larger group came out of the house, the two tourists still jabbering away at each other, pleased with whatever discoveries they had made. The two watching over them were relaxed but vigilant. As they passed by Joseph this time, though, they looked over at him and stopped, curious now to examine the creature.

Joseph flushed hot. A heartbeat... another.

I'm an idiot.

He let out a breath and took in a fresh one. He rose slowly to his feet, his legs shaky.

The Shylmahn showed little emotion beyond a pleasant curiosity. The two serving as escort were more guarded than the tourists, and had their stun sticks ready; but they showed nothing in the way of real concern in their manner.

The female in the group said something to Joseph. Her voice was smooth and as soft as her appearance, delicate to the ear. She took a step nearer, and a second. The others followed, not wanting her to go beyond their protection. Joseph took a step, out and away from the rubble of the house. They stood there, then. Human and Shylmahn, Earthman and Invader.

She didn't look like an invader. Even at this distance, Joseph could see the bright, golden flecks in the dark brown of her large eyes. Her features were as all the Shylmahn; slight, delicate. Her hair was the same golden color as the flecks in her eyes and held the same shimmer. It was shoulder-length and had a gentle wave to it. In an alien way, he found her strangely attractive. It was a pretty creature.

She tilted her head a little to one side, studiously.

EsJen, bohn. EsJen mes leht, she said. Then, *Ba-Cheh, leht buhn.*

He had no idea what she was saying, but it was obvious that she was trying to communicate with him. He didn't think she was planning on hurting him. At least, not yet. Maybe they wouldn't be taking him away after all.

What did she want? He shrugged his shoulders stupidly.

Chehnon leht buhn? she asked, apparently a question.

Joseph watched as different expressions drifted across her face, none hostile. The Shylmahn beside her spoke to her, and she mumbled something back, then turned again to Joseph.

Shylmahn, she said, indicating herself, then pointed to Joseph, *Chehnon.*

"Yes," he said, glad to have gotten something. "Shylmahn," pointing to the four of them. "Human," pointing to himself. "Human. I am human."

The female nodded, pointed to Joseph. *Human. Chehnon.*

Progress, then. Sort of.

EsJen, she went on, pointing to herself, then pointed to Joseph and waited.

"Britton," he said suddenly. "Joseph Britton."

A flurry of words between the aliens, then EsJen said, *JosephBritton.* It was a single word, and sounded very alien.

EsJen bohn, JosephBritton buhn?

"Joseph." He wondered how the hell he had gotten himself into this, and how he was going to get out of it. "Jo-Seph. Just Jo-Seph."

JoSeph.

"Yes. You are EsJen, I am Joseph."

EsJen took another step towards Joseph, examining him more closely. This time her companions did not follow, but appeared quite able to at the slightest provocation. She spoke over her shoulder, as if relaying back the information that she discovered. She spoke again to Joseph, continuing her interrogation.

Dahl kahr buhn, she said, then pointed to the rubble and repeated, *Dahl kahr buhn?*

"No," said Joseph. "No. Not my house." He shook his head, waved his hands negatively. EsJen nodded in understanding, and waved her hands as if to ask 'where'. Joseph indicated south. "Long way away. Long way." He looked at the ruin and mumbled to himself, "Looks about the same, though."

EsJen again nodded understanding, said something to her companion. He spoke back, appeared to smile. EsJen spoke cheerily in response, turned back to Joseph.

JoSeph bav-cheh meschu? she asked, already knowing this creature would not understand. She brought her hands together, locking her fingers. *Meschu, JoSeph fa ...*

The other Shylmahn spoke then, directly to Joseph. He pointed to himself and EsJen. *MehnTec EsJen meschu. MehnTec fa EsJen. Meschu JoSeph?*

"A mate? Spouse?" asked Joseph.

Ba-Cheh JoSeph. Ba-Shyl MehnTec. Bav-Shyl EsJen.

"I have no one," said Joseph uncertainly. They could be talking about damned near anything. But then, they probably didn't really have any idea what he was saying, either.

EsJen pointed to Joseph and said, *Ba-Cheh.* She pointed to MehnTec, *Ba-Shyl.* She pointed finally to herself, *Bav-Shyl.*

"I understand!" he cried out. He pointed to himself, "Man. Earth man." He pointed to MehnTec and then EsJen. "He is a Shylmahn man. You are Shylmahn woman."

EsJen figured that the gibberish meant that the creature had understood. She knew the syntactical structure and the content of many of the Chehnon languages, though her discipline had not been linguistics. She regretted there had not been a greater focus on practical execution of the main Chehnon languages during the journey from Shylmah. Her hands-on studies here in the early stages of the migration would have benefited, as those in other areas of the migration were likely benefiting from their expertise.

She nodded her approval to the Chehnon.

Ba-Cheh, she said. She pointed to the space beside him. *Bav-Cheh?*

"No. I have no woman. No wife."

Meschu La-Cheh? she said, holding her hand waist high.

"No children." He had a sudden thought then, pointed to EsJen, then to the empty space beside her, "Ba-Shyl? La-Shyl?"

EsJen clapped her hands excitedly, practically jumped up and down. It was as if her pet had learned a new trick. Joseph was both glad to have managed communication and angry at this allusion to inferiority.

Ohpjehtu. Ohpjehtu, she said, shaking her head happily. *Ohpjehtu meschu EsJen.*

Apparently she didn't have a mate. This fella with her must be a traveling companion, a fellow team member on this mission of theirs. MehnTec spoke to her, resting a hand on her arm. She waved impatient acknowledgment.

Chohn kehta, she said, backing away now. Those behind and beside her retreated with her until they reached the sidewalk. She stopped then, called up to Joseph, *Muhtla. Muhtla kahlmeh chohn. Ba-Cheh stehcho JoSeph.*

The four turned about and went down the sidewalk, continuing their tour. They found a house that looked promising and went inside. As they did, Joseph heard a noise from the other direction and hurriedly moved back into the shadows.

He saw two humans being pushed and prodded by two Shylmahn with stun sticks, while a third followed along beside them, his voice raised and yet calm as he spoke to the newly acquired humans. They stopped in front of the shuttle and the prisoners were forced to their knees. The Shylmahn in charge squatted down onto his haunches and spoke to one human, then the other. One was quite a bit older than the other, and Joseph suspected they might be father and son. Perhaps they had allowed themselves to be captured so that the rest of the family could get away. He had seen that happen more than once in the last week.

The Shylmahn turned his attention back to the older prisoner, and hissed a series of Shylmahn phrases mixed with English words. The man, still on his knees, lifted his head up to look his captor in the eye. He spit bloodied saliva at the feet of the alien. The two escort began beating him and stunning him with their sticks, while the interrogator continued speaking, calmly yet forcefully, in that strange mix of English and Shylmahn. Rather than angry, he sounded and acted as though pleased with the responses that he was witnessing.

Knowledge gatherers, thought Joseph.

The man lay unmoving on the street. The younger man knelt in silence beside him. The interrogator continued speaking to the prone figure before him. Joseph couldn't tell for sure, but he didn't think the man was conscious.

Joseph didn't believe the Shylmahn interrogator was trying to get information directly from the prisoners, but was trying to learn about how these humans would act and behave while under interrogation. *Trying to learn our ways...*

With his face held close to the face of the prone figure, the interrogator turned his head in slow deliberation until he was looking up at the younger human. He spoke, barely above a whisper at first, his voice growing louder and sharper as he continued. He raised himself up finally, tilted his head from side to side in curious study.

EsJen and her companions came out of the house. They crossed the street and casually approached the shuttle. The accompanying escort moved off to one side, near the shuttle door, and stood in silence.

MehnTec stepped near the human prisoners and examined them thoughtfully. He asked the Shylmahn who had been performing the interrogation a question. The interrogator rose to his feet, answering MehnTec as he brushed himself off. EsJen pressed between them and knelt to examine first one, then the other human. She asked a question then, nodded at the response, then looked curiously at the younger of the two humans. She asked the young prisoner a question, knelt to look at him more closely, then stood.

There was apparently some discussion about what to do with the humans, and it was finally decided to bring them along. There were a few anxious moments when Joseph feared they might come back for him, might take him as well, but none of the Shylmahn took notice of the human hiding in the nearby shadows. They and their prisoners loaded themselves into the alien vehicle, the older of the two prisoners having to be carried aboard. The shuttle door closed and moments later it lifted from the street, rose a hundred feet or more, then headed north in a slow ascent. It left behind an oppressive silence.

The sill of the tiny window was shoulder high. Daryl was standing now, as most evenings, with his face near the glass and his eyes closed, feeling the setting sun's warmth radiating through the small pane. The minutes rolled slowly through his thoughts until, when all outside had dulled to a cold, misty gray, he turned and sat on the narrow cot.

The cell's dimensions were such that he could lie down in either direction with little left to spare. It was richly carpeted and wallpaper covered two of the walls. A light fixture hung from the ceiling in one corner of the room, but the light switch was outside the solid door. Daryl guessed this had once been one corner of a bedroom. The building itself had probably been a large manor in the pre-Shylmahn days, now converted into some bizarre prison.

Every day or so he was taken from his cell and led into an examination room, where he was poked, prodded, examined, interrogated, and occasionally experimented on by a Shylmahn who had been given the name Dr. Black. Daryl wasn't sure where the name came from, but suspected it was a mangling of his Shylmahn name "BehLahk" by one of the prisoners.

Physically, Daryl hadn't yet suffered any permanent damage that he could point to, as painful as some of the examinations had been. Mentally, he was sometimes out of it for hours at a time, but always returned to himself, finding himself back in his cell. He sometimes heard other prisoners screaming out, crying out, in pain or anger or fear or confusion. He had not been allowed to see any other humans, but he guessed there were a fair number locked up here along with him.

Daryl slid over to one of the two-gallon cans. One was for water, the other served as his toilet. Using the plastic cup, Daryl took a drink from the water can and tossed the cup back in. The toilet he wouldn't use until morning, as that was when the guard exchanged it for a fresh one. Daryl didn't want the smell with him any longer than necessary.

As he sat back, leaning against the wall beneath the window, he heard noises in the hallway outside his cell. There were two voices—one human, the other that of the guard. The door to the next cell was unlocked and opened.

New neighbor. There had been someone in the room directly next to Daryl's during his first two days here, but there had been no sound from there since. His comrade in chains here at the manor had been led away one morning and had not returned.

A few moments later the neighbor's door closed and locked, then his own opened and the figure of the guard stood in the opening.

"Daryl," said the Shylmahn.

"Good evening."

Guard pointed down the hall. "BehLahk."

"I'd rather not," said Daryl. He was still sitting on the cot beneath the window. "Thanks just the same."

"No trouble, Daryl," said Guard. His English was improving each day, and he understood much more than he was able to speak. Probably more than he was willing to admit. "No trouble."

Daryl looked carefully at the Shylmahn guard for several seconds. Daryl knew more than to be troublesome. "No trouble." He slid off the cot and slowly rose to his feet. "The good doctor should call first. I had other plans for this evening."

"Quickly, Daryl," Guard was waving him out of the cell and into the hall.

"All right, all right. I'm coming. It isn't like he's going to start without me."

Daryl had been eight years old when his parents were killed. With no other family, Bril, who had just turned twenty a few weeks earlier, selflessly took on the task of raising his six much younger brothers and sisters. He looked to Joseph and Jason, just into their teens, to help out as they could, but their lives were just beginning to open up. Lizzie and Carolyn, seven and six years old, helped with two-year-old Kenny whenever they were not in school, and the daycare helped.

Daryl, stuck in the middle, found himself often on the outside looking in. It wasn't anything the others did or didn't do, it was simply the way things had fallen into place and the world had formed itself. Bril was so much older than the others, with his role defined by events, his life revolving around keeping the family together and the family finances in balance and beating off the social workers. Joseph and Jason were just entering a phase in their lives that didn't include eight year olds, though they were nice enough to him on those rare occasions when they happened to stumble over him.

His sisters, hardly much younger than Daryl, did appear to go out of their way to ignore him. They became very possessive of baby Kenny and made every effort to keep Daryl out. Bril, pleased that his daughters-by-default were willing and able to help with the baby, when he had so much to deal with and didn't see how he would ever get it all taken care of, either didn't see, or didn't want to see, that Daryl was being pushed aside by the girls. Maybe he didn't see the importance.

As the years went by, Daryl adjusted to his role in the family. His responsibilities were minimal, which gave him opportunities to seek out and explore interests outside the family, and he took advantage of these opportunities whenever they came. He grew farther apart from the family, as the others grew closer. In all those years, he never blamed his brothers and sisters for the way things were, for they were no less victims of circumstance than he was, but it still hurt. His brothers and sisters never saw his distance from them as their doing, but rather something intentional on Daryl's part. They loved him, and assumed and accepted that he wanted that distance.

He didn't. He hated it. That space between them was a dark chasm that had separated a little boy from the only people he had left in this whole, scary world.

Bril helped Susan and the children out of the small boat and onto the shore. As soon as they knew who it was, Kathryn had hurried into the house to grab a kerosene lantern. It was pitch black out. She met them coming up the path, Bril holding Susan about the shoulders, guiding her along. He frowned at the lantern, which was a break in security protocol, but said nothing. The two children followed close behind. Kathryn turned uphill and led the way back to the house, where her son Peter waited on the porch.

"Hide the boat, Peter," she said, climbing the steps. Peter gave a silent nod and left to put the boat in the boathouse with the charter and the dinghy.

As Kathryn went to make coffee and cocoa, Bril helped Susan to a chair. The children climbed into it with her. When Kathryn came back in from the kitchen, Susan told them what they had gone through and what had happened to Daryl.

Several days after the Shylmahn invasion, they had set out to go to her sister's house. They made several efforts at driving there, each time forced to abandon the car and return to foot. It took them a week to get there, only to find the whole community had been turned into some sort of labor camp. They decided to try to make it here to the island. Traveling grew more dangerous each day. They woke one morning to find the hotel they had slept in was surrounded by Shylmahn. One of their mobile command posts had been established outside the building.

She told them then of Daryl's desperate sacrifice to keep the Shylmahn from finding his family. The alien command station moved on two days later, and Susan continued working her way to the island. That she had made it here was a miracle. Time and again they had eluded capture. They had slipped through collection parties, sometimes on hands and knees, circled around alien encampments in the dead of night, come face to face with aliens and had literally run for their lives.

At one point they had been forced to hide in the bushes beside a wide dirt roadway. Hundreds, maybe thousands, of humans were being led down the road to a camp in the foothills. Many of the prisoners had seen her and the children as they passed. Several even managed to give the children a wink.

Now that Susan had brought her children safely to the island, she wanted only one thing. She wanted Bril to find Daryl and bring him back.

"Come on, Susan," said Kathryn, standing and reaching for her. "Why don't you lie down for a while?"

"Yes... yes, all right. For a few minutes."

Bril watched Kathryn lead Susan and the two little ones to the back of the house. He fumbled for his coffee cup. He felt almost helpless. His work on the defensive systems across the island was something he could hold onto, was some comfort to him, but he was often overwhelmed with a sense of grabbing out at empty air. He felt threatened by this latest threat to his family, and fought to keep hold of his wits. He needed his family here, together. He needed the unity. Rather than his family coming together, however, to take on the battle together, they were scattered out beyond his protection, beyond his help. Beyond the protection and power of the family. More than ever before, they all needed the strength of the family. They had all sensed it. It was what had drawn them all here, had brought them all here to begin with. Whether they knew that it was what had pulled them to this island or not, they had come, enduring tremendous hardship to do so.

He had no doubt that one day soon Jason would come, and Kenneth, also. Little Kenny, who had joined the army against his wishes and was now most likely half a continent away. He too would come.

Yet even those who had come to the island had left again. Each with their own reasons, yet they had all left. Joseph had gone in search of his ex-wife, and of Daryl and Susan. Perhaps he would find Barbara quickly, and when he found Daryl and Susan gone, he would return. Carolyn, he hoped, would come to her senses and also return. She had gone to find the resistance, she had said, an underground that had to be there, fighting against the Shylmahn invaders. Bril had tried to convince her that the family should make their own stand, here, together, but Carolyn was determined to take the fight out to them. Well, when it came time, she would be back.

Elizabeth had taken her family and fled in some absurd effort to escape the madness, harboring some pie-in-the-sky belief that somewhere beyond the horizon things were better. Bril was most concerned with Liz and her family. Their leaving the island was the most desperate, the most unreasoning. Their actions were akin to Bril's own sense of grasping out at empty air. He knew this to be the most dangerous act of all.

And now, this latest with Daryl. What to do about Daryl? How could he possibly find Daryl, much less rescue him and bring him back to the island?

Bril stood and went to the front window, threw aside the heavy black curtains. Dawn had come to the island. As he gazed out the window, Kathryn returned from settling Susan and the children in. She took hold of his arm and put her head on his shoulder.

"Oh, Bril," she said softly.

"I feel so helpless."

"You?"

"Don't make fun, woman."

Kathryn smiled fondly. "You will find him, and you will rescue him, and you will bring him here and return him to his family."

Bril grit his teeth, stared sharply out at the growing light. "I don't mean just Daryl."

"We will get through this." She spoke with quiet confidence. "I have no doubts about that."

"They're scattered all over the countryside."

"Think about what they are doing out there." She gave Bril a warm, loving look. He had raised them, his brothers and sisters. "Husband, what more could you possibly ask of them?"

Bril's answer came quickly to his mind, but he took his time voicing it. He was afraid that he wouldn't be able to get the words out. "I would have them here. With me."

Chapter Nine

June 15

This was their sixth car since leaving Bril's island. They had also spent time on foot and had traveled by bicycle for almost a week. They hadn't seen another vehicle on the highway for weeks; at least not one that was moving.

Robert drove now, careful and with one eye out for Shylmahn, always mindful of their surroundings in the event they had to make a dash for cover. The kids did their best to watch for Shylmahn as well, but it was difficult for them to keep it up for very long, and they spent as much time fussing about in the back seat as watching out for bad guys.

Elizabeth kept constant vigil, with an eye for escape routes toward cover. They sometimes went for hours, even as much as a day, with no sign of Shylmahn. Other days were spent rushing from hiding place to hiding place, at times abandoning their car and frantically scrambling to escape, perhaps for their lives. These back highways usually offered more opportunity for cover, and since the human population was less dense, there were also fewer Shylmahn about to collect them up. This, for Elizabeth, was the rationale.

They had made it out of Washington, and then through Oregon. With each day, with each mile, Robert showed signs of growing weaker. His ability to cope with the events around him visibly diminished. He fought to keep his anxieties hidden from his wife and the kids, but his struggles were all the more evident as a result. Too much was happening, and it was coming from too many sides. He wished they had stayed on the island, where it was all so much simpler. He could deal with the situation there. The family was on the island, and Bril was in charge. If the Shylmahn came, Bril would tell them what to do. The plans were made, they all knew where they stood and what had to be done.

Robert could deal with that. Everything was defined and clear cut. The responsibility was gone. *Nothing more was required.*

This was madness. What the hell was he doing out here? When Elizabeth had first brought up the idea of going to California, Robert had eagerly reached out to the promise of seeing his family as the one faint light of hope in this horrible darkness. Without really thinking, he had gone along with it, accepted Elizabeth's need to get away, on the surety that she was right, that it was true, that it would be safer in northern California. If they could just get out of the Northwest, all would be well.

They would be getting out, getting away from those hideous creatures. He would also, for all her family to see, be doing the brave thing, the courageous thing. He would be sneaking through the Shylmahn, outwitting the enemy, leading his family to freedom. Right? Better than hiding out on Bril's island, waiting for the inevitable. Right? And he had been hiding out, hiding behind Bril. Hadn't he?

Shouldn't I do the brave thing?

"Shuttle," said William, very matter-of-factly.

"Cover." Elizabeth pointed to a stand of trees off to the right, but Robert had already seen it, was already slowing the car and easing it onto the shoulder of the road. Once slowed to a safe speed, he turned toward the shadows beneath the trees. They hadn't quite stopped when the shuttle passed slowly overhead, descending beyond the hill.

With the car stopped, Robert turned off the engine and laid his head back.

"I think it was landing," said William.

"Yup," said Sean, more curious than concerned, despite the tension in the car.

Elizabeth unfolded a map and spread it out in her lap and across the dash. "I think we're about here," she said, half in thought. "There's a town just up ahead. I'll bet they've got themselves a command station there."

Robert's eyes were closed, but the muscles in his face were taut. He tried to keep the tension out of his voice. "Must be Beckler."

"That's right. Just over that rise."

"Then we're stuck here. We're only two hours out. Or we were. Two lousy hours."

"We can get around 'em." Elizabeth continued combing over the map, looking for a way around Beckler.

"It's no different here, Liz," said Robert, opening his eyes and straightening up. "Here, or Washington, it's all the same."

"No. It's not," said Elizabeth, without looking up from the map. "It's not the same at all. This is the first sign of them all day."

"They're here."

"They were everywhere... up there." She looked up then from the map. "Down here, I can breathe."

"Elizabeth, it won't be any different here."

"It's a damn sight different."

"Liz-"

Elizabeth had opened the car door. "It was filthy there. The air smelled of them. If I'd stayed another day, I'd have vomited." She climbed out of the car.

"Where are you going?"

"To see what's up ahead." She walked away from the car and out from under the stand of trees. There was a sloping hillside beyond, steeper and higher than she had thought before starting up, and she found herself out of breath as she neared the crest. She bent low as she scrambled the last few feet, then went to her hands and knees, and plopped down onto her belly.

Beckler had been a crossroads on the highway, little more than eight buildings at an intersection. There were houses scattered about the surrounding hills, but the town proper was the blur of buildings the highway traveler saw when he rushed through on his way to somewhere else.

Beckler was now enclosed on all sides by a high fence of mesh and barbed wire. Large gates stood where the fences crossed the road at either end. The enclosure looked to be half a mile on a side. Inside the camp, on either side of the original buildings, several hundred small buildings formed up in line after line. Elizabeth could see several thousand people milling about amongst the buildings.

She looked behind her as Robert crawled up to join her. Far below, the children were sitting beside the car in the shade of the trees. They spared a quick glance to their parents before returning to whatever game they were playing.

"Holy shit," said Robert. He had settled in beside Elizabeth on the crest and was peering down at what had once been a struggling roadside stop.

"Concentration camp, looks like," said Elizabeth, turning back around and giving her attention back to Beckler.

"Labor camp." Robert pointed to the nearer gate. It was being opened and a line of humans were being led out. They weren't being led to any waiting vehicles and there were no work sites in view. The group was being marched down the highway, to no apparent destination. If they continued their current course, they would follow the road right past the stand of trees now hiding the car and the children.

"Could be a labor camp," Elizabeth agreed. "Could be worse. Hard to tell from here."

"Yeah, well I'm not curious enough to get any closer. I say we backtrack and not dally about thinking about it."

Elizabeth gave Beckler one last look and nodded. "No argument from me," she said.

"Damned magnanimous of you," Robert mumbled, scampering back a few yards before turning and working his way back to the car.

Finding a road that Elizabeth had seen on the map, they worked their way through the hills around Beckler and near nightfall located the county road that would take them back onto the state highway some miles beyond Beckler. Once it got dark, they pulled well off the road for the night. They risked a small fire and heated up canned foods for dinner. Afterward, the children slept in the car with the doors open toward the camp, while Elizabeth and Robert took turns at watch.

It was midmorning the next day before they reached the coast. Following it south, they came to the little bedroom community north and east of Eureka where Robert's parents lived, where Robert had grown up. He was at once in a place as familiar as anything in his life and as foreign as another country.

There was no damage that they could see, but the neighborhood had a ghostly quality. The streets were clean and quiet, the windows in the homes were dark. The lawns were yellowed and dry and there was a dusty smell in the air.

Robert looked through the steering wheel at the gas gauge in the dash. "We'll just make it, I think."

Though we won't have much to spare.

"Great," said Elizabeth absently. She looked carefully at each house they passed. Each was as the house before, dark and empty. She had an idea where they all were.

So did Robert. He knew that his parent's house would be empty. If they were still alive, he could guess where they would be. Perhaps they had been too hasty in backing off that labor camp the day before. Perhaps they should have taken the time to get a closer look at the people being held there. He turned right at the next intersection, then turned left two streets further down, always maintaining the ten to twelve miles per hour he had been driving since coming into the neighborhood.

Robert turned down another street, finally pulled up to the curb of one of the houses. He put the car into park, but left the engine running. He and Elizabeth stared blankly at the home. The front door was standing ajar.

Robert looked down at the steering wheel, rubbed at it with his fingers, then with the palm of one hand.

"We're alone, Liz..." he said. "We are all alone."

From the back seat came the sound of the children just waking. They were at Grandma and Grandpa's house.

EsJen followed her escort out of the ground vehicle, smiled at the warm sunshine that brushed her face. It was a pleasant morning.

MehnTec and NehLoc followed after her. The loosely related occupations of the three now frequently brought them together on their field trips. It no longer bothered EsJen. She had grown used to their company and their peculiar habits.

She indicated to the escort that she wished to walk up the narrow side road. They led the way, always observant, quiet and unobtrusive. EsJen and her two companions followed a few paces back, maintaining a calm, pleasant demeanor. The local inhabitants were skittish and easily frightened off; any that remained would be doing their best to hide from Shylmahn eyes. While the chances were slim, there was always the hope there would be direct contact, though of course this was not the purpose of this particular expedition.

The group traveled in a long, circling path that would eventually bring them back around to the ground car. They found a number of interesting artifacts along the way, and they discovered several open-air habitats that were obviously in current use. EsJen and the others suspected the Chehnon that were living in them were nearby, waiting for them to leave. They found a Chehnon vehicle that was in working order and looked to have seen recent use. The houses nearby were inspected and one of them looked to have been recently occupied. NehLoc made a note of all this. He and his staff would be watching. When appropriate, suitable action would be taken.

EsJen and MehnTec had their own perspectives on all of this and made careful observations of the rooms and the items they found in each. If only they could talk with the Chehnon that were living in this dwelling.

EsJen asked NehLoc about contacting the security director of this area. Perhaps a flyby of the area; perhaps they could spot the Chehnon from the air.

NehLoc grunted at the suggestion. They could not be bothered with such a trivial request. Besides, it would accomplish nothing.

Trivial? Who was NehLoc to judge her request trivial? Did he think her studies trivial?

EsJen finally let it go, but insisted on being included in the observation of this group of Chehnon. It promised to be very interesting. Once agreed, they continued their walk, though now much less congenial than it had been; the strain from their discussion followed them.

As they came to the top of the hill, where the road turned and ran along the ridge, MehnTec stopped suddenly and pointed. Following his line of sight, EsJen saw a group of the local inhabitants around a small campsite set up in the 'back yard' of a human dwelling at the bottom of the slope. The camp was well hidden, even from the air. There were a number of trees and a high wooden fence surrounding the yard, and it was by sheer chance that MehnTec had spotted them. He pulled out the visual enhancement gear in order to better see them. After a few moments, he grew very excited and urged EsJen to look quickly, asking several times if that was indeed him.

JoSeph, she said. Yes, it was. She was sure of it.

JoSeph was one of a number of Chehnon that she had been keeping under field observation. He had traveled some distance. Not in the direction of his home, if he was to be believed. She had found that the Chehnon were not always truthful.

MehnTec agreed that JoSeph had indicated his home to be in another direction entirely. EsJen's records were correct. They wondered, then, about his travels. They had lost track of him and this discovery had come as a pleasant surprise. This was EsJen's second sighting of a subject today, though the other had been expected. The activities of the other human subject had been much more predictable than this one.

JoSeph was different than most of EsJen's subjects in many ways, though this had not been obvious at first. His movements, his bedding habits, his daily activities. Now, as then, EsJen found this one fascinating. For what purpose was he traveling? Why here? What of those he was with now? Were they of his tribe? Were they companions? Were they also traveling? Were they traveling companions of JoSeph? While there were many Chehnon in hiding, quite a number were also on the move. If these were travelers, what were they doing here?

It was decided that these Chehnon would have to be collected. Following questioning and examination, they would be released and observations would continue. Careful note was made of the location, and they started back down to the ground vehicle. Once there, they would make their way around towards the collection site. NehLoc would coordinate the process with the security in the area.

Carolyn watched the activity around the ground car from inside a nearby house. Two Shylmahn guards. The ground car was no doubt a detachment from the large transport shuttle that had come down a half mile to the east. Looking up the street, she could see the group of Shylmahn returning from their walk. Two guards and three brass.

She saw movement behind a window of the house across the street.

Easy, boys... she said to herself. She looked quickly at the two Shylmahn. They were not positioned to see the window and could not have spotted the movement. She signaled for those at the window to get ready.

The group of aliens was getting nearer the ground car. The three brass continued to chitter away.

You just keep on chittering.

Jenzie was at the window in the next room. His weapon was equipped with a grenade launcher and he was in possession of two grenades. Everyone would wait for his first shot. He was going to put a grenade right into the ground car. Then all hell would break loose.

The Shylmahn creatures were still a dozen paces away when one of the brass stopped abruptly and held out a hand, halting the others.

He saw something!

Carolyn heard the grenade launcher fire. Jenzie had no other choice. Now or never. The ground car exploded. First one, then a second ball of fire pushed toward the sky. Both guards beside the car appeared to vanish. Even before the explosion, the three Shylmahn brass scattered and the two escorts with them knelt and aimed their energy weapons at the nearby houses. Amid the sound of the energy blasts, Carolyn heard her comrades open fire. The grenade launcher, reloaded, let go the second grenade. Carolyn managed to get off several rounds before an energy blast knocked her to the floor.

She groped about, dazed, uncertain about up or down. She pushed her hands out in search of the wall and fought to regain her senses. She felt a hand grasp her arm and try to lift her. She found her weapon, took hold of it and used it to push herself to her feet. Another shuddering boom almost knocked her back to her knees.

"Move! Now!" she heard from the back of the house. Finally able to stand on her own, Carolyn followed the other two out to the back yard and across toward the back of the house next door. As they crossed, Carolyn could see that one of the Shylmahn brass was down, the other two were bent over it, looking after it.

Carolyn stopped and went to one knee, brought her weapon up to sight. She was still shaken up, and sighting was difficult. As she fought to clear her vision, a shadow covered the area. The sound of the large transport shuttle moving in overhead pounded right into the bones. Carolyn paused, had to look up. It was right above them.

Screw it. She brought her weapon back to sight. She could see the three alien brass huddled between the two houses across the street, two of them working on the third, wounded and perhaps dying.

She fired.

The two kneeling beside the wounded Shylmahn threw themselves to the ground. But she had missed.

She did, however, have their attention; theirs and perhaps a few others.

Shit.

An armed Shylmahn appeared suddenly in the line of sight between Carolyn and the brass. It was in the street and hurrying towards her. She jumped to her feet and ran after her companions, who were no longer to be seen.

The sun was just beginning to set behind Hurricane Ridge, and the distant horizon was becoming awash in reds and purples. Kenneth took little notice. The sky overhead, still a pale, late afternoon blue, seemed to crack wide open as the alien energy blasts shattered the world around him. Gray, willowy smoke rose up from the blackened field. The ground itself was on fire. Shylmahn fighter craft thundered low overhead. Human soldiers continued to advance, constant, steady. No one knew where the next energy blast would strike. The nearer they got to the Shylmahn command center, the more frequent and the more concentrated the blasts became.

Bobby walked several paces ahead of Kenneth, taking the same steady strides as those around him. A step, then another. Kenneth followed him, matching him step for step. Then, for no reason that Kenneth could see, Bobby stopped. Kenneth continued forward and came up beside him.

"What's the matter?"

Bobby shook his head, turned and looked at his friend. He said nothing. He showed no fear, no panic. He didn't really show anything at all. He glanced up at the sky.

"Bobby?" Kenneth was growing scared.

Bobby looked like he might be shutting down. Right in the middle of the battlefield. An odd look shadowed across his face. Not really confusion, but something akin to it.

"I... I don't think I want to do this anymore, Britton." He smiled tentatively. "I just don't think I... you know..."

"What are you talking about?"

"What the hell's going on?" Sarge called out, striding heavily up to them.

"I don't know, Sarge. I think we're losing him."

Three energy blasts, one—two—three, and the world lit up around them. A second later, an alien ship raced overhead, leaving thunder behind it. The ground continued to smolder, to smoke.

Sarge stood directly in front of Bobby.

"What's the problem, Corporal?"

Bobby looked at Sarge, but said nothing.

"See what I mean?" asked Kenneth. "He said he didn't want to do this anymore, and then..."

"Bobby," Sarge's voice went calm, authoritative. *Make the boy think.* "Son, you listen to me, now. We got forces from all over in on this one. You understand me? We're gonna make it work, but every one of us has to do his part."

Sarge gave Bobby a friendly smack on the shoulder.

"You hear me? Huh? We all gotta do our part. We each gotta play it right... Bobby?"

Bobby continued to stare at Sarge.

"They're counting on us," said Sarge. "On you, Bobby."

A few moments, then Bobby nodded slowly.

"You got it?" said Sarge, encouraged. "We gotta keep our line going. All right? Let's go now. "

Bobby nodded again. He said nothing. He made no effort to move.

Several soldiers had made it to a small grove of trees growing beside a narrow ravine that ran alongside the field. Seconds after they disappeared into the ravine, an energy blast turned the grove into a cloud of hot, glowing powder. A rush of air struck Kenneth and the others full in the face, pushing them back a step. Kenneth hurriedly brushed the dust from his face. He grabbed Bobby and pulled him around. Their faces and frames were aglow from the nearby flames; shadows from the smoke danced around them.

"Come on, man!"

There was a bright flicker in the eyes. Maybe it was comprehension. He appeared to know what was going on around him. He just didn't care anymore.

"We can't stay here, Bobby!" Kenneth's grip on his shoulders tightened. "We can't stay here, and we sure as hell aren't going back. We don't have any choice. We have to get out of here!"

The look on Bobby's face began to change, slowly shifting as the shadowy smoke crossed his face.

"You with us, Corporal?" asked Sarge.

Bobby's words are whispered and distant. "Where else would I be."

Kenneth sighed relief. "Are we going now?"

"S'pose so."

Jason Britton pulled back the canvas flap and stepped into the command tent. An army colonel and several resistance leaders hovered over a large map that had been spread across a wooden table. They looked up as he came in, the colonel nodding curtly.

"Britton. Welcome to the action."

"Wouldn't miss it, Colonel."

The colonel was already turning back to the map, waved a hand over it, "Your people put on this show. Getting what you expected?"

Jason didn't know if he was being baited or not, but he didn't much like the tone. He moved to the table, stepped around it to face the colonel.

"This may be my party, Colonel Williams, but you are here because you graciously accepted the invitation."

The colonel stiffened. "Exactly so, Mr. Britton."

"I'd like to get this over with, please," said the short, squat, middle-aged man standing to Jason's left.

Jason turned his head slowly and gave the man a slight smile.

"Of course, Mr. Brett," he said. He leaned forward and examined the map. After a few moments' study, he cleared his throat. "This," he said, pointing, "is the route I took coming in. At that time Alpha Company had made it as far as the road and should by now be cresting the low ridge to the north. Another half hour and they should be in sight of the target."

"Bravo Company is here," said Colonel Williams.

"I know we've gone over this... but timing is everything. Everyone has to be in position at the final assault."

"The Shillies know that. They have to see it," said Brett.

"They can dig in and fight, or they can pull out by air. If they stay, we hit 'em. If they pull out, we cheer a minor victory and we try again somewhere else."

"This isn't our kind of fight," said the man on Jason's right. Jefferson had signed on very reluctantly. He was shaking his head slowly and frowning. "Any people I have left after this will not be attending another of your parties."

"That is completely up to you, Mr. Jefferson," said Jason.

"We're hit and run. That's what we do. This frontal assault crap is too damned expensive."

"I appreciate that, Mr. Jefferson. Signing on for this couldn't have been easy for you. I'll not forget."

Brett leaned forward, "Listen, we all agreed to go in on this, knowing full well the cost. We're accepting the losses, like it or not, because Britton here bought and paid for 'em. He may be here because he believes all his talk of the importance of getting hold of that Shillie technology, but the rest of us are here because he's handing out toys. So let's cut the bullshit and get on with it."

The room fell silent and Jason stared down at the map, an imperceptible smirk crossing his face and quickly vanishing. The truth was, right now everything was in the hands of the line commanders. Brett had four cells coming up on the supply depot from four different locations out of the northeast. Jefferson had a large group coming down the valley from the northwest, accompanied by several smaller resistance forces that had agreed to coordinate with his group. The west was completely inaccessible. From the south came Alpha Company, from the west came Bravo, these being the last of Colonel Williams' battalion. Three separate resistance forces were approaching from the southwest, wedged between Alpha and Bravo.

Each force had followed specified routes in their approaches to the target, beginning their advances several days earlier. They followed these routes as unobtrusively as possible, hoping to engage the Shylmahn at the last possible moment. Each force had designated coordinates they had to reach by the final assault time, which now a little over two hours away. At that moment, all forces would move on the main supply and redistribution center for the Shylmahn outposts in this area. Jason's goal was to grab hold of as much Shylmahn hardware and technology as possible, then spirit it away for study. They hoped to discover more about the Shylmahn as a result, and perhaps turn the Shylmahn technology against them. It could change the course of the war.

Once Jason had managed to bring all the local forces together on this, his superiors had authorized an artillery barrage. There was very little armament left, and the barrage in itself would not actually be effective. Its main purpose would be as one more simultaneous assault on the target, one more front for the Shylmahn to deal with. Because of these arguments, Jason had been able to place an artillery assault force in the hills southwest of the target. There would be a five minute barrage at the moment of the final assault. It would take just over five minutes for the ground forces to reach target from their final assault positions. Any personnel reaching target were to begin search and destroy operations within their target zone coordinates.

Once arriving, they would make no effort to leave the target zone. If the assault was not successful, escape was unlikely. If they survived and managed to reach the depot, and then failed to take it, the chances of them surviving a retreat were virtually zero. This was going to be all or nothing.

The canvas flap opened and an army corporal came in and handed the colonel a message. Colonel Williams read it, looked down at the map, and pointed to a spot northwest of the target.

"Jefferson's people are here. They are having some trouble due to the terrain, but are expected to be in position well within the specified time." The colonel straightened, "Thank you, corporal. Advise Bravo that I will be joining Alpha at one hour to final assault. Tell Captain Hiller I wish him and his people all the best. I'll see him at the target."

"Yes, sir."

Colonel Williams turned back to the map as the corporal left. Studying it, he scratched fretfully at his days' old beard.

"Well," he said, "that leaves your group, Mr. Brett."

"They'll be there."

"No doubt."

Jefferson had moved to the corner of the room, now began pulling on his gear. Brett grunted and joined him.

"It's about that time," he said.

Jason glanced at his watch, breathed a final, heavy sigh over the map, then went to the gear that had been stored for him. As the three of them put on their equipment, Colonel Williams stood at the table, arms folded across his chest. The kerosene lamp sitting beside the map threw strange shadows across the room and over the colonel's face, giving him an apocalyptic look that Jason didn't much like.

"We'll be waiting for you at target, Colonel."

"You all plan on getting there on your own, do you?"

"We'll be just three more in the crowd. Besides, Brett and Jefferson gotta be there to greet their troops." Jason pulled on his utility belt, then nodded to the map, "We'll be moving right along with the rest of you."

The three of them started toward the door. Jason held the canvas open and allowed the others to pass through. Before pushing through himself, he looked back at the colonel, who was still staring down at the map, perhaps searching for that one last tiny advantage that could make the difference.

"We've done all we can, Colonel. In this situation, under these circumstances, with what we have, we've planned it as best we can. It's not up to us, anymore."

The Colonel continued to study the map.

"There is always something else, Mr. Britton. I've come face to face with that fact time and again." He turned to Jason, "I shall search for it until the last possible moment."

"Good luck then, Colonel Williams."

"To us all, Mr. Britton."

Chapter Ten

The sky was a pre-dawn gray and was growing brighter with each passing moment. Kenneth sat with his back against the metal siding of the large warehouse, watched the eastern horizon change color. He stared at the brightest spot and watched as the new sun was born. The gray skies took on a pale blue tint, the few wisps of cloud shown pink. He turned his face full against the shining sun and felt the warmth melt away the chill in his body.

Bobby lay beside him, asleep or unconscious. Around them, smoke and fog intermingled in the slight breeze. Kenneth could hear Sarge talking to brass inside the warehouse. The sergeant gave a tired *yessir* before he stepped out the door a few yards away. He stopped and admired the sunrise a moment, turned and saw Kenneth and Bobby.

"You all right?"

Kenneth nodded. He cast a glance at Bobby, looked at Sarge and nodded again for Bobby.

Sarge looked away, at the scene around him, and stepped off.

It had been a tough night. Bravo Company had reached Final Assault Point at eighty percent strength and considered themselves lucky. They had gotten word that others had fared far worse. They had steeled themselves for the attack on the depot. They all knew the success rate on such assaults and tried to set aside the numbers. This was going to be different. They could feel it. This wasn't just another assault. This was highly thought out, highly coordinated, and all-important. Everyone knew it would be costly, and everyone had trouble looking at one another. It wasn't the fear of losing friends and comrades that made it impossible to look each other in the eye. It wasn't the concern about the pain of knowing that most of the faces looking back were the faces of the dead. It was something much worse, much more painful, something much deeper and more basic.

It was guilt. Guilt and shame. Not the guilt and shame of cowardice; there were no cowards here. The men and women who had fought their way across the land and to this battlefield were courageous beyond measure and trusted by one another beyond question. Each had laid their lives on the line for their comrades again and again.

And yet, as Final Assault grew nearer, as they waited in the growing darkness, something crept into the thoughts of everyone.

Don't let it be me.

Unspoken, unbidden, unwanted, and fought down as unseemly and shameful, it hung heavy in the air. Many had died arriving here. Many more would die in the coming hours. Despite this, there was always the knowledge that no matter how many might die, it would always be the other guy. That was what made the charge successful in the face of overwhelming odds. That was what kept the line moving forward. Each soldier had the inner knowledge that it would never be him.

That meant it had to be the other guy. To keep the numbers right, that meant somebody else had to die.

The longer they waited, the more anxious they became, and the more the doubt regarding this hard-and-fast *other guy* rule crept into their subconscious thoughts. There was some nervous talk, a few stupid attempts at graveyard humor, but mostly there was silence. Deadly silence.

Let it be someone else.

Kenneth's company had moved out at the first sounds of the artillery fire. Within seconds, the alien energy blasts began, but they were less concentrated than he expected. He could hear blasts in the distance. Everyone was getting their fare share.

The ships and ground assault vehicles that had come out to meet them pulled back as the aliens concentrated their efforts at the depot. As Kenneth's group came up over the rise, they saw their target clearly for the first time. Three large warehouses surrounded by a number of smaller buildings. Settled in amongst the buildings were more than half a dozen alien freighters, a dozen or more large shuttles, and as many smaller craft. There were half a hundred Earth-designed vehicles and dozens of Shylmahn ground vehicles. Shylmahn fighter craft flew overhead. Kenneth could see fighting on all fronts. The artillery barrage stopped. Artillery Hill was in flames.

It was another hour before Kenneth reached flat ground. With Bobby beside him, he rushed ahead and into a small grove of trees. Reaching the other side, Kenneth stopped beside a small, twisted tree, grabbed at Bobby before he could rush past.

"Stop, man," he said. "Look."

There was a thick shimmering some thirty feet beyond. A heavy bombardment of the concentrated energy blasts. The CEBs. Each blast took out an area of fifteen or twenty feet. Detonated frequently enough, and dispersed closely enough together, they formed an almost impenetrable shield.

Sarge came up beside Kenneth and Bobby, and stopped. The three of them squatted down and studied the clearing ahead.

The shimmering began about ten yards into the clearing. Another twenty yards beyond that, a row of small sheds signaled the outer perimeter of the complex.

"What do we do now?" asked Bobby.

Sarge turned suddenly and looked behind him.

A soldier was rushing up at them through the darkness. He plowed headlong past them, not knowing what lay ahead, before anyone could stop him, screaming unintelligibly all the way— into the clearing, through the CEB shield, through the row of sheds, into the complex beyond.

Sarge turned sharply to Bobby. "You heard the man." He stood and called out. "Chaaaaarge!"

Sarge rushed forward. Kenneth and Bobby followed after Sarge. Others, huddled along the line of trees, surged forward. The CEBs kept on coming, kept pounding at them. Kenneth felt the intense pressure from the blasts beating unceasingly against him.

The asphalt of the tarmac suddenly hit him in the face and chest. There were several seconds of confusion as he struggled to figure out what was going on. A blast had knocked him to the ground, hitting him from behind. He pushed himself up and scrambled forward, was knocked to the ground again. Looking forward, he saw Bobby ahead of him, Sarge further ahead still.

Bravo Company crossed the energy blast field in three waves, the second and third following after Sarge's dramatic charge. Of those making it to target, half made it through the shield. They hoped the other forces had done better.

Sarge led his group through the maze of buildings and flying ships and ground vehicles. They wasted little time as they rushed forward. Their goal was the center of the complex. This was where the majority of the energy blasts were originating. Take those out, and the other forces could come through intact.

Jason stepped carefully among the men and women who were sitting or lying sprawled out on the small lawn, climbed the steps to the front door of the low wooden building. An aroma nostalgic from long ago swept him up as he came into the room.

"Coffee?" he asked.

Brett held a cup tightly in both hands. Jefferson, standing near an open window, drank quietly.

"We discovered a full can, unopened." said Colonel Williams.

"Smells great," said Jason.

The colonel poured a cup for Jason as he spoke. "I have several pots going now, and I have people out scrounging up a cafeteria pot. Everyone will receive a share in the bounty."

"It has been a long time," said Jason. He took a delicate sip. It was almost too hot to drink. He blew into the cup, took another sip. "Oh, that's good."

"Well," said Jefferson, watching Jason take a seat behind one of the three desks in the room. "Then I guess you'd have to call this a successful operation."

"Yes, I would. You wouldn't?"

"We took the depot. You got yourself some toys... and coffee."

"It was expensive," Colonel Williams agreed, "but we knew that going in. My fear had been that lives would be lost to no purpose. That fear has not been realized, and the depot has in fact been taken."

"The Shylmahn escaped," said Jefferson.

"Don't forget the real goal here, Jefferson," said Brett. "The toys."

"Yes," agreed the Colonel. "Our supplies were at a critically low level prior to this engagement, Mr. Jefferson. I do not believe that we were alone in that respect."

"You pegged it there, Colonel," said Brett.

Colonel Williams sat on the edge of the desk and gave Jefferson a sympathetic look. "How much longer could you have continued without the provisions that Mr. Britton's people provided? How much more effective will your fight be with the supplies that we will all take with us from this facility?"

"Very expensive supplies, Colonel."

"I'll not argue that. But without them, the fight was all but lost." Colonel Williams nodded in Jason's direction. "And let us not forget the technology that was left behind."

From Jason's perspective, retrieving this technology had been the only reason for the assault. "The value of that alone is incalculable," he stated flatly.

"I can calculate it," said Jefferson.

"That would be cost," said Brett. "Not value."

Jason managed to speak up before the two resistance leaders came to blows. "I'm sorry about those that didn't make it, Mr. Jefferson. I really am. But this was a major victory for us. This was big. Who knows what our people will be able to do with the technology we captured?"

Jason looked down into his cup briefly, then looked up again at Jefferson. "I'm sorry, man, but we needed this stuff."

At that moment, a young, boyish private dressed in a uniform two sizes too big for him came through the door juggling three automatic drip coffee machines, and was about to lose the glass carafes.

"Sirs," he said, pleading.

Colonel Williams looked despondently at the boy. "A cafeteria pot, son. A big, metal pot."

Kenneth dipped two cups into the big aluminum drum, filling them with the hot, black liquid, walked back and sat beside Bobby.

"Enjoy," he said, handing Bobby one of the cups.

"Almost makes it all worth it."

"It's the new army." Kenneth took a big swallow, then set the cup down and picked up his mess plate. They were eating good, too. Food supplies had been found in several of the sheds. Kenneth was finishing up his second serving.

Bobby glanced up at the skies for the hundredth time.

"Stop that. You're making me nervous." Spotters had been posted all around the area. If the Shylmahn came back, there'd be warning. "We won this one. Enjoy it, damn it. We don't get many like this."

"We don't get any like this."

"So don't waste it." Kenneth set his plate down and picked up his coffee.

Until now, Kenneth hadn't thought they had a chance in hell of winning this war. But now? Maybe. Just maybe. A chance in a thousand? The odds were probably worse than that. But because of what had happened here, because of what they had done, the odds were better than zero. Their odds were better today than they had been yesterday.

There was hope now, and he was part of the reason.

Several hundred yards away, unknown to Kenneth, his brother Jason was going through some of the Shylmahn equipment, trying to make some sense of it before crating it up and starting on the dangerous trek to where scientists and engineers impatiently waited in their small underground complex a long night's journey away. Jason thought the chances of human victory over the Shylmahn were slimmer than the one in a thousand his brother gave, but he would have agreed that they were better than they had been a day ago.

Back outside, Kenneth held his metal cup to Bobby. "To victory," he said.

Bobby smiled weakly, reached down and picked up his cup. He tapped it against Kenneth's.

"Sure," he said. "Why not?"

Chapter Eleven

July 03

Bril pushed up on the long pry bar, maneuvering the log atop a wall that was already six logs high.

"Okay, let it go," he called out. A few feet away, young Peter released the end of the rope. Block and tackle shook and jingled and the notched ends locked the log into place.

"Peg it," Bril said. Peter was already scrambling onto the wall with long, wooden dowels in hand. Holes had been pre-drilled into the log and Peter placed a dowel into each one and began pounding them in with a wooden mallet.

Bril turned and looked out from the island. The sun was setting into the horizon of the distant shoreline. That shoreline was silent these days. Motionless. He found this more unnerving than having the enemy in sight. Put 'em too damn close, perhaps, but at least then he would know where they were. He took two steps over to a small table and picked up the binoculars from among the jumble of tools. For the thirtieth time that day he carefully scanned the mainland. Peter stopped work, as he always did, and calmly watched his father. He knew that one day his father's muscles would stiffen, that he would turn and call out for him to get ready—that *they* were coming.

This time, though, as he had every other time so far, his father lowered the binoculars, squinted and looked out with naked eyes, then turned away and set the binoculars down.

"All clear," said the boy, returning to his work.

"All clear," said Bril, now able to give the new wall a closer examination. Yet another bunker dug into the hillside. This front wall would be buttressed inside and out with dirt. The small door was made of two layers of wood with a middle layer of metal, all set on heavy hinges.

A network of bunkers was strategically built around the island, some of them already connected by tunnels, with plans to eventually connect them all, though that would take time. Booby traps had been placed at the bunkers, along the paths, at the lagoon, and at other key positions on the island.

Bunker One, the main bunker near the house, was much larger and much more heavily fortified than the outlying bunkers. It was connected to the main house by a tunnel that was more of a hallway addition to the house, having wood floors, paneled walls, and a string of lights. A solid door stood at both ends of the hall, each with its own double-set of deadbolts. Bunker One had been near completion at the time of the invasion. Though alien invaders hadn't exactly been what Bril had been preparing for, he felt himself damned fortunate for having taken the responsibility to ready his family for disaster, whatever that disaster finally turned out to be. There was also, he had been sure to point out, some level of vindication to be applied here. Recent events had justified his efforts.

"You 'bout done up there, son?" he asked, and began cleaning up his tools.

"Done now, Daddy."

"Be dark soon."

Once the tools were cleaned and put into the bunker, Bril scanned the horizon once more with the binoculars, then the ocean between shore and island.

"All clear," said Peter.

"All clear," said Bril, handing the binoculars to the boy. He tilted his head back and checked the skies, "All clear."

Back at the house, Bril and Peter cleaned themselves up at the large basin on the porch. It was a warm, clear day, and though the sun had gone down it was still evening bright and pleasant. Susan's kids were playing in the front yard and the sounds of children's laughter made the day all the brighter, all the more pleasant.

Kathryn brought out a tray of food and set it on the porch table. Sandwiches, slices of fruit and vegetables, carrot cake and banana bread. She hurried back into the house and came out again with a pitcher and a stack of glasses.

"Milk from powder, but it's cold and plentiful."

"Nice job," said Bril, smiling as he dried himself off. An outdoor buffet would be a nice change, a nice diversion.

Kathryn turned her attention to the children and clapped her hands together loudly. "Clean up now!" she called out.

As Little Daryl and Sharon and washed at the basin, Susan came around from behind house, covered in dirt from head to foot.

Peter pointed, laughing through a mouthful of sandwich.

"Oh, my," said Kathryn.

"Digging in the dirt is a dirty business," she said. "Don't let anyone tell you different."

"Well, clean up, clean up. We're eating outdoors tonight."

By the time Susan was cleaned and changed, with a plate of food resting on her knees, her children had finished their dinner and were running in circles around the yard, cheeks bulging with banana bread. Peter tried his best to be more adult, but he was only seven after all, and soon he was out there with the other children. They tumbled, wrestled, played tag and a half dozen games they made up as they went along. All the while the adults looked on. For brief moments they managed to push back the thoughts of war and death and Shylmahn invaders. They smiled and laughed and called out *be careful!* as one or another of the kids would take a painful tumble or one would fall on another, forcing out a breathless groan. Here, on this island, with the children, it was possible to forget the world out there, if only for those few fleeting moments.

Then reality would force its way back to the forefront. The children would make a dash toward the bottom of the hill and Bril would have to call them back. *Stay clear of the traps!* Or Little Daryl would turn and look up at the porch, and it would be impossible not to see his father in that innocent young face. Everyone would silently wonder where Daryl was, whether he was still alive. Memories of his sacrifice would come flooding back. With thoughts of Daryl would come thoughts of the rest of the family. How were Elizabeth and her children? Were they all right? Were her children able to play, as these children were playing now?

"Tomorrow's the Fourth," said Susan.

"Mmm," said Bril.

"Are we going to do anything?"

Bril continued to watch the children. The three of them were in a pile, a mass of arms and legs and mats of dirty hair. How could they stuff themselves, and then roughhouse like that? Bril picked up the coffee cup sitting at his feet.

"We'll celebrate."

"That's good." Susan drank down the last from her own cup, reached behind them and picked up the metal coffee pot. Refilling Bril's cup, Kathryn's, then her own, she stated flatly, "We've about finished off the pot."

The children were again working their way further down slope.

"You mind what I said!" Kathryn called out. "Stay in the yard! Stay clear of the traps!"

The three sat silent then. The sky grew darker as night closed in on them. The children continued to play, but they were showing signs of wearing out. They would have to take baths before they went to bed. Likely as not there wouldn't be enough hot water to go around for everyone. By the time Bril got into the shower, the water would probably be cold.

Bril woke to a low beeping sound and a blinking red light above the headboard. He jumped from bed and was half dressed by the time he reached the door.

"Intruder," he called out, low but harsh. Kathryn, too, was up and dressing. As Bril went out the door, Kathryn was waking Susan and the children.

Checkpoint One. The lagoon. Probably human, then. The aliens would most likely come by air. Still, who knew? Who knew about aliens?

Bril moved into position at the fortified foxhole that overlooked the landing. Another minute and Kathryn would be in position across the clearing. Susan and the children would be safe in Bunker One, with Susan at guard.

Even if the intruders were human, that didn't make everything all right. Out of the six billion people on the planet at the time of the invasion, only a handful had been worth a shit. The rest had been either mindless sheep or selfish exploiters.

Which is most likely to land on my island?

Those that are worth a shit, the mindless sheep, or the selfish exploiters?

Bril set the ammo box on the shelf, opened it and took out two of the grenades. These he placed within easy reach. He took out three ammo magazines, set two beside the grenades and quietly slipped the third into his weapon. He gave it a final push with the heel of his hand and felt it lock into place. It wasn't until he heard the sound of an electric outboard motor that he pulled the bolt back, which sent a round into the chamber and readied the weapon for firing.

Electric outboard. Human, then.

Small motor. That meant small boat. Most likely one or two people.

Or someone with kids? Liz? Possible. Could be Liz, or one of the others.

Or could be some psycho. Bril kept his finger on the trigger guard, ready to slip it onto the trigger at the slightest provocation. He had taught the others to do the same. Don't rest the finger on the trigger, as it is too easy to fire off a round before you're ready.

He could just make out a dark silhouette on the water. As he watched it draw nearer, he continued surveying the banks of the lagoon, the water around the boat, and the entrance to the lagoon. This small boat could be a decoy.

He could see now that there was one figure in the boat, but he couldn't make out any features. It could be anyone—friend or foe. The boat turned slightly now, the bow pointed toward the landing.

Five boat-lengths out, the engine cut out and the boat drifted toward shore. Two boat-lengths out a voice called softly, "Permission to come ashore."

Bril stiffened at the unexpected break in the silence. If his finger had been on the trigger, the intruder would have been a dead man. The boat ran aground. The figure remained seated, unmoving.

"Identify yourself," Bril said at last.

"Oh, about six feet tall, hundred and seventy pounds, blue eyes, dark brown hair. A rather handsome sort."

Bril relaxed, his tensed muscles suddenly aching. "Kinda' skinny, ain't ya'?"

"I prefer to consider myself trim."

"Permission granted," said Bril, repacking the ammo box. "Stand down," he called into the darkness. As he climbed out of the foxhole, he could hear Kathryn popping the round out of the chamber and putting it back into the magazine.

Jason was working his way up from the lagoon.

"Figured you'd be skulking out here in the dark, ready to blow my brains out."

"Damn you, Jason, I was afraid we'd lost you. I should have known better." As they met, they locked into a powerful bear hug. Bril fought back tears. "Where the hell 'you been?"

"Working."

They hugged again, then started up toward the house. They could see Kathryn ahead of them, disappearing into the shadows. She would give the stand down call to Susan.

"So, what's this now, then?" asked Bril. "You here on vacation?"

"Something like that," Jason smiled, but there was a somberness barely hidden by the smile. Once in the middle of the clearing he stopped and looked carefully around him. The house was up the hill, the lagoon below, with woods on either side. Dawn would be here in an hour and Jason could just make out the dark shadow of a structure to one side of the house. Kathryn was going inside. In the woods, some animals would be just bedding down for the day, others just rising, readying to forage for food before daylight. He could hear some of them, though most were too cautious; the silent prey.

"Rough out there, I guess," said Bril.

"Out in the real world? Pretty bad."

"I don't suppose there's much left that I'd recognize. 's what I hear."

"You could say there's been some changes. The major cities are pretty much gone; the places we knew..."

"Damn."

There's a new world in the making out there, thought Jason. Whatever Bril was up to here, he wasn't going to be able to stop that world from rolling over this sanctuary of his.

"Have you seen the others?" he asked.

"All except Kenny. I don't suppose—"

Jason slowly shook his head. So, if Kenneth wasn't here, he must have stayed with his company. It was what he had expected, but he didn't want to think about what that might mean. "Everyone else is here, then?"

"Come and gone. Susan's still here; and the kids."

"Where'd the others run off to?"

"We'll talk over an early breakfast," said Bril. "And what about you? You here to stay? Oh, right. Vacation."

"Wish I could. Just came to see how everyone was doing." Jason opened his arms as the kids ran down from the house. He gave them all a hug, then hugged Kathryn and Susan. They sat on the porch, wrapped in blankets, drinking hot cocoa, talking of family and of good times and bad, and watched the morning come. Bril told of what he knew of the others.

Jason listened to it all quietly, and overall took it all rather positively. Truth be told, he had expected much worse. He told them then that if Daryl had been taken captive, there was a good chance that he was still alive. Entire cities may have been obliterated, but if you were taken alive, odds were good that you would stay that way. He told them that if Elizabeth was damned lucky, and damned careful, she might have made it to California; and that if she hadn't, the Shylmahn were more likely to take a family captive than to kill them.

"Is it any different in California?" asked Kathryn.

"Not much. Some." *We do seem to have more than our share of bad guys here in the Northwest...*

"Hmm," Bril grunted.

"As for Carolyn, she could have joined up with any of a dozen groups. All tough as they come, but to be honest, only a couple are of any real consequence."

He didn't know what to say about Joseph, particularly with the locally heavy concentration of Shylmahn. There were still a lot of people on the loose. One man, unobtrusive, by himself... if he was careful... maybe.

Joseph clambered among and over the bricks and masonry, slipping and almost falling as he made his way back to the open asphalt beyond the rubble. All the buildings along the north side of the street had collapsed and fallen into themselves, splashing broken brick, mortar and stone onto the road. Once he was safely beyond the worst of it, he stopped to catch his breath. It would be night before long, and he would have to find a place to sleep.

He turned his head to a whistling sound and muffled explosion. There was a burst of fiery color in the sky several blocks up the street. Another burst, then another.

The Fourth of July?

Rocket after rocket went screaming into the sky. It wasn't quite dark yet, but it was dark enough. He recognized these as rockets strapped to three-foot sticks, like those he used to pick up at the Indian reservation come the last week of every June. Back when he and Barbara were still...

Those things'd go a hundred feet or so into the air and set off a sky display in miniature. He would pound three or four hollow pipes into his back lawn to use as launchers. Slip the stick of a rocket into each one, then light them one after the other. Put on a great show. Stupid, really, and not exactly legal.

Joseph hurried down the street, rushing toward the celebration. He ignored the shadows that dusk had brought out— the shadows that waited in the corners, the alleys, behind the broken walls and the shards of broken windows.

The sound of an alien ground vehicle finally brought him up short, and he quickly backed into one of those beckoning shadows. The vehicle came out of the side street and stopped in the intersection not more than thirty feet away. After half a minute, the side door opened and two Shylmahn stepped out, a female and a male.

It couldn't be the same...

She was looking right at him. They had known he was here. How the hell... had they been watching him? Following him? Were they finally coming to take him?

Another set of rockets screamed into the air. The bursts were bright enough, and near enough, the sky now dark enough, that the shadows were pushed back from Joseph's face. The aliens turned, startled, and looked up at the sparkling sky. As the display faded, they turned back to Joseph.

"It's the Fourth," Joseph said, strangely calm.

The female smiled faintly. "Fourth?" she asked.

She had understood him. More than that, she talked back in English, and quite clearly. An unreasoning sense of panic threatened to overwhelm him and it was several long seconds before he could respond.

"The Fourth of July. It is a day of some importance to humans. Some humans. We celebrate it each year."

Both aliens turned back to the sky. There were more rockets. There were firecrackers going off as well, and Whistling Petes, and probably a lot more. The celebration couldn't be more than a block and a half away and one or two streets over.

"I... understand," said the female alien.

"I doubt it."

"I believe that I do." She turned to her companion, "Wait for me, will you?"

The companion spoke hurriedly, *EsJen... Ba-Cheh haht buhn goht. Ahpesfehtohp—*

"I shall be fine, MehnTec." the alien said in English. "This is my function. Wait here."

MehnTec appeared ready to argue, but stopped himself. He took a step back, stood ready in case he might be needed, and watched the *Ba-cheh*. The female gave him an understanding smile, then turned away from him and back to Joseph. Joseph shifted nervously under the alien scrutiny.

"What do you want?" he asked.

"To talk, Jo-Seph."

"How do you—it is you, isn't it? The same one that...?"

"My name is EsJen."

"Uh, huh. You following me?"

"We have kept you under observation—have lost and found you several times. We... monitor... movements and activities of a number of Chehnon... *humans*."

Joseph felt as though a smooth, solid wall had suddenly flipped up and smacked him.

"What do you mean, monitor? Wha... why? Why are you following me?"

"I...," EsJen paused a moment, in thought, "*evaluate* humans. The *thoughts,* of humans."

"You read minds?"

"No," she said quickly, then rethought her words. "I observe humans. I observe human... life. I watch your activities and from this I make judgments as to how you... *think*."

"Some sort of psychologist?"

EsJen paused in thought again, then said finally, "A psychologist, no... Perhaps... a behaviorist. Our knowledge base requires to know how Chehnon react, respond, behave, under varying conditions."

EsJen stopped again, thought again, considered her words again. "This is necessary so that the... transition... can be completed smoothly.

"In order for this to occur, we *behaviorists*... gained as much information as was possible prior to our arrival here so that subsequent... direct... observations... would be more... effective."

"How's it been for you? Rewarding?"

"I have gained much information. I have expanded the knowledge base."

"By observing me?" he asked edgily.

She stepped nearer Joseph, almost close enough for him to touch her, though not quite. "You gain nothing by such... attitude... Jo-Seph. You only lose knowledge that might be acquired by talking with me in... civil manner."

"Joseph."

"Yes."

"No. I mean *Joseph*. Not Jo-Seph."

"JoSeph."

"Close enough. Thank you."

"You are welcome."

"Fine," he said.

EsJen smiled. Joseph could not help but smile back. But... this was the enemy. These were the bad guys. *She was a bad guy.* Joseph had the strange feeling that she had no comprehension of that fact. What could she think was going on here? What did she see from her vantage point? From her unique point of view? Could they be so alien that she was incapable of understanding the horror of what they were doing to this world? These invaders, these conquerors, how did they interpret their actions? How did they see what was going on? How do they see these humans?

Perhaps there was something to learn from talking with her.

"You speak my language very well," he stated.

"It... improves."

Joseph looked at EsJen very carefully. After several seconds, he took another step further from the shadows. "All right. I'll talk with you."

§

There was a small campfire burning. Carolyn sat a short distance away, on the sill of what at one time had been a large window. The wall was now broken and jagged, as were all the brick walls of the old warehouse. She could see Danny standing guard near the far wall. There was the silhouette of another guard beyond the left wall. The rest of the group was gathered near the fire. Terry pulled something from the box beside him and poked it at the flames.

It was a sparkler. When it came to life, he walked over to Carolyn and handed it to her. He hurried back to the fire and lit more, began handing them around.

"Sing something," someone called out. Terry nodded agreeably, stepped over the rubble to where their supplies were stacked and came back to the fire with a worn and beaten guitar. He made himself comfortable, gave Carolyn a warm look, and then turned his attention to the guitar, the fire, and the music.

It was a ballad. It was sad, warm and human. Jenzie, kneeling beside Terry, stared into the flames as he listened, falling into a numbing melancholy. He stood finally and tossed the stub of his firework into the glowing coals. As Terry continued singing, Jenzie moved away from the heat and light of the fire toward one of the four crumbling walls that formed the camp perimeter. He turned and looked back to the group. The flames of the small fire were showing brightly on the walls and rubble surrounding the camp, smiling faces flickering and shimmering in firelight. The encampment shone into the night like a beacon.

Danny shifted about from his post at guard along the wall, looked over at Jenzie and then back at the camp to where Terry was playing and singing. Some of the others began tossing their dying sparklers into the fire. Danny smiled contentedly to Jenzie before returning his attention to his duties. The boy had only looked to the light for a few seconds, but it would be enough to destroy his night vision for several minutes. Jenzie thought to chastise him about it, but decided to let it go.

Jenzie was in his late forties, the oldest member of the group. Ben Soo, the group leader, had surreptitiously maneuvered him into a position as the wise old uncle to these kids, of which Danny was the youngster. Just a boy, sixteen years old, Danny had been fired up by the call to arms made by the others.

Carolyn. Fierce independence, strong personality. A lot of the passion of the group came from her. The day Ben Soo accepted her, this band of renegades had truly come alive. She was rebellious, outspoken and dedicated.

She was also growing infatuated with Terry. He was in his late twenties. Quiet, modest and soft-spoken; rather warm and cuddly; the poet in the midst of anarchy. He had a romantic eye on the world, on humanity, and he was head over heels in love with Carolyn. Jenzie thought they made a peculiar and yet somehow perfect couple. They complimented each other well. The Bard and the Revolutionary.

In Ben Soo lay the heart and soul of this band of resistance fighters. Thirty years old, though he looked younger. Jenzie suspected that Ben Soo had ordered his body not to age and it was reluctant to disobey. His was a blistering, zealous personality, always at the edge of bursting, of exploding through all that he said and did. The aura about him was intense, and his own demanding independence made Carolyn's seem placid by comparison. He would be chained in neither mind nor body.

Above all, Ben Soo was born to lead. There could be nothing else. Others, who were no more a follower than he, such as Carolyn and even Jenzie himself, were drawn to Ben Soo as their leader. And while he demanded loyalty and dedication to duty from those he would command, what he insisted upon in equal measure was that they hold independent thought and will and voice. There would be no blind rush into oblivion by those he would lead. They would hurl themselves into the great void with eyes opened wide.

Ben Soo stood now behind Terry, gave him a pat on the shoulder as he finished his song, "Very nice, Terry." He continued around the fire, then, and stopped near the box of assorted rockets and other fireworks. They had liberated the cache from a storage shed on a nearby Indian reservation. He glanced over at Jenzie, who was already grimacing.

Sorry Jenzie... thought Ben. *Gotta be done.*

"Boys and girls," he said, kneeling before the box. "I think it's about time we let the people of the Great Northwest know that we are here."

Bril watched from the highest point on the island. The skies all up and down the mainland were lit up with Fourth of July rockets. To the south he saw large fireworks exploding out over the Sound. All about him the skies were glittering with the strength and energy of the human defiance.

Bril felt a pride rekindled. We are not lost, yet. Hell no. The human race would not give up so easily. Every square foot of ground the invaders took was going to cost them, and in the end these alien bastards would know that there had been a fight.

Bril would wait his turn. He would bide his time and prepare. The pull to take the fight out to them, to stand beside his human comrades in combat, was strong. It was almost overpowering at times, especially when his brothers and sisters came and went. And tonight... The sense of comradeship was overwhelming, the fireworks of freedom lighting the skies in the distance, beckoning him, beckoning all, to join in the celebration of that freedom and the struggle to keep that freedom. The Fourth of July, long a celebration of the birth of independence for a people, had now become the call and cry of the fight for freedom for all people. It was a celebration of the survival of the spirit of the peoples of the Earth.

But Bril knew also that his place in the great struggle was here—on this island. It always had been. The battle would be unseen, unheard, lost among the million tiny wars that were to be fought in this time of great peril. He knew even more certainly that here was where he would make the greater difference. Whether that difference would matter in the big picture was not the point. Here was where he would leave his mark. Not out there. Each struggle against the invasion was its own world, had its own purpose, its own life, its own soul. This island and the inevitable conflict to come was to be his time and place. He would strike his blow for freedom here.

In the clearing below, at the base of the ridge, the island celebration was in full swing. The afternoon picnic had shifted to an evening of campfire singing, ghost stories and burnt snacks. At the moment, Jason was fending off a particularly violent attack by the children. Bril managed to catch Kathryn's attention, and finally made her understand that they should all come up.

It took twenty minutes to get everyone up the hillside. Once on the top of the ridge, they huddled together against a cold wind and watched the fireworks. Tiny rockets spun up from darkened neighborhoods. Big blasts detonated out over the Sound in deafening defiance.

On this night, no one felt alone.

Chapter Twelve

July 05

Daryl woke to a pounding headache. The birds outside his small window, normally a pleasure to him, now only focused the pain, directing it toward the back of his brain. He swung his feet around and onto the floor and held his head in his hands.

In the past week his headaches had grown more frequent, as had the sessions with Dr. Black. They were more numerous and more intense, though there seemed to be little point to them. There was nothing special or important about the information Dr. Black was gathering, whether he acquired it by interrogation or physical examination. Daryl saw no rhyme or reason behind the information Shylmahn wanted or the methods he used to get it. Sometimes Daryl would just sit in a chair and respond to questions; questions about his work, his breath, the color of his eyes, about trees or fish or frogs. He was asked about cities and societies. He was asked about hair styles and clothes. He was asked about food and eating habits. He was asked about the stars.

He would be laid out on an examination table, fully clothed one time, and stripped the next. Here too he might simply be asked questions, or he might be probed and prodded by silent technicians, or wired to a machine and interrogated, all the while being accused of lying. On a number of occasions he had been put through a series of physical exercises, each time under varying circumstances. Once he was stripped, ordered to perform the exercises, then was returned to his room naked. Throughout this particular session, Dr. Black had stood silently by, half-hidden in shadow against the far wall. Daryl wasn't sure if he had been observing the human body in motion, or his prisoner's reactions to the situation. Daryl was beginning to question whether he was reading too much into everything, but what the hell else was there to do?

"Daryl?"

Daryl lifted his head from his hands and looked toward the door.

"Daryl, wake up. You all right?"

"I'm awake," he said softly. Softly or not, the words echoed in his skull and it felt like his brain was pulsating. It made him nauseous.

"Daryl?" It was Frank, in the next room over.

Daryl stood up slowly and delicately walked to the door. Leaning against it, he spoke loudly to the closed slide that was set into the door at eye level. "I'm awake, Frank!"

"Don't give me an attitude, Daryl. I could make your life miserable, you know."

Daryl had to smile. He waited until he was able to lose the grin before speaking again. He slid to one side, nearer the shared wall. "I have a headache the size of this room."

"I was worried about you. They brought you back kinda late."

"Yeah," said Daryl. "I'm all right. Dr. Black was as gentle as ever."

There was silence on both sides of the wall. Daryl closed his eyes, remained standing with his back against the wall.

"Helluva show last night," said Frank.

Daryl opened his eyes, then, uncertain about what had just been said. He said nothing at first, but finally curiosity won out. "What?"

"The fireworks."

Daryl thought about that for a while, finally looked over at the small window, his only connection to the outside world.

Fireworks...

"Right in their faces, Daryl," said Frank, the words somehow distant. "Right in their fucking faces."

Guard called out from down the hall. His voice was authoritative and confident. "Quiet down the hall."

Daryl slid tiredly down the wall until he was sitting on the floor. "Sounds great, Frank," he said.

Kenneth knelt, brushed the soot from the object with his blackened hands. Sarge glanced briefly over at him from twenty feet away, then continued on, kicking up clouds of ash and dust as the three of them searched the field. Bobby was twenty feet to the other side of Sarge, managing to appear both sincere and bored.

Kenneth picked up the small weapon and looked it over carefully. They had come across several of them in the past; Sarge had even used one once against a Shillie in an ambush. They were like the stun sticks, but were effective at greater distances and had more punch, making it an actual battle weapon rather than a control or punishment device.

The cost for the greater range and power was that the blaster could only be fired three times before having to be recharged. For this reason, when the Shillies used hand blasters they usually stayed in groups of four or five, surrounding an *energy pod* containing a couple of dozen blasters. In addition to the blaster reloading function, these small pods were also capable of launching energy blasts similar to the CEBs, though these the Shillies used sparingly. Once a pod fired off an energy bomb, its reload capabilities were down for ten to fifteen minutes.

No one had yet managed to get hold of an energy pod, or had even seen one up close. When threatened with capture, pods were detonated, destroying everything and everyone within a wide radius. Larger pods were known to be installed in all alien ships and vehicles, in alien buildings, and they ringed the perimeters of Shylmahn installations. Even larger versions were thought to be installed on the great ships and in several Shylmahn facilities. It was widely believed that the pods were the actual power sources for all alien equipment.

Kenneth put the weapon into the bag attached to his belt and continued across the field. They had won this skirmish, minor though it had been. The Shillies had set up a camp here, perhaps a survey crew or observation post. The usual contingent for a group like this was a guard escort of four to six, the flight crew of two, and a work crew of three to six. The work crew could be made up of scientists, engineers, military, or just about anything else. The makeup of this small camp had never been determined.

Lieutenant Parker came across the field from the creek that ran the length of the valley, the dust cloud he kicked up drifting ahead of him and toward the three soldiers. Beyond the creek, eleven others searched the far field for little treasures the Shylmahn may have left behind during their escape.

The lieutenant stopped as soon as he thought Sarge could hear him.

"Sarge, you and your boys come on up to the Command Center. The colonel wants to have a chat."

"Yes, sir," said Sarge, then waved Kenneth and Bobby over.

By the time they reached the creek, those from the other field had already joined the lieutenant and Colonel Williams. The colonel jumped up onto the large rock near the edge of the clearing and waited for the group to gather 'round.

"Gentlemen and ladies... Job well done. Without serious injury or loss of life. I commend you all." The Colonel paused a moment to let his verbal pat on the back register. "Our numbers have grown small on our journey, but we've grown tough along the way and we've learned much about our enemy. We've learned how to take him on. Sometimes at great cost, but absolutely necessary if we are to one day attain final victory. This victory, I am sure, will come. It will come through the small successes like this one.

"This you already know. You know also how proud I am of each of you. You are much more than my troops. No collection of men and women can go through what we have without growing very close. We have become a family, and this has helped us to endure.

"Unfortunately, this closeness makes the loss of fellow comrades all the more painful. The death last week of Jenny Brennan and the injuries to Tom Allen and young Sean are bitter reminders of the high cost of our struggle, these incidents following what had been a period of very few injuries and no loss of life. We will miss them, and we all wish Tom and Sean well."

Colonel Williams paused, looked past his troops. He took a deep breath and grew thoughtful. He tried to smile, but the feeble attempt quickly faded. He clasped his hands firmly behind his back.

"Lieutenant Parker has returned from Colonel Drake with news. You are all familiar with our situation per last orders. We have been operating as an independent unit for some time based on those last orders. We were to seek out and destroy the enemy anywhere and wherever we may find him. These were our last and only instructions and we have carried them out to the best of our ability.

"Unsettling new information has been brought before me and I feel it vitally important that each of you be given the opportunity to reassess your individual situations based on this new information.

"The Federal government, which has up to now been struggling to hang on in some limited form, is no more."

Colonel Williams was visibly shaken at having to speak the words aloud. Several in the crowd were also shaken, and there were a few gasps. "There is word that while most state governments have dissolved, a few have gone underground and are continuing to operate in some minimal capacity. We should take heart in that, and can hope and pray that the Federal government, at some level, continues to exist as well, and will one day return."

One of the soldiers interrupted, "What about overseas?" he asked.

"We have no word on foreign governments, but we can assume that they have fared no better." The Colonel seemed not to mind the breach of protocol, but after answering, did take a moment to stiffen his resolve before continuing.

"What this means is that the flag under which you fight no longer exists in an official capacity. If I understand history correctly, such was the case when it was born. The ideals that make up the fabric of that flag still live, and always will. For us, those ideals have kept us going long past any reasonable human endurance.

"You have all given far more than can ever be repaid. You have fought, and many have died, with unquestioning devotion to duty and country. However, the circumstances have changed. I feel that it is my responsibility, and your right, that I now give each of you the opportunity to choose whether to stay or leave. Some of you may wish to try to return to your homes, to find your families. To those who choose that path, I fully understand and will support that decision. All who wish to leave may do so, with honor, with our gratitude, and with our prayers for a safe journey. I salute you.

"To those electing to stay, I will be proud to continue to lead you. Colonel Drake has two full platoons encamped thirty miles from here. He has asked that we and Major McBain's Riders join him on an assault of a Shillie distribution center that he has had under surveillance. We will start out first thing in the morning."

July 09

EsJen followed the winding dirt path through the trees and into the clearing that straddled the top of the hill. Sidewalks circled the clearing, winding their way around flowerbeds and narrow strips of lawn. She could see that it had at one time been well looked after by the Chehnon, but now nature was quickly reclaiming what had once belonged to her.

There was no one else in the small park. EsJen walked to the bench at the far end of the clearing and sat down to wait. From here she could see the remnants of a small community below. Fifty or sixty Chehnon dwellings lined several meandering streets. Below, as here on the hilltop, lawns had overgrown and some were beginning to turn brown. Shrubs and hedges were showing signs of neglect.

The homes looked lonely. Windows were dark and lifeless, a few doors stood ajar. It was all eerily still. She knew, despite appearances, that a number of Chehnon were living down there, in that neighborhood. There were several families and a couple of isolated individuals. It saddened her, somehow; the more so as she grew to understand these creatures. This had been unexpected.

It had been difficult. Even now, when she would feel she had a concept within her grasp, it would often slip away. Piece by piece, though, the true picture of the Chehno native population was forming. As this picture became clearer, the Chehnon view of the Shylmahn migration to Chehno was becoming clearer to her as well. She was astonished at this view, if not a little frightened. At every level of Chehnon mind and spirit, virtually every Chehnon subject now under study emanated anger, frustration, and even pain, at the situation.

It was all very perplexing. It was no wonder that ShahnTahr had seen it necessary, from the very beginning, to assign individuals such as EsJen the task of studying these creatures and developing an appreciation of the complex emotions and intricate discourse that arose as a result of the arrival of the Shylmahn colonists, an appreciation that must necessarily include an understanding of the Chehnon perception of the migration.

Joseph had been a stupendous find. EsJen had had no idea that those first cautious attempts at communication would reward her with such a wealth of data. Their sporadic encounters had slowly evolved into regular dialogues as Joseph grew more trusting, and more comfortable, around her. EsJen had carefully sought out and nurtured those first seeds of confidence and assurance, went out of her way to make him feel safe. One of her earlier discoveries had been Joseph's maddening necessity for independence of will and the illusion of choice. When she had identified these traits in him, she knew that she had found something important. Carefully handled, those forces within him could actually make Joseph more accessible, and the knowledge she might gain would have a perspective that would make it much more valuable than if it were acquired by more traditional methods, if it could have been acquired at all.

Her efforts were paying off. She felt that she was indeed beginning to develop an understanding of the Chehnon. She had been forced to cast aside a number of earlier misconceptions, and had developed a number of theories on the 'hows' and 'whys' of these strange beings. ShahnTahr was continuing to encourage EsJen in her studies.

Despite the new insights, and in spite of the fact that she thought she was gaining a clearer picture of the Chehnon, she was all the more bewildered by this knowledge. The structure and organization of their thinking was truly bizarre. It was very hard for her not to put Shylmahn mores into their reasoning, yet it was absolutely essential that she not. When looking at the actions of the Chehnon from the Shylmahn viewpoint, they were quite insane, irrational beyond belief. Only when she was able to apply Chehnon reasoning to their actions did they make any sense at all. This she was able to do only very rarely, and only in the most limited sense, in spite of what she knew. She was simply not Chehnon. She was Shylmahn. It was as if these Chehnon creatures existed in a perverted universe where one of the traditional dimensions had been replaced with some new, slightly altered dimension. She might be able to understand it, she might even be able to document how the inhabitants of this altered universe would perceive their world, but she could never actually see it. She would never know what it was like to be an inhabitant.

The closest she could ever come to being Chehnon would be to experience what it was like being a Shylmahn being a Chehnon. Even this level of understanding she had yet to truly attain. EsJen had only just touched the shadowy realm of Chehnon thought.

Yet she *had* touched it.

The Chehnon Joseph appeared suddenly and sat down on the bench beside her. She watched his expressions as he glanced at her before turning his attention to the community below. He said nothing yet. They often went through this. It was an awkward few moments. She had thought at first that it might be some Chehnon ritual, preparatory to two forces meeting. She now believed it to be more individualistic, dependent upon the participants, the situation, and the emotions involved. She wondered if Joseph was this way with other Chehnon.

"You look well," she said.

"I'm doing okay."

"If a bit tired."

"My world has become an exhausting place." Joseph continued looking out across the vast scene splayed out before them. "You know... I had a vision once, before... all of this. Or a dream... hallucination, something."

"A vision? What did you see?"

"I was here," said Joseph. "I was sitting on this bench. It was very relaxing. It was evening, and I was watching the neighborhood below as it settled in. Families coming together after being apart from each other all day. Dinners cooking, televisions coming on, kids arguing. And then..."

"Yes?"

"And then... then it looked a lot like this."

EsJen thought this curious. "Do you believe that you saw the future?"

"I doubt it. I was probably just freaking because we all thought you were a meteor storm."

"I see," EsJen wondered. "Are such visions common among Chehnon? Among humans?"

"I don't know," Joseph leaned back. "Maybe. Not me. Never happened before. Hasn't happened since."

"Interesting."

"Just one of those weird things that happens."

"I would not dismiss it so readily, JoSeph."

"Not a whole lot to do about it," he sighed. He seemed to be through with this line of thought. For the moment, EsJen wasn't sure how to pursue it further. This was definitely something that required additional research. ShahnTahr would be most interested. This may be an entirely new field of study.

She shifted her weight on the bench, looked back over her shoulder at the small park behind them. "As I was waiting for you, I was thinking about home; my old home; my old world."

"You must miss it." *I sure miss mine.*

She shrugged. It was a very Chehnon gesture, she realized. "Sometimes," she said.

"So what was it like?"

"It does not matter. This is my home, now." She looked out at the panoramic view, then down the hill. "There are several Chehnon families living below."

"I know."

"I am sometimes saddened by what I see."

"You ought to see it from our side."

"I do try." EsJen smiled her most human smile. "It is not an easy thing to do."

"We're not all that complicated."

"You are very alien to us."

Joseph thought about that. He looked out at the world spread out before them. It was his world. He was a product of that world. "Humans are the children of Earth," he said. "The human psyche is born from that. I don't think that you can ever actually see through our eyes, not as we see. You are children of a very different world."

"An interesting correlation."

"Earth as mother? As old as the human race."

"Ah, well," she smiled sadly. "Shylmah pushed her children away from her. We were not the best of offspring, and Shylmah was not a forgiving parent."

Joseph struggled through a polite pause.

"What happened? Back home?"

"It makes no difference, now." EsJen grew still.

"I'd like to know."

EsJen shook her head slowly, "Let us simply say that you had your wars, we had ours. Let it go at that."

"This isn't one of those 'we destroyed our world, we have to find someplace else to live' stories, is it?"

"No... No, not as simple as that... We... we altered our destiny." EsJen looked carefully at Joseph, finally decided to continue.

"Many hundreds of years ago, we had our 'Great Conflict', as we called it. A romantic turn of phrase. Two simple words that removed two billion people from existence."

"There is nothing romantic about war."

"It set into motion the forces that finally brought us here."

"You guys destroy your planet a thousand years ago and that's why you're here taking ours now?"

"As I said... it is not that simple. And you are trying to reintroduce old arguments."

"Okay," Joseph held up both hands. "I'm really interested. I would like to know what happened."

She turned her head slightly, slowly lifted her gaze to a puzzle of clouds hovering above them. It appeared as though Joseph would get nothing more from her, that she would speak no more of it. She finally said, almost to herself, "Thirty million survived the initial war, and it wasn't enough. The main warring factions continued to slaughter each other, until, in the end, the very land they walked on, the air itself, was killing them... and still they fought."

Sounds almost human, thought Joseph.

"The last survivors, a few million, no more, had no choice but to attempt the dangerous crossing to the South Continent. Not a hospitable place. Many times we had tried to colonize there. But now there was no alternative.

"The South Continent was not made for my people. At the time of the Great Conflict, only a handful of tiny communities existed on its southern coast. Less than seven thousand people lived there."

"What was wrong with it?"

"The Veltahk dwells there. A vine-like plant that covers the entire land mass. It grows very fast and it cannot be destroyed.

The vine is eight inches thick; it grows along the ground, twists up into the air, twenty feet, thirty feet, branches and branches again, takes root anywhere and everywhere. The roots dig deep into the ground, sixty feet down, with root offshoots a hundred feet long and more. It is believed that the vines covering the continent are all connected, that it is all one plant."

Joseph tried to imagine a plant the size of a continent. "Still, there had to be ways of controlling it."

"Thousands of years before the Conflict, and in all the centuries since, you think we had not tried?" EsJen shook her head. "The South Continent belongs to Veltahk. It was never meant for us."

"And so you had to adapt to a new way of life on your world."

"They were ill prepared for this new world. Most of those who had survived the crossing landed along the northern shores. Some stayed there, but most went inland, trying to reach the settlements to the south. Starvation, injury, food poisoning, exhaustion. Thousands more died, but many reached the settlements and their populations swelled. From seven thousand to almost a hundred thousand in a matter of months. They began turning people away."

"I guess it must have been pretty bad."

"There was no way they could sustain such populations. More than half died that first year, and it was much worse outside the settlements, in the wilderness.

"My people were never the same after that. Too much had happened to them. Many of those who survived had done terrible things in order that they might live."

EsJen had seldom spoken of her world, and Joseph was fascinated by it. Here was an alien history, the story of a world so different from his world, yet with similar emotions and passions. He thought at first that she was trying to lay some excuse on him about how they had no choice but to come and take his home, that they were driven from their world and this was their only hope for survival. As she told her story, though, and from what little he had already learned of her and her people, it was clear that such a thing as making excuses, particularly made to a Chehno native, would never have occurred to her. He knew also that while EsJen wanted, even needed, to understand the ways and thoughts of the human mind, she would never concern herself with changing the opinions of a Chehnon native. She would see no purpose in that. The Chehnon were, after all, Chehnon. Understanding them was one thing, changing Chehnon opinion was something that would not cross a Shylmahn mind.

This didn't make sense, but it was very Shylmahn.

EsJen was telling her story because doing so either served a purpose in her dealings with this human, or she simply wanted to tell someone. She needed to speak the words. Joseph hoped that this was so. It seemed to fit. She knew these events intellectually, had grown up with them, but she had never known them emotionally. They had been the facts and figures of the past. Facts and figures were safe. Now, perhaps because of her arrival here, possibly as a result of her work here on Earth, her history was rising up and becoming something real for her.

EsJen had gone quiet. Joseph watched her, saw totally alien expressions cross her face.

"But you did survive," he urged. "Your people survived, recovered, and eventually you reached the stars."

"Yes. We did."

"EsJen..." Joseph hesitated. "How does any of this justify taking our world away from us?"

EsJen gave Joseph a curious look. She spoke calmly, without frustration. "Now it is you who cannot see our actions through our eyes."

Joseph held back a frown. He wanted to cry out *justify yourself!* but resisted. Justification wasn't in her. Besides, it wouldn't accomplish anything. And he wanted to hear more of where these invaders came from. After more encouragement, EsJen did tell him more.

After the first few years following their war, the population in the five communities leveled off at about 40,000. Scores of tiny bands managed to survive *in the vines*. By the end of the third year, the Shylmahn knew the fate of the North Continent. It would be uninhabitable for millennia. They had destroyed their only real living space on the planet, and were now left with trying to survive in an environment totally alien to them, and nearly as hostile.

Life in the settlements was extremely hard, and some Shylmahn fled into the vines hoping to fare better. Those that stayed behind constructed great stone walls around the communities to try keep the vines out and to protect animal herds and plowed fields. More hours were spent keeping walls clear and rebuilding what the vines destroyed than perhaps at any other endeavor. An open field one day was often covered by the Veltahk the next.

Then they discovered that if they built great moats of sea water around the communities, just beyond the walls, the Veltahk could be kept at bay. It was still a fight, but if the moats were deep enough, and wide enough, the vines could be kept out.

Later generations concentrated on such things as intensive agriculture, population maintenance, building architecture, and the social and political structures required in the environment in which they found themselves. At some point, a road following the coastline between two of the communities was constructed. A trench of seawater three times the width of the highway had to be built along the inland side in order to keep the highway clear of the vine. Crews worked constantly to maintain the road.

As the cities grew higher and deeper, and as the agricultural sciences were perfected, the populations were allowed to slowly increase. Four hundred years after the Great Conflict, six hundred years before the migration to Earth, a moon base was established on the largest of the two moons. By then the population of the five communities had been allowed to grow to over one million. It was a near-miraculous achievement. A society of only one million had managed to reach beyond their planet.

The Shylmahn were looking for a place to grow, a place to go. The million or so on Shylmah knew their existence was not a normal one. Four hundred years had not changed that. Each city was a small, crowded, isolated world. Shylmah was livable, with its mixtures of joy and sorrow, but it was no longer their world. It was their home, but it was no longer home.

The moons were barren, with no atmosphere. With time, the other planets circling their star were explored, and though these were little better than the moons, small bases and a few distant outposts were established. Technology advanced, but travel beyond the solar system was still a long way off. As science moved forward, the outposts expanded to accommodate larger populations. Still, none of these bases was ever more than a collection of prefabricated canisters joined together in a maze of rooms and halls. The necessities of air, food and water had to be manufactured or brought in. And the shelters had to be protected against the radiation from their star.

From these remote outposts they searched beyond.

They sent out three small sleeper ships to three nearby stars. One was expected to take forty years round trip, one sixty, the last sixty-four years. Two of the ships returned, sending word ahead at light speed that the planets they had found were uninhabitable. The sixty-year ship was never heard from, its small crew lost.

Some had said that science would catch up with the sleeper-ship technology and that Shylmahn colonists would be waiting for the sleepers when they reached their destinations. While this didn't happen, technology had indeed outpaced those first crude attempts at star exploration. Something the Shylmahn called

Computer Network sent out a series of high-speed unmanned probes to distant stars.

The reference to computers caught Joseph's attention. Here was something that perhaps the two worlds shared.

"What's this Computer Network?"

"ShahnTahr now, but back then it was the Computer Network. Without it, I don't think there'd be a Shylmahn alive today. In the beginning, a small computer system was developed to run a few of our systems, but by the time of the probe ships it was doing much more. Two of our cities were governed by the Dahltahr, the largest governing body of the time. The Dahltahr had integrated most of the cities' operations into a single computer system, the Computer Network. The other cities allowed some of their systems to be operated and maintained by Computer Network, in a limited way, and all of the outposts were operated by the Network as well."

Joseph was beginning to see the Shylmahn from a whole different perspective. From their earlier wars, to their battle with nature, to the exploration of space, to the foray into the realms of computer technology. Up until now, he had seen only the invaders.

"What sorts of things did this Computer Network do? Did it, like, run the lights and communications?"

"Early on, it controlled the utilities, assigned the work details, tracked and recommended population growth, authorized and guided construction. With the passage of time, the more complicated our society became, the more technologically advanced Computer Network became; the more we depended on it, even for our very lives."

Let it go for now. Don't appear too interested in the computer.

"So what happened with the probes? One came here, I guess."

"They sent back huge amounts of data, all gathered by Computer Network. It collected and interpreted the subtle clues that might identify any likely locations for habitable planets as it deciphered the secrets of the universe."

In the meantime, though, they continued having their problems back on Shylmah. They had their little wars. As isolated as they were from one another, they managed to irritate each other. Then, about four hundred years ago, a plague struck one of the cities. It ran eight months and killed more than ninety percent of the population of the city. Once the disease had run its course, the remaining population cleaned and purified their community. Prior to the outbreak, the city had allowed some of its operations to be run by Computer Network, and this had been a key factor in the city's ultimate survival. During those months,

Computer Network expanded its responsibilities and by the end it was operating the city virtually on its own.

The survivors had an empty city to themselves, and Computer Network kept things running smooth. The people in the other communities saw this as a chance to gain some breathing room and sent some of their populations over. So they had more fighting. In the end, three of the communities were operating within a single government.

And Computer Network, always upgrading, evolved into ShahnTahr. It eventually developed to the point of self-upgrade, far beyond the ability of those who had originally built it, and those who helped to maintain it.

"Over time," said EsJen, "the remaining communities joined the three, and we had one government."

And ShahnTahr.

Joseph could scarcely imagine the Shylmahn history that was being laid out before him; this strange world, with its strange people; forces that guided them inexorably forward into a future that would eventually bring them to Earth. A society that was a thousand years and unbelievably far away, destined to eventually come crashing into Joseph Britton's peaceful existence.

The Shylmahn people had thrived under ShahnTahr. Over the centuries, it took control of all decision-making on Shylmah. It ran the communities, now under a single government. It managed material and supply flow, controlled the work force—who should work, when, and on what; what should be made and in what quantities. It directed the survival of the communities, and of itself. It enforced the laws and dispensed justice, made the decisions as to future advancements and social tolerances.

"But," Joseph had to say something, "that's the kind of stuff people like to do."

"In a society like ours, as tightly controlled as it had to be in order for us to survive, we needed to have those processes taken over by ShahnTahr. We grew and prospered under ShahnTahr, where otherwise we would have died."

At a terrible cost, thought Joseph, but said aloud "And it brought you here." *At a horrible cost to us...*

Carolyn leaned against the low wall that ran the length of the hilltop park. Looking behind her, she watched her companions step carefully along the path that wound its way through the forest grove and down the hill to the road. Terry turned back to her once and waved before leaving her and disappearing into the evening shadows beneath the trees. Carolyn held up a hand in return, brought it down slowly and turned back to the clearing. Joseph was sitting on the overlook bench at the far end of the park, talking with a Shillie. They were too damned friendly.

The plan had been to kill the Shillie and her Chummie, following an intensive interrogation. When she recognized Joseph, Carolyn had persuaded the others to walk away from it. It had been asking a lot. It wasn't every day they had a chance to grab a Shillie who was off by herself, so when they had learned there was one frequently seen alone with a Chummie companion, Ben Soo and his group saw it as an opportunity they just couldn't pass up. Ordinarily they wouldn't have even have been in the area, but being as they were, it was the second chance in as many days to strike a blow for human kind.

Carolyn had been surprised that the others had given in to her request so easily. She figured they were probably uncomfortable with the situation. Who could blame them? The fact that your brother was a Chummie was bound to cause disconcerting feelings among your friends.

They pity me.

Carolyn waited and watched, until finally Joseph's friend stood and left the park. When the Shillie was out of sight, Carolyn pushed off the wall and moved from the shadows, dreading the impending confrontation with her brother. *What the hell does he think he's doing?*

Oh, he's a dead man...

Joseph turned and stood at the sound of her approach. He held out his arms when he saw who it was.

"Carolyn!"

She hugged him in spite of herself. It had been six weeks or more since they had last seen each other. A lifetime, these days, and apparently neither of them had been playing it safe. She pulled away slowly.

"What are you doing here?" asked Joseph. He could see then that something wasn't quite right. "You don't look so good. Something's wrong."

"You could say that."

"Kenny?"

She shrugged from his grasp. "What the hell's the matter with you? The only reason you're not dead is that it was too awkward to kill my brother with me watching."

Joseph was stunned. He turned away woodenly, took the half dozen steps back to the bench. He sat. Moments before, he had been sitting there with EsJen. They had talked pleasantly. He had listened to her story of the history of the Shylmahn. He had even felt for her at times.

So that was it.

"Oh."

"Yeah."

"It's not like that," he said.

Carolyn sat beside him. "What the hell are you doing?"

"Carolyn, just what do you think is going on?"

"We hear there's a human and a Shillie spending a lot of time together. That makes you dead."

"I'm not a collaborator."

"Hey, that's great!" Dripping with sarcasm. "I'll let the folks back home know."

"I don't have to answer to you."

"You need me on your side. You answer to me, or you answer to those who aren't in the mood to listen."

Joseph leaned slowly forward, rested his elbows on his knees. "Carolyn, I swear. I'm not collaborating with the Shillies. We talk. That's all. I'm trying to learn about them. I am learning about them. Each time I meet with her, I learn a little more."

"Yeah? And what's she getting out of it?"

"What can she learn from me that they don't already know? Hell, what do I know? Besides, do you really think we have a chance against them the way things are now?"

"So now you're saying that fighting them is a waste of time? Let's hold hands and be friends?"

"You know me better than that."

"No. Apparently I don't. Not anymore."

"What I'm trying to say is that we need better tools, better weapons, if we're going to take our planet back. Information. Knowledge."

"And you are going to get this knowledge for us?"

Joseph suddenly looked very weak. "I can try."

"Oh, Joseph," said Carolyn, sadly. "This is bad."

What was she supposed to make of this? Okay... in a way, it made some sense. If he could get some inside information that might help in the fight... still... *oh, crap...*

"My brother has taken it upon himself to infiltrate the enemy and win the war against the Shillies... singlehanded."

The muscles in Joseph's face went weak. He turned away from her, let his shoulders fall. He felt very tired.

"You fight them your way. I'll fight them mine."

"Joey, you're walking on very dangerous ground."

"We need to know how they think, how they feel, what gods they worship; Hell, why they're here. How sophisticated are they? How smart are they? Do they make mistakes? How much, or how little, do they know about us?"

"Do you have the answers to any of those questions?"

"Yes."

Carolyn looked at her brother very carefully. She sat back, finally, and looked out across the neighborhood below. It was completely lost in the evening shadows. A cold breeze was climbing up the hillside and numbed Carolyn's face.

The struggle against the Shillies could benefit from what Joseph might learn, might have already learned. But Joseph had to be careful. Their defeat at the hands of the Shillies could be the result of what he unwittingly gave them; not secrets in the traditional sense, but the same kind of information that he was getting from them. Their reason for wanting this information was undoubtedly far different from Joseph's. The Shillies were looking for ways to control what they had already won. Joseph was looking for ways to win back what had been taken.

If nothing else, Joseph had been right on one point. Carolyn may not want to admit it, but she saw little hope of winning this war without something new and drastic being introduced into the mix.

"Damn," she said softly. She got to her feet, took a step, looked out across the devastated landscape. She'd listen to what he had.

"All right, let's walk." She started away from the bench and toward the trail.

Chapter Thirteen

July 13

Bril and Joseph walked the trail down from the ridge and came around from behind the house. Bril had accomplished a lot, and he had been eager to show what he had done. Joseph had been willing to take the tour, and he was impressed with what he saw. His brother had done a good job. It was well thought out, well designed, and quality work.

Yet he knew perfectly well that if the Shylmahn were serious about collecting these few humans, these defenses weren't going to stop them for long; and if these humans should become too much trouble, the island and those on it would simply be eliminated.

Jason was standing on the porch, watched Bril and Joseph approach.

"So, Joseph. What do you think?" he asked.

"Bunkers, underground tunnels, booby-trapped trails, spiked pits." He looked at Bril. "You've been busy."

Bril took the steps up onto the porch, turned and sat on the rail. "They may take me, but they'll know I didn't want to go."

"They may come, or they may not," said Jason.

"If they do, you're as ready as you're ever going to be," said Joseph. Safe enough. He turned to Jason, "So, what do you think of Carolyn's plan for getting Daryl out?"

Jason shrugged heavily, "As good as any other. When coming up against the Shillies, you never know."

"What about this group that she's tied herself up with?"

"They've created themselves a bit of a reputation."

"Good or bad?" asked Bril.

"Ben Soo and his band of revolutionaries." Jason had to think about that. They were a frightening bunch, all right. "Calculating, ruthless, determined, and extremely dedicated to the cause. They take chances and they're willing to make sacrifices. But they do pick their fights carefully."

"I'm not sure that answers his question," said Joseph. "They must lose a lot of people."

"They are very good at what they do. Their core personnel has remained fairly intact, but they do go through the recruits. To tell you the truth, I think a lot of them get scared off. Those that stay, and live, usually become as extreme as the rest of the bunch."

Bril grunted. "Sounds like just the kind of folks we need to get Daryl out."

Joseph was a little more wary. "Why are they willing to help us?"

"Daryl is Carolyn's brother," said Bril. That should be enough.

"You doubt their motives?" Jason asked Joseph. "You don't believe they're doing it to get a couple of dozen humans out of the clinic? When one of the prisoners is the brother of one of their own?"

"As you say, they pick their fights very carefully."

Jason gave a vague smile, "Joey, I do believe you're growing cynical."

"Something's up, and you're in on it; or you know about it."

Jason put on his thoughtful look, the one he always wore just before he was going to bestow words of wisdom upon his audience. Joseph and Bril both recognized it immediately, having been the audience upon which Jason had spent years practicing.

"You can't ask someone like Ben Soo to put his people on the line for the sake of a freeing a few prisoners. Not during times like these. Not even for Carolyn's brother."

"Then there is another target."

"Destroy the lab," said Bril, quickly.

"I don't think so," said Joseph. "More than that..."

"Quite right," said Jason. "Ben Soo won't attack a building just because it happens to be occupied by the Shylmahn. Or if he did, it would be from a safe distance. And he wouldn't be going inside."

"But?"

"If the odds show there's a chance of success, he just might attack a building in an attempt to get his hands on an energy pod."

"What the hell's an energy pod?" growled Bril.

Joseph sat on the top step and clasped his hands together. He sighed unenthusiastically. "It's a device the Shillies use to charge their weapons."

"And perhaps much more," said Jason. "It may be central to much of the Shillie weaponry and transportation. If we were to get our hands on one intact, we may be able to learn a lot about their technology. It could turn the war around for us."

"Then this isn't about Daryl at all," said Joseph.

"Oh, we'll get Daryl out," Jason said soberly. "And the others."

"But that's not the mission."

"No. It's not the mission."

Bril's face was turning bright red. "That's your brother you're talking about. You damn well make it the mission."

Jason leaned softly against the post, but said nothing.

Joseph, still sitting on the step, breathed out heavily. "He's right, Bril."

"Like hell."

"Getting Daryl out of there may be all important to us, but a few humans in the face of the millions already dead is nothing. Grabbing an energy pod intact could conceivably save millions more."

"What's the good of winning the war if we lose who we are?"

"What's the good of saving a man if we lose the war?" asked Joseph.

"We'll get Daryl out." Jason pushed gently off the post. "In spite of your cotton candy sentimentality. Freeing the prisoners is key to the mission succeeding."

"Don't give me cotton—"

"We're the diversion?" asked Joseph, cutting Bril off.

"The prisoners are what makes this is a viable target."

Joseph was getting to his feet. "So, we'll be freeing Daryl and the others, and meanwhile Carolyn's people will quietly slip in and haul away the pod."

"That's the plan."

Bril wasn't ready to accept this. "With half our forces going after this energy pod, we have much less of a chance of getting Daryl out."

"This works for us, Bril."

Joseph rested a hand on Bril's arm. "Let them have their mission, Bril," he said. "We have ours. We'll provide the diversion they need, and they'll provide the additional firepower we need. They get their pod, we get Daryl."

Bril glared over at Jason, then looked back at Joseph, the features in his face softening finally, if just a little. He grumbled under his breath and stalked into the house.

Jason took the steps down off the porch and walked out away from the house. Joseph followed slowly after him.

"How'd this all come together, Jason?" he asked, calling after him. The two of them stopped, Jason looking back at the house, then at Joseph.

"Waddya' mean?"

"Come on, Jase. The Brinkman Mansion has been there since the beginning."

"So?"

"So you found out Daryl was in there. You had to find a way to enlist the help of Ben Soo's group in order to get him out."

"We need the energy pod."

"I'm not arguing that. But I think you'd do whatever it took to free Daryl, even if it meant winning the war."

"I think you have that backwards, brother. And now you're getting all cotton candy on me, too."

"You found out that Daryl was in there, quickly figured out this two-pronged mission, made sure Ben Soo would find out about it, and the rest is just details."

Jason turned and walked away without responding.

Joseph grinned and turned toward the door, mumbled to himself, "...and he calls me cotton candy."

Dinner was a loud, hectic affair, as they always were when the family got together. None of the arguments ended; they just evolved into new ones. Many were about the Shillies, in one way or another, but a surprising number of the arguments had nothing to do with the invaders or the invasion, or the mission to rescue Daryl. Many were the same, run of the mill, everyday family fights that cropped up over and over, year after year, at every one of the Britton family get-togethers.

Throughout the day, Carolyn's thoughts had continually returned to the matter of Joseph and his business with the Shillie. He had put himself into one hell of a fine position, and put Carolyn in one that she found very uncomfortable. She didn't like it one damn bit. The longer it went on, the more unpleasant it would become; all the worse because she had little or no control over the events. Her only participation in the whole matter was going to be to support her brother and try and keep him from being shot in the back of the head.

Still, like it or not, the more she thought about it, the more she had to agree with him. For all her doubts, for all her concerns, Carolyn had to admit that no matter what her own feelings might be, Joseph was probably doing the right thing. In all the world, with all the confrontations between human and Shylmahn, with all the sacrifice, with all the death, it may well come down to a whispered word between this Shillie and Joseph. Or, as Joseph had said, it may not be the spoken secret, but rather a sudden burst of understanding that he may realize about these invaders.

She watched now as Joseph went over to Susan and gave her a supportive hug. She had been bubbling tears since hearing that Daryl was alive and that a rescue was being organized. Joseph knelt before Daryl's children and gave them hugs and kisses, whispered something to them that Carolyn couldn't hear. She envied his relationship with all the kids, and the way he had of making their faces light up whenever he was around.

Joseph went to the front door and stepped through the blackout curtains and disappeared outside. A single conversation continued in the living room, but Carolyn felt outside of it now, outside the scene, as if she were looking in on the room from some distant place. Earlier, she had been as involved in the quickly shifting discussions as any of the others, but as the evening wore on she had unconsciously pulled back.

She looked again around the room. Susan was still sitting quietly in the stuffed chair against the far wall, her face flushed with emotion, her children playing quietly at her feet. Kathryn had gone into the back of the house, ostensibly to clean up, but Carolyn knew she was simply tired of the arguing. It got boring after a while.

With Joseph outside, and Carolyn acting as silent observer, there was only Bril and Jason left to keep things going. In years past, it would more than likely have been Bril and Elizabeth in the throes of discussion, with Carolyn and Joseph there to provide variety. Jason, Kenny, and Daryl were usually the quiet ones hovering around the edges of heated debate.

Carolyn listened inattentively for a minute more, then followed after Joseph.

It was quite dark now, the stars and what little moon there was were hidden from view by thick clouds. Joseph was standing in the yard a few paces from the porch, lost in thought, his hands stuffed into his pockets.

"Fresh air?" she asked.

"Getting a headache." Joseph looked occasionally at the black, heavy sky, but mostly just stared out into the night.

"He has that affect on people."

"Maybe we should send him to the Shillies."

"I'll talk to Ben about it." Carolyn looked down the slope towards the lagoon. It was too dark to see even half the distance. Her group could do a lot of damage on a night like this. *We're wasting a perfect night.*

"Thanks for not bringing up the uh, you know..." said Joseph.

"The little affair between you and the Shillie?"

"The... arrangement."

"You're doing what you have to."

"Really?"

Carolyn shrugged, turned away and looked out at the night. "You're in for rough times."

"I'm glad you're with me on this."

"This whole thing sucks."

"Then you deserve my thanks all the more."

She gave another shrug. "Like I said, you're in for rough times."

"I guess I hadn't really seen it from any other point of view. I just, you know, did it."

"You hadn't thought about how others might perceive it?"

"No."

"How about your place in history?"

"I'm thinking about it now, thanks for that. My place in the present doesn't look too good, either."

"Well," Carolyn grew genuinely thoughtful, "After careful consideration, I'd say don't worry about it. If you are successful, hey, you're a hero. If you're not successful, there'll be no one left to condemn you. So, what the hell?"

"I hope you didn't expect me to find comfort in that."

Carolyn turned around to head back to the house. She placed a hand on her brother's shoulder as she passed. The only comfort she had for him.

It wasn't uncommon for TohPeht to come away from communication with ShahnTahr feeling both exhilaration and confusion, and this latest session provided a substantial amount of both. Success continued for the Shylmahn. All was well, and ShahnTahr was enthusiastic in the praise that he bestowed on TohPeht for his efforts and his leadership. At the same time, however, TohPeht sensed that ShahnTahr was anxious about matters and subjects that he had thought settled long ago, or had simply not been worth the effort.

He would never openly question ShahnTahr's plans nor its orders, but the fact that these thoughts had entered ShahnTahr's consciousness at all concerned TohPeht. The Shylmahn people stood now on the threshold of a new era due solely to the wisdom and guidance of ShahnTahr. ShahnTahr's selfless and untiring labors, with a foresight that spanned centuries, had given the Shylmahn a new world, a new home.

What possible justification was there for TohPeht to second guess ShahnTahr now?

None. Absolutely none.

He pushed such thoughts aside. They served no useful purpose and could not possibly affect any action he would take. TohPeht held the greatest of all privileges, to direct the Shylmahn people as ShahnTahr instructed. From this role he would never waiver.

GahJen arrived for their meeting and they set about preparing assignments and task timetables. There were dozens of figures to go over, and operations to initiate that were dependent upon those numbers.

Of the surviving human population, over half remained at large in those territories of the planet not yet annexed by the Shylmahn. Of those humans in the occupied zones, over eighty percent were now under Shylmahn supervision on twenty four reservations, two hundred thirty smaller managed communities, and more than six hundred work camps. The facilities were now automated to a large extent, but were still a considerable management effort, with a staff that comprised more than ten percent of the Shylmahn population now on the planet. With the adjustments to staff personnel that ShahnTahr was calling for, and the development of the new equipment that it had recently designed, they should be able to absorb the remaining Chehnon at large into the facilities without additional staffing. This estimate relied on the projected mortality rate resulting from normal collection operations.

Though the reservations took large tracts of land, they were by far the most efficient in Shylmahn-to-human ratio, and were well suited to automation. The work camps, at the other end of the spectrum, by their very nature required the greatest number of Shylmahn staff for the fewest number of humans. The largest of these work centers, with a population close to 13,000 humans, would be disbanded and the laborers taken to the nearby reservation once they had completed construction of Operations Center 12. Half the Shylmahn staff there would be reassigned to other centers, and the remaining would be sent to prepare a new, smaller work center on the southern coast of the continent. The new facility would be the first to incorporate several of the new monitoring devices that ShahnTahr had designed.

The research facilities were to be expanded, with several new avenues of study to be explored. This would require some minimal increase in the staffing of these locations and the acquisition of suitable subjects. The new staff personnel would be reassigned to these facilities from other research operations as completion of their current assignments allowed.

Expansion into as yet unoccupied areas of the new world was ongoing.

The next fleet of ships was scheduled to arrive in six and a half days. The plans for their disembarkation and placement had been worked out long ago and only minor adjustments had been made to these plans in recent weeks. The primary responsibilities of these new arrivals were the construction of the *dahlsehts* and the establishment of agricultural programs. While much of the physical labor would be performed by the Chehnon population, the expertise would come from the Shylmahn.

The last matter that TohPeht and GahJen discussed would have confused GahJen if he had thought enough to be confused about it. If he had thought at all on the matter, he would have assumed that ShahnTahr, or perhaps TohPeht, was simply curious. He did not think about it. He simply noted as instructed.

Request confirming data from test subject 41a53ca/site241.

Probable connection subject to minimal concentration at island 43359621ar.

Probable connection subject to antagonist force 12432256dw/subject31s/site43358911e.

Probable connection subject to antagonist US83210a2/site43358923w.

Probable connection to natural study subject 8642611josep/site4359132tc/observer33213.

Probable connection to antagonist force ML3451196/subject52a/site43359597d.

EsJen dreamed.

She walked the streets of her dahlseht. They were crowded with all those she knew. Friends, relations, those she worked with. It was a soft, warm and pleasant dream. The city enveloped her, wrapped itself around her like a favorite blanket. Those rushing past her were a soothing elixir that she took in along with the air in long, slow breaths. The wind whistling through the narrow canyon streets tickled the skin on her face, brushed back her golden hair. All was well. She felt joy.

Minutes passed. EsJen continued her gentle stroll, offering salutations to all she met and greeting those she knew with courteous pleasantries before they hurried on about their business, promising to visit longer when they could. Such was the life in her dahlseht. It was home. She was home.

A strange face appeared in the crowd of faces. An odd face. An unpleasant face. It was hard and rough and large.

It was a Chehnon face. *Human.*

The Earth man stood tall above all those around him. Large and grotesque. EsJen grew frightened, sensing that at any moment the Chehnon might sweep his arm angrily about him, brush her friends violently, distastefully, aside. She was about to cry out, to warn them, when the moment passed, the sense of imminent danger subsided. The man turned and looked directly at her. There was recognition then. It was him. It was JoSeph.

She knew that it would be. Somehow, she had known all along. Of course it was JoSeph. He was here. He had come here, to her home. JoSeph had come to see her.

He approached her now, moving slowly through the crowd, stood finally before her. She held out a hand and he took it. It was tiny in his grasp. She felt his strength, and his gentleness. They pulled closer together and he wrapped his arms around her. With her head against his chest, EsJen heard JoSeph's heart pounding deep within. She felt him take one of those powerful hands and softly brush at her hair.

The pedestrians continued hurrying about their business, stepping around the two lovers. It should have been a strange sight, a frightening sight, yet they seemed not to see, seemed not to notice. This large, horrific creature had grasped this tiny Shylmahn, was embracing her with its massive arms, and yet those of her dahlseht were ignoring the two of them.

But this was a dream.

A warm, comforting, emotionally cleansing dream.

Chapter Fourteen

Daryl lay strapped securely to the table. The Shylmahn researcher hovered over the sensor equipment table nearby, tracking brain, perspiration, pupil, and blood chemical data of the human.

Daryl watched Dr. Black make adjustments to the equipment. The rest of the room was hidden in the darkness that lay beyond the tables. There was a faint hum coming from somewhere, and Daryl knew that Guard was in the room, out of sight, watching the interrogation preparations.

"Please feel free to speak other than the truth," said Dr. Black. "We are studying this human characteristic as well."

"Do what you want." *There is purpose behind everything he says...* "It won't make any difference."

"What will not make a difference, Daryl? And to what?" Dr. Black was calm and excruciatingly patient. Daryl didn't answer. Dr. Black continued fussing over his equipment. "Is it that you believe the results of your participation here will not impact the migration?"

"Migration?"

"Do you believe that your participation in our activities here at this facility will make no difference in the relationships that may form between Shylmahn colonists and members of your family?"

"I have no family."

"I see," said Dr. Black. He watched Daryl a moment, then smiled a very human smile. It looked odd on a Shylmahn face. "Perhaps I have been misinformed."

"Yeah."

"No matter. It was a side issue in any case. Perhaps it is better not to wander too far afield on such unrelated issues."

"Whatever."

"To more engaging concerns, then. For instance, I would be interested in hearing your views on the various political structures that existed on this planet prior to our arrival."

"I have no opinion."

"Do you feel the United States of America had the best form of government?"

"Still does."

"You see? You do have an opinion. We are making progress." There was a quiet pleasure in Dr. Black's voice. "Let us continue. What are your views on the history of human rights on this planet prior to our arrival?"

"Strange question coming from an alien with a human tied to an examination table."

"Do you believe that improper actions are ever justified by their outcome?"

"That's a leading question."

"All of my questions are leading, Daryl. You know that."

"I see no reason to cooperate with you."

"Do you feel violated by this process?"

"Yes." Daryl could hear Dr. Black working with his equipment.

"There will be no pain during this meeting," he said, taking more readings. "Does your fear subside?"

"I have no fear. I have anger."

"I must disagree with you on that point."

"I don't really care."

"What do you think Jason would do in this situation, what with him being, *in the business*, as it were?"

There was a moment's hesitation.

"I don't know any Jason," said Daryl, but of course the Shillie wouldn't have brought up Jason's name if he didn't already know all about him. And, of course, all of the equipment that he was attached to was spotting every lie.

"Do you wish that you were fighting beside him?"

"I wish I was fighting."

"You would die beside him?"

"If it would help defeat you."

"Bravado. An expected human response, Daryl."

"Then why ask the question?"

"Would you willingly die to save Jason?"

"Is that a choice I can make?"

"I am not a threat to him."

Then why bring it up?"

"I merely ask," said Dr. Black, too smoothly. "Would you give up your life if the action would save your brother, whatever the threat might be?"

"Yes."

"Of course you would." He turned away from his instruments for just a moment. "That is the kind of person you are, Daryl. The sacrifice that you made for your wife and children is evidence of that."

"If you say so."

Turning back to his equipment, Dr. Black was smiling. "Would you make the same sacrifice for Carolyn or Kenneth? Would you give up your life for Bril and his family? For Elizabeth and hers?"

"Am I supposed to be impressed? So you've collected information on my family. It wouldn't take much digging to come up with all this. Anyone can get as much in a few minutes on a computer."

"Not anymore." Dr. Black smiled subtly. "Do you believe that Joseph would trade his life for yours?"

"Is such a concept beyond your understanding?"

"Not at all," said Dr. Black. "Do you know that Joseph is having a—*relationship*—with a Shylmahn?"

The room was silent but for the faint hum in the background, a faint whining of the equipment on the table.

"I see," said the doctor.

He paused a moment over a sensor, humming softly to himself. He nodded contentedly. The shadows on his face danced as the monitors revealed the human subject's medical data.

"Let us discuss your brother's island for a moment, shall we?"

Robert turned the station wagon into the alley and drove down the narrow, graveled road. Backyards were hidden behind high wooden fences. The only sounds to be heard were those of the roughly idling engine and the tires rolling over compact crushed rock. The neighborhood was as quiet as every other they had been in these past weeks.

"There it is," he said to Elizabeth, pointing to a gate with *313* painted on it. Robert brought the car to a gentle stop and Elizabeth jumped out and pushed the gate open. Robert drove through and parked the car in the back yard.

"Is Uncle Brad here?" asked William.

"I don't think so, son," said Robert. "Wait here."

His half-brother's house looked empty and alone. He climbed out and went to the back door. Elizabeth closed the gate and hurried to her husband, stood beside him.

"No one?" she asked, more of an observation than a question.

"Doesn't look like it." Robert tried the door knob, but it was locked. "They could be hiding."

He looked through the window. There was no movement, and it didn't look as though anyone had been in the kitchen for some time.

"I'll try this way," said Elizabeth, and she started her way around the house. The kids were out of the car by now and followed after her. Robert went the other way.

All the windows were locked. He had to pry one of the back windows open. Once inside, they assured themselves that Brad and his family had left. There was no message anywhere indicating where they might have gone. The cupboards were empty, but Robert and Elizabeth had brought enough supplies for two weeks or more. By midmorning they had emptied the station wagon and had settled into the house. They covered the car with an old tarp they found in the garage. In the house, they hung blankets over the existing curtains covering the windows to prevent anyone from the street seeing any movement within.

They had a cold lunch and the kids climbed into the twin beds of the middle bedroom for an afternoon nap. They went to sleep almost immediately, which gave Robert and Elizabeth the freedom to discuss their options. There were few.

Robert held his hands out in front of him. "Our choices are simple. We go back to a place we've already been, we stay here, or we continue looking for someplace they're not."

"There's no place we've been that I really care to go back to," said Elizabeth. They sat side by side on the couch. Elizabeth drank water from the plastic cup, set it on the coffee table in front of them. "Before deciding to stay, I would want do to some investigating first. We don't know the situation here."

"We know that the people here have gone or are in hiding. That tells us something."

Elizabeth breathed out tiredly. "Let's stay a day or two, anyway. We need to rest."

The skies outside had started to cloud over. With the graying day and the covered windows, the room was dark. The two of them sat quietly now. Elizabeth reached over and took Robert's hand. Their eyes closed and eventually they slept.

They awoke with a frantic start.

Robert ran to the front window and pulled the blanket and curtain aside enough to see outside.

"Right out front," he said anxiously. A Shylmahn shuttle had settled onto the street directly in front of the house. Several

Shylmahn were standing beside the ship, a number of others were walking up the street.

The children ran down the hallway from the bedroom and rushed to their mother. Elizabeth held them, pulled them with her as she went to the window.

"How did they know we were here?" she asked.

"I'm not sure they do." As Robert watched, another Shillie stepped out of the shuttle. It had yet to look directly at the house; rather it appeared to take in the entire neighborhood. He held an instrument up to his mouth.

"Folks," said the alien in thick English. "Folks, may I please have your attention?" He looked from one house to another, up and down the street. "In a few minutes I will be asking you to step out of your homes. I will require that you board the buses that will soon be arriving. I beg you, do not to attempt to leave the area. All routes are being watched. I assure you, there is no way out of this situation other than to do as I ask."

"Oh, my God." Elizabeth held tightly to her children.

"I can't believe this," said Robert. "We showed up at exactly the wrong time."

"Please do not be frightened," said the Shylmahn. "I promise you that no harm will come to you. You will be joining those of your neighbors who have attempted to leave this area over the past days and weeks. They are safe, as you will be safe. There will be food, water, clothing and shelter."

When the alien paused, Robert and Elizabeth could hear another alien voice speaking from another street. The same scene was likely being repeated on street after street throughout the neighborhood.

"I don't know how we're going to get out of this one," said Robert.

Elizabeth turned away from the window, sat on the couch, William and Sean sitting on either side of her.

"We're not," she said.

"Here comes the bus," said Robert. A converted transit bus came up the street and stopped beside the shuttle. A family was already coming out of one of the houses across the street. A woman was walking up the center of the street towards the bus. Robert ran to the back of the house. He came back moments later.

"I can't see anything, but I heard something going on in the alley. I think someone was trying to get away."

There were two gunshots from some distance away. Robert hurried back to the window. Humans continued coming out on their own. One teenage boy was being prodded along with one of the stun sticks.

The alien speaker ignored this and spoke again to the darkened windows of the homes.

"I wish to thank you for the orderly fashion in which you are conducting yourselves. I urge that this behavior continue. Please, I ask now that everyone come out. For those uncertain what they should do, look to your neighbors for guidance. They understand the situation as it truly is. They are saving themselves and their families from unnecessary pain and mental anguish."

The alien paused a moment and looked for reaction to his words. He continued then.

"Please... in a few moments, my companions will begin searching the dwellings. If you are found at that time, there will be unpleasantness. I do not want for such to happen."

Robert turned from the window to his wife. "Elizabeth?"

They could hear the sounds of families coming out of their homes and working their way to the buses. There was an occasional human cry as someone attempting to escape was brought down by an alien energy weapon.

"Elizabeth?" Robert asked again.

"That's it, then," said Elizabeth, at last. She stood and firmly led her kids to the door.

Joseph sat beside Jason on the hillside, overlooking the old mansion in which Daryl was being held. It was after midnight, but was still light enough to see the details. The black sky was ablaze with bright stars.

On the other side of the ridge behind them, twenty men and women were camped, Bril among them. Below, in a shadow of brush and misshapen trees halfway down the hillside, Carolyn and several of her group were making final adjustments to their plan. In the flat of the valley below, beyond the meandering creek and a small grove of alder, the square squat research clinic waited. It was surrounded by a large lawn, now overgrown, which was bordered by a low rock wall. There were two military trucks, a Shylmahn shuttle, and one of the rare Shylmahn ground vehicles parked in front.

The small security force was visible. Two Shillies were on the roof, with equipment, two more were down near the shuttlecraft, and several others were walking the grounds. Powerful lights hung from each corner of the building, and more were mounted along the walls surrounding the facility.

The plan was a simple one. Get as close to the target as possible without being seen. Then, before attacking, a sharpshooter from a god-awful distance away would take out the Shylmahn on the roof. Since they controlled the energy bombs that were the Shillies' main defense, it should be relatively easy to storm the building once they were taken out.

Joseph shifted about to look over at where the sharpshooter, one of Ben Soo's group, would take up position, down the slope and to the left, as the hillside swung around nearer the complex. The road coming into the small valley was just beyond. The position was a little above the vertical level of the top of the building. Joseph tried to visually space off the distance, not for the first time.

It had to be a thousand yards.

Could someone really do that? Twice?

Carolyn was confident that this Danny kid could do it. He seemed sure enough.

Chapter Fifteen

Jason ran quickly but quietly across the clearing and slid to a stop behind the line of brush. It was another ten yards to the rock wall. The group he was leading followed after him. Joseph scrambled noisily up beside him and peered through the bushes. The others, including Bril, were quiet as mice by comparison.

Jason tapped Joseph on the shoulder, and when Joseph turned, Jason raised his finger to his lips in a fierce gesture for him to be silent. Joseph was apologetic, if not a bit apprehensive. Jason gave his brother a supportive pat on the shoulder and looked to the next stretch of ground they had to cross.

He led his group along the strip of brush, and when he saw the way clear, ran the distance to the wall. The Shylmahn had cleared the area along the wall, and the ground was covered with cut vegetation and short stalks sticking up out of the soil. He heard the others following behind him, stumbling their way through. Once they were all at the wall, they crawled their way along to their final position.

The side entrance to the house was just over a hundred feet away. The shuttle and other vehicles were around near the front of the house. Carolyn and fifteen others would be coming in that way. Another small force would be coming in through the back. The remaining assault force would stay outside the compound to protect the escape route of those going inside.

There was a hint of gray in the night sky. The stars were gone. A sudden sound from the house made Jason and the others stiffen. More noises then, but none sounded as though they were coming near. Jason slid up the wall and peeked over the top.

Three Shylmahn had come out the side door of the house and were walking around towards the front. The door to the shuttlecraft opened as they approached. A few moments later the shuttle started; a smooth sound.

§

From his cell, Daryl heard the shuttle lift off. He rolled over on his cot and looked up at the small window. It would be dawn in an hour. Another great and glorious day. He stood and stretched, slowly, and began his morning ritual. This involved cleaning himself up, performing stretches and exercises, cleaning himself up again, and then dressing. His breakfast tray would usually arrive about then.

Midway through his exercises he heard energy blasts outside, not far away. Moments later he heard gunfire; gunfire and more energy blasts.

"Daryl!" Frank called out from this next cell.

"I'm not deaf, Frank." Daryl began hurriedly pulling on his pants. He picked up his shirt and ran his arms through the sleeves. He heard Frank begin to whoop.

"Sounds like we have company!"

"I do believe it is time to go home, Frank."

"Yeah. Yeah. Here comes the army. I knew it. I knew it. Damn Shillies; lying bastards. The U.S. of freaking A!"

There was a noise out in the hall. Daryl went to the door and looked through the open slat. Guard was standing in the middle of the hallway. He looked confused.

"Life getting you down, Guard?" asked Daryl.

Guard turned sharply, in surprise. The look on his face was one that Daryl finally took for bewilderment. He had been around Guard long enough to recognize most of the facial and body expressions of the Shillie. This expression, though, was new.

"I am sorry," said Guard.

It took Daryl a few heartbeats to process and recognize what Guard said. It was definitely not the response that he had expected. What the hell did he mean by that? Was he afraid of what might happen to him now that his prisoners were being rescued?

"I'll put in a word for you," Daryl said at last.

The look on Guard's face told Daryl that he was as perplexed by what Daryl just said as he himself had been by Guard's comment.

"I do not understand," said Guard.

Something wasn't quite right here. It was like they had two different conversations going.

The fighting continued outside, but Daryl could now hear commotion in the house as well. An explosion shook the walls. Daryl had to brace himself against the door to maintain his balance.

"Here they come!" Frank cried out from the next room. "Here they come, you sonofabitch!"

Guard stared over at Frank's door, then looked back at Daryl. "This does not make sense."

Daryl felt a sudden chill.

What the hell's going on?

"We're going to be free," he said. It was almost a question.

"This... does not make sense," said Guard. The attack on the clinic was apparently beyond his comprehension.

Frank laughed. "We're free, you freaking freak!"

Guard took a stumbling step to Daryl's door. "No sense. No sense."

"All the sense in the world," said Daryl, calmly, almost sympathetically.

Guard shook his head in a human gesture. What strange creatures these humans were. He unlocked the cabinet and took out one of his weapons, looked up and down the hall. He stopped again, for a moment, at Daryl's door, then continued to the end of the hall, to the far door on the opposite wall. Daryl watched him use the key stick to unlock and open it, being careful that its occupant did not rush out at him. He moved into the doorway. A moment later he came away, leaving the door standing ajar.

He stepped reluctantly to the next door.

"What's happening there, Guard?"

"What the hell are you doing?" Frank called. "Daryl! Daryl! What the hell is he doing?"

Guard used the key stick to unlock the next door. The woman inside could not have seen what had just happened, but she knew that something was wrong. Her room was too far down for Daryl to see inside her cell, but Frank saw her move back as Guard stepped into the door.

Daryl heard the woman, almost pleading. "What is it, Guard?"

"Jump him!" Frank cried out. "Jump him! Jump him!"

Guard came away, moved to the next room, directly opposite Frank's.

"Murderer!" Frank was screaming now, frantic. "Fight him! Fight the fucking bastard!"

Guard looked to Frank, saw him through the slat. There was genuine sadness on the Shillie's face. Sadness. Confusion. Something else. There was something in that face that Daryl, watching him from his own door slat, couldn't make out.

"Don't do it," said Daryl. "Stop this."

Guard looked over at Daryl. "Why would they do this, Daryl Britton?" he asked, but he was already turning back to the next door in line.

"<u>You</u> are doing this," said Daryl, panic rising up within him. "You are doing it! Stop! Just stop!"

Daryl swung about and leaned back against the door. Frank continued to scream out obscenities. From the sounds across the hall, this next victim didn't go as quietly as the last, but went nonetheless. By now, everyone in the block knew what was happening.

Guard pulled a fresh weapon from the cabinet. The man in the room directly across from Daryl was yelling at Guard even before he inserted the key stick into the lock of the cell door. Another energy blast outside again shook the walls. The humans had yet to gain control of the facility, but the gunfire and energy bursts inside the house told Daryl that at least the fight was continuing.

Loud gunfire came from close at hand. Commotion in the hall brought Daryl back to his door. Guard was at the door directly across, the human occupant lying dead in the room behind him. Guard aimed his weapon cautiously down the hall and fired once. Gunshots rang out from within the hall itself and Guard backed into the room, reached around and fired again. Bullets shattered the door and jam around him.

Guard looked down at the charge indicator on his weapon. With a sign of resignation, he moved slowly back, farther from the door, until he was standing in the middle of the room, his last victim lying at his feet. He looked up at Daryl's door across the hall. Lost, confused, bewildered.

"His weapon is empty!" Daryl cried out. He took several steps back from the door and stared at the open slat.

"Get him!" he yelled out. "Get him!" There was a burst of noise and activity. Then silence. Outside, and elsewhere throughout the house, the fighting continued; but for a few, brief moments, it all seemed very far away.

Then voices were calling out. Cheers from the other rooms, triumphant cries of success from the rescuers. Frank was jeering happily. Daryl sat heavily on his cot. He stared blankly at the wall opposite.

A voice came from beyond the door. "Somebody here order a Canadian bacon and pineapple?"

"Chicken and garlic," said Daryl, drained of emotion.

"My mistake. This order is for Apartment B."

Daryl smiled thinly, stood and walked back to the door. The figure beyond had turned away and was searching the body of Guard. He ran then to the end of the hall and began opening doors. There were angry cries as the dead prisoners were discovered in the open rooms. When Daryl came out of his room, he could see a wounded rescuer being attended to at the end of the hall. Frank was running up and down saying something about the great U.S. of freaking A., and the floor around Guard was beginning to puddle.

Daryl was growing numb.

He noticed then that none of the rescuers was wearing a uniform. Some had long hair, some short, one had a beard. Their weapons were all of different models.

Not the army that Daryl was familiar with.

The wounded man was helped to his feet and assisted out.

"Let's go, let's go!" said the leader of the group. The freed prisoners were rushed out of the block and into the main hall of the house. The prisoners released from the other block were just coming in from the other side of the house. Among the rescuers bringing them out was Bril. As everyone hurried to the front of the house, Daryl saw Joseph standing in a doorway, urging everyone forward.

Daryl ran outside, his first exposure to open air in six weeks.

Someone took a strong hold of Daryl's arm and pushed him ahead, directing him out onto the lawn and across the yard. It wasn't until they were beyond the wall that he looked over and saw that it was Joseph.

"Through there!" Joseph released his arm and pointed to a newly blazoned path through the brush. Others along the trail hurried the freed humans along, directing them ahead to safety.

Joseph waited. Jason and Carolyn were still in the house. Once inside, Joseph and Bril and a few of the others had sought the prisoners, while Jason and Carolyn had gone in search of something more important.

Jason moved smoothly down a stairwell, weapon at the ready. At the foot of the stairs, the hallways T'd in two directions—one directly ahead, the other to the left.

Alien weapons fire came from the hallway to the left. Ben Soo was directly at the foot of the stairs, while Carolyn stood out of the line of fire in the hallway ahead on the other side.

There were two dead on the stairs.

Ben Soo looked up behind him as Jason came near.

"They knew, Mr. Britton."

"Then we'll never get the pod out of here," he said. Even if they did, they'd never get it away.

Ben gave Jason a curt nod, then turned to Carolyn. "Let's get out of here!"

"The pod!" Carolyn called out angrily.

"Never gonna happen," said Jason.

Carolyn, fuming and frustrated, looked across at Ben and her brother. She made a mad dash across the line of fire. Once safely across, she started immediately up the stairs.

"All right, God damn it. Let's go," she said.

Dr. Black stood beside a small, round table with glass inlaid in its center. He tapped a small sensor with one finger and an image of a hallway appeared in holo above the table. Cell Block A looked empty. He knew that several humans were dead in their rooms. He tapped the sensor again. Cell Block B had blood on the floor of the hall. As with Block A, there were several dead humans in their cells; as was ChonTuh, the Watch.

He showed no emotion as he calmly scrolled through the images. The lab was destroyed, several dead on the floor. The main hall was a shambles, with the blood of both human and Shylmahn on the floor and walls. There were two dead on the roof, several more on the grounds.

Dr. Black watched the last of the humans hurrying into the wilds beyond the complex. He spoke then, without turning, to a Shylmahn standing silently near the door, patiently awaiting orders.

"Observations only. For now."

The young Shylmahn turned and left. Dr. Black stared thoughtfully at the last image hovering above the table. The last of the Chehnon had passed through the brush and the scene was still.

This was becoming truly interesting.

Chapter Sixteen

July 15

Joseph stood the final watch of the night. As planned, they had set up camp in the ruins of a large warehouse the evening before. A number of the rescue team had already left, returning to their own affairs, but the bulk of the force, and most of the freed prisoners, remained.

Some were beginning to stir from restless sleep. As they did, Joseph went about waking the others. A new guard was posted outside, another at the window. Someone began cooking breakfast. Several began going over the equipment they had neglected to clean the night before.

"'morning," said Jason.

"Quiet night," said Joseph.

"Didn't expect any trouble. Not once we got clear."

"They could have come after us."

"They don't usually do that. Not once the attack is broken off." He gave a quick glance around. "We might see something yet, but not because of yesterday."

"Well, I didn't sleep much."

"No, I expect not." Jason smiled.

"I still can't believe we did it."

They had reached the breakfast fire. A small collection of flames was flickering beneath a large metal pot of coffee. Another pot was filled with rolled oats just beginning to cook.

"Not everyone made it," said Daryl. He was sitting beside the fire watching the coffee.

"No. No, but we got twelve out," said Jason.

"Don't get me wrong, I'm glad I'm out."

Bril came to the fire. "Damned frightening to see just how far these little bastards will to go to prevent their prisoners from being freed." He picked up one of the metal cups and dipped it into the coffee. "At least now they know we'll not leave our fellows in their hands."

Joseph turned his head sharply and looked at Jason.

"They had no idea we would try to rescue our people. Did they?"

Jason shook his head soberly.

Bril puffed up his chest. "They damn well know it now."

"You don't get it, Bril," said Joseph. "It didn't even occur to them."

"So, now they know better. They know they're dealing with people who care about their own."

"That's not a good thing," said Jason. "They may be all the quicker at going about the business next time."

"Damned sick," Bril said into his cup.

"They don't think the way we do," said Joseph. "We don't know their reasoning."

"We know the results."

"I'm not arguing that. And I'm not justifying what they did. I just think it would be better for us if we tried to understand why they do what they do." Joseph was growing more than a little uncomfortable. What had happened made it all the clearer to him the importance of what he was doing, and though the others didn't know of his activities, he still found himself trying to rationalize his relationship with EsJen.

Carolyn, meanwhile, was huddled with the rest of her resistance group. Their own plans had failed miserably, and they were discussing their next move. The freeing of the prisoners had been no diversion at all. At the first sign of attack, the pod had been considered by the Shylmahn to be the target. In any event, the location of the energy pod, down in the basement, meant that it would have been nearly impossible to bring out, even if the diversion had been effective.

By now a large crowd had gathered at the fire in search of breakfast. Joseph and his brothers set aside their own discussion and instead set about to serve up the coffee and oatmeal. It was several minutes before they found themselves again alone at the fire.

"If they're so set on not letting prisoners out alive," said Daryl, once things had begun to settle down, "why didn't they track us down and wipe us out last night? It couldn't be that difficult to figure out where we are."

"I have no doubt they know exactly where we are," said Jason.

"Then I don't get it."

"It doesn't suit their purpose," said Joseph matter-of-factly.

"Exactly," said Jason.

"But then why shoot us in our cells rather than allow us to be rescued? Why hold us at all, for that matter?"

"One misconception is that you and the others were prisoners."

"Of course they were prisoners," said Bril.

Joseph shook his head. "They were specimens."

"In the truest sense," said Jason.

"Prettying up the manure pile doesn't stop the stink," said Bril.

"However we may see it, they believe they are simply exploring this new world they've come to."

"But it's like we're nothing to them," said Bril bitterly. "How can things like that look down on us as... inferior?"

"It's not a matter of inferiority or superiority," said Jason. "I don't think they have the capacity to conceive of any beings as existing on the same level as themselves."

Joseph nodded. "Yes, and more than that, they'll never be able to see us as anything other than just another component of the world they intend to colonize; a resource to be utilized."

"And an issue to be resolved," agreed Jason.

Carolyn joined in the circle around the fire. She held out her empty cup and Bril took it and filled it for her. She took a drink. "It looks like we'll be seeing these folks get to where they need to go, then we're getting back to work."

"Tell the others I appreciate their help in this. I'm sorry that we couldn't come away with the pod," said Jason.

"Hey, at least we got Daryl out."

"That is the important thing," said Bril, throwing the gauntlet out one last time. No one took up the challenge. "What about the rest of you?" he asked at last. "You coming out to the island?"

Daryl, of course, would be going to the island. Susan and the kids waited for him there. Jason declined, saying that he was being *called out of the area.* Joseph looked uncomfortably at the others, finally stated flatly that he had been distracted of late and that he had better get back to his reasons for being out here to begin with. The last he had been able to discover, Barbara was alive. He had lost her trail, what little he had found.

He would try and pick it up again.

No time to go wandering after lost loves, thought Carolyn, and immediately felt guilty about it. It was just that now that she had accepted Joseph's not-so-covert activities, and had become somewhat a part of it, she was impatient that he get on with it. Damn it, he had a job to do.

§

Elizabeth and her family were near the back of the eighth bus of the twenty-three bus convoy. The convoy grew by several buses at each community, neighborhood or town they passed through on its way to wherever they were going. Elizabeth and Robert sat side-by-side, with the children in the seats directly ahead of them.

Now, with the children asleep and the convoy traveling an open highway, Elizabeth spoke of the fears she had at being at the mercy of these horrible Shillies. She had been the first to accept the fact that they had no choice but to surrender, but she had also been the one to vehemently insist they run to California in the first place. Her fear of being near the Shylmahn was near to being a phobia. The mere thought of them made her skin crawl, made her stomach turn. To have willingly surrendered herself and her family to them had surprised Robert. He would have thought she would rather they had all died in that house rather than be taken by them, no matter how genuine the promise of safety had been. He had been impressed at her composure throughout this entire incident.

As she spoke now, almost two days later, Robert could sense the facade beginning to crumble. For the sake of her family, she fought to hang on, but Robert feared that if they didn't reach their destination soon, she wouldn't make it there at all.

He was terrified at the thought of being alone. Elizabeth was his strength. She always had been. There was no way that he could survive in this new world without her. He wouldn't know what to do. For the sake of the children, she had to hang on. He knew that their lives depended on their mother hanging on. And she knew it, too. She knew their situation as well as he did, despite her current condition. It was that one thread of knowledge that kept her from going altogether. It was her one handhold on reality. Without it, she was lost, and without her, they were all lost.

The bus came to a sudden, violent stop. Passengers were thrown from their seats and into the aisle or against the seats in front of them. William and Sean struck the backs of the seats and fell to the floor, bruised and bleeding. People throughout the bus were screaming, crying out in pain or fear.

Elizabeth was thrown across the top of the seat in front of her. As she tried to recover, she heard gunshots, then two explosions. Then she heard the alien energy blasts. She leapt around to the seats in front of her and knelt on the floor, wiping blood from her eyes and pulling her children up. Robert leaned over from behind and examined the children as Elizabeth placed them back in their seats. There were no broken bones, but both William and Sean were sore and very frightened.

"They're attacking the convoy!" someone called out.

"We're being rescued!"

Cheers rang out amidst the crying and sobbing and screaming. The gunshots continued, explosions that may have been planted charges going off. Energy bursts from Shylmahn hand weapons and the larger energy blasts began to light up the surrounding fields. Shylmahn ground vehicles raced up and down the convoy.

The Shylmahn within each bus were busy trying to keep order in their vehicles. Their wards were either rushing about taking care of injuries, cheering the battle outside, or attempting to escape and help their rescuers. It was turning into complete chaos.

A mass of humans charged the buses. A Shylmahn ground car exploded just outside the bus in which Elizabeth and Robert hovered over their children, those inside applauding their rescuers on even as broken glass exploded in on them, splashing blood wherever it struck flesh.

As the situation became clear, as it became obvious just what the attacking humans were attempting, the Shylmahn within the buses began the process necessary to prevent the release of the human creatures placed in their care. Positioned at both the front and rear of each of the vehicles, with weapons sitting in their chargers, they began. On some of the buses, panic began almost immediately, and many humans were injured before their elimination. On other vehicles, the humans didn't realize what was happening until the very end, and in these situations their demise came without undo fear.

Many of the humans had an unreasoning belief that they were to be joining the humans that were attacking the convoy of buses.

Dobbs climbed over the dead Shillie lying on the steps at the door of the bus. Another lay near the driver's seat. He could see sixty or seventy human bodies slouched in their seats, laying in the aisle, atop one another, or curled up under the seats. Mothers lay over their children in desperate attempts to protect them.

It was beyond comprehension. Dobbs found himself shaking uncontrollably as he worked his way to the back of the bus, checking each body for signs of life.

It didn't make any sense. How could any intelligent being do this? Shillie or not, there was absolutely nothing to explain or justify an action like this. To be able to do something as barbaric as this, the Shillies had to be completely without conscience or compassion.

We know where we stand, thought Dobbs. *Our day will come.*

He pulled a young boy aside to examine a girl lying face down on the floor of the bus.

"Here! This one's alive!" he called out the window. In a moment a doctor was hurrying onto the bus and climbing over bodies to reach Dobbs and the girl. She looked to be in her early teens, and from her appearance had been on the run for some time before being taken by the Shillies.

The Shillie hadn't missed, but the wound hadn't killed her outright. The doctor nodded hopefully at Dobbs and went to work on her, calling out to an assistant outside the bus for materials and equipment. In the meantime, Dobbs continued his search.

They had found several still alive, including one small child who had escaped unharmed; physically anyway. The survivors were being made as travel-ready as possible in preparation for departure. Everyone expected the Shillies to come down on this place like a heavy boot.

The body of a woman lay across two small children. A man lay over the back of the seat. Seeing these families was the hardest for Dobbs. He knew exactly what it was like to be there, to watch your children butchered.

Butchered... Butchers, goddamned butchers.

The woman had been shot at least twice; once in the upper back, and a glancing shot across the side of the head. Dobbs held her by the arm and reached in to check the children. Dead. Both dead. He could see now that the woman had been shot in the shoulder as well.

The Shillies had got her coming and going, most likely as she tried to protect the little ones. He laid her back down across the children and checked the man. He had been blasted in the face and chest. A river of blood, slowed now to a trickle, had soaked the seat beneath the youngest of the children.

Dobbs pushed himself away from the family and turned to continue his search. Something made him stop, though, and take another look at the woman. There was nothing to indicate that she was alive, but something, *something,* made him look at her again.

Dobbs slowly moved his hand down to her forehead and delicately pushed her hair aside. There was still nothing. He lowered his cheek to her face and tried to feel a breath. He put his hand to her chest...

He pulled her around and cradled her head.

"Doc. I think I have another one for you."

The very air seemed to be on fire. Kenneth took in cautious, shallow breaths through clenched teeth as he lay face down beside the shattered brick wall of the large warehouse. Hot smoke billowed out of the row of windows that ran along this side of the building. He felt a sudden pressure take hold and threaten to crush him as another blast shook the world. More broken brick rained down on him and he pushed himself more tightly against the wall. He was cut and bruised, and thought that he might have internal injuries, but he doubted that he would live long enough to actually have to worry about them.

The air grew still and quiet. Kenneth slowly relaxed his tense muscles. He lifted his head and looked down along the wall. Bobby's body lay among a group of others piled up beside the main doors to the warehouse. Kenneth knew that Sarge's body was in there too, but he couldn't see it. A shadow drifted across the scene as a Shylmahn shuttle passed overhead. He laid his head back down on the pavement, watched discretely as the ship landed a couple of hundred feet away. A door opened and a group of Shillies hurried out and scattered, going in half a dozen directions. Several of them went into the warehouse through the open door near Kenneth, giving the human bodies piled there only a passing glance, ignoring the lone human figure lying farther along the wall.

Minutes passed, Shillies coming and going. A second shuttle came and went, this one to collect two humans that had been brought in, marching past Kenneth. He continued to be taken for dead, and to all appearances he looked it.

He recognized the two human prisoners as officers in Colonel Drake's force. They looked disheveled, but not seriously injured. For all Kenneth knew, these were the last two left alive. This second joint venture with Colonel Drake would be the last.

The shuttle lifted off just after dusk. Kenneth waited several minutes before sliding away from the wall and rolling over onto his back. It felt good to change position after hours of lying immobile. He pushed himself into a sitting position and leaned against the wall.

He had to go to the bathroom. He had to find food and water. He had to find somewhere to spend the night. The first place to look was inside the warehouse, now abandoned. He glanced to Bobby and the others, ten yards away. He would have to walk past them to get inside.

Kenneth rolled over onto his knees and rose shakily to his feet.

Chapter Seventeen

October 04

Jason kicked at a small stone lying in the narrow dirt roadway. It clicked loudly as it struck one, then another stone, before finally bouncing into the tall grass. The sound startled him and he checked his surroundings nervously as he walked on. It was late afternoon, cool and damp. It had been gray and threatening to storm all day.

He had been dropped off more than three miles back and would have bet that he would have been rained on before reaching Johnson's headquarters, still another two and a half miles distant. It was now even money whether he would stay dry. Shifting his small pack, he set in earnest to cover some ground.

Jason had been out of the Northwest sector for more than two months. In that time, the alien grasp on the region had grown even tighter, human resistance more ineffectual and more scattered. There were few humans left in the area who were not under the direct control of the Shylmahn. The Shylmahn now enjoyed freedom of action with little fear of retribution or retaliation. Their control of the sector grew more complete day by day.

Jason stopped, brought up short as a distant sound penetrated his wandering thoughts. For the second time in as many miles he found himself taken unawares. A thick, low wall of brush ran parallel to the road about ten yards up the slope to Jason's left. From there, he watched as a small Shylmahn convoy passed by. It was made up mostly of alien ground vehicles, now becoming more popular and more common. They were manufactured here on Earth and Jason guessed that perhaps this type of vehicle would not have been suitable back on the Shylmahn home world. This would explain why they were so similar to human design.

When he was again alone, Jason crawled from the bushes and walked back down onto the road. He would be getting wet after all. The rain was holding off, but the air was growing thick with moisture. A chill mist washed over his face. He wiped at his eyes and brow, held his head down against the weather and started again towards Johnson's headquarters. His hope now was to beat the coming nightfall.

Joseph walked down the center of the street, a well-worn olive-drab backpack slung over his right shoulder. The small town was abandoned and the wide main thoroughfare was showing serious signs of disuse. Tall grass and weeds grew from cracks in the concrete sidewalks and the asphalt surface of the roadway. Dirt was collecting in crevices and gutters and on the sills of the darkened windows.

He stopped at the wooden bench halfway down the block, sat down and dropped his pack at his feet. He rubbed his eyes and pulled his hair back from his face. He felt tired all over. At the sound of a shuttlecraft passing overhead, he considered stepping into the shadows of the nearby awning. By the time he decided against it the ship had already come and gone.

He was not all that concerned about the Shillies taking him. Joseph had been confronted a number of times during his search for Barbara, and had been allowed to continue on his way every time. Two days earlier he had turned onto a street where a group of Shillies had just come out of a building and were preparing to get into one of their ground cars. On seeing the human, they had talked among themselves for several moments before climbing into the vehicle and driving off. He had become an acceptable feature of the landscape.

Joseph leaned back and closed his eyes. He pulled his jacket around him and let his body warmth fight off the damp chill that had hung in the air for most of the day. He was about to fall asleep when he heard a sound in the distance. Sitting up straight, he watched an alien ground car round the corner and come down the street.

It stopped directly in front of him. EsJen stepped out alone.

"I am pleased to see that you are safe," she said. She came around the front of the car. "Have you been waiting long?"

"I just got here."

EsJen walked to the bench and sat down directly beside Joseph. Oddly, it was good to see her again, and he found himself strangely warmed at having her beside him.

"I am... concerned... for you, JoSeph."

"I'm doing all right."

"I do not think you will find her. You should stop these dangerous trips."

"I have no choice."

"Humans are quick to boast of their freedom of choice."

"We also have a duty to choose what is right even if it is the less desirable option. I can't give up. It's bad enough I waited as long as I did. If I had gone for her in the beginning, she might be safe now."

"You do not know that she is not safe. She may be better off where she is."

Joseph half smiled, "Is there something you're not telling me?"

"There is much that I am not telling you."

Joseph laughed. "I mean something about what we're talking about."

"I have no information about your mate," she said.

"Ex-mate."

"I have no information about your ex-mate."

"Of me, then?"

"You continue to be of interest to many," she said. "As does our association."

"Yeah, well I'm a bit curious about that, myself."

"ShahnTahr continues to grant approval of the study."

"And that's the important thing, right?"

"Yes."

"And when your computer says stop, that's it?"

"I do not understand."

"You do whatever the computer says."

"I don't know what you mean, JoSeph."

"Have you ever done anything against the wishes of your ShahnTahr?" Joseph knew damn well that to even think of doing something against ShahnTahr's wishes was completely beyond EsJen's imagination.

Yet, somehow, EsJen was at least able to take hold of the thread of Joseph's thinking. She gave Joseph that patronizing smile that told him his thoughts were drifting too far from reality.

"We each have our function, JoSeph. You, I, ShahnTahr, everyone. That is the way."

"Not my way."

"It is *the* way."

"Okay... let's say that I give you that. I don't, but let's say that I do. Just what is ShahnTahr's function?"

"I don't understand."

"EsJen!" Joseph grabbed at the bench in frustration. Sometimes, talking to EsJen was to talk in circles. "You just said we all have our function. So I'm asking... what function does ShahnTahr play in all of this?"

"But, ShahnTahr—*is*."

"ShahnTahr is."

"ShahnTahr serves, that we might serve."

Joseph stood up, walked around the bench and leaned against the pole holding the bus schedule.

"It is impossible to get a straight answer when it comes to your master."

"What you say is not true. And ShahnTahr is not master."

"Maybe... maybe you don't know. Maybe you can't know." Joseph took a long, surrendering breath. "We have changed, you and I. Haven't we?"

EsJen paused, then spoke simply. "In the time that we have known one another, you have changed, as I have changed. I believe it to be to the good that there are those such as we... gaining the knowledge, the insights, the viewpoints... that can be acquired no other way. ShahnTahr understands this, or the research would end."

"Of course," said Joseph. "There are many who have serious misgivings regarding the possible consequences of our... of my... cooperation."

"I know."

Joseph smiled again, halfheartedly. "There is probably very little that you do not know." He looked up at a break in the clouds. There was blue sky. There might be a change in the weather before the sun went down, as was often the way this time of year. Joseph moved back to the bench and sat down beside EsJen.

"I fully understand your position, JoSeph, and the dangers that you face as a result of your association with a Shylmahn. I know that you must move cautiously."

"And you know that I am not a collaborator."

"I know your reasons for pursuing our relationship. You know ours."

"Yep. Definitely strange times, EsJen."

She turned to face him. "JoSeph," she began, then stopped. Joseph stirred uncomfortably. EsJen seldom found it difficult to speak her mind. She usually had these meetings well planned.

"What is it?"

"You understand," she began again, "this project goes beyond just you."

"I'm not so self-absorbed as to believe the universe revolves around little ole' me."

EsJen pushed ahead. She turned to face him. "You are the center of this study, but you are not alone in it. It began with you, but because of circumstances, it was expanded to include others."

"What are you talking about?"

"This study, it encompasses other members of your family."

Joseph suddenly felt very cold. "Okay, hold it," he said, raised both hands defensively. "Stop. Stop, stop... that's not in the deal."

"Deal?"

Joseph's thoughts were jumbled. He tried to think. "What—what does... what does this mean?"

EsJen turned subtly away from Joseph, placed her hands in her lap and looked down at them.

"Many in your family have become involved in the activities of our migration to this world to such an extent as to draw the attention of ShahnTahr. Individually, each has no unique qualities that differentiate them from any of the thousands of other humans under observation. It is, rather, their relationship to each other, and in particular to you, that is of... interest."

"Why? I mean, what's so... as you say, there are thousands involved in this war. Millions. Everyone on the planet. What's so special about us?"

"Each member of your family is quite different from the other," she said patiently. "Each of you approaches this situation in a different way, and each of you has, individually, come to our attention. Together, as a single entity, your family offers a compelling focal point of study."

"Great."

Her features grew soft. "You have a very interesting family, JoSeph."

"Great," he said again. He would have to rethink everything. This could have serious implications; any actions could have serious repercussions. For now, though, "What's going to happen to them?"

The clouds overhead had closed up again. In the past several minutes the day had grown darker. "I do not know."

Bril pointed to the boat running parallel to the shore a quarter of a mile out.

Daryl raised the binoculars. "Shillies," he said. He and Bril were in a camouflaged bunker on the main spit, looking out over the waterway between the island and the mainland.

"They're using boats, now. Manmade boats."

"Could be running short of their own stuff. They can't seem to make it fast enough."

"Probably just too damned many Shillies running around," said Bril.

"There may be something to what you say," said Daryl. He lowered the binoculars. "They're not stopping."

"They never do. By air or sea."

"They know you're here." Daryl turned away from the window opening, "I imagine they know we're all here."

The brothers made one more stop, the lagoon, where they checked the condition of the boats and the camouflage netting, before working their way up to the house. Young Peter was playing outside, having finished his chores. He called out a hello to his father. Bril waved back, but was looking distractedly at Elizabeth, who was sitting on one of the porch chairs.

"She's not getting any better, Daryl," said Bril. Elizabeth had hardly spoken a word since being brought to the island by those who had rescued her. Most of her time was spent in silent contemplation. She spoke occasionally of times past with her children and husband, and more rarely of the Shylmahn and her hatred of them. Mostly, though, she sat and let the world continue without her.

"Give it more time."

"We should have seen some sign of improvement. Any sign." Bril thought her physical injuries were healing fine, but her mind... he hadn't seen any improvement at all.

"For now, Bril, it's enough that she's here and that she's safe. Let's be grateful they brought her back to us."

"If only we could see something."

"It will come."

As they approached the house, Kathryn came out, tea in hand, and placed a cup on the small table beside Elizabeth. Susan and the children followed Kathryn out, the kids rushing around the adults and bounding off the porch to the lawn below.

"I hope so," said Bril. "I guess Suzy wasn't really all that much better off than Liz, till we got word you that were still alive."

Daryl had to step through a mass of young arms and legs to get to the steps. "It seems the kids are doing all right."

"And what about you?" asked Bril.

"I'm fine." The headaches were getting worse, and he had trouble sleeping. When he did sleep, he often woke from terrifying nightmares.

Susan gave Daryl a hug, looked out at the kids, and smiled at their play. For several moments, everyone on the porch was quiet and there were only the sounds of children.

A darkness fell over the features on Susan's face.

"Have you seen the way they look at Elizabeth?" she said, her voice suddenly very sad. Hers eyes never left the children. "They try not to look at her at all, but they can't help but see her. When they do, they see... I don't know... an *empty* place where Robert and the kids are supposed to be."

Kathryn was standing behind Elizabeth, brushing the woman's hair from her face. Elizabeth didn't appear to take notice. She watched the lagoon, smooth and dark at the bottom of the hill, but what she saw was not what the others saw. The sounds she listened to, with just the slightest turn of the head, were not what others heard. Somehow, the children knew that.

Chapter Eighteen

October 06

The black curtains were pulled across the windows. On the coffee table, one small candle gave off the only light. They used the generator rarely these days. It was late, but no one thought of going back to bed. Bril sat in his chair, occasionally glancing up at the ceiling, as if to see the alien ships that were continually passing overhead.

Daryl paced near the window. Elizabeth was sitting on the couch, trembling uncontrollably, with Kathryn doing her best to comfort her. Peter sat beside them. Susan huddled with her children in the large chair near the door leading to the kitchen. No one spoke. Since first being jarred from sleep by the strange alien sounds, no one had said much of anything. Not in those first terrifying minutes, and not later when they realized the Shylmahn weren't landing.

But they kept coming. They passed from east to west, and back. A new route, perhaps, or a new project. It had been going on for several hours now; every few minutes a distant hum that grew steadily louder, steadily sharper, until the shuttle was directly over the house. The sound would begin to fade then, slowly, to the point where one couldn't be sure if what they heard was actually there or just the lingering memory.

Bril waited now for the next ship. The silence was as bad as that damned Shillie whine. The waiting. Knowing that it was going to come, knowing that it was out there, knowing that it was going to pass right over his island. Further invasion, further assault.

"This is damned hard to take," he said at last.

"What's going on, Bril?" said Kathryn.

"Damned if I know."

Daryl continued his nervous pacing. "Probably some new Shillie complex going up nearby."

"Hell of a coincidence, them passing right over my island," said Bril. He stopped at the sound of another approaching Shylmahn shuttle. It came from the east. He stood, rubbed his hands nervously on his pant legs, and watched the ceiling. His movements had caused the candle flame to flicker and it created shadows that danced around the room. The ship was directly overhead, then continued west, toward the peninsula.

"I doubt they planned their route for our benefit," said Daryl. Not that they didn't have it in them to do it. In fact, he thought Dr. Black would really be enjoying this. But aside from them coming down and asking their feelings, he didn't see how they're going to get any data.

"I don't like the coincidence, Daryl."

"Nooooooooooo," Elizabeth cried out in a sudden, slow, mournful wail. She was looking across the room, but she was blind to all but her nightmares. Her trembling grew more violent. She began flailing her arms, then kicked out angrily, desperately. "No, no, no," she said, louder, more frantic. She screamed then, terrified. Kathryn managed to take hold of her, fought to keep her from hurting herself. Bril rushed to the couch and reached in to grab her arms.

Another ship approached. The hum grew to a whine, sharp and piercing. The candle flame struggled to stay alive. Kathryn and Bril finally managed to still Elizabeth's movements, but she kept screaming, crying out, living out and reliving horrors that the others could not see.

Daryl was standing near the window, his attention torn between his sister's wrenching anguish and the enemy overhead, when the candle lost its fight and the room went completely dark. Elizabeth let out another scream, then her cries turned to sobs, as if she was finally surrendering to whatever fate lay in store for her in that other world to which she had fled, to where the demons had followed after. Daryl stumbled in the dark towards the coffee table and fumbled about for the matches, finally managed to get the candle relit.

Bril and Kathryn looked as though they were getting Elizabeth calmed down. Peter was standing safely to one side. Elizabeth looked awful. Kathryn had Peter bring a damp cloth and she used it to try and clean her up. Daryl turned and sat on the table. It was then he noticed his wife and children.

They had left the chair and were standing in the corner of the room, in the shadows beyond the reach of the candle. They looked more terrified than he had ever seen them, more so than on that horrible day when he had been taken by the Shylmahn. Daryl rushed to them, scattering furniture as he went. The fear in their eyes was heart-wrenching, gut-wrenching. He reached out to his family and held them, promised them it was going to be all right. He knew it was going to be all right. They shouldn't worry.

Everything was going to be all right.

October 07

From what Jason had seen the past three days, this Oregon town looked to be drawing quite a crowd. Carolyn and the rest of Ben Soo's group were here, had been in at least one skirmish that he knew of, and perhaps others. Joseph was around here somewhere, as well. He had come in late the night before with that Shillie girlfriend of his.

There could be just one reason for Joey showing up here.

Jason had seen Joseph's ex-wife with a group of civilians the day before, and had spoken with her briefly in the evening. Barbara was all right, but she and her friends were constantly on the move and spent most of their time hiding in shadows. Considering the situation here, Jason didn't see how they would remain free much longer.

He didn't like to admit it, but some people would be better off living on the reservations until this entire matter was taken care of. The one and only service that civilians provided out here was to occasionally busy up the Shillies who went about collecting them. Such a benefit wasn't usually worth the supplies these people consumed, what little food there was to be found on grocery store shelves and in warehouses; Supplies that those in the resistance could use and wouldn't be getting.

Damned cynical of you, Jason old boy.

His own role here in Oregon had been to locate a facility the Shylmahn had in the area and design an assault strategy with the objective of acquiring equipment, supplies and information. During his reconnaissance of the facility and the surrounding area, he had seen a number of collection patrols out and about gathering up humans.

He shifted position. From his vantage point on the top floor of an old office building, Jason could see the apartment building directly down the street. Barbara and her friends occupied the four apartments that made up the second floor. They knew of the collection patrols in the area, had been dodging patrols just like them for months.

They talked a good line, but Jason could see how frightened they were. They knew that it was only a matter of time.

He returned to the north window. Jason had been observing the comings and goings of the alien ground car manufacturing center since well before dawn. Over the previous two days, from locations not nearly so distant as this, he had run an extensive recon of the facility. He had mapped out each of the buildings, the purpose of each, various time schedules, number of personnel, and so on. Utilizing such data, he would soon have a complete picture of the facility.

The place was putting out a lot of vehicles. That had to mean that either there were a lot of Shylmahn here on Earth, or they expected a lot of company. Or both.

Jason heard sounds from the street below and hurried back to the other window.

Several of those Shillie ground vehicles were pulling up outside the apartment building where Barbara and her friends were staying. Jason could see other vehicles disappearing around behind the building. A number of Shylmahn had just gone inside, with more following. Still others looked to be securing the area.

Jason opened his window a little, in order to better hear what was going on, then stepped back and to one side. One thing he didn't need now was for one of those Shillies to casually look up and see him staring down at the scenery.

Do Shillies do things casually?

A window of one of Barbara's fourth floor apartments shattered; glass and what looked like a chair came raining down onto the street below. Jason could faintly hear people screaming. Angry screams. A few moments later he heard gunfire.

Come on... give it up, damn it.

Smoke began coming out of several windows. Jason guessed that it was probably the result of the Shillies' weapons, but the fire could have been set by humans.

He caught movement along a side street approaching the apartment building.

Focusing his attention, he saw nothing.

He watched the shadows and the edges of the blind spots.

Again, nothing. Then...

Shit. Carolyn.

Jason tapped absently at the windowsill, uncertain about what the hell to do. With Carolyn and her group coming into the picture, there was sure to be more killing.

This isn't the time.

It just wasn't worth it. Let these people be taken to some nice, quiet, safe reservation. We can deal with them later.

Hell no... Not Carolyn.

But then, Jason doubted very much that Ben Soo's resistance group was out to save these humans from life on the reservation. More likely, they had seen these people as bait. That would be more Ben Soo's style.

They approached the Shillies from the south, coming up both sides of the street, fading in and out of the shadows. Jason caught sight, then, of several others coming in from a bisecting street.

There was a sudden flash of back-blast near Carolyn's position, coming from a weapon's launch, and a thin vapor trail corkscrewed to one of the Shillie ground vehicles parked outside the apartment building. The vehicle exploded.

An almost immediate response came from three directions as Shillies along the secure perimeter activated one of their coordinated response plans. Carolyn and her team continued moving slowly forward.

Another ground vehicle approached the apartment building from the opposite side of the ongoing conflict. It slowed as it came near, and was passed through the perimeter by the Shylmahn securing the area. It stopped at a side entrance to the building and a Shillie climbed out. It met with two of the posted guards. After several moments a human stepped out of the vehicle.

Shit. Shit, shit. God damn it.

The whole fucking Britton family.

The Shillie guards didn't look to be too obliging. A heated discussion was going on. They apparently weren't very pleased at having this uppity human walking around as if he owned the place. Jason continued grumbling as he angrily opened his weapon case.

Joseph had an odd mix of nervous anxiety, anger, and barely suppressed panic. EsJen wasn't getting anywhere with these morons, and he didn't like the way they were looking at him. He readied himself to run, and even briefly considered charging through them and into the building. For the moment, though, he let EsJen continue her efforts to get them through.

Meanwhile, the battle continued all around them. Great timing. If they had only been one day sooner. Hell, one hour sooner. Instead, he found himself in one really weird situation. He was attempting to talk his way past Shylmahn guards and into a building that was at present being assaulted by Shylmahn who were trying to capture humans, while the attacking Shillies themselves were under attack by other humans.

One of the guards suddenly stiffened, and there was a perplexed look on his face. He reached up and placed a hand on his chest. He brought it away and stared at it. He held his hand out for the others to see. It was bloody. The expression on his face changed slowly to one of disorientation.

Joseph stared unbelieving. The Shillie had been shot. He had to force his eyes from the bloodied chest and began scanning likely positions for a sniper. He could see no one. As he turned back, the second guard stumbled back at the impact of a bullet to the shoulder. He slid to the ground as a second red spot flowered in the middle of his chest. The first guard, hand still held out for the others to see, carefully knelt down on the concrete walk, his life slowly draining from him.

"Come on!" said Joseph, recovering enough to move. He took EsJen's hand and stepped over the dying guards. EsJen allowed herself to be led into the building. She had grown numb, her thoughts trapped in that fraction of time when the eyes into which she had been looking sparkled suddenly, then quietly emptied.

EsJen followed Joseph into another world. It was gray and hollow, with gray and hollow sights and sounds and smells. The activities around them were irrational and unconnected. Shillies and humans ran past each other without seeing one another, as if each were on different planes of existence, as if the two worlds existed half a second out of time with one another; as if the purpose of each was unrelated to the other and therefore the realities of each were invisible to the other.

Small fires were burning now on a number of floors; smoke swelled out of doorways and rolled down the halls. Walls were cracked, some had holes that exposed the apartments beyond. Here and there the carpets were stained and damp. On the second floor, the walls of a long, narrow hallway were splattered with blood. EsJen clutched at her arms. Noises echoed deeply within her.

The collection of this group of Chehnon had gone terribly wrong. Despite the collection team's efforts in anticipating and in preparing for the unforeseen, what should have been a routine operation had resulted in a number of Shylmahn casualties, along with the deaths of a significant percentage of the Chehnon being collected.

EsJen considered herself fortunate in being witness to it all. From this truly unique perspective in which she found herself, she was gathering information that could not have been acquired from any other observational standpoint. Beyond the data to be utilized in improving future collection operations, which was unquestionably important, lay the wealth of information of both human and Shylmahn frame of mind brought to the surface by this extraordinary experience. She found herself awash in the emotion and aura of this surreal situation.

They found Joseph's mate (ex-mate) on the second floor with six of her companions. They all appeared very resolute to their situation. They were frightened yet defiant. It would take quite an effort on the part of the collection team to gather them.

Barbara stepped around from behind a tall, thin man, the leader of these Chehnon.

"Joseph?" she asked.

"Barbara," Joseph said sheepishly. "Believe it or not, I'm here to rescue you."

"What?"

"Yeah."

All in the room eyed EsJen warily, and looked at Joseph with suspicion. The leader stepped back in front, analyzed the situation, tried to decide how best to respond to Joseph.

He looked questioningly at Barbara, turned again at Joseph.

"All right." He gave a curt nod. "Rescue us."

Jason watched Carolyn's band make a major push on the front of the apartment building. The Shillies pushed back just as hard, and the humans were forced to fall back, finally taking a stand several hundred yards down the street.

During the heaviest of the firefight, Jason saw a group of humans slip out the side door of the building. Joseph and his Shillie friend led seven humans to the vehicle they had arrived in.

With the intensity of the conflict elsewhere on the perimeter, Jason wasn't too surprised that Joseph was let out of the area once the patrol saw the Shillie in the front passenger seat of the Shylmahn ground vehicle. After all, they had passed her and the human through to begin with.

Meanwhile, another four humans were led out the front of the apartment building and into the back of the waiting trucks. Over the next hour, more were brought down in groups of one and two and three. The bodies of the dead were piled to one side.

Carolyn's group finally withdrew. They had suffered in the assault and probably considered the attack a complete failure. They couldn't yet know that it was because of their efforts that Joseph had made it inside and that he and Barbara had gotten out alive.

As Jason watched the Shillies gather the last of the humans and take them away, leaving the apartment building to burn, he carefully cleaned his rifle and put it back into its case. He tried not to think on his moment of weakness, in which he had exposed his mission, his position, and therefore himself, for personal reasons. At the moment he was not expendable. During the past few days he had gathered together information that was vital to the upcoming operation. If he were to be killed or captured now, the operation would not succeed.

In the end, though, Jason did not regret his actions. He had been instrumental in helping Joseph get Barbara out safely. Joseph had completed a successful operation, and Jason felt good about that; all the more so because Joseph didn't know what the hell had happened.

Jason smiled broadly. He and Joseph had worked together on two successful operations. Two for two. Great stats, considering just how rare success of any kind was these days.

Chapter Nineteen

October 10

Joseph stepped carefully between the sleepers and squatted next to the fire. It was a cold autumn morning. Ben Soo sat silently opposite the fire, calmly watching him. Joseph found the man's gaze unsettling and the man himself eerie.

"Good morning," he said, little more than a whisper.

"Mr. Britton." Ben placed several more sticks of wood into the fire. He filled a ceramic mug with something from the pot that rested on a warm stone and handed it to Joseph.

"Thanks," said Joseph. He took a cautious sip. "It's good. Some kind of tea?"

Ben nodded silently. He and his group made their tea from ingredients they collected as they traveled, and its character changed depending on what they found.

Joseph looked around the encampment. The Columbia River was below them, with Washington State to the north across the river. A figure stood watch on the hill above them, another upstream, a third downstream near the bridge. To the east, the sun was just coming up above the horizon and orange sunshine was beginning to splash across the sleeping bags and blankets.

Carolyn was asleep in a bag beside Terry; her soul mate, Joseph was told. The poet and balladeer. Nearby was a boy not yet out of his teens, and someone named Jenzie, and several others. Farther off, huddled together in blankets and bags, were Barbara and her six companions.

It had been a rough few days for her and her friends. They were tougher than they appeared, and seldom complained, but they had reached the very end of their endurance. At the time Joseph and EsJen had pulled them from the apartment building, they had been near collapse from exhaustion and hunger. Now they were getting food and rest.

Following the escape from the apartment building, once they were safely outside town, EsJen had left them. Joseph didn't know whether or not she had been given the authority to do what she had done, and so didn't know whether she had to face up to her superiors, or even perhaps to that ShahnTahr master of hers. She didn't seem concerned. He suspected that whichever way it went, she was going to turn this to her advantage. EsJen always looked at every situation as something to learn from, a new and wonderful well of knowledge to draw from. This may have been simply another of those experiences. She would use it to ease the process of the migration.

The human refugees had been left with very little in the way of supplies. To the few items Joseph carried in his backpack and on his utility belt, Barbara's group contributed two canteens and three pistols. Two of them didn't have jackets and none had caps. Almost everything had been lost, what little there had been, back at the apartment building.

They had traveled north. It was twelve miles to the next town, and they didn't reach it until late into the night. According to the sign posted at the city limits, it had a population of thirty-five hundred. Now, however, not a light shone, not a car moved, not a sound disturbed the silence but for a faint breeze brushing past the ears. The town was empty of life.

Too bad, perhaps, but so much the better for their needs. Joseph sent two of them in search of a van, utility truck, or large wagon, preferably with four-wheel drive, that would hold them all and their supplies. He sent two others to search the nearby homes for anything they could use in the way of food, clothing, weapons, first-aid supplies, utensils, and camping gear. The remaining five in the group searched the dozen or so shops that lined either side of the main street, skipping the video store, credit union and bank.

The community had been gone through more than once before, and they weren't in any condition for hard work, so the search wasn't easy. Nevertheless, by morning they had managed to come up with a van that would hold them, enough fuel to take them to the next town, clothing and some camping gear, and an assortment of canned goods.

They settled into a house at the north end of town, ate a cold meal, and slept for several hours. By early afternoon they were on the back roads to Portland. They had no real plans, other than ultimately Joseph wanted to get Barbara to Bril's island. As for the others, he assumed they had destinations of their own, but for the moment they were traveling together.

The back roads were in rough shape, and they made poor time. They drove cautiously, to avoid the potholes and debris, and were continually detoured onto ever more obscure roadways or sent back the way they had come in order to get around some obstruction or another.

Then, the evening before last, as they neared Portland, Joseph rounded a curve and suddenly found himself driving headlong towards a Greyhound bus that was lying on its side and completely blocking the road. He turned hard at the wheel and went into the tall grass and brush, hitting and bottoming out on a stump. Their injuries had been minor, but their van was beyond repair and they were again on foot. The sun was just setting, and they spent the rest of the evening and half the night walking the rest of the way into Portland.

It had been cold. The City of Roses was a dark and hollow place, as if the very soul of the city had died and its graying carcass lay now over the landscape, the barren streets and abandoned buildings forming the weatherworn skeleton of the once proud community. The empty void seemed to draw the air from Joseph's chest. His breaths grew more shallow and he grew dizzy to the point where he had to rest a hand on the walls of the dead buildings as he walked. They were all tired and needed a place to sleep.

They settled into one of the large hotels, selecting one of the finer downtown establishments. They doggedly climbed the stairs to the fifth floor. Being five floors above the streets somehow gave them a greater sense of safety. For a time they crowded in a single suite, talking till they grew so tired they were dozing off in mid-conversation, then went to their individual rooms.

Once in his own room, Joseph stood at the window and looked out on the black city. He had thought that at this height he would be able to see all and beyond, but with no lights and the sky overcast, he saw nothing. He could just as well have been in a basement. He turned finally from the window and fell heavily onto the bed. It swallowed him up and he slept soundly till well after sunrise, the thick drapes keeping the daylight away.

They all gathered in the ground floor restaurant at midmorning. There was no food to be found in the kitchen or pantries, so they were forced to take from their own supplies. Still, these were pleasant surroundings and their spirits were up, more so than in some time. There was talk of staying a while, perhaps for a long while. There had to be plenty of untapped supplies in a city of this size. Even Joseph was drawn into it, thinking that he might return here with some of the family. The Shylmahn weren't thick as flies here, as they were further north around Puget Sound. There was less destruction here. A small group of humans could get good and lost in a city as large as Portland.

Several hours of relaxed breakfasting and ever-warming conversation and planning were interrupted by Ben Soo and his group, who appeared as if from nowhere and sat noisily at the tables around Joseph and his startled companions.

They were loud and cocky and full of themselves. Carolyn introduced Ben Soo as the leader, after which she explained that Portland was used by the Shillies as a major collection point. Humans were drawn to the city and tended towards certain locations, such as this hotel. The Shylmahn around here made regular sweeps and had become quite skilled at gathering immigrants coming here to make a home.

Carolyn had crossed paths with Jason the day before, and she had been told to keep an eye out for Joseph and a scruffy little band of refugees. Ben Soo and his people were making their way north and had decided to spend a morning checking the most likely collection sites. A big, beautiful hotel like this, easily accessible to exhausted humans traveling from the south and dodging Shillies was a *can't miss* location.

That Ben Soo would just assume that Joseph would naively walk into a Shillie collection site was frustrating; their patronizing attitude had been even more annoying. That Carolyn withheld comment on the matter didn't help, but Joseph grudgingly appreciated her silence. They kept their own exchange brief, leaving their reunion for later. They had several weeks' worth of stories to swap.

Everyone was packed into the resistance group's two vehicles, and they began working their way through the streets of Portland and finally out of town.

Carolyn walked around the fire and sat beside Joseph. Ben Soo handed her a cup of tea, mentioning that it was particularly good today.

Carolyn blew lightly into the mug and took a sip. "Mmm, you're right. I think we're onto something here."

"I think so, too."

Carolyn took another sip. *Good blend...*

"I wish we had more time here," said Ben. "I would have liked to gather more of these ingredients. There is so little of it farther north."

"You don't think we could stay one day?"

"Perhaps if it was just us."

Joseph took their exchange in silence. He was curious that this tea of theirs held such an important place in their lives. This band of warriors, facing conflict and suffering and death day after day, seemed to be obsessed with this tea thing. So much of their time and thought and conversation was devoted to it. Shouldn't they be spending a little more time at the business at hand?

Even as he thought this, a possible truth struck him. The business at hand was always there, always in front of them, always facing them. It constantly shadowed their lives and invaded their thoughts. They lived the business at hand 24 hours a day, every day. Maybe the tea, the quest for the perfect blend, was their one escape from the constant state of the war and the darkness that threatened to overwhelm them. What better choice than seeking a better tea? Here was an ongoing project with endless possibilities and countless paths to explore. Every field and meadow, every flowerbed, every wood, was an opportunity to escape, for a few moments at least, from the ominous presence that was their existence. The daily ritual around the fire, during which they tested and experimented with new blends, was a pleasant diversion from the day to day planning of the activities to come or discussions of the days gone past.

Maybe this tea, in fact, was necessary. It was probably the most important factor in their lives. Joseph wondered then if they knew what role it played, whether it had been a conscious decision on their part or if it had been a subconscious, random selection from any number of other possibilities that could have filled this vital role.

Ben Soo stood and left his place at the fire. It was time to get the camp stirring.

Carolyn turned her attention to Joseph. "Have you been back to the island?"

"Not since you and I were there."

"I keep meaning to," she sighed. How else to get the latest? "No word on any of the others, then?"

"Nope."

Carolyn hovered over her tea. "Your Shylmahn friend, she helped you find Barbara?"

"Couldn't have done it without her."

"Hmm," Carolyn gave a slow nod. "You and Barbara... you had a chance to talk?"

Joseph made a face and looked into the fire. Beyond, the camp was beginning to wake. "Let that go."

"Hey, I'm not the one who's been crawling around amongst the heaviest concentration of Shylmahn on the planet trying to find her. Don't blame me if I get the wrong idea."

"I felt obliged to find her; I found her."

"And now?"

"She wants to go to the island. I'll take her there."

"Okay," Carolyn said flatly.

"Yeah," said Joseph. He and Carolyn had the same thoughts concerning the island. "Sooner or later, we're probably going to have to leave the Northwest."

"Probably."

"EsJen says there's a group of humans operating an escape route; some sort of underground railroad that's helping people escape to the south. It might be a way out."

The Shillies were looking the other way for now, because the humans that were leaving were difficult to collect. This way, most were ending up in one big group down in New Mexico or Arizona somewhere. Joseph figured the Shillies thought it was easier to keep an eye on them this way, and that it'd be easier to gather them up when they were ready.

"You're going to try to get the family to leave?" asked Carolyn.

"Maybe. If we went by way of the underground railroad, we could take off on our own once we got south."

They were quiet then. Everyone in the camp was up and about. A few had gathered near the fire. Carolyn and Joseph stood, walked slowly toward the edge of the camp.

"Bottom line, Joey. This is our home. My fight is here."

"Hey, I agree. I'm not going anywhere just yet. But the day will come when we may have to make a choice."

"You mean whether to stay or go?"

"More than that. The way I see it is this... We fight now because it's impossible to accept that they've taken our planet away from us, and they did it so easily. But when there's nothing left but to believe it, we'll have to choose about how to go on with the new order of things. If we can't beat them, the best we might expect is to be allowed to share our Earth with them."

"I'll never accept that. I want them to get the hell off my planet, and I'll keep fighting till they're gone. I'll never give up."

"Don't misunderstand me, Sis. I will not surrender to them; and I will not be going to a camp, no matter what happens, no matter how bad things look. But then, I don't have children asking for food or clothes or a warm place to sleep. I can afford to keep my fight out here."

"Then what about this *new order* that you're talking about?"

They were down near the water now, both looking across the river toward Washington on the far shore. Political borders held little reality these days, but were still as visible to Joseph as a white picket fence.

"If it comes to that," he said finally, "then we'll have to move into the shadows and show some patience. We'll have to take our steps carefully and create our opportunities. Our methods will have to change to fit the new situation."

"Geez, you sound just like Jason."

Joseph grinned, "Sorry. Hazard of the job."

Carolyn knelt down and picked up a small stone. She almost tossed it into the river, instead rolled it in the palm of her hand. "I guess by now you see the world quite differently than anyone else on Earth; human or Shillie."

"No two people ever see anything the same way."

"Yeah, but your perspective is particularly unique."

"I suppose so." Joseph was growing increasingly uncomfortable with the direction of the conversation.

"It was the plan, after all," said Carolyn.

"So far, it's not doing us much good."

"We both knew you wouldn't find a big red button. You hang in there. Remember, I'm in this with you."

"Thanks." Joseph turned to see Barbara coming toward them. "Good morning," he said, once she was near enough to hear.

"Good morning," she said. When she reached them, she stopped and wrapped her arms about herself. "The others won't be coming with us."

"What do you mean?" asked Joseph.

"They're not coming. They're going back to Portland."

"That's crazy."

"I know."

"That figures," Carolyn grumbled, tossed the stone she had been playing with.

"You heard what Ben said," said Joseph. "If they go back into Portland, they'll be walking right into the Shillies' hands."

"They believe that if Ben tells them where to say clear, they can avoid the Shillies. They say Portland is big enough to get lost in."

Joseph looked past Barbara and toward her friends. They were packing their things, talking conspiratorially amongst themselves.

"Hell," he said at last.

Carolyn shook her head in resignation. "Well, at least they're more likely to be taken alive in Portland than up north. They're doing a lot less collecting and a lot more clearing once you cross the river."

Barbara gave Carolyn a questioning look. Carolyn glanced once at Joseph, then looked back to Barbara.

"The Shillies are touchier up north," she went on. "Less inclined these days to take prisoners. Most of the humans they come into contact with up there are more fanatic and more likely to put up a fight."

For some twisted reason, Joseph liked the sound of that. Maybe he was becoming more like Jason than he realized.

Joseph seldom let the speedometer go much over thirty, and was averaging closer to twenty-five. Even at this, he was careful not to take his eyes off the road. There were downed trees and other vegetation, an occasional abandoned vehicle, and bone-jarring potholes. Now, as evening drew near and the mists of the damp, gray day closed in around them, the chance of something untoward happening grew greater. They certainly couldn't afford to wreck the vehicle or have an injury out here.

They pulled into an overgrown campground while it was still light enough to see. They found an old, weathered trailer parked beside the shower building and the bathrooms. The trailer had been closed up tight, so while it may have been musty, it was dry and had not been bothered by animals. As Barbara set about to clean it up, Joseph gathered wood.

They built a small fire three or four steps from the trailer, and brought a picnic table and benches near, so that the camp was enclosed by the shower building, trailer, their Bronco, and the table. They set out a hot dinner prepared from their provisions, and after they had finished eating sat near the fire and drank rich, black coffee that bore the taste of campfire smoke and camp coffee pot metal. The flames from the fire played shadows and light against the tall trees that stood in a great circle around the camp.

"I miss this..." said Barbara.

Joseph smiled inwardly. "Remember when we took Liz and Robert camping?"

"Right after they got married. Talk about a city boy."

Joseph stared into the fire. "He got better," he said.

"He didn't have much choice in the matter, did he?"

"He never does," said Joseph. He smiled, then his face darkened. "I sure hope they're all right."

Barbara poured herself more coffee, held the pot to Joseph. He looked into his cup and shook his head. Barbara set the pot back and settled again into her chair. She held the cup tightly with both hands.

"My God, I can't believe this is happening."

Joseph stared silently into the fire.

§

In the morning, Barbara stepped out of the trailer, a blanket wrapped about her and her hair a mess. She approached Joseph, who was struggling to get the fire going. The morning was cold.

"You could have slept in the trailer, Joseph."

"I don't think so," he said without looking up.

"I wouldn't hurt you."

Joseph leaned back when several small flames flickered up from the half-burnt wood from last evening's fire. He held a stick in his hand, occasionally poked at the half-hearted flames.

"Joseph," Barbara tried again. "There are several beds."

Joseph leaned back towards the fire. "I know," he said. There was no way he could look at her and have this conversation.

I'm not ready for this... this is way too close...

Barbara looked suddenly ready to burst into tears. The evening had been so nice... She had thought that maybe...

Joseph finally looked up. He started to say something, but couldn't. Barbara trembled.

"I am sorry."

Joseph tossed the stick into the fire.

October 20

Jason stood just outside the small park, which served as the center of the little town. He could see the lawn was being maintained and the few bushes were kept trimmed. It was an unnecessarily conspicuous nicety in this day and age.

An old man was sitting at the only bench, tossing out bits of carrot that he took from a brown paper sack. Three rabbits hopped about the freshly cut grass in front of him. Jason watched the old man and his rabbits for several minutes before starting into the park. The old man appeared not to notice him, continuing calmly about his business. It wasn't until Jason sat on the bench beside him that the old man acknowledged his presence.

"You have disturbed my rabbits," said the old man. His voice was soft and pleasant, but still managed to make Jason feel uncomfortable.

"Sorry." The rabbits had moved a few feet off, but were already coming back, however cautiously. There were a dozen or more pieces of carrot lying about on the lawn. "They look well cared for."

The old man looked at Jason for the first time, finally shrugged his shoulders and turned back to his pets. He said nothing.

"My name's Jason Britton." Jason said. He would try again. "I don't see many people these days."

"There aren't many to see."

"True enough," Jason nodded, slowly leaned forward. He rested his elbows on his knees. "Do you have any family or friends around here?"

"Nope."

Jason rubbed his hands together. *You old fart.*

"Anybody else living around here?"

"Just me."

"It must get lonely, being here all by yourself."

The old man only shrugged. Jason looked about the park, then at the buildings that bordered it on all four sides. This had at one time been a nice little community.

"It's awfully quiet nowadays," said Jason. On top of everything else, the old man was beginning to make him feel damned melancholy, "Sometimes... too quiet for my tastes."

"Peaceful," said the old man, tossing another piece of carrot out to his fat pets. "Things were crazy those first weeks, that's for sure. After a time, though, everything settled down. Folks got killed, or were taken, or just drifted off... till finally... there was just me." He looked down into the bag, saw that it was empty. He sighed heavily and frowned; the rabbits continued chewing away happily. After a few moments, he leaned back, perhaps content, perhaps resigned to fate. "People came through now and then, none stayed long. Now, I hardly see a soul. There's just me. Me and mine. But I don't mind, ya see. Don't mind at all." The old man took a satisfying breath. "Fact is... I kinda' like the quiet."

As Jason left the park, the old man's last words brought back his meeting with Mr. Johnson days earlier. He had checked in with his supervisor and provided him with the data that he had collected during his mission to Oregon. During their conversation, Mr. Johnson had also talked of how quiet the world was becoming.

The noise of humanity is being silenced, he had said. There appeared to be nothing that anyone could do about it.

"It is no longer a matter of how long we can hang on," Mr. Johnson had said. "We are not hanging on, there is nothing to hang on to. There are skirmishes, random acts of rebellion. The

Shillies sometimes have to pay a little for what they take or do. Little more, though. Little more."

"It's not over," said Jason.

"We go on, Mr. Britton. We always go on. But without a silver bullet, we will have to fight a very different war; a quiet war, a secret war that the enemy does not see, does not even know that it is fighting."

Jason had smiled faintly. "You're sounding like my brother." He grew thoughtful. "We're studying the Shylmahn technology. That may yet yield us something. And we do have the occasional victory on the battlefield; their numbers are not so great that they can afford many defeats."

Mr. Johnson shook his head tiredly. "There are too few organized groups out there to provide those defeats. Ben Soo, of course. He has a way of irritating the Shillies. And there is the Earth Resistance League in North Carolina; a few others in New England. Perhaps a handful operating in Europe."

"I'll admit that—"

"But we won't win this with resistance groups alone, no matter how we coordinate them. It will take technological advances jumpstarted through the acquisitions you've managed; and perhaps through alternative means, methods such as those that your brother is attempting."

Chapter Twenty

October 26

Bril ran. He was dirty and sweaty, having been working on the north shore bunker all morning. The cold, wet October air was brittle against his face. His damp shirt chilled him. The cramp in his left leg, something he had been fighting with sporadically for several weeks, had him hop-skipping along the narrow path, dodging the booby traps and the obstacles.

Kathryn had given him the word over the intercom.

Kenny is coming into the lagoon.

Bril hadn't waited for any more. He ran.

The boy was home. The boy had made it home.

Kenny is alive.

Bril's dirty face was streaked with sweat and tears as he came out into the clearing above the lagoon. Kenneth was in a small boat, still ten yards out. Everyone waited along the bank, calling to him, laughing, crying. Bril could hear him answering their questions as he guided the boat in.

Bril stood above them and tried desperately to hide his tears.

Kenneth made it to land and Daryl helped him climb out of the small boat. The crowd surrounded him then, smothering him in welcoming hugs. The children, caught up in the excitement and emotions of the adults, were jumping and laughing.

All the while, Bril stood silent. He was composed, now. The hard, gray midmorning pushed at him; he could feel the cold dampness deep down inside, chilling his bones.

He stood and waited for the boy.

The crowd brought Kenneth to him. Bril held out his arms and Kenneth came into them. Bril held him, squeezed him and cried again. He wouldn't let go. His tears fell into sobs and then Kenny was crying, too.

Kathryn walked past them and started up toward the house. One by one, the others followed. Finally, with the children hovering around them, Bril and Kenneth followed Kathryn up the slope.

While Bril cleaned himself up and Kenneth was getting settled in, lunch was made ready. As they ate, Bril filled the boy in on all that had happened in the months since the invasion began. He spoke of Daryl's capture and eventual rescue, of Carolyn's wild adventures with her resistance group, of Joseph's wanderings, of Jason's comings and goings, and of Elizabeth's ordeal.

Mostly though, he talked about his island and the preparations.

Kenneth watched the family. Daryl and Susan, with their kids; Bril and Kathryn, and their son Peter; silent Elizabeth. The table held them all. There was room yet for the others. For Joseph and Carolyn and Jason.

Robert and the boys were gone... *Poor Elizabeth.*

Yet Kenneth couldn't help but be... if not happy, something akin to happy.

My family is alive.

He felt guilty and selfish and happy. For perhaps the hundredth time that morning, he began to cry.

Kathryn rushed around the table and held him to her. She kissed him and brushed at his hair. Meanwhile, Bril sat at the head of the table, stone-faced, hands held tightly before him. The great patriarch had shown enough blubbering emotion for one day.

November 17

"He doesn't talk much about his time out there," said Daryl. He and Jason were at the jetty bunker, set into the tip of the spit of land that formed the lagoon. From here they could watch the waterway between the island and the mainland.

Alien traffic was heavy these days. It was mostly air traffic, but they could see a Shillie hovercraft, a few of the big boats, and from here they could see the Shillies moving along the shoreline.

Jason had arrived on the island just that morning. He was planning to stay a couple of weeks, wanted to spend Thanksgiving with the family. This Thanksgiving was more important than most. Such things took on greater significance these days.

"No one has had it harder than Kenny," said Jason.

Daryl looked back out over the water, took note of the single hovercraft, used the binoculars to study the activity on the far shore. Opening the logbook, he entered the date, time, and what he observed from this station.

"Onward," he said. They continued on Daryl's rounds. They would check the condition of every bunker, booby trap and detection device on the island. It would take over three hours. Every adult on the island made the round at least once a day. Bril made it twice. He thought of the second trip as Elizabeth's. Even Peter had a round to make, though his was less extensive. Now that Jason was here, he would also have to make the rounds.

This round with Daryl was his introduction. He had no objection. He saw some value in all of it, though perhaps not as much as Bril placed on it. He had even asked for copy of the records on the Shylmahn comings and goings, for there was real value in that.

As he saw it, the greatest merit of the constant inspections was that, when the time came and the island was overrun, everyone would know the trails intimately. Anyone who had to run down a path in the middle of the night would be able to avoid the traps without even thinking about it.

"What's it like out there these days?" asked Daryl. He used his walking stick to point to a booby trap. Near their feet a wire crossed the path. Well hidden in the brush, a spiked branch was bowed back and held in place. "And don't give me the canned version you gave the rest of the family. What's going on? How goes the war?"

"The war? Hell, the war's over."

"What?"

Jason maneuvered around the trap, indicated that they should continue. "Oh, there are still a few of us around, stirring things up, making a nuisance of ourselves, but for all intents and purposes, it's done."

"But... how can that be?"

"Just is," said Jason.

"How can they just take over a planet with billions of people?"

"By taking all the right steps, in the right order. It also helps if you turn the billions into millions."

They stopped again at a point along the path that overlooked the cove. Daryl took hold of Jason's arm.

"Jase—"

"The most recent estimate we have is that we lost half of our population in the first hour. Those losses were very specifically targeted."

"But, how can you know? For sure?"

"Admittedly, it is an estimate. Most communications were lost in the first few minutes."

"So you can't know. Not really."

Billions... such a loss was beyond the mind's grasp. It was too great a number to be simply a planetary loss; it had to have been felt across the galaxy. *Billions.*

"The estimate is conservative," said Jason.

They started walking again. They walked in silence for a time, Daryl continuing to indicate the traps set along the path.

When Jason finally spoke again, he sounded far away.

"From the Shillie point of view, the war was over a few hours after it began. If they ever really thought of it as a war. Everything since then has been clean-up."

"That's what they're doing now? Cleaning up?"

"And moving in." Jason waved his arm at the view of the island. "This island... this island is smack dab in the middle of one of three major Shylmahn centers on the North American continent. And they have their own Shillie city right near here, with a spaceport."

"But, what are they doing with all the people?"

"With us? Well, there's a couple of big reservations in Wyoming, another in Arizona. Around here, there's a small one over near Moses Lake. Work camps operating around that city of theirs, and a couple of detention camps where they keep a few hundred of us."

"Then... it is lost."

"I didn't say that. I said the war is over."

They had reached the inside trail that led along the small cove toward the boathouse. Daryl indicated the booby trap. Fishing line was pulled taut across the trail, half an inch above the ground, every four inches for three feet. Any pressure placed on the fishing line released a series of spiked branches back along the trail that would incapacitate not only the individual setting it off, but many of his companions as well. Just as importantly, the release of the branches would set off an alarm.

The trap had been activated once since being put into place, killing a doe and her yearling. Bril had hoped to allow the yearling to breed several years before taking it down, but the meat wasn't wasted.

Daryl checked the trap, logged it in the book, and showed Jason the way safely around the trap and on to the boathouse. Here they examined the camouflage and the readiness of the boats.

"Why haven't you told the others about this?" asked Daryl.

Jason climbed aboard Bril's charter boat and sat heavily in one of the fishing chairs. "They didn't ask."

"That's not an answer."

"Sure it is."

"You don't think they should know the numbers?"

"They know. So did you. It just makes you uncomfortable having it confirmed."

Daryl frowned. "Maybe you're right." He leaned against the large boat. "What are they going to do with us?"

"Use us." Jason's words were sharper now. "Listen, it's never been a war of conquest with them, or enslavement, or a desire for domination. We are just that much more stuff that came with the planet."

"Are you giving up?"

"Oh, hell no. You know me better than that. Now comes the real war, the one we have a chance of winning. They've had centuries to study us... now it's our turn. And we're doing just that. I have labs studying their technology. Joey is studying who they are and how they live. Carolyn, how they fight. We'll get more from you, and from Kenneth. They won. And we'll let them go right on thinking so."

"This is going to take a long time."

"You got any other plans?"

Daryl gave a cursory once-over of the small boats that he and the others had brought to the island.

"And on and on and on?"

In answer, Jason leaned far back in the chair and spread his arms out wide, looked down and Daryl and gave a slight shoulder shrug.

Thanksgiving Day

Bril was awake long before dawn. It was common for him to spend twenty or thirty minutes organizing his day before getting out of bed. Today's planning was simple. He would help Kathryn, if asked, but otherwise he would sit on his butt and give thanks that his family was relatively intact.

A lot of horrible things had happened since that day back in May, but there was also a lot to be thankful for. It was true that Elizabeth had lost everything that she felt made life worth living— her husband and those two wonderful children—but the rest of the family was grateful that she at least was alive and had been brought back to the island. Bril gave thanks for that. He took a moment in his thoughts to remember the kids and the joy they had brought to everyone in the family, and thought of the companionship and love that Robert had given to Liz, then gave thanks again that she was alive and was here with the family today.

Bril's thoughts turned to Daryl. He and his family had also gone through some difficult times. Daryl had been captured and put through experiments and examinations that he still wouldn't talk about; but just look at how his brothers and sisters had come to his rescue... and he was safe now. He and his family were here on the island and Bril could give thanks for that.

And Jason, the man of mystery and shadow. What covert situations had Jason slipped into and back out of in the past seven months? How many enterprises had he initiated that he could not, or would not, discuss? What did he know that he could not tell us? Bril was thankful that there were those like Jason around to fight this invasion, and that Jason was alive and here to share Thanksgiving with the family. Bril was proud that Jason had felt it was important to make the journey to be with his family.

Kenny had made it home! Thanks, dear God, for that. The boy had fought and sacrificed and witnessed so much death and suffering, but he had survived and had come home. He still wasn't saying much about his experiences, but what little he did say from time to time conjured up images of a great, terrifying war being fought out there; a war with few victories, but with many shining moments of great humanity. Kenneth had fought beside mankind's finest representatives, and because of them the boy was alive and safe here on the island.

Where was Carolyn, that whirlwind of fire and tooth and nail? Jason had said that he had last seen her down in Oregon, taking on the bastards and kicking ass. It was just like her to jump onto the monster's back and try to ride it down. The world could be thankful that she was out there giving it all she had. Bril was thankful that at least she had joined up with a group that was as tough and as dedicated as she herself was, and that she had comrades strong enough to protect her back, and he was thankful that he had a sister like Carolyn out there representing the Britton family.

Jason had also seen Joseph down in Oregon. He had finally found and rescued Barbara. Bril couldn't help feeling a bit melancholy about Joseph; quiet, thoughtful, the conscience of the family. In some ways, Joseph was like Daryl. He could be quite reserved, and was prone to keep his opinions to himself, to let the louder voices of the family stand unchallenged; but he was more liable than Daryl to take a stand against the odds if you got his hackles up.

On this day, as Bril took careful examination of his family, he couldn't help but be most concerned about Joseph. If he had planned on bringing Barbara back to the island, he really should have been back by now. It had been six weeks since Oregon.

Jason said that he felt confident that Joseph and Barbara were fine, and since Jason had a way of knowing these things, Bril accepted Jason's optimism and was thankful that Joseph, *the man with the bulls-eye on his back*, as Jason often referred to him, was alive. He was thankful that Joseph had found Barbara in good health. Perhaps in the midst of all of this chaos Joseph and Barbara had rediscovered one another. That would certainly be something to be thankful for.

Bril was most thankful for Kathryn and Peter. He couldn't help but grimace at all the bullshit that Kathryn had endured over the years because of him. Could he possibly be worth it? Yet together, they had built this home and forged this defense against any and all comers. If he had gone to God with a list of requirements and asked for a companion, the only person God could have found would have been Kathryn. He may not always show it, and he may not often say it, but Bril worshipped Kathryn and thanked God every day that she had chosen him to be her companion, as well. He was thankful beyond all imagining that she and Peter were here now with him. When he looked at Kathryn, and felt her touch, Bril saw and felt the reason to live. And when he looked at Peter, he saw the purpose in keeping the future alive.

Bril rolled onto his back and tucked one arm under his head. He was wide awake now. He felt ready to take on the day. Yes, there had been and continued to be suffering and anxiety and loss. In spite of that, there was so very much to be thankful for. The Britton family had survived this year, particularly the past seven months. Much of the family would share this day together. Carolyn and Joseph, though not on the island, would be in the thoughts of those present, and Bril knew that the two of them would each take a few moments of their own to reflect on those here.

Bril and the family would be taking time on this day to wish peace to those close to them who had not survived since the last Thanksgiving, to all those who were no longer here to give thanks, and to all who now bore the grief of loss and the struggles of the times.

With that, Bril climbed out of bed and began to dress. Kathryn woke at his movements, looked over at the clock and sat up. It was dark. The sun was a late riser in the Northwest at this time of year, and dawn was still a long way off, but Kathryn had work to do and breakfast to get out of the way. Once that was done, she and Susan would have to get going on the Thanksgiving dinner. The Britton family always had their Thanksgiving meal in early afternoon, and despite the annual loud balking to the contrary, the men in the family were of little help. Whatever they might say, many of the 'shared duties' in this family still fell along gender lines.

Kathryn stood and pulled on her robe. By the time she left the bedroom, Bril was already outside. Thanksgiving Day or not, he had the morning rounds to make. He would be gone three hours. Kathryn would have his breakfast ready for him when he got back.

Daryl watched Bril disappear into the shadows of the path that ran behind Bunker One and into the woods. He zipped up his coat and sat on the top step of the porch. It was cold out now, but Daryl thought the day would turn out nice. A bit cool, but not too bad for late November.

Most of the stars had gone out. This was the dark time before the skies grayed and signaled the coming of the sun. Daryl was often awake at this hour. He still had the headaches and the nightmares. He was afraid they would never go away, that his experiences with Dr. Black would follow him to the grave. For all he knew, they would follow him beyond and into whatever lay in the life after.

The lab did not haunt just his dreams. Much of his waking hours were spent back there as well. Guard, and Dr. Black, and Frank, were still a major part of his life. He thought often of his eventual escape, and of Guard's last moments. Daryl relived Guard's march from cell to cell. He saw, again and again, the look in Guard's eyes during that last moment...

Daryl found himself in Dr. Black's laboratory again and again, experiencing those tests again and again, enduring the probing and the experimenting and the interrogations again and again and again...

He did not believe that Dr. Black would have looked on the rescue as a setback. If anything, it was an opportunity for further investigation. Might Dr. Black even now be continuing his studies, perhaps even with the same subjects? Is there any way that he could still be watching?

God, I'm paranoid. I'm a paranoid human lab rat...

He tried to shake off the anxiety, to turn his mind to something else, but his thoughts continued to circle the same points of reference.

What was Frank doing now? The last couple of days especially, Frank had been on Daryl's mind. When they had said good-bye, following the rescue, Frank was off to join the resistance. But Frank was not a healthy man. His time before his capture, hiding and alone, and his later experiences at the hands of Dr. Black, had taken a severe toll on Frank. What would he do if none of the local groups took him in? Would he have gone off on his own and gotten himself killed? If he had been accepted, how could he have withstood the harsh realities of life in the resistance? Such a life wasn't easy. It took a lot of stamina to survive the life of a resistance fighter. It took much more than just a fire in your soul. It took physical strength, mental alertness, the stamina to endure little sleep, little food, bad weather, poor living conditions, psychological stress and hardship, and the mental endurance to live the life of calculated killing and the constant shadow of imminent death.

On this day of giving thanks, Daryl hoped that Frank had been picked up by the Shylmahn and was now living on one of the reservations. There were times now when Daryl wished that he, too, was living safely on one of the reservations with Susan and the children. The fear that at any moment the Shylmahn would drop in on them from out of the sky was almost as bad as sitting in his cell, listening for the sound of Guard getting ready to open the door and tell him it was time...

He heard the door behind him open and close. Susan sat down beside him, placed an arm across his shoulders. She did this most mornings when she woke to find him gone. She would dress and follow him out, and sit quietly beside him. They would watch the day begin. In the gray between the night and the day, they would hear the animals in the forest go about their pre-dawn activities. Behind them, the sun would finally rise, the lagoon below would slowly gain color, the trees on either side of the clearing would turn from black and gray to a myriad of greens and browns and yellows.

Susan held tightly to her husband. She would never let him go. Not again. They would live together, or they would die together. They would never, ever, be apart again.

Now, on Thanksgiving, she was happy. In spite of all that was going on, or maybe because of it, she felt a joy inside her. They were alive and they were together. Whatever problems Daryl was having, he was alive and with her and the children. She could take anything, put up with any hardship, so long as she and Daryl and the kids were together.

The sky overhead was just showing the hint of gray.

§

Jason woke late. His room had been dug out of the side of the mountain and had no windows. The walls were of solid wood, the one door opened to the tunnel that ran from the back of the house to Bunker One. The room was dark and quiet, and it suited Jason just fine. He was here to recuperate and see the family, and getting a good night's sleep, each and every night, did a lot to recharge his batteries.

He had made the last rounds the night before, inspecting the defenses, and had found the trip to be relaxing. A quiet walk around the island in the late evening could do a lot to soothe the nerves. The only real anxiety that followed after him was the fear that he might set off one of Bril's traps in the dark. This had been his first shift on the night rounds. He had traded with Daryl, who wasn't getting much sleep these days. Maybe the early evening inspection would better suit him.

Coming into the main area of the house, Jason found the rest of the family had been up and busy for some time. A holiday mood was already beginning to set in. The children were playing, Kathryn was in the kitchen working on something that smelled real good, and Bril and Daryl were playing a card game in the front room. Susan was gone on the midmorning rounds. The midmorning tour was an abbreviated inspection. She would go to each of the primary bunkers and log any activities she witnessed off-island. In going from bunker to bunker, she would pass by the main traps and detection devices, noting if any had been tripped. Under ideal circumstances, an alarm would sound if these main traps activated. Such had not been the case in several inadvertent activations. This was one of the reasons for the constant inspections.

Jason ate a quick breakfast of dried fruit, warm bread and coffee. He offered to help Kathryn in the kitchen and was shooed out. That was fine with him.

There wasn't a cloud in the sky. The sun had been at work all morning trying to burn off the mid-Autumn chill. It was going to be a beautiful Thanksgiving Day. From the porch, Jason could see Kenneth and Elizabeth sitting in a small boat out in the middle of the lagoon. There were two fishing poles, one hanging over either side.

Jason stepped off the porch and began down the hill toward the lagoon. As he walked, watching Kenneth as he gently worked with Elizabeth, talking calmly and patiently with her, trying to draw her back from whatever world she had gone into, he couldn't help wondering if maybe she wasn't better off wherever her mind had taken her.

Perhaps, where she was, her husband and children were still alive. Maybe where she was billions hadn't died. Maybe half the planet hadn't been blown to dust where she was. Did we really want to bring her back here, to this?

Today was another booby trap, like all those booby traps Bril had laid out around the island. The sun was shining here. The family was here. Children played. People were playing cards. Wonderful smells were coming from Kathryn's kitchen. It was the perfect day to climb into a small boat, row out into the lagoon and do a little fishing.

Come back to us, Elizabeth. Come back, feel the sun warming your face. Your brothers and sisters are waiting for you. We love you. We want you with us.

Come watch the Shillies take out the rest of your family.

Damn, Jason...

"Good morning, Jason," said Kenneth.

"Catch anything?" Jason had reached the bank. It was only a few yards out to the boat. It was quiet.

"Elizabeth got one." Kenneth smiled at Elizabeth. She looked at Kenneth, then over at Jason. She didn't say anything, but she was there, with them; if just a little.

Give it time, she'll be back.

"How long have you two been at it?"

"All morning."

Jason looked behind him at the sun. "Near midday; I doubt you'll get much now. You could try again come dusk."

"Doesn't matter. It's nice out here. Isn't it, Liz?"

"Nice," she said. It was a flat, hollow sound, but she meant it. She spoke little, but she always meant what she said.

"I won't argue that." Jason squatted down and sat on his heels. He stayed there with them. It was nice.

Kenneth sat on the tree stump at the edge of the clearing. Jason sat beside him. Elizabeth was up on the porch, drinking coffee with Bril and Kathryn. The Thanksgiving dinner had gone well and Kathryn had been strutting about proudly.

Kenneth sat silent for a long time, occasionally looking down at his iced tea. Jason waited patiently, watching sympathetically, looking now and then at his own drink. He could tell that Kenny had something to say. He always knew when someone had something to say.

When Kenny finally spoke, he did so without looking up at his brother. The words were hard enough in coming.

"Jase... have you ever known you were going to die?"

Not exactly what I expected...

"Wow. That's heavy for Thanksgiving," he said. He thought a long moment. "We all die."

"That's not what I mean, and you know it. Have you ever believed, known for a fact, that this is it? You know... 'Now. Right now. I am going to die'."

Jason let out an anxious breath. "Oh," he started, then drifted, settled in again. "I've come face to face with death. I've overcome it. But, to be honest, no matter how bad it's gotten, no matter how hopeless it looked, I don't think I've ever really believed that I was about to die. This little guy living in my head always speaks up. He's in there saying *'we're going to get out of this. 'There's a way out, Jase. There's always a way out.'"*

Kenneth nodded silently, stared into his glass.

"I'm immortal, Kenny," said Jason.

"Yeah," Kenny said. There was a faint smile. "Well, my little guy gave up. He and I both knew that it was over."

"You gotta get another little guy."

"When you're in the middle of a fight, you don't think about living and dying. You do your job. The thinking comes in that empty time before a battle, in those miserable hours between battles, when there's nothing left but to think and to wait. Even then, even when you're thinking about death, there's always this thin thread of hope that keeps you going. You have to have that."

"Kenny, you've had to face that more than me. You're the expert here. Not me." *Not absolutely, totally, completely true, but appropriate to the situation...* "What happened?"

Kenny wasn't sure. He couldn't put it into words, but he felt he had to. There was an ache, and this ache had brought on a doubting, and a searching. He struggled with his thoughts, but the more he tried to grasp at the meanings, the more confused his thoughts became.

In the last weeks with his platoon, he had gone into battles knowing that he was the one about to die, and not the soldier beside him. He was going to die. Death was walking beside him, became the shadow hovering over him. Even his friends had seen it, had seen the shadow as it lay across his face. Even Bobby saw it. Bobby, who had, to everyone's surprise, come to rely so heavily on Kenny's strength, had seen it.

Still, Kenneth survived the next battle, and the next. All the while, his friends continued to die.

"After the last battle, I was laying there, and the Shillies were everywhere; they didn't pay any attention to me. Even they could see it. I was dead. They saw that I was dead."

"Kenny, it sounds to me like you met it head on. You've come face to face with it and come out alive."

"No. No, that's just it, Jason. If it had been like a life-after-death experience, that would have been one thing. This, this was *death in life*. When you realize that you are about to die, you don't sense immortality, you confront mortality. Nothing is as cold as knowing, believing with absolute certainty... that you are going to die."

"I can't offer you any words, Kenneth. I've never had to come to grips with my own mortality."

"I'm not looking for words, Jason. Words are useless."

"Then I don't know what you want from me."

Kenneth frowned, grimaced, then fell thoughtful. Just what was it that he wanted from his brother? Was there any way to put it into words? Hadn't he just said that words were useless?

"Forget mortality. Have you found your immortality?"

"I already told you. I'm immortal."

Kenneth set his glass down, rubbed his hands in frustration, stuffed them back into his jacket pockets.

"Everyone knows the old saying that there are no atheists in foxholes, and maybe that's true; I don't know. You certainly don't want to think that it's all over if you die out there. You always keep a sliver of faith, just in case..." He went introspective again, and Jason waited. When Kenneth spoke again, there was a faint desperation in his voice.

"I never felt the immortality that you're supposed to feel. I had to accept my mortality, like I said. I experienced my mortality. That's fine. But I never felt the other, never felt the warmth. I never saw the light... I didn't see anything after. I didn't sense... anything."

Jason stared uncomfortably into his glass. He couldn't look at his brother. "It's there, man. No other choice."

"Yeah," said Kenneth. "That's what they say."

From the porch, Elizabeth drank her coffee and watched.

Thanksgiving Day - Carolyn

"Take a break," said Ben. He let his pack slide off his shoulder and fall to the ground. A cloud of ash billowed up and rolled out in all directions.

"Oh, yes," groaned Carolyn, letting her own pack fall. She sat on it. She pulled her canteen free and drank. Terry sat beside her. Carolyn held her canteen to him. He shook his head and pulled his own from his belt.

"Afraid of germs?" she asked.

They sat in a circle, facing out. Nine souls, crossing a barren, desolate land. There was no color but for shades of gray. There was no form, but for abstract lines and misshapen curves. They walked now, had been for several days since abandoning their vehicles at the edge of the desolation.

Jenzie was going through his papers.

"How are we doing, Jenzie?" asked Ben.

"Happy Thanksgiving."

"Really?" asked Carolyn.

"By my calculations."

Ben Soo shifted. "Well?" he asked impatiently.

Jenzie pulled out a map book. He opened it up and began studying it.

"So?" Ben urged.

"Perhaps a mile beyond that ridge."

"Is that good news, or is that bad news?" asked Carolyn.

"We shall look into the jaws of death..." Jenzie was stuffing the map book back into his pack.

"...and laugh," sighed Carolyn, tiredly.

They had fallen on hard times. Their supplies never went far enough, their weapons needed repair, their ammunition was always low, their clothes were ragged and dirty, and they were constantly on the run.

"Happy Thanksgiving," said Terry, leaning close to Carolyn.

"You, too."

"Turkey, mashed potatoes, cranberry sauce, pumpkin pie, corn on the cob, green salad, rolls, ice cold milk."

Carolyn put on a satisfied smile. "Mmm, I'm stuffed."

"Football games, screaming kids, and the brother-in-law you can't stand."

"What a day."

"It'll take tomorrow to recover."

"And thus the four-day weekend."

Ben Soo called Danny and Billy the Kid over to him, had them start to the top of the ridge. They were to survey the area beyond, check the scene around and behind them to make sure all was clear. Ben didn't like being out in the open like this, though of course there really was no choice. The Shillies had leveled everything for miles in all directions. That was part of the reason for Ben Soo and his group being there.

Jenzie completed his note-taking, stuffed his paperwork back into the plastic bag, and slipped the bag into his backpack. He then used the backpack as a pillow.

That paperwork was the purpose of this mission. Jenzie was there to complete that paperwork. Everyone else was there to protect Jenzie.

Danny and Billy the Kid finally reached the ridge top. They studied all points on the compass, then gave the all clear signal to Ben. He signaled them to hold position.

From there, the boys should be able to see the alien city. The Shylmahn called it a *dahlseht*. High walls surrounded it, and a ring of vegetation encircled the walls. Beyond that lay this band of desolation. It was part of their defense against intruders like Ben Soo and his friends.

Ben gave his people a few more minutes, then ordered them up and ready. They had a lot of ground to cover before nightfall.

Thanksgiving Day - Joseph

"Thanksgiving or not, that was a great dinner," said Joseph. He picked up their two plates and took them into the trailer. Barbara began clearing the dinner from the picnic table.

"It is Thanksgiving," she said.

"I'll get the fire going," said Joseph, coming back out. "It's starting to get cold. Isn't it?"

Evening shadows came early to the campground. The surrounding forest was thick and the trees grew tall and thin in their search for the sun. There were streaks of sunlight reaching down through the canopy, but the shadows kept the camp cool.

"I keep a close track of the days, Joseph," said Barbara. She came out of the trailer with a freshly readied coffee pot. She placed it near the fire that Joseph was preparing.

"Today's as good a day as any, I guess," he said.

"It is today," she stated firmly.

"All right," said Joseph. He managed to bring the coals back to life. He placed fresh firewood expertly into position, moved the coffee pot over the heat to brew, then stood and plopped himself into his chair. "All I meant was that maybe the specific day doesn't matter. Yesterday, today, tomorrow... does it really make that much of a difference?"

"Yes. It does." Barbara sat in her chair opposite the fire from Joseph.

"All right..."

"It matters as much as it ever did. More so."

Joseph interlaced his fingers and set his chin on his hands. "Then it's a good thing I have you here to keep track of these things. Isn't it?"

There was a sound from beyond the clearing, from the front gate of the campground. Neither Joseph nor Barbara acknowledged it. Both continued looking into the fire.

Their weekly supply shipment had arrived. They had been expecting it all afternoon. Joseph would bring the boxes in after he had his coffee.

The Shillies treated them well enough. They got what they needed, and sometimes a few extras. There was hot water in the showers. There was propane enough to keep the refrigerator going if they were careful about how much they used at the stove in the trailer. To conserve, they did a lot of their cooking over the open fire.

They had clean clothes, blankets, toiletries, even playing cards and books and other odds and ends. They had the freedom of most of the campground. An invisible fence had been put in place on the other side of the creek and along the main road that ran along the east side of the campground, consisting of mechanical probes that watched the boundaries, hovering silently out of sight or sitting unobtrusively at the base of a tree or behind a rock.

If Joseph approached too near the boundary, a warning sounded. If he failed to heed the warning and did not back away, a warning energy beam would strike out, near enough to Joseph to let him know that he was in danger, far enough away to let him know that it was a warning.

He knew that the next shot would be more painful, if not fatal. He had yet to challenge the probes any further.

Other than the boundary probes and the weekly provisions, Joseph and Barbara were left completely alone. They hadn't seen EsJen in six weeks. Joseph didn't know if their imprisonment had been her idea, or if it had come from someone else and she was just going along with it.

It might be something she would come up with. Now that Joseph had found Barbara, his 'ex-mate', maybe they wanted to see if they could get the couple 're-mated'. Cute experiment.

Joseph had slept out by the fire those first few nights, while Barbara slept in the trailer. Then came a night that was particularly cold and wet, and Joseph came into the trailer and out of the weather. At first, he slept in the second bed. It was another week before anything else happened.

This change in the arrangements brought about no reaction from their Shylmahn captors. All continued on as before. Two days later, on schedule, the supplies arrived inside the gate— nothing new in the boxes, nothing taken away.

Each night they would huddle together in the small bed, warmly and affectionately, and they would whisper of all they had seen that day, and of how they might escape.

The coffee was ready. Joseph poured a cup for Barbara, and one for himself.

"Happy Thanksgiving," he said.

"You too, Joey."

Chapter Twenty One

December 04

TohPeht turned from the communications console and faced GahJen. He had spent much of the morning in conference with ShahnTahr, and GahJen had patiently waited. TohPeht indicated that GahJen should sit.

He relied heavily on his assistant these days. There was much to do, and he could not do it all himself. The coordination of the migration of an entire people was a complicated affair, and though TohPeht treasured the assignment, such responsibility was exhausting. He had had little time to relax since their arrival on Chehno, and it would be some time before ShahnTahr released him from his position and allowed him rest. It was good that GahJen was here to help share the burden.

He was very tired, but the day had only just begun.

The facts and issues rang in his ears. Each item, whether a problem to be dealt with or a status to be reviewed, would have to be addressed.

The construction of the dahlsehts was continuing on schedule, though there were a number of concerns to be resolved if they were to remain on schedule.

The manufacturing facilities were producing at full capacity, and the agricultural centers reported that they would meet their timetables. The development facility producing the next series of robotic probes designed by ShahnTahr reported that they were on schedule.

The next migration fleet was due to arrive in three weeks. The assignments of the newly arriving personnel were unchanged.

There were no problems of serious consequence. The reason there were no serious problems was that TohPeht dealt with the dozens of little problems identified by ShahnTahr before they became serious problems.

He spent the next several hours reviewing every item with GahJen, presenting ShahnTahr's resolutions where they had been provided, sorting out their own solutions where they had not. It wasn't until after the midday meal that he was ready to meet with those whom he had called to come before him.

NehLoc came into the room and stood at the end of the table. TohPeht quietly eyed his manner. NehLoc was an ambitious sort. He had risen quickly through the levels of responsibility and would continue to do so. TohPeht saw no reason why he would not. His work consistently met or exceeded all requirements.

"NehLoc."

NehLoc stood silent.

"NehLoc, the sector assigned to you was a particularly difficult one, and ShahnTahr has indicated the highest approval of your efforts and your results."

"I am very honored," said NehLoc.

"ShahnTahr fully understands the complications that were inherent in gaining full control in this sector, and appreciates that any delay was due to your efforts to comply with ShahnTahr's requests for implementation of research and knowledge operations."

"My only purpose is to serve the needs of the migration. ShahnTahr understands far better than I how I might best fulfill my responsibilities."

"You have met your responsibilities very well." The results of his early research work in this sector were instrumental in both the design and implementation of collection and restraint procedures that were now in use throughout the world.

"I ask to continue to serve."

"And so you shall."

NehLoc stood quietly waiting for word on how he would continue to serve.

"You have served well in the security of the Chehnon holding facilities and work camps in the sector," said TohPeht. "You are now given the responsibility for the security of the dahlseht and all Shylmahn facilities as well."

"Honored."

"You are now responsible for all Chehnon in your sector."

"Yes, TohPeht."

"You are pleased?."

"I live to serve. ShahnTahr knows how I might best attend the needs of our people."

"There is nothing wrong with being pleased, NehLoc."

"Thank you, TohPeht. I... am pleased."

"Very good," said TohPeht. "ShahnTahr would like for you to coordinate the final collection activities of the sector. This is a controlled area, and as such we must have complete confidence in our ability to move about freely."

"Understood."

NehLoc was indeed pleased with that request. That much was clear to TohPeht. He leaned back and gave NehLoc a gentle nod, "You will do well. You always have."

NehLoc bowed in silent acknowledgement. He was dismissed. He turned and left.

TohPeht took a few moments to clear his thoughts and ready himself for the next audience. He took in a breath and let it out slowly.

More human issues. These Chehnon were but one small element in the midst of a hundred elements of the migration. Why was it that he spent so much time dealing with human issues?

BehLahk was let into the room. BehLahk was one of the leading scientists in the field of the human mind. He was called Dr. Black by most of his study subjects, initially because of a misunderstanding of his name, encouraged later by BehLahk because he liked the emotions that he was able to evoke by such a nickname.

"Good morning to you, TohPeht," he said.

"And to you. Have a seat."

"Don't mind if I do," said BehLahk, sitting. He smiled. "It has been a long morning."

"A curious turn of phrase. *A long morning...*"

"A Chehnon expression. I find many to be quite... quaint. I fear I am becoming a bit too acclimated."

"BehLahk, your studies will do much to aid the human integration to the new order."

"I would do no less than serve, and as much as I am able."

"That is known," said TohPeht. "Your communications with ShahnTahr have reflected your dedication."

"I am pleased."

"How refreshing."

"Yes?"

TohPeht waved off the query and began the meeting in earnest. "As the migration enters a new phase, it is necessary that certain of your projects accompany this shift, or be brought to a close. Your work necessarily must look far ahead of where we are at any moment in the migration."

"I have been preparing for the changes." BehLahk was much more relaxed than NehLoc had been. This made this meeting a much more comfortable one for TohPeht.

"As you know," TohPeht continued, "all work with the Chehnon has been shifting away from the wild subjects and to those now under controlled management. Your own work has explored both environments, particularly so since the release of the subjects from your primary research facility."

BehLahk nodded. "The most enlightening experiments are often those resulting from the most unexpected turn of events."

"You have several as yet unresolved projects involving wild subjects. While these are exploring issues that may be of interest to future interactions with Chehnon, ShahnTahr feels that you should draw these experiments to a close as soon as is feasible. You should focus your attention on your remaining projects, and several additional that will be presented to you and your staff."

"I am eager to serve as ShahnTahr finds appropriate."

"It is important that you provide us with the tools necessary to ensure that the Chehnon population is fit and prepared to accept their role in our society."

"Such has always been my goal. My responsibility is my life. I live for nothing else."

"The future of the society is assured due to the dedication of its people."

"And the spirit of the Shylmahn people lives within us," said BehLahk.

TohPeht was warmed by his conversation with BehLahk. The scientist was sincere. He was in the truest sense the life force of the Shylmahn spirit.

"ShahnTahr will continue to give you the widest latitude in your studies, BehLahk. Bring the projects in question to a close at your discretion, and continue on course with those that focus directly on the future role of Chehnon in the new order."

"Understood." BehLahk stood.

Once BehLahk was gone, TohPeht again cleared his mind in preparation of the meeting to come.

"EsJen," he said. This one would be the most difficult.

EsJen came into the room and stood at the end of the table.

"It has been some time," said TohPeht. "I am glad to see you again, though I am uncertain as to the reason."

"I wish to communicate with ShahnTahr."

"So GahJen has informed me. GahJen is your supervisor."

"I need to communicate with ShahnTahr."

"You provide the information to GahJen. He provides it to me. I provide the information to ShahnTahr."

"Yes, TohPeht. I understand the procedure."

"Then utilize the procedure."

"I have done so. I serve."

"Then the issue is settled." It was as much a question as a statement. TohPeht was deeply concerned with EsJen's struggle, as he sensed that she was indeed struggling: with herself and with her situation.

"I believe that in this instance I can best serve by direct communication," she said.

"Such has been the case on several occasions since our arrival... each at the behest of ShahnTahr. If ShahnTahr again seeks direct interaction, you will be notified... through GahJen. That is clear, is it not?"

"Yes, TohPeht."

"EsJen, do you question ShahnTahr?"

"I do not." The very thought was horrifying.

"Do you doubt me, then? You know that all data from your studies is provided to ShahnTahr. Absolutely nothing is left out. The data you provide is but a small fraction of the information that ShahnTahr is given. ShahnTahr utilizes its entire knowledge base in determining the correct courses of action."

"Yes, TohPeht. I understand this. I do not doubt you. I do not question ShahnTahr's instructions, nor the methods by which I am provided with those instructions."

TohPeht let out a gloomy sigh.

"You believe that you can provide additional data by direct communication."

"Yes, TohPeht."

"It is not your place to make that determination. By pursuing this matter beyond your initial inquiry, you are questioning the abilities of ShahnTahr and the methods that it has established for acquiring and disseminating information and instructions."

"I do not question. I serve."

TohPeht laid his hands flat on the table. He stared down at them, no longer wishing to look at EsJen. He feared for her, feared for what was happening to her. He did not want her to see that fear. It would not help. He knew that she must be as frightened for her sanity as he was, and knowing that he shared in this concern would only make it worse. It was a concern that ShahnTahr also held. Their apprehension was the reason for granting EsJen's request for this meeting. EsJen's behavior was cause for grave concern as to her condition.

This matter would have to be dealt with carefully. They did not want to lose her. EsJen was one of the most valuable researchers they had. She had done more for the knowledge base of the human psyche than any other single individual on the planet.

The sixteen subjects under study by her and her staff spanned the entire human spectrum. Through her research had evolved the current methodology of collection procedures and storage of the human population. Her studies were the building blocks that NehLoc and his people used in the design and structure of their operations.

At this late stage in the research, most of EsJen's wild subjects had been collected and were now in the camps, the projects now complete. TohPeht knew that the issue at hand almost certainly involved the JoSeph project, which included JoSeph and by extension a number of secondary subjects. Through the JoSeph project, EsJen had reached and explored a number of dark and dangerous levels. Throughout the research, she had been under the cautious, watchful scrutiny of ShahnTahr, TohPeht, and GahJen. They had feared for her from the very beginning, but had agreed that the possible return was worth the risk.

The return had been rich indeed. Now, perhaps, their original fears were being realized as well. It had been inevitable that such a degree of submersion into the world of these creatures was bound to have had an impact on her psyche. Her constant exposure to these creatures was playing havoc with her mind.

She had sacrificed herself for her people; willingly, with no regard for own well-being. Here was yet another example of the unfailing Shylmahn spirit. TohPeht would work hard to bring her back.

EsJen's initial request to hold communication with ShahnTahr, which had been included as a part of her report, had been unorthodox but not unheard of. EsJen had been in communication with ShahnTahr on a number of occasions. There had even been an unofficial protocol established for her on those occasions when ShahnTahr advised that she be brought in for conference.

It was her subsequent verbal requests to GahJen that were now of concern to TohPeht. ShahnTahr had conveyed no intention that there be direct communication with her; not following her most recent report nor at any time since then. That matter was ended. The matter did not exist. There was no reason for her to communicate directly with ShahnTahr.

This was further evidence, alarming evidence, that there was something wrong, something unstable, with EsJen's mental condition.

"EsJen, I am reassigning MehnTec to assist you in bringing your remaining projects to a close."

"MehnTec?"

"You have worked well together in the past. Since recovering from his injuries, he has shown interest in working with you again."

EsJen nodded in silent surrender.

"Once done," TohPeht continued, "you are to take supervisory role of a research project under development at the South Continent Reservation."

"I serve as I am needed," said EsJen. There was a strong tone of resignation and acceptance.

"We all do. It is our reason."

EsJen stood in silent submission.

December 12

NehLoc's shuttle landed gently within the walls of the *dahlseht*. He allowed his escort to lead him out of the vehicle. He could hear the sound of human weapons in the distance, and the satisfying sound of the Shylmahn response. The escort moved out ahead of him, in the direction of the tall gray building standing at the landing pad perimeter.

"Status," he stated flatly, upon entering the room. It was sparse; a few tables, bare walls, no windows. Three Shylmahn worked at communications holo-tables, overseeing the conflict with the humans. A fourth Shylmahn sat at a small console in the far corner, in communication with ShahnTahr.

The supervisor hurried over to NehLoc.

"All continues well, NehLoc."

"Of course it does. I would like facts." This skirmish had been a last breath push by the Chehnon. NehLoc had been observing their maneuvers, their reconnaissance, their efforts to consolidate their forces in what was obvious to him to be one final desperate assault on the Shylmahn. NehLoc had been ready.

The *humans* had to have known the Shylmahn would be waiting. Perhaps it was suicide. NehLoc would put nothing past the creatures.

"Loss is minimal, NehLoc. Two dead, three wounded. The west wall outpost was destroyed when its energy pod had to be eliminated. An assault shuttle has been moved in to replace the outpost."

"No other damage?"

"The Chehnon have not been able to come within range of the dahlseht since the attack on the west wall."

NehLoc turned and went back outside. The sun had reached its zenith and was just beginning its fall. At this time of year, this far north, the sun was not in the sky very long. Still, just now, it shone over the wall and did what it could to warm the dahlseht. There was little wind. NehLoc's golden skin glistened faintly and his flesh felt warm.

There was similar action being taken around the world. As the planet turned and darkness slowly swept across the land, as a great Shylmahn hand might sweep a table clear, the last of the feeble resistance by the native creatures of Chehno was crumbling. These petty and often irritating altercations would very quickly become a thing of the past.

The Chehnon were destined to become an integral part of the great new Shylmahn society. NehLoc himself would guide them, shape them, forge them into an effective tool for use by the Shylmahn in the building of this grand new future.

NehLoc understood his role in this future. He had seen it all along. He knew the roles of all those who would help shape that future, for it was a future that he had helped to design and create. He had guided and pushed and manipulated, and served.

NehLoc served. He knew the power of ShahnTahr. He understood its strengths. These, there were many; strengths that had brought the Shylmahn people from the edge of oblivion out to the stars, and on to a new world. These were strengths that would take hold of this new world and make it the home world of the Shylmahn.

NehLoc had seen this. He saw the strengths that were a part of what made ShahnTahr the vital component of Shylmahn society. Unlike his fellows, NehLoc had not been content. Society and the needs of society had not totally blinded him. He had observed. He understood. He respected. But NehLoc was never content. He had also seen the weaknesses of ShahnTahr, and those of the Shylmahn people. These, the weaknesses as well as the strengths, he chose to use. He used the blindness that total obedience and total subjugation to ShahnTahr had created in his people to create and exploit opportunities. He used the blindness of ShahnTahr in its expectation of blind subservience of the Shylmahn people to take advantage of opportunities he himself would create.

NehLoc loved his people. It was for this reason that his actions were necessary. NehLoc served. He was guided by his service to the Shylmahn. His purpose was the same as the purpose of all Shylmahn, and of ShahnTahr: the survival of the Shylmahn people. His role was to serve as an invisible guiding force; a gentle hand, shepherding his people.

NehLoc returned to the shuttle, his escort hurrying ahead of him and opening the access door. Once inside, he ordered the pilot to take them over the battle area. He wanted one last look before returning to headquarters. He would be witness to it. The last gasp of Chehno, the birth of New Shylmah.

Jenzie reached the trees. Dusty gray ash, shaken from the leaves, encircled him like a fog. He hurriedly waved the others in and under cover. Carolyn rushed past, then Danny and Terry. They ran twenty yards on before stopping in a small clearing, exhausted and unable to go further. Jenzie slumped down against a fallen log. Overhead, above the treetops, he could hear alien ships hurrying to and from the alien city in the distance, unhindered by the humans, unconcerned by any human threat.

"Where's Ben?" asked Danny. There was desperation in his voice. He started up, but Terry held him back, pulled him down.

They had all seen Ben Soo go down. Danny had seen him go down. He had screamed then, tried to run to him, but a second blast had knocked Danny back and off his feet.

"He's gone, Danny," said Jenzie. Danny looked blankly at him. There was nothing on the boy's face, no comprehension, nothing at all. Then, as Jenzie was about to turn away, uncomfortable and uncertain of what to do or say, he saw a shimmer in Danny's eyes. "I'm sorry, son," he said, and then he did turn away.

There was only the four of them left, now. Terry sat next to Danny, holding him by the arm, trying to comfort the boy. Billy the Kid was dead; and the others. Carolyn sat a good distance away, her back to a large tree, staring away, a good distance further still. She held her rifle across her knees. It was the only weapon they had left.

Jenzie shut his eyes to all of it. It was over. They had nothing left to give.

What were they to do now? Where were they to go? It would be dark soon. It was cold now, and it would get a lot colder. They couldn't start a fire here. They would be seen, even here under the trees. They would have to move on.

Maybe they should surrender. Sooner or later, they would have to go to one of the labor camps or reservations anyway...

"Let's move out," said Carolyn, standing. "We have to put some distance between us and them before we make camp."

"It's over... isn't it?" asked Terry, looking at Jenzie. Perhaps he saw the surrender in Jenzie's eyes.

"Never over." Jenzie stood. Whatever his thoughts, he wasn't ready to speak them aloud.

"What are we supposed to do? Look at us! I don't even have a weapon."

"We rest and we regroup," said Jenzie.

"Regroup?" Terry broke into a laugh.

"Come on," said Carolyn. "I don't want to walk these woods in the dark."

"Walk where, Carolyn? Where do we go?" Terry stayed put, still holding Danny by the arm. Danny watched and listened in silence.

"Where it's safe to make a fire. I'm cold and I'm tired."

"Maybe it's time we gave up."

She turned on him as if she would strike him. "I will not give up. I will never give up."

Terry let her words fade away before lifting his gaze to look directly at Carolyn.

"You don't even have any bullets for that thing," he said, nodding toward the rifle she held.

Carolyn shook angrily, tossed the rifle aside. "I will fight them with rocks and sticks, with my bare hands... I don't need a rifle to fight."

At that moment, it didn't matter if the others followed. Carolyn left the clearing. Jenzie took two steps toward the others and pulled Danny to his feet. Danny started after Carolyn. Terry looked up at Jenzie, frowned, finally held a hand up to the aging uncle. Jenzie pulled him up, and they followed after the other two.

Bril and Jason stood on the ridge top, looking east, out across the Sound to the mainland. Bright lights put a glow to the low clouds far in the distance, off towards Seattle. Construction went on day and night. The world was being rebuilt in the Shylmahn image.

There was nothing but bad news over the short-wave these days. The Shillies were on a worldwide offensive. The last, desperate attacks by the humans were failing. The only good news coming over the short-wave was that there was any short-wave activity at all. At least there were still people out there, people not in the camps.

Jason continued to hope that the scientists would come up with something. A magic bullet; a bacteria that would kill the Shillies but not hurt humans; a super weapon that could break through the Shillie defenses. Something...

Jason and Bril both turned at the sound of Kenneth climbing up to join them. Reaching the top, he turned and pointed silently to the west, behind them.

The clouds were glowing red and violet.

The Olympic Peninsula was burning.

Chapter Twenty Two

December 14

Shillie eyes were everywhere. The day after Joseph had begun digging the hole in the shower room floor the Shillie guards had come to let him know that they knew. They made no attempt to fill in his feeble beginnings at a tunnel, but warned him that sensors would pick up the movement should they use such an escape, and they would be eliminated by the guard probes as they emerged on the other side.

Eliminated.

He tried building a rope bridge up in the treetops, hoping to rise above any tracking devices, but was again warned off, this time by one of the probes moving up from below and hovering silently beside him. The implied threat was perfectly clear.

When Joseph and Barbara tried to lay in ambush of the Shillie transport bringing in the regularly scheduled supply delivery, the delivery simply did not arrive. They were forced to ration their remaining stores until the next delivery, which did arrive, on schedule, the next week.

Unless something happened to alter their circumstances, it seemed they were going to remain where they were until the Shylmahn chose to move them.

Joseph rolled out of bed and dressed. It was damn cold. Stepping out of the trailer, he saw that it had snowed overnight. There was a thin layer of white over everything.

"Freakin' great," he mumbled, and jogged across the camp to the restroom. Inside was as cold as outside. As he was taking care of business, suspecting the Shillies were watching even that, he heard a noise from the gate.

This was not the day, and certainly not the time, for the supply delivery. Looking through the air vent set high in the left wall, he saw two Shillie vehicles coming down the dirt road from the gate to their camp. One was a small two-seater, the other a small transport able to carry six Shillies in the back.

Definitely not the supply delivery.

Joseph moved to the door and opened it just enough to see the trailer. Barbara was looking through the window, first toward the gate, then toward him. She moved out of sight.

The vehicles came into the camp and stopped. The passenger of the two-seater climbed out and stood in the middle of the clearing as the back of the transport emptied. Three Shillies moved towards the trailer, stopping beside the door. The others moved toward the shower and restroom facility, stopping just outside.

"Bar-Ba-Ra. Please step out of the trailer," said the Shylmahn leader. He turned then to the shower and restroom building, "Jo-Seph. Come out now."

"Son of a bitch," Joseph whispered. "I'm busy!" he called out.

"Do not complicate," said the Shylmahn. "Come out."

"I said, I'm busy!"

"They will go in for you." The Shylmahn nodded to his three companions.

"Spying on us isn't enough for you anymore? Now you gotta hold my hand while I pee?"

"I will not argue."

Both the Shylmahn by the trailer and the restroom started forward, pulling their stun sticks from their belts.

"All right, all right," said Joseph and he went quickly to the door and stepped outside. "I'm finished."

He saw that Barbara had also come out on her own.

"What do you want?" Joseph asked.

"This project is ended."

"Yeah? Great. I'm outta here."

"You are to be eliminated."

Eliminated.

Joseph forced a smile.

"And about time, too. You bastards have been threatening me with that one for months. I'm tired of listening to your whining."

One of the Shylmahn standing behind him prodded Joseph with a stun stick and he collapsed to his knees. He had to reach out with both hands to stop from falling on his face.

"A little torture, first?" Joseph's words were so slurred he was almost unintelligible.

At that moment, a vehicle pulled into the gate and started down the road toward the camp. The leader held a hand out for his team to stand by. One of the escort moved to stand between the leader and the incoming vehicle.

The Shylmahn passenger car stopped and EsJen climbed out. *Very good. I am in time.*

She nodded curtly. "Tyh Muhtla. Bohn gohtrah."

"Come to watch?" asked Joseph.

EsJen couldn't understand his slurred words. She ignored him in any case, and instead approached the Shylmahn leader.

"Chuhn mes kehopt fe bohn." *These two are to come with me.*

"Chuhn mes kehta kahropt." *They are to be eliminated.*

"They are to come with me."

"The project is ended."

"And I would know. It was my project. I am to deliver them to BehLahk."

"Their elimination has been ordered."

"BehLahk has the authority to rescind such an order. He has done so." She stood her ground, staring the squad leader down. She said nothing more, and neither did he. She did not know who he was, but he knew of her and he certainly knew of BehLahk.

The members of his team began shuffling about nervously. By his statements and his actions, their leader seemed to be going beyond his position. He could not question EsJen's authority. She had stated that BehLahk wanted these humans. Therefore, they could not eliminate them.

The Shylmahn leader turned to his squad. "Bind them," he said.

EsJen returned to her vehicle and waited. Once Joseph and Barbara had been placed in the back seat, she started the engine and drove out of the camp. She did not acknowledge the Shylmahn squad leader.

Joseph had understood only enough of the Shylmahn conversation to know that EsJen had thrown her weight around to get them out of there. Barbara hadn't understood a single word, but she had also figured that much.

EsJen's hands were trembling. She drove without thinking what she was doing or where she was going.

There had been no time. There had simply been no time. She had been left with no other option but to act, then hope that she could clean up the mess afterward.

Not a Shylmahn course of action.

What am I going to do?

She must report her actions to TohPeht, of course. But what could she say? What justification was there? The project was ended. That was a fact. Due to the volatility of the situations surrounding the subjects within the project, the elimination of all subjects was ordered. This too was a fact.

There had been no time to request a postponement for review. She had only become aware of the order a few hours earlier.

She knew also that no postponement would ever have been granted. The order was valid and fully proper. There was no justification for her actions. She had been wrong in any event. To arbitrarily countermand an order for elimination, to out and out lie...

She should take them back. She should return them for elimination. It was the right thing to do. It was the only thing to do.

It is the Shylmahn thing to do.

Take them back, assist in the execution of the order, then report her misbehavior to TohPeht.

EsJen slowed the vehicle. Finding a wide shoulder on the road, she pulled over and stopped. Joseph and Barbara sat quietly in the back seat, watching, uncertain. EsJen pulled her hands free from the steering wheel and turned off the engine.

"Come closer," she said, shifting about and reaching over the seat. "I will undo your bindings."

Joseph slid forward and offered up his tied wrists. "Thanks," he said. At least he was able to get the word out without slobbering on himself.

EsJen began unfastening the bindings. "I will take you as far as I can, but I do not have much time."

"We're going to the island."

"No," said EsJen, flatly. "You cannot."

"I'll get my family out and we'll leave." His hands free, Joseph untied Barbara. He felt a strange hollowness in his stomach.

"The project is ended."

"So I heard."

EsJen had turned to the front and was looking through the windshield of the alien vehicle. She gripped the steering wheel; a yellow glow shone from the dash panel.

Barbara held onto Joseph's arm as soon as her hands were free. "Joseph?" she whispered.

"EsJen?" Joseph leaned forward. "EsJen, what's going on?"

The project is ended...

EsJen took two deep breaths. The yellow glow on the dash shifted to pale blue and the vehicle started. She continued to hold tightly to the wheel, until the muscles in her fingers grew sore and she forced herself to relax her grip.

Joseph began to feel cold all over. The realization of what they had been telling him began to seep in.

The project is ended...

"My family," Joseph mumbled to himself, then spoke out sharply. "My family."

EsJen continued to stare out the windshield. Her words were precise and formal.

"You and the other members of your family pose an inordinate instability risk to the planned societal structure of this world."

"What the hell does that mean?"

"Once the project was ended, the order for your elimination was inevitable."

"EsJen."

"I should have seen it." EsJen lowered her head. Her golden hair covered her face. "I did see it. I simply ignored what was obvious."

"They have nothing to do with this!"

"That is not true."

"Take us to the island," said Barbara. "Please."

"I cannot."

Joseph slid back into his seat. He spoke now without emotion. "As close as you can, then."

"There is nothing you can do, JoSeph." said EsJen. "I was wrong to help you."

"You saved our lives," said Barbara. "How can that be wrong?"

"It was not Shylmahn. I was not Shylmahn."

"It was human."

"That is a bad thing for me to be." EsJen stared at the lights on the dash, which continued to indicate the status of the vehicle. It was ready to go.

EsJen wasn't ready. She didn't think she would ever be ready.

"EsJen," said Joseph. "EsJen, you are my friend."

December 23

Much of the Olympic Peninsula had burned, despite the wet weather and the huge amount of moisture in the vegetation. It was Shylmahn work, then. Joseph could not imagine why they would to this, but the evidence was all around him.

Some of the moist ash was days old. Some of the burnt out husks of the grand, old trees were smoldering, as if set to blaze within the last few hours, perhaps as recent as the night before. The contrast of black charcoal against the bright white snow from the pre-dawn flurry was blinding in the midmorning sun. It was the second snowfall of the year, and the season hadn't even started. Joseph feared they were in for a long, cold winter.

"There," said Barbara. The two of them had been following the narrow road that followed the shoreline. Barbara had stopped and was looking down the slope toward the water. Joseph stood beside her. He could see a small, planked dock jutting out twenty feet from the bank. Looking up and out across the water, he saw Bril's tiny island as a shadow on the horizon.

"No boat," said Joseph, looking back to the dock.

"We'll have to find one, then."

Joseph raised his hand to his brow to shade his eyes. He could see nothing. The island was too far off to see any detail with the naked eye.

Barbara suddenly grabbed at Joseph's arm and pulled the two of them down together. "Look," she whispered.

There was movement down the slope, halfway to the dock. Someone was walking through the trees.

"Hello," came a voice from behind them. Turning quickly, Joseph came face to face with Carolyn, an old hunting rifle cradled across her forearm.

"Damn it, Carolyn. You scared the hell out of me."

She nodded to the activity below. "We have a fire."

"Is that safe?" asked Barbara.

"The forest is burning, Barbara."

Despite the comment, the camp was fairly well hidden beneath an unburned cluster of trees. Joseph and Barbara sat close to the fire and Terry handed each of them a cup of tea.

"It's not strong, but it is hot."

"Thanks," said Joseph. "I'm near freezing."

Carolyn sat opposite the fire. She looked tired. More than tired, she looked empty; empty of spirit, of heart... of energy. There was little left of the intensity that had been the body and soul of Joseph's little sister. What fight remained looked forced.

"What are you doing here?" asked Joseph.

"Waiting," she looked over her shoulder, toward Bril's island. "For a boat. Jenzie and Danny went searching."

"They've been gone three days," said Terry.

"What about the rest of your people?"

"There are none."

Joseph held tightly to the cup in his hands. "I'm sorry."

"We all knew the odds."

"Doesn't make me any less sorry."

Carolyn looked thoughtfully at Joseph, finally nodded in acknowledgement. Terry stood and walked toward Carolyn. He picked up the hunting rifle resting beside her.

"I'll stand watch," he said, started from the camp.

A strange mix of smoke and steam rolled through the campsite. The wind was light but constant, and the whorls of gray and silver swam continually through the trees and among the group huddled around the fire.

Joseph didn't ask, perhaps he didn't think to ask, but Carolyn saw the way he looked around them, at the destruction, at what had once been one of the most beautiful places on Earth.

"The forests here were full of people like us," she said. "I guess the Shillies decided it was time to come in and clean us out."

"Why fire?" asked Barbara. "If they're really serious about it, why not just level the place and be done with it? They certainly have the means."

"Fire is a great cleanser," said Carolyn. "It flushes the rebels out, takes away their hiding places, and in a matter of months green is poking up through the ashes and the animals are coming back. In the thickest forests, where fire hasn't reached in a long time, the flames burn a little hotter, and the destruction may be more complete, but even there life eventually returns."

Barbara set her jaw tight. "The fires force the rebels out—"

"And they are killed."

"Eliminated," Joseph mumbled.

Carolyn nodded grimly. "Eliminated."

"Anything from Bril?" he asked.

"No. Fire there, too. I can still see the smoke." Carolyn pulled her coat tightly around her.

The project is ended, thought Joseph.

"They could still be all right," said Barbara.

Carolyn almost managed a chuckle. "I wouldn't want to be the first Shillie setting foot on that island looking to find out."

Joseph had to grin at that, but in spite of the image of Bril lightly tossing Shillies aside, left and right, waving an axe like some berserker, the thought of what may wait for them on the island lay heavy over the camp.

He cleared his throat and spoke against the sudden silence. "What brings you back here? I mean, bringing your friends here?"

"What few of us are left?" Carolyn turned an eye to Terry walking up near the road. "For some of us, the fighting is over, one way or another. For some, we just need a place to rest. Bril's island may not have been the best choice."

"We'll soon see."

"If Bril needs help, I'm glad we showed up when we did." Carolyn tried another smile, but it didn't look like much. Joseph moved around to be close to her.

"You okay?"

"Yeah." She took a shaky breath. "I'm fine. Did I tell you it was good to see you? I don't think I did."

"Good to see you, too."

Carolyn laid a hand heavily on his arm. "I really need to stop for a while."

Jenzie and Danny returned with a boat just before dawn. Putting six aboard made for a tight fit, and an unstable ride, but Jenzie hadn't been expecting company. They managed to push out from shore, leaving their few scant supplies behind, and started for the island.

Jenzie was an old man now. He had always had the air of the wise, elderly uncle, but Joseph knew him to be only in his forties. Always in the past, he had looked in his forties; healthy, strong, and vigorous. Now he was old. Old and tired and without hope.

Danny was also very different from what Joseph remembered. He was no longer the bright-eyed young rebel. The teenage boy had seen too much; he had lived an ugly life and every day of that life shown now in those dull, weary eyes.

Carolyn and Terry sat together at the back of the boat. Joseph remembered Terry as the romantic. He had been the bard of the group, as well as its conscience. He had been with Ben Soo since the very beginning. Ben had told Joseph that when he first formed the group, he had sought Terry out, feeling strongly that his band had to have someone like him if it had any chance of surviving the dark times ahead.

Joseph wondered now whether Terry would have stayed with the group if Carolyn hadn't joined them. She had been his opposite in every way, yet he had fallen head over heels in love with her. While he may very well have stayed with Ben in any case, once Carolyn came into the picture, the poor guy never had a chance. He would have followed her to the ends of the earth and then into hell.

So he had. He sat by her side now, the idealistic spirit torn slowly from him till there was only Terry. That force within him that Ben had felt so vital to the group was gone. He was hard now, and dark. The soul from which originated the ballads and the folk songs was gone. That beat up guitar was nowhere to be seen. Looking at him now, Joseph hoped that someday, if they survived this, Terry would regain that inner light; that he would once again see the world as so few were able. He wanted Terry to sing again. The world was going to need that.

Joseph could smell the wet charcoal in the thick, black mist that rolled out from the island to meet them. As they drew nearer, the chill that he had felt since beginning the crossing seeped deeper, reaching finally into his bones. The cloud that lay over the island was heavy with moisture, soaking everyone as soon as the small boat entered the lagoon. Joseph was shivering.

It was the same island, but a different world. It was an alien world of gray and black. Many of the trees were now bare, black snags rising up like spires to the dark gray sky. The ground was black, and hovering just above it, barely moving, was slate-gray fog, thick with ash and moisture. Just above the spires, low clouds rolled over the island.

Bril stood waiting for them, thirty feet up the hill, defiant, his rifle ready. He watched in silence as the boat reached the shore and Joseph and the others climbed out. Joseph and Carolyn went to him alone first, the others choosing to wait by the boat until they knew what was happening.

"Is everyone all right?" Joseph asked.

"Alive," said Bril. He had changed, as well. He must feel it too, then; the alienness of the world they found themselves in. Such a thing would affect Bril more than anyone. He looked up, at the clouds, at the sky. "They won't land. We didn't even see them. We heard them, but we didn't see them."

"They'll come," said Carolyn.

"Let's go inside," said Joseph.

Bril nodded, turned and started up toward the house. It looked undamaged, but was coated in a layer of smoke and ash. Kathryn and Kenneth stood on the porch. Jason watched from the open door to Bunker One. He was wet, and covered in soot.

Chapter Twenty Three

Christmas Morning

Joseph woke before dawn. He had spent the night clean and dry. The house was warm. Coming to the front of the house, he found Danny and Jenzie asleep in the living room. Kathryn mumbled a quiet good morning when he came into the kitchen, and she poured him a cup of coffee. He took it and went back through the living room and out onto the porch. There stood Bril.

The clouds were gone. The sky was a clear morning gray. Puffs of fog and smoke lay about amongst the burnt trees, rolling slowly into the clearing below them.

"Do you hear that?" asked Bril.

Joseph turned his head to listen, but could only hear the faint breeze. "No."

"Birds," Bril almost managed a smile. "Not all the island was burned, you know. You can see a green band right there, and there's a good stand just a few hundred yards over there, and another back beyond the ridge."

"That's good."

"Damn right, it's good. It means the island will be back in no time. The trees and brush will seed. Meantime, the animals have places to ride things out until the island is healthy again."

Joseph sipped at the hot coffee. *Same island, different world.*

Bril gave a heavy sigh, almost as if he had heard Joseph's thought.

"I guess they'll be coming soon..."

Joseph wrapped his hands around the cup. "Yes."

Bril was staring down at his own cup. He nodded thoughtfully.

"I didn't really believe it, you know. I thought I did, but... despite all my planning and preparation... oh, I probably figured they wouldn't want to bother with this crummy little speck."

"It's part of some prime real estate, Bril," said Joseph. "Mostly, though, it's us."

Bril managed to grimace and grin at the same time. "The Britton family managed to make a stink out there, eh?"

"We got noticed."

Bril looked away from Joseph, away from the house. He looked down toward the cove. "I know we're not going be able to fight them off. Not for long."

"Sure we will," said Joseph, too quickly. He stopped then, set his cup on the porch rail and stuffed his hands into his coat pockets. It was very cold out.

Bril said nothing, didn't turn around.

"No," said Joseph. "No, I don't see how. If we become too much trouble, they'll just wipe the island clean. I've seen them do it a hundred times."

Bril continued to look out at the scene laid out before him. He finished his coffee. "That's about what I thought."

Joseph and Jason stood halfway up the slope, watching Carolyn walk slowly up from the cove. Jenzie, Danny and Terry were in the small boat, heading out.

Carolyn stopped when she reached her brothers. She looked back at her departing friends, already halfway out of the cove. She turned then again to her brothers, but spoke without actually looking at them.

"I'm sending them out to make ready for our trip out of here," said Carolyn.

"Good idea," said Jason, giving her the lie.

Carolyn looked defensively at Jason, then at Joseph. Joseph turned away from her gaze, but Jason returned it.

"We can't have the family wandering blindly around the Northwest asking about the underground railroad, now can we?" she asked.

"No. I guess not," said Joseph.

She surrendered then under Jason's gaze.

"It's not their fight," she said sharply. "Damn it, I can't get Bril to listen to reason."

"Neither can I," Jason said softly.

"But we could get the family out. We can have them in Arizona inside a month."

"He's not leaving the island, Carolyn," said Jason. "And none of us has it in us to leave him here."

"So this is it, then." Carolyn looked back toward the boat, nearly to the mouth of the cove, then up the hill at the house. "What a load of crap."

Kathryn hurried Susan, Little Daryl and Sharon to the back of the house and safely into the tunnels. Elizabeth followed after, still not in any shape, physically or mentally, to be of any help against the Shylmahn. She could best help by staying with the children, and along with Kathryn serve as the last line of defense at the family's last position of retreat. Bril and young Peter took up position at the tunnel entrance within the house itself.

Daryl, Jason and Kenneth took their positions at the slotted openings in Bunker One. From here, they had a sweeping view of the slope below the house most of the way to the water. They could also protect the front of the house and, if necessary, could move back into the tunnel and finally to where Kathryn and the others waited.

Joseph slid into the foxhole near the tree line down by the cove. Carolyn and Barbara were already there, watching the entrance to the cove and the main trails that led into the woods across the clearing.

Carolyn tapped Joseph's arm and pointed toward the trail running along the shore, just inside the trees. A Shylmahn probe the size of a volleyball, hovering eight feet above the ground, was working its way along the trail toward the clearing.

"They are all over the island," she whispered.

"We had guards like that at the camp," said Barbara. "Maybe they plan on keeping us prisoners."

Carolyn groaned low. "I doubt it. I've seen this a couple of times. The Shillies are getting smart. They send these things in first to map out the situation and attack anything resembling humans. It makes things a lot easier for the Shillies when they do finally come in."

"What kind of sensors do they have?" asked Joseph. "Those we saw were pretty sophisticated."

"Some are really intelligent, but even the drones have a full range of sensors, and they're sensitive. That one there is listening to us, registering our location. If it had a clean shot, it'd be firing at us."

"Then what the hell are we doing talking?" asked Joseph in a harsh whisper.

"Don't sweat it," she answered calmly. "They've a good idea where everyone is."

They could see Bunker One near the top of the slope, on the other side of the clearing, and the house beside it. There was a probe near the bunker, and another one coming up over the top of the house.

Carolyn continued to watch the probe across from them working its way into the clearing.

"Okay." She shifted position. "The bunker is immobile, but defensible, and it can protect the front of the house. Our own defenses here are weak, but we can move. I say we do some hit and run, maybe confuse them a little."

"Sounds good to me," said Barbara.

"Certainly," Joseph agreed. "My feet are freezing."

Carolyn grinned, turned, and took aim at the probe. She fired. The probe spun about, sparked, returned fire twice as its weapon swung about to face the foxhole. It was off target and tiny pins of light struck the ground in front of Carolyn. She fired again and the probe came apart, pieces flying in an expanding circle and falling to the ground.

"Let's go," Carolyn called out, climbing out of the foxhole and rushing across the clearing in the direction of the destroyed probe. Joseph and Barbara scrambled after her, weapons and ammo in their folded arms. Carolyn reached the foxhole on the other side of the clearing, moved around behind it and waved the others down into it.

"I'm going up slope," she said. "You take out the next probe that shows itself, then follow after me. By then, I should be on the other side. We'll run this a few times, see what happens."

Then Carolyn was gone.

"Elizabeth, what are you doing here?" Daryl asked as his sister rushed into the bunker from the tunnel.

Kathryn rushed in frantically after her. "She got away from me," she said.

"I'm staying here," said Elizabeth. She walked to the front wall and planted herself at one of the view slots. Each slot was four inches in height, eighteen inches wide.

Jason gave Elizabeth a hurried study, then turned and spoke to Kathryn. "It's all right. You go back to the hold. Be ready for us. We're likely to be coming in fast."

Kathryn nodded and disappeared back into the tunnel.

Those in the bunker could hear shots from down near the cove, but other than a brief glimpse of a hovering probe, they had seen nothing. As the waiting wore on, Daryl grew more and more anxious.

"Damn, damn, damn." He moved back and forth before his view slot, looking for some activity, some sign of the Shylmahn.

"Patience," said Kenneth.

"Listen to the voice of experience," Jason told Daryl. If anyone had experience at patience, and at fighting the Shylmahn, it would be Kenneth.

There was the sound of another rifle shot. Still they saw nothing.

"I can't see anything," said Daryl.

"It'll come," said Jason. "They won't have all the fun."

"They might be getting killed, and all we can do is sit here and listen to it."

"You just watch your sector," said Kenneth. "If you leave your position, the Shillies could walk in on us and we'd never see 'em."

"I know, I know," Daryl groaned as two more shots were heard.

"There's Carolyn," said Jason. He could see her making her way across the clearing and into a small stand of unburned trees on the other side. Kenneth and Daryl didn't have as clear a view, their own defensive arcs not directly encompassing that same area, but they did manage to swing around and steal a quick glance.

"She made it," said Kenneth. *Go, Carolyn...*

"Where are the others?" asked Daryl.

"Looks like they split up."

Jason saw a probe move slowly into view and glide gently across his target area. He calmly shifted his weapon into position and fired one shot, paused, then fired one more. He relaxed.

"What are you shooting at?" asked Daryl.

"Probe."

"D'you get it?"

"Well, yeah," said Jason. He winked.

A shadow passed across the front of the bunker.

"Uh, oh," Kenneth mumbled under his breath. Another probe was directly above them.

Jason looked for Carolyn, thinking at first that she might be in a position to shoot down the probe. He didn't see her. Elizabeth started toward the door, but Jason caught her movement out of the corner of his eye, reached out and pulled her back down.

"No you don't, Sis. You stay right here with us."

"Fight is out there."

"We're doing just fine from in here."

"*They* are out there!"

"Yes they are."

Elizabeth glared hard and cold, shook free and turned back to the view slot. Her hands gripped hard at the sill. There were more shots coming from far down the slope. Across the clearing, there were pins of light tracing through the trees as probes fired at targets that those in the bunker couldn't see.

"Everyone seems busy but me," mumbled Daryl. Kenneth and Jason only smiled. They had to smile. Smiling kept their nerves in check, just as Daryl's incessant complaining served to keep his own from taking control of him.

Kenneth fired suddenly at two probes coming down over the top of the house. He caught then a shimmer of sunlight on metal at the far corner of the house. It quickly vanished.

"I think there's a smart probe at the far side of the house."

Jason had the best view of the area beyond the house, though the angle was beyond his sector. He gave a quick look. "I don't see it."

"Where'd these things come from?" asked Daryl. "They didn't have these things."

"Shillies are inventive," said Jason.

"I see it. I see it!" cried Elizabeth, though her angle of vision was worse than Jason's.

"You watch for it," he said. Maybe it would keep her busy. "Tell me when it sticks its nose out again."

"Yes."

All fell quiet. The minutes began to drag on, until even Kenneth began to grow restless. Once the probes had finished scouring the island and reported their findings, their masters would be coming. The last batch that had come through had probably moved in from the quiet areas of the island to support those here.

"I see it!" said Elizabeth. Everyone whirled about to look at the corner of the house, but there was nothing there to see.

"Slippery little bugger, isn't he?" said Jason, shifting back around to stand vigil over his own defensive arc.

They waited. The sun moved to its highest point in the sky, but it was still cold. Even in the best of weather, the Northwest didn't have much daylight in late December. The sun barely made it above the trees, and it never stayed there long. It was already beginning its slide back into the forest, though a little more visible now through stands of bare, blackened trunks.

Jason turned to a flash of movement in time to see Carolyn scurrying along the tree line. Pins of light raced almost invisibly towards her from some place beside the bunker.

"It's still with us," said Jason, "moved down next to the bunker."

"I saw," said Kenneth. "Did it get her?"

"I don't think so."

No one saw Elizabeth slide from her place at the view slot and edge toward the door. It wasn't until the door was opening that Daryl sensed movement, turning in time to see his sister about to go outside. He cried out as he hurried to stop her, but she was out before he could reach her.

A pin of light struck her in the shoulder. She spun about and rushed at the source. Outside with her now, Daryl grabbed at Elizabeth again but missed. Jason, scrambling after the two of them, pulled Daryl down as pins of light flew at them from across the clearing. From inside the bunker, Kenneth was firing at the probe that had moved just into the clearing from the blackened trees directly opposite the bunker. He managed to destroy it, but not before Daryl was hit in the leg.

Elizabeth struck at the probe beside the bunker with her bare hands. It bounced wildly about in the air, chaotically firing pins of light all around the clearing in front of the bunker and the house. Daryl cried out and fell, hit again, and began crawling toward the trees. The probe glided back into position only to be struck again by Elizabeth before backing a safe distance away. Jason, lying out in the open, fired two quick shots and the probe swept erratically to its left, skimming across the top of the bunker and falling in a heap on the other side. Elizabeth ran into the trees behind the bunker, her shoulder colored in red.

Jason, afraid to move, afraid to draw the attention of any other probes that may still be around, looked cautiously over to where Daryl had crawled and was now laying. He couldn't tell if Daryl was alive or dead.

He heard Kenneth fire three quick shots. Twisting around and looking behind him, he saw one probe fall and another come into view from around the corner of the house. With Kenneth continuing the cover fire, Jason jumped up and ran back into the bunker, closing the door behind him. He stalked silently back to his view slot.

"Where's Daryl? Where's Liz?" Kenneth's attention was torn between the view from his position and Jason, who was now sullenly gazing out beyond the bunker. "Jason?"

Jason turned to Kenneth, and the two looked almost calmly at each other. Jason turned away first, returning his attention to his post. Kenneth turned back then, carefully studied the terrain outside.

§

The sun shone from the west, shining directly on the slope and the house. For Carolyn, Joseph and Barbara, if they were fortunate enough to be in the sunshine and out of the breeze, it probably felt warm. Inside Bunker One, though, the day had turned from cool to cold.

Looking out, Jason saw the sun's rays shining through the forests of bare, black tree trunks in the burnt out areas of the wood, and a shimmering of damp green in the few stands of trees nearby that had been untouched by the fire. Patches of white snow still lay in the shaded areas.

He had tried once to go out for Daryl. Several probes had come out of hiding, firing at him as he stepped outside the door. He had been struck once in the arm with one of their pins. It still felt like fire.

But for that brief moment of activity, it had been quiet most of the afternoon. Jason frowned, struggled to ignore his throbbing arm.

"Sitting here is getting us nowhere."

"You tried going out," said Kenneth.

Jason looked back toward the opening leading into the tunnel.

"I could go back through the tunnel," he said, thinking aloud. "From the house, I could make it into the woods, make my way around to him."

Kenneth said nothing. Jason was talking out of misplaced guilt, and way out of character. If only he could have reached Daryl. If only he could have gotten to him and brought him back into the bunker.

The house was being watched as closely as the bunker. He would have as little chance reaching Daryl from there as from here.

Kenneth stiffened. He had twisted about and was looking out and to the right, toward the sky and the sun.

"Shillie fighter coming in."

"That's it, then."

They both knew what the likely target was. Kenneth was already moving to the back of the bunker. Jason followed after him. He stopped to turn around and pull closed the thick door that separated the bunker from the tunnel.

Joseph watched the fighter pass low over the island. It fired once at the bunker and moved off, possibly to another target on the afternoon schedule, perhaps somewhere on the peninsula.

The explosion left the front of the bunker completely demolished, with a thick fog of dust and ash and smoke laying over it. As the fog thinned, Joseph saw within it broken concrete, splintered timber and dark soil. The only movement was the settling of the rubble, and smoke and dust pushing slowly away from the scene.

Carolyn gave him a smack on the shoulder and turned his attention back to the sky. Two alien shuttles were coming in from the same direction as the fighter, but from a much lower altitude and apparently with plans on landing.

The lead shuttle passed over the cove and turned to the north, disappearing beyond the trees. The second came directly over Joseph's position down near the water, Carolyn and Barbara hunching down low beside him. It moved slowly up the slope and landed in front of the house. Smoke and dust continued to hang over the remnants of Bunker One to the left of the shuttle.

"We have to get up there," said Carolyn, climbing out of the foxhole. "We gotta shoot any Shillie that comes out of that ship!"

Joseph and Barbara found themselves once again hurrying after Carolyn. They hadn't gotten more than a quarter of the way up the slope though, before they found themselves in another firefight with three probes rushing down to meet them. They made it to cover, Carolyn rolling frantically from one side to the other, cussing and spitting and holding onto her leg. There was very little blood, but the flesh beneath the smoking denim was seared.

Joseph and Barbara tried to help, but Carolyn angrily pushed them away.

"Get up there! Get up there!"

"Bril is waiting for them," said Joseph, but he knew that Bril wouldn't be able to hold them off for long.

"We have the mobility. We have to keep the fight out here."

Carolyn had rolled onto her belly and was trying to stand up. Another energy pin struck the ground in front of her, missing her only because Barbara managed to wing the probe just as it fired.

Joseph and Barbara continued to provide cover for Carolyn as she made her way, stumbling and limping forward, through the trees beside the open slope. One of the three probes followed after her, staying far inside the trees and twenty feet up. The other two stayed near Joseph and Barbara until Carolyn was near enough to the shuttle to pose a serious threat, then broke away and hurried after her.

Joseph jumped from cover and fired after them, striking the probe that Barbara had hit earlier. It spun about, rose high into the air and disappeared up over the treetops. The other was directly over Carolyn within seconds, darting back and forth, calculating and recalculating an accurate shot. Carolyn hugged close to the nearest tree, moved around it and fired at the shuttle, then rushed to the next tree and repeated.

Meanwhile, Joseph and Barbara had gotten close enough to begin firing at the open shuttle door. They saw movement then on the front porch of the house. There was a shadow at the door. The Shillies were already inside.

Bril thought he was ready for them, but hadn't expected those flying probes to be able to move so quickly inside the house. He knew there were at least three Shillies in cover near the door, but couldn't take the time to consider how to deal with them. There were two probes firing at him and Peter, moving so damn fast in and out of cover that they couldn't get a clean shot.

"Open up on 'em, son!" he said, emptying one rifle, then picking up the shotgun, hoping to at least knock one out of the air. Beside him, little Peter took careful, quick shots with his .22, once hearing the *ping* as one of the slugs struck the casing of one of the fast-dodging probes.

"Save the twenty-two for the Shillies, boy! Use the Winchester!"

Peter took the 30-30 and pulled the stock snug against the shoulder. The sharp kick hurt; he knew he'd really feel it later. He pushed the lever down and back, struggled to get a bead on the fast-moving targets, fired and missed, tried again.

"They're too fast, Daddy!" he cried out.

"Just keep 'em hoppin', son! You're doing great!"

There were splinters flying from the bullet holes flowering suddenly in the wood paneling, and the air was filling with smoke from the rifle discharges and the smoldering of the energy pin strikes in the walls and floor. Bril pulled the trigger again, and the shotgun blast knocked one of the probes back against the front wall. It spun about and rushed at Bril and Peter, coming at them so quickly that neither could get off a shot. Once directly between them, it began pummeling them with the energy pins. Peter struck at it with the butt of his rifle, knocking it back.

"Into the tunnel, boy!" Bril cried. Peter took another swing, but the probe moved safely back, continuing to fire the energy pins with devastating accuracy.

Kenneth came rushing from the tunnel behind them. He fired three shots with the pistol and the probe exploded in the middle of the room. Shards of metal filled the air, digging into the walls, floor and furniture. One of the Shillies stepped out into the middle of the room, and slowly and quietly crumpled to the floor.

Kenneth knelt between Bril and Peter. They were both down. He could give them only a quick glance before the second probe hurtled toward him, with the other two Shillies showing movement as well. Kenneth concentrated on the probe, emptying his pistol and then picking up Bril's rifle and swinging it like a bat as it reached him. He turned and ran back into the tunnel, stumbling and regaining his footing. The probe followed, with the Shillies following more cautiously behind.

Jason couldn't move. He was buried beneath concrete and heavy timbers. From his position, with only his head and one shoulder exposed, he could see where Daryl lay.

Bunker One, and the mouth of the tunnel that ran back to the hold where Kathryn kept Daryl's family safe, had collapsed. He guessed that Kenneth had made it far enough into the tunnel that he hadn't been trapped. He was probably with Bril and Peter.

Fight on, kid. That little guy in your head is full a' crap.

Jason could see a probe hovering over Daryl. It hung there, unmoving, six feet or so above him, as if it was monitoring Daryl for signs of life. It was as if the probe didn't want to waste any pins if the human was already dead, but was eager to let loose at the slightest indication.

Jason still had hold of his rifle, fought to pull it free, but the rifle, his hand, his arm, and the body it was all attached to, were trapped. There was barely enough room for him to take a breath, and even at that he had to keep them shallow.

The probe moved slowly off, finally, and Jason froze in his efforts. He didn't want the thing coming to investigate him. The last thing he needed was to have his head filled with holes as he lay there trapped and defenseless.

Once the probe was gone, Jason relaxed and watched his brother.

How twisted can it get? he thought. He had spent hours trying to reach Daryl, now here he was half buried, unable to move, positioned so that he had no choice but to watch over him. Never to reach him, never to look away...

Damn it, we are not going to die like this.

Jason continued to carefully scrutinize his brother for any movement, just as the probe had done. He wanted desperately to see an eye open, a hand move, Daryl's chest to rise just a little as he took in a breath.

There is a way out of this. There's always a way out.

§

Joseph glanced up at another shuttlecraft passing overhead, its windows glowing in the dark. It passed from sight, and he couldn't tell if it was going to stop on the island or not. There was a lot of activity on the peninsula tonight, and shuttles were crisscrossing above the island every few minutes.

Barbara sat in the foxhole beside him, her head back and eyes closed. She held a shotgun in her arms, and there was a pistol tucked in her belt. The ammo belt slung across her chest was almost empty.

They had found that the best way to handle the probes was to try to take them out with a 30-06 as they hovered at a distance. Failing that, blast them at close range with the shotgun and if necessary finish them off with the pistol. The problem with the close range stuff was that the probes tended to let loose with a barrage of energy pins when hit with a shotgun blast, and to erupt into a deadly, exploding mini-nova of shrapnel when destroyed.

"Here she comes," said Joseph.

Barbara nodded, imperceptibly, eyes still closed, arms still wrapped around her shotgun. Carolyn slid down into the foxhole beside them. She groaned painfully as her wounded leg took her weight, and she shifted onto her good leg.

"Everything's quiet," she said.

"You okay?" asked Joseph.

"Fine."

"What about the others?"

"I can't get close enough to tell."

Joseph turned and stared out into the dark. Nothing moved, but he knew they were out there.

"What are they waiting for?"

"There aren't many of them here," she said. "Three went into the house, none came out. There are a few others out there, somewhere; probably resting comfortably in that shuttle that landed up on the ridge. They're not in any hurry."

"Why should they be?" asked Barbara, her eyes still closed to the world. "The probes are doing fine."

"I think they're holding back."

"I think you're right," said Joseph.

"They've lost a third of their probes, and they can't be too happy about that. They have no qualms about killing us, and they have us dead to rights... but they haven't finished us off. Why not?"

Barbara opened her eyes and sat up. "If they want to take us prisoner, why don't they?"

Joseph took Barbara's thought to the next step, speaking to Carolyn.

"Because they know we're not likely to surrender?" he asked. "They have to beat the fight out of us?"

"I don't know."

"They were eager enough before to kill Barb and me... and you."

Carolyn gave a gentle mental shrug. "Whatever their reasoning, their methods do provide us with possibilities."

"Like what?"

"So long as we're not feeling the full brunt, there's a chance we can slip out."

Barbara grimaced. "In case you haven't noticed, this is an island, dear heart."

"What's your point?"

Barbara frowned, laid her head back again and closed her eyes.

Joseph, however, managed to smile.

"Where there's a thread of hope, there's a way to win."

Barbara kept her eyes closed. "If they take us prisoner, and don't *eliminate* us, there's the chance we could escape."

"I suppose that's so," said Carolyn. "I'd rather not think about that particular option right now. I plan on all of us getting out of this, if you don't mind."

Elizabeth leaned against the tree. The woods here along this part of the ridge hadn't burned and the bark of the hemlock felt comforting somehow. It belonged here, just as she belonged. There was a connection between her and this grand, earthly creation. They were of the same stuff, these two. And they had both suffered at the hands of *those creatures*.

She surveyed the shuttle that was squatting in the clearing like an ugly white slug. She could see occasional movement inside, and this only added to her image of a grotesque, fat bug. She had to fight back the urge to vomit.

There were probes scattered about in the woods surrounding the clearing. Elizabeth had become quite adept at spotting them, and even killing them. There was one now, not more than ten yards in front of her, between her and the shuttle. It rested in the night shadow at the base of a tree. Another hovered off to the left, nearer the clearing. She had seen several others moving about within the clearing and in among the trees.

One of the Shillies stepped out of the shuttle. The light from within washed over the little monster and created a dark silhouette outside the flying machine. Elizabeth turned around and again pressed her back against the trunk of the great tree. She checked the shotgun that she had acquired from the north bunker.

She had two shells left, both loaded in the gun. She shrugged off the pain in her shoulder and wiped her bloodied, matted hair from her forehead. Spinning away from the tree, Elizabeth rushed toward the shuttle. The resting probe, as expected, rose quickly and fired at her, struck her in the stomach. Elizabeth, already holding the shotgun in position, fired back and continued moving. The probe began sputtering, firing pins in all directions. Elizabeth was into the clearing then, and fired the second shell at the alien.

Turning quickly, she swung the empty shotgun at the unsteady probe now rushing at her, striking it and sending it flying. Hurrying after it, she hit it again and it fell to the ground. Behind her, the Shillie outside the shuttle had fallen to one knee. Another had come to the door of the shuttlecraft, aiming a weapon in Elizabeth's direction. Two probes rose up above the shuttle and began firing.

But Elizabeth hadn't stopped. She was back into the trees, heading directly for the probe that she had seen hovering nearby.

It had moved, as Elizabeth had known it would. These things were fast— and quick learners.

Elizabeth turned down a narrow trail, ran ten yards and jumped into the brush.

The probe was hovering in the dark another ten yards ahead. From earlier, painful experience, she had known that it would be somewhere ahead of her. The probes tended to work in pairs, and when one was attacked, the other would move into silent position ahead of Elizabeth's escape path.

There it was, though she hadn't actually seen it until she was already off the path. It was luck that had placed the booby trap two steps farther along the path, between Elizabeth and the probe now laying in ambush. She knew exactly where every trap was set and avoided it.

The probe rushed at her the second it saw her move off the trail, and was above her a second later. Elizabeth threw the empty shotgun toward the trap, releasing the catch and setting the wall of small, wooden spears swinging powerfully across the trail. One of the spears hit the probe, sending it against a tree trunk twelve feet above the ground.

It moved slowly back from the tree, hovered, rose three feet higher and stopped.

Elizabeth had found her shotgun and was ready to take another swing at the probe, but it made no effort to come at her.

Deciding quickly, she backed into the woods and disappeared before another probe could come looking for her.

Chapter Twenty Four

"It's getting light," said Carolyn. The stars had long since disappeared, and the skies had been turning gray for some time. The sun, though, would have to climb above the east ridge before it would reach them here on the jetty.

Because of the recent fires, they could see through the trees to the slope and the house. With binoculars taken from the jetty bunker atop which they sat, they were able to keep watch, particularly now that it was starting to get light.

The Shylmahn shuttle was still sitting just below the house, and now and then they could see probes moving about. Bunker One was in rubble.

"There's Daryl," said Joseph. His hands shook, then stiffened. He kept the binoculars in place. "He didn't make it."

"Oh, God," said Carolyn. Barbara clasped her hands tightly together, but said nothing.

"Something moving in the house," said Joseph. The women jumped to their feet and tried to see with the naked eye. The house and shuttle were still in the shadow of the ridge, and they could see very little.

"Well?" asked Carolyn.

"I don't know."

"Let me look."

"Just a minute," said Joseph, pulling away.

The front door opened and people walked out onto the porch. Joseph refocused the binoculars.

"Well?" Carolyn was ready to rip the binoculars from him.

"Susan, the kids," said Joseph. "Little Daryl, Sharon."

"Thank God for that," Barbara sighed.

"Shillies coming out with them. A couple of 'em coming out of the shuttle, too."

"Shuttle." Barbara was looking up at the sky. The other shuttlecraft was coming down from the ridge. They watched as it landed downslope from the first. Joseph quickly turned back to the house. He watched as Susan and the kids were led to the first shuttle. He saw Kathryn come out of the house then.

"Kathryn looks all right."

Kenneth was helped outside. He looked hurt, and had to be assisted down the steps. Then Jason came out. He appeared to be able to walk on his own, but he looked ragged.

That was it. No one else.

"I don't see Bril, or Liz," said Joseph. Another half-minute passed. He lowered the binoculars. Carolyn snatched them up and brought them up to her eyes.

Joseph sat on the roof of the bunker. "Peter's not there, either."

"Oh, no," cried Barbara.

Joseph was rubbing his hands on his face. Kenneth looked real bad. Daryl was gone. Bril, Liz... Peter.

Carolyn continued to hold the binoculars up to her face. She was trembling, and it made it difficult to see. She finally gave up and shoved the binoculars toward Barbara. Barbara took them, squatted down and watched the house and shuttles.

Several minutes passed. The first shuttle closed up and rose into the air, followed by the second.

"They're leaving," said Barbara.

Carolyn sat unmoving. Joseph slid down off the top of the bunker.

At least some of us made it... some of us are alive...

"Are they just going to leave us?" asked Barbara.

Carolyn slowly lifted her head and looked in the direction the shuttlecraft had taken. It took a moment for the nagging in the back of her mind to make sense.

"Shit. We have to get out of here." She stood and started toward the head of the trail.

Joseph and Barbara obediently followed.

"They are, right?" Barbara grew increasingly anxious. "They're leaving us, right?"

"We have to get to a boat."

"They'll spot a boat," said Joseph.

Barbara spoke calmly then. "Oh, God. They're gonna blast this place."

"We can't swim it," said Carolyn. "The water is too cold and the mainland too far. We go by boat."

"All right then, boat," said Joseph.

Carolyn stopped, suddenly, as Elizabeth stepped out onto the trail. She stumbled toward them, walking stiffly among the burnt snags of trees.

"Liz!"

Her hair was heavily matted, caked with blood and mud. Her shirt was dark with blood, riddled with holes. Her pants were torn and bloodied. She continued in their direction, stiffly, awkwardly. Carolyn rushed to her, grabbed her and helped her gently to the ground.

Joseph knelt beside them. Carolyn looked at him, then back at their sister.

"Oh, Joey."

Elizabeth was in bad shape; really bad shape.

But they had to get out of here.

"I'll carry her," said Joseph.

EsJen moved into the passenger compartment of the shuttlecraft and sat in the seat nearest the door. MehnTec was sitting in the seat opposite. She looked out the small, round window at the blackened skeleton of the peninsula landscape as it passed below. The island was behind them now. What remained of it, and of the Britton family, would soon be gone. The only survivors were in the other shuttle, on their way to the main collection site on the peninsula.

EsJen had done her best, within the confines of her loyalty to ShahnTahr and her duty to the Shylmahn people. In the end, it seemed she had accomplished little. She had managed to pluck a few of the family from death, and she was sure that Joseph was glad of that, but her real hope had been to bring Joseph and the majority of his family out alive. That hope was gone now. They had left no alternative open to her.

She had ordered the boats destroyed. She could not have them slipping away at the last moment. Left on their own, they would only continue to cause trouble for the Shylmahn. Their only way off that island was as captives, to be relocated. This, EsJen knew, they would not do voluntarily. She had hoped to force it upon them, for their own good. She had held out hope, however slim, to make them part of the Shylmahn dream.

Perhaps there had also been something inside her that wanted Joseph to die fighting for these futile illusions the humans still held. EsJen knew that Joseph would rather die in the struggle than live as what he had sometimes referred to as "a tool" of the Shylmahn.

He had gotten his wish...

EsJen placed a hand against the smooth, cool window. She felt a tug deep in her chest. Her mind was filled with human thoughts, all of which fought with every memory, every experience, every thought that made her a Shylmahn, that made her what she was, or what she had been.

"You could have done nothing else," said MehnTec.

"I know."

MehnTec did not fully understand EsJen's feelings for this Chehnon and his family, but he knew that JoSeph had been important to her.

"You have saved much of JoSeph's family," he said. "You have shown this Chehnon much more respect than his due."

EsJen managed a slight smile, but it was a sad smile. She continued to watch as her new world passed beneath them.

"I was his friend," she said.

Joseph pulled four survival suits from the storage cabinet on the damaged charter boat. With these, they could survive the cold waters of Puget Sound. It would be an awkward and clumsy swim, but if they could make it off the island in time, and get far enough from the island in time, they could make it to shore.

Every boat... destroyed. Holes in every hull. They really didn't want anyone getting off this island.

Joseph tossed the suits down to Barbara. Carolyn was sitting on the floating boathouse floor, holding Elizabeth in her arms.

"She's not going to make it, Joey," said Carolyn.

Joseph ignored her. "We'll go to the end of the jetty and suit up there." He jumped down onto the deck and knelt beside Elizabeth. He picked her up and carried her, calling back over his shoulder for Barbara and Carolyn to bring the suits.

Somewhere along the way, as Joseph struggled and stumbled with Elizabeth in his arms, he felt her take her last breath. He didn't stop. He didn't say anything. When they reached the end of the tiny peninsula that formed the island cove, he sat her down and carefully laid her head back. Joseph, Carolyn and Barbara put on their suits in silence.

They were several hundred yards from the island, the water about them as black as the sky above them, when they heard the sound of alien fighters coming from the south. Moments later came the sound of first one, then a series of explosions from the island. All about the three human figures in the water, the surface reflected the bright, explosive flames of the island behind them.

Joseph stopped and turned, looked back at what had once been Bril's escape from the real world. It was now a massive orange and red ball, growing and rising from water.

He turned then and continued swimming toward the far shore, Carolyn and Barbara beside him.

Chapter Twenty Five

March 02

ShahnTahr completed its conversation with TohPeht and disconnected. It entered the new information into its database, examined and weighed this information against current known facts, assigned values and flags to the information and merged it with existing data.

TohPeht was doing well. TohPeht served the Shylmahn people and ShahnTahr.

TohPeht would remain in his current position.

As ShahnTahr continued about its duties and responsibilities to the Shylmahn people, the sole purpose for which ShahnTahr existed, it applied its overlay of the requirements that it had defined as necessary for the continued survival and success of the Shylmahn population to the newly updated database. From this it extrapolated the current situation and identified any modifications that might have to be applied to the current stratagem.

Four dahlsehts were near completion and currently being inhabited. The remaining dahlsehts were also under construction and on schedule for completion.

Additional Chehnon creatures were to be assigned to assist with the construction of dahlseht A3, for while it was, in fact, on schedule, the pattern was consistent with similar circumstances in which construction expectations had subsequently failed to meet expected milestones.

The Shylmahn population was satisfactorily integrating into the ecosystem of the new world. It was adapting well to varied climatic environments around the planet. The slow introduction of local flora and fauna into the Shylmahn diet was progressing on schedule.

Introduction of Shylmah-originated plant life into the Chehno ecosystem was beginning in isolated test environments.

Three of the medium-level Chehnon work facility populations had reached completion of phase two adaptation and the order was to be given for individual interrogation and review for selection of phase one training.

Order to be given for expansion of the search and examination process of reservation inhabitants for appropriate candidates for all phases of Chehnon level tasks.

Research and development operations of all five probe lines was continuing along scheduled advancement projections. The R6FRA2-A "Guardian" probes would begin receiving the ADR439C enhancement in nine days.

Order to be given for installation of fixed position sensory input devices in one location each at each of the dahlseht ShahnTahr facilities. Installation to begin in sixteen days.

Internal self-enhancement tasks were continuing on schedule.

Collection of the remaining wild Chehnon populations was falling behind schedule. Of the eighteen major concentrations of free Chehnon remaining worldwide, only eleven collection activities were meeting current projections. The order was to be given for the elimination of seven populations deemed unrecoverable.

Six hundred and four minor concentrations of wild human populations had been identified and were not on the current schedule for collection. There was at present no indication that these remaining minor concentrations would be moving voluntarily to specified collection points, as requested by Shylmahn collection teams. Order was to be given for the elimination of the six hundred and four populations.

NehLoc was performing as anticipated in his current position and despite noted tendencies remained well beneath the societal threat threshold. Current level of observation satisfactory. NehLoc continued to serve the Shylmahn people as required and would continue in his current capacity.

The basement was musty. The only light was from the oil lamp that sat at the center of the folding table. There were no windows, and only one door that opened to a narrow stairwell that lead to the kitchen upstairs.

Carolyn stood silent in the shadows of one corner of the room, arms folded across her chest, cautiously observing and listening to the others. Jenzie sat at the table, Danny beside him. Three others, none of whom Carolyn fully trusted, sat opposite Jenzie.

Jenzie shook his head, not for the first time.

"It won't work," he said, looking up at Jones. "Not any more. Probes are smarter now, and convoy probes aren't any different. They make 'em smarter all the time."

"With this plan, we can take it. In and out before any help arrives."

"We'd never get through the probes. The Shillies send two ahead, two follow behind, and there's always at least one on each flank. They coordinate at the first sign, and they have help in minutes, if they ever need it."

"I know the pattern," said Jones, defensively. When he turned his big, red head from one side to the other, Carolyn could see the broken veins in his cheeks brighten in the dull, yellow light of the lamp. He pointed to the pile of papers on the table in front of him. "In fact, I'm counting on it."

Jenzie breathed heavily through his nose, leaned back in his chair and stared at Jones. Finally, he spoke over one shoulder to Carolyn. "What do you think, Carolyn?"

"We need food."

"That doesn't make the odds any different."

"Desperate times call for desperate chances," said Danny.

"That's not true," said Jenzie.

"There's nothing desperate about this plan," Jones said angrily. "We know their route, we know their pattern, we know their strength, and we damn well know their weakness." He stabbed at the papers with his finger, "This takes it all into account. Three of us can't do it alone. I don't like it, but we need your help."

Carolyn's laugh came out of the shadows. "You're making a mistake, wanting to join forces with us. NehLoc has made it his personal mission to track us down and stomp on us."

"You're no worse off than anyone else, *missy*." Jones turned in the small metal chair. He looked at Carolyn, his eyes cold. "With Ben Soo gone, you're no more a threat to the Shillies than any of the rest of the stragglers. Come down off your white horse, Princess, and walk with the peasants."

Carolyn shrugged, pushed herself casually out of the shadows. "This asshole would get us killed, Jenzie. He may need us, but we sure as hell don't need him."

Jones stood slowly, glaring fiercely as she passed. Carolyn wasn't nearly as casual as she put on, carefully taking in the man's demeanor as she moved towards the stairs.

Jenzie straightened his chair and stood.

"You heard the Princess," he said with a shrug.

"Jenzie," said Jones ominously.

Jenzie and Danny followed after Carolyn, leaving Jones steaming.

Joseph pushed the drape aside and climbed through. Once inside the house, he reached back out and pulled in the cloth bag that he had been carrying. Barbara, waiting inside, repositioned the drape and set the board back into place. She waited for reassurance from Joseph that he hadn't been seen or followed before turning on the lamp.

The doors were boarded up from the inside. The windows had heavy curtains and blankets over them, nailed into place with plywood or planks. Despite these precautions, they only lit the one lamp, and this they kept turned low.

"I found a few things," said Joseph. He knelt before the coffee table and began emptying the bag. "Enough to keep us a couple of days."

"How do things look out there?"

"No Shillies. Saw a few probes, though."

"Those things are a plague."

"And effective, too." Joseph picked out a can of tamales, scooted around and sat on the couch. Using a small can opener that he kept on a chain around his neck, he opened it and pulled one tamale out. He handed the can to Barbara. She took it and handed Joseph a paper towel. His tamale was dripping all over him.

"How's your ankle," asked Joseph. She had twisted it two days before as they were climbing over rubble that had fallen into the street. They had been working their way out of the Northwest, trying to get out of the controlled area. In the past few weeks they had seen few Shylmahn, but the probes were everywhere, looking for wild humans.

They no longer tried to capture humans. Any that were found were eliminated.

"The swelling is down."

"Well, stay off it. We're safe enough here for a few days."

"Are you sure?"

"Positive. I'll go out again tomorrow, stock up on traveling supplies."

Barbara moved close to Joseph, slid under his arms, reached around him and held him. Joseph wrapped his arms around her and held her.

They had a long way to go, and they couldn't know if what was outside the Northwest was any better than what they had now. They did know that they couldn't survive here. They couldn't fight the Shylmahn. The Shylmahn were out of reach, living behind their dahlseht walls, coming out only to build more, to spread their Shillie world until there would one day be nothing human left.

They had no choice but to try to get out now and could only hope they would find something human still out there... somewhere.

Chapter Twenty Six

March 12

The sound that woke Carolyn was not a good sound. She rolled quickly to one side, pulling herself up to a sitting position with her back to the wall and her pistol pointing toward the open door.

There was the silhouette of two men, one man holding another in front of him.

"Danny?" she asked. She only had three bullets left, and she had to be careful how she used them. To her left, she heard Jenzie moving, positioning himself.

"They came up on me," said Danny. "I didn't think—"

"'morning, Princess," said Jones. "Sleep well?"

"I always sleep well." She kept her pistol trained on the silhouette. Jones was a big man, and Danny wasn't. She could take him out now, but she was afraid Jones would kill Danny in reflex.

"All we want is some supplies."

"You don't say." Carolyn didn't want to waste time talking with him; it would only give him time to analyze the situation.

"Drop your guns or things get messy," said Jones.

There was a shuffling of feet and the shadow that was Jones and Danny began moving to one side. There were others coming in behind them. Carolyn would have to do something—now.

She squeezed the trigger. Beside her, Jenzie did the same. They each rolled quickly from their positions as the room exploded with the sound of gunfire. Carolyn fired her second bullet at the movement near the door, then crawled quickly to the bathroom and closed the hollow door. She heard several more shots in the other room, one shot splintering the door beside her. She went quickly to the small window, climbed through and fell onto the narrow sidewalk that ran along the side of the small house.

She could hear the sounds of yelling and more shots coming from inside the house. Scrambling to her feet, she ran around to the back of the house. As she came around the corner, Danny was stumbling out the back door. He took two steps out, fell to his knees, hurriedly climbed back to his feet and ran out into the yard.

Carolyn dropped to the ground and slid back against the house just as one of Jones' companions came rushing out the door, chasing after Danny. Carolyn fired her third and last bullet as the man took his third step. It struck him in the center of the back. He fell to the ground, turned and fired two shots at Carolyn. One struck the house just above her head, but the other struck her in the soft spot of the shoulder. She felt a faint *thump* as the bullet passed through her and buried itself in the wood siding.

She dropped her arm to her side, the gun clattering on the cement walk, and stared at the man. Satisfied that he was now safe from Carolyn, he struggled to get back to his feet and followed after Danny. He stumbled to the back of the yard and disappeared into the trees that bordered the property.

The world grew quiet. Carolyn listened for any voices or sound of movement from inside the house, but there was nothing.

The sun was managing to peek through the trees, and a mist began to form above the tall grass and weeds of the yard as the sunshine washed over the morning dew. Several minutes passed, and the silence continued. Then, as Carolyn watched, there was a barely perceptible stirring of the grass blades a few feet away. She realized, finally, that a small animal was working its way across the yard. It stopped now and then, probably to investigate some possible treasure, and she would hear a faint rustling as it worked with whatever it was that it had found.

It took at least ten minutes for the little creature to make it all the way across the yard and to the fence that ran between the two houses. Carolyn thought she saw a flurry of gray fur as the animal worked its way under the wood fence and on into the yard of the house next door.

She smiled faintly.

Damned strange...

Killed by a human...

Should a' known...

The air was still cold, but the sun had begun to warm the wood of the house against which she was leaning and the cement of the walk on which she was sitting.

No one came out of the house.

Jenzie...

He could be alive, but hurt. He could be dying.

Carolyn had nothing left. She closed her eyes.

Damn...

She heard a bird. It was in the tree in the yard next door.

When Carolyn woke, there were two humans in the room. A woman was sitting at a small table, and looked to be playing solitaire. A man sat in a wooden chair beside the bed in which Carolyn was laying.

She tried to take in the situation, but there was nothing familiar for her to hold on to.

"Where am I?" she asked, finally.

The woman at the table stopped her solitaire game and smiled, if a bit cautiously, and the man straightened, as if startled from sleep.

"We just call it the Village," said the woman. "The Shylmahn have some official name for us, but we ignore them as much as possible." She stood and took two steps toward the bed. She looked at the man.

"Go get the doc, and tell the council she's awake."

"You sure?" asked the man, slowly standing.

"She's not going anywhere."

The man stared down at Carolyn uncertainly but finally stepped away from the bed.

Carolyn watched him go, then looked again at the woman. The woman studied Carolyn a moment longer, then turned away and moved back to her table. She sat and looked down at her cards.

"There are some questions regarding the, uh... *circumstances...* of your injuries," she said.

Carolyn said nothing, and after a moment the woman returned to playing solitaire.

"The Shylmahn do not use bullets," she said.

"How did I get here?" asked Carolyn.

"A supply party found you. Three days ago."

Three days...

"You were lucky. The Shylmahn let them bring you back. If you had been moving about and they had seen you, the Shillies would have shot you for practice. They do that now, you know; to the wild humans."

"What about my friends?'

"You were alone."

Carolyn laid her head back down. The woman leaned back in her chair and observed in silence. A few minutes later, the man returned with two others. Behind them came a short, thin woman who pushed her way through and began examining Carolyn.

"I take it you're the doctor," said Carolyn.

"That's me," said the doctor, sitting in the wooden chair. "Janice Horn. Janice."

"Carolyn Britton."

At that, there was some activity and shuffling about by others in the room.

"Hello, Carolyn." The doctor continued fussing over Carolyn, looked at the dressing of her wounds. "I'll bet you didn't expect to open your eyes onto this world again."

"I'm not finished here just yet. Still have work to do."

"You'll be taking a little vacation, hon. I'll let you know when you can get back in the action."

"I'd appreciate that, Doctor."

"Call me Janice," said the doctor. She made a few more obscure comments about how lucky she was, how much blood she had lost, and that there appeared to be no permanent damage. Her body was going to take its time recovering from the injury because of Carolyn's overall poor health.

As the doctor hovered about Carolyn, redressing her bandages, securing her arm, taking her temperature, and advising her on taking things slow and easy, the others in the room skulked about impatiently and whispered in the shadows.

Janice indicated those behind her. "Now, it's part of my job to get in the way of the pseudo-government officials around here. So send for me if they tire you out."

"I can take it," said Carolyn.

Janice nodded and stood up. "I'll drop back by this evening."

As Janice stepped aside, one of the men thanked her and moved in to sit in the chair the doctor had been sitting in.

"Miss Britton," he said, shifting the chair into a comfortable position. "I'm John Shelby."

"You a pseudo-government official?"

"As you like." John Shelby looked friendly enough. "In some manner unknown to me, I find myself serving as the representative of this colony."

The man who had gone to find the others, now standing at the foot of the bed, spoke up. "You did you say your name was Carolyn Britton?"

"That's right."

"Ben Soo's Carolyn Britton?"

"I was."

The man nodded, apparently satisfied. "We were all really sorry to hear that he got killed. And you, you were one of his key people, huh?"

"We were a very small group. We were all key people."

The man smiled and nodded again, as if what Carolyn had said was exactly what the Carolyn Britton would say.

"Do you mind?" John Shelby was looking up at the man in frustration. "I do have a few questions of my own."

"We can trust her, John."

Shelby gave the man a long *'are you a complete idiot?'* look, before shifting around again to face Carolyn.

"Sorry, Miss Britton," said John. "At some point, we'll need to know how you came by your injuries." He looked sharply back at the other man, "And perhaps we should find someone who knows Carolyn Britton by sight?"

Carolyn watched the man standing at the foot of the bed nod briskly and leave. She looked back at John.

"As if the Carolyn Britton would be incapable of wrong-doing?" she asked.

John Shelby smiled. "Let's just say that, apparently, the word of Carolyn Britton will carry a little more weight, justified or not."

"I see."

"In the meantime," said John Shelby, "despite how all of this may appear, a person is still presumed innocent and we do welcome you to the Village. You need not fear being dragged out to the hanging tree just yet."

"Thanks for that."

John studied Carolyn's face for a moment, then nodded and straightened.

"Your injuries... came from humans?"

"Yes."

John shook his head heavily. "Times like these, to have humans killing one another."

"Look at our track record," said the woman at the table.

"Yes, Brenda but, I would have thought... oh, I'm not sure what I thought."

"There wasn't much human about the men who attacked us," said Carolyn.

"Yes, well," John could see that Carolyn was growing tired. "We'll pick this up again later, all right?"

"Thanks."

John stood and waved everyone out, following after them and closing the door.

Carolyn found herself alone. It was then she realized that, though she was tired and weak, she was also very hungry. A few minutes later, just as she was debating whether to call out or to try and get out of bed, the woman who had been standing watch over her brought in a tray of soup, bread and milk.

As Carolyn ate, Brenda told her of the Village. The site was fairly new, the land having been cleared and the buildings constructed by the people now living here. There were two thousand humans in the Village—men, women and children. Some of the people in the community thought it was an experimental facility, a kind of "all purpose" community at the beckon call of the Shylmahn masters. Apparently it wasn't like any of the other facilities anyone had heard of, but rather a merging of functions. It wasn't like the massive reservations found in the Midwest, nor the work camps that were scattered about everywhere.

For the most part, those in the Village were left to handle their own affairs, and were allowed to go about their business unhindered. There were fences to let the inhabitants know their boundaries, and there were Guardian Probes to ensure the inhabitants abided by those boundaries. Other than this, the inhabitants saw little of the Shylmahn—with one exception.

Each evening, John Shelby reported to the main gate, where he was given instructions as to what project was on the schedule for the following day and how many humans were to be included in the detail. One hour after dawn the next morning, the requisite number of humans reported to the main gate for the detail. They were always back by sunset.

"There's not much technology here," said Brenda. "Not even electricity. But we do get by. We're not too uncomfortable. The Shylmahn even let us go out on foraging expeditions, like the one that found you. They check everything we bring in, but we usually do pretty good. It all helps. The little things, and the important things. Most of all, though, we feel safe again."

"It sounds sad," said Carolyn.

Brenda shrugged, "We do okay."

Carolyn lowered her spoon delicately into her bowl of soup and stared down at it. She finally lifted the bowl and set it carefully onto the food tray. Her silence betrayed her thoughts.

"My kids are alive," Brenda's voice turned defensive and her body stiffened. "They have food and a roof. They play, and they laugh again."

"I'm sorry," said Carolyn. "You're right. You're absolutely right. Your kids need a safe place. Families like yours need a place where you can hang onto something of what we're fighting for."

"It is," said Brenda. "Safe. All things considered. It isn't like we were asked if we wanted to come here. But since we are here, we make the best of it."

"You take care of your babies. That's exactly what you're supposed to do."

"Yeah, well..."

I'll see there's a place for 'em when they grow up, thought Carolyn. *That's what I'm supposed to do.*

Carolyn could feel Brenda's defenses were still up, though the woman did appear willing to accept Carolyn's apology. Once again, Carolyn had put her foot in it. Better to keep her mouth shut and accept the hospitality of the place. She might be here for a while.

Carolyn had a feeling the Shillies had ulterior motives in sending out those scavenging parties. The cost was minimal to send the humans out scrounging among the remnants of human civilization, and it did provide supplies the humans needed if they were to survive to serve the Shylmahn. It kept the humans happy. Most importantly for the Shylmahn, and Carolyn believed the primary reason for the foraging expeditions, was that it took supplies away from the humans that were still on the loose and still causing headaches for the Shillies.

"Are you feeling better now with some food in you?" asked Brenda.

Carolyn pulled herself from her thoughts and put on her satisfied smile. "Much. I think I should rest, though. Janice told me not to overdo it."

"Of course," said Brenda, taking the tray from the small table beside the bed. "I'll come back by later. We'll clean you up for your doctor's visit."

"Good morning."

Carolyn woke slowly, a reaction to the medicine, her injuries, and exhaustion. The voice she heard coming through the fog was familiar, but out of place. She opened her eyes and tried to focus on the figure pulling up the wooden chair and sitting down beside her.

"Jason?"

"How are you?"

"I'm—" Carolyn was coming wide awake now. "What are you doing here?"

"It's where they brought us."

"The others?"

Jason nodded. "Kenny's here; Susan and the kids."

"Wow…"

"Wow, right. I thought you were dead. How about—"

"Shelby didn't tell me you were here."

"He sent for me. Identity check." Jason took a long breath. "You know about…"

"Yeah. And Liz. Liz didn't make it, either."

Jason nodded knowingly. "Joseph's all right then?"

"We were together up to about six or seven weeks ago. He and Barb were going to try to get out of the Northwest."

"Not you, though."

"I decided to stay with Jenzie and Danny." Mentioning their names brought back a flood of emotions. Jason reached out and took hold of her arm.

"I can come back," he said.

"Hell," she mumbled, fighting back tears.

"I'll bring Kenny by this afternoon. Janice says that if the weather holds up we can wheel you outside for a few minutes of fresh air."

Jason stood and started toward the door. He looked back and gave her another smile. "I'm sorry about your friends. They were good people. Terry seemed like a nice guy."

"Terry wasn't with us," she managed. She smiled at Jason's awkward nod. "He didn't belong in this fight."

"Then I hope he made it out all right."

"Me, too. People like Terry… it's what we're fighting for."

Carolyn stood with Jason and Kenneth beneath the awning that protected the gathering area near the main gate. They watched as John Shelby went to meet with the Shylmahn representative and get the information for the next day's task.

"Who's that?" asked Carolyn. She had been up and about for less than a week, and she spent each evening observing Shelby as he went to the main gate to talk with the Shillie. Today, the Shillie had brought a friend.

"That," said Jason, "is BehLahk."

"Dr. Black? Daryl's Dr. Black?"

"That's him."

Carolyn watched Dr. Black. The Shylmahn scientist wasn't saying much. He listened to Shelby and the other Shillie, occasionally looked through the gate at the humans walking about inside. He glanced only once in Carolyn's direction.

"What's he doing here?"

"He comes by now and then."

"He hasn't hauled anyone out yet," said Kenneth. "I think he runs this place."

"That's scary," said Carolyn.

Shelby finished with his meeting and turned away from the gate. The Shylmahn representative walked back to his vehicle.

Dr. Black stayed at the gate, observing the quiet evening activities going on in the large clearing just inside the fence. After a few moments, he turned and looked at the three humans standing beneath the awning a dozen yards from the gate. He then looked directly at Carolyn, and nodded. It was a distinctly human gesture. It was a sign of acknowledgment. It was a sign of recognition. Carolyn couldn't move.

Dr. Black spun slowly about then and walked away from the gate. He climbed into a small shuttle, followed by an escort of two Shylmahn bodyguards that seemed to appear from out of nowhere. Several moments later the shuttle lifted off and headed away north.

"Did you see that?" asked Carolyn.

"I saw," said Kenneth. "He knows who you are. By sight."

"No, no. Not that," said Carolyn. She had already shaken that off. She'd live with it. Or she'd die with it. "The bodyguards. He has bodyguards."

"So?"

"They still need protection," said Jason.

Carolyn suddenly had a smile on her face. "Nothing like a bit of good news to lift the spirits."

They stepped out from under the awning and started back into the heart of the Village. Carolyn took her steps slow and soft. It would be some time before she would be anywhere near ready to take on the Shillies again.

The three of them walked down the main thoroughfare of the village at Carolyn's pace. Kenneth relied heavily on his cane, suffering from ongoing physical problems that he kept mostly to himself. Jason had recovered fully from the injuries suffered at the bunker explosion. He looked now at his brother and sister.

"What a pitiful sight," he said.

"And you," said Kenneth, "are unbelievable. Buried in tons of rubble, and, as always, you walk away with hardly a scratch."

"In case I haven't mentioned it lately, young man, I am immortal."

They passed a number of cabins. At one, Susan was standing on the front step. She gave a light wave, but nothing more. The three waved in reply.

"She doesn't want anything to do with us," Kenneth said to Carolyn as they continued on.

"Let her grieve, Kenny," said Jason. "We'll be here when she needs us."

"You, maybe," said Carolyn, taking steps as if each might break her. "Me, I'm getting out of this dump."

Jason smiled, spoke in a light, patronizing tone.

"All right," he said. "First though... dinner." They had reached a large building with a sign hanging above the door that read 'Mess Hall'.

Jason helped his sister take the steps. Kenneth followed her in. Jason stopped. He watched a guardian probe move slowly down the thoroughfare, forty feet above the heads of the villagers. As it neared the mess hall, it stopped and hovered.

It was almost as if it recognized Jason and was watching... waiting...

A small shuttle sat in the middle of the hilltop park. EsJen was sitting on the bench, looking out over the neighborhood that was spread out below. No one lived there now. The last of the Chehnon had been gathered up long ago.

MehnTec stepped out of the shuttle and down the ramp, walked slowly over to the bench. He stood a moment, then sat down beside EsJen. He didn't want to disturb her, but he wanted her to know that he was there for her, should she feel the need of his company.

"JoSeph had a vision of our arrival," she said at last. She did not look at him. "Well before we reached this world."

"Is that so?"

"Yes."

"I see." He thought about that. "Is that normal for Chehnon?"

"I do not think so."

"I see," he said again. "What does ShahnTahr have to say about it? I assume you reported this."

"Of course," she said. "I have not been advised as to what ShahnTahr thinks about it. I have not been given direction as to how to pursue it further."

"This bothers you," MehnTec stated flatly.

EsJen said nothing.

"So," MehnTec continued. "And what of JoSeph's vision of our grand arrival? What did the Chehnon see?"

Again EsJen said nothing. She looked sad. As sad as MehnTec had ever seen her.

"EsJen?" he urged.

He waited. He gave her time. EsJen still did not respond.

"EsJen?" he urged again, now with a hint of disquiet. He rested a hand on hers.

She did not look at MehnTec when she spoke.

"The future. Perhaps."

The two sat silent then, on the Chehnon bench, and looked out across the panoramic view of hundreds of empty Chehnon dwellings lining empty Chehnon streets, an island of abandoned Chehnon landscape lost now in a Shylmahn world.

Chapter Twenty Seven

Joseph slid down the embankment and followed Barbara out onto the road. He adjusted his backpack and started down the center of the two-lane county highway. The painted stripes were faded and peeling, and there were weeds poking up through the asphalt, some growing to several feet high. He had to step around some of the more assertive vegetation, which had grown to bush proportions.

It felt good to walk on smooth, level ground again. They would make good time from here on out.

They hadn't seen a probe now for three full days and Joseph was confident that the worst was behind them. They had made it to the uncontrolled lands that had been rumored to exist out here. The Frontier.

For the first time in a long time, they could breathe easy.

Joseph fought the urge to stop and look behind him. Back there was his home and his family.

He could hear their footsteps. The sound made the world seem a very empty place. He suddenly felt very alone.

The world was very quiet.

It was an alien world, even out here. It belonged to the Shillies now; all of it. Joseph and Barbara walked it now as strangers; as invaders.

Welcome to the new Shylmahn home world.

No. This is my world. This is my home.

Now Joseph did stop. Barbara took another two steps, then she stopped also, to see what was wrong. Joseph looked all around him. The sun was warm and the air was dry, but the breeze was cool on bare skin. If he listened very carefully, he could hear the breeze pushing at the dry grass on either side of the road.

It was all so strange, so alien, and yet it was still home.

Joseph had the odd sensation that he and Barbara were the only two humans left on the planet. The cool wind, or perhaps it was that thought, made him shudder.

He turned his back to the wind, to the thought, and continued down the road. Barbara walked beside him.

Somewhere out there, they would find others like them... the wild humans.

End